Dimension Travel IV:
The Story Continues From The Original Dimension Travel Trilogy

Dimension Travel IV:
The Story Continues From The Original Dimension Travel Trilogy

Joseph Salvatore Pidoriano

Copyrighted Material

Dear Reader,

I hope that you enjoy this book. I believe this book is for all ages and all kinds. This book might contain some scenes that are filled with violence and death. In addition to that, there are some political controversies in this book that might be misunderstood by some. There are also some historical inaccuracies in the book. The reader must keep in mind that this is a fictional book. It might be confusing at first, but when you dive into the pages of this book, you'll understand the story. In spite of the controversies, I mentioned that this book was age friendly. The reason it appeals to younger audiences is because the different settings that are featured teach the younger audiences some important morals. The reason why this book appeals to older audiences is because some people might take a stance and pose an argument. for the older audiences, try not to be extreme with those arguments. There is also an anomaly of things that have taken place throughout the story. Be intelligent and respect others' opinions. Overall, I am basically writing this letter to you to state that I hope that you enjoy this book. I definitely enjoyed writing it for you.

Sincerely,

Joseph Salvatore Pidoriano

6

To:
my family, friends, teachers,
and God, who gave me the
ability to write this book.

Acknowledgements

Donna Marie Foti, Lisa Ann Esposito,
Mario Strong, Kitty Brown, Mrs. Mary
Katherine Scally,
Ms. Marianne Teta

Thanks for all your help in creating this
book

Contents:

Characters:

Rubi Worschinskiwitz...

Will Von Alien...

Light S. Cycle...

Sarah Rosenthal..

Buck/Brutus..

Sheriff Joe Arpello..

God..

Commissioner Clayton...

Enkel..

Officer Valencia...

Abraham Lincoln and his family (5 characters).............

Tom Jackson..

Jacqueline Langyaw...

King Haggoth...

Serpianto and Korbian..

Mitchell...

Jobe Rosenthal...

His Sons (2 characters)..

Prologue

Man lives in a world where there must be a constant fight for justice and fairness. Unfortunately, the fight for justice may never be over. Some folks say that it is okay to honor evil. it is not okay to honor such a wicked idea. It is totally wrong. History will also repeat itself. In this book, you will learn about how some folks are influenced by the evils of old history and politics.

Although this book is a political, historical, and religious allegory it is friendly for all ages. In addition one will understand that it will take a lot of guts and glory in order to fight for true justice. Justice is a relative subject. One might see justice by "doing good" for others; others might see justice by doing evil. In this book, you (the reader) will have to decipher who is on the good side and who is on the evil side.

Chapter I: "Good" Morning

The hallowed halls of the Alien Estate were adorned with drapes that were the colors of Red, Yellow, and blue. These were the colors of the flag of Starmos City. The old government was destroyed and a new democracy was set into place. A new leader has taken over Starmos City. The gold engraved tiles in the hall of the old dictator's face were removed and tiles signed by every citizen in Starmos City were put into place to represent that the Alien Estate belongs to the aliens.

Balloons lined the hallway because of the jubilation that had taken place last night. And all men, women, and children now have all rights. The portrait of Cornelius Von Alien was removed, and it is being replaced by a picture of the Starmos flag. The Royal Quarters is now inhabited by a new and heroic leader, Will Von Alien. He was the rescuer of Starmos City. He built a liberal society and removed the straight-laced, tyranny of Cornelius. Colorful confetti lined the stone floors of the estate's halls. The new leader was asleep in a regal, canopy, king-size bed. The canopy made one feel like he or she was in some sort of a rainforest or swamp. It would spray mist that had the scent of cologne every ten minutes.

Adjacent to the canopy were two wooden nightstands, which featured two modern lamps. These lamps were one thousand kilowatts and if one touched the light bulb while the lamps were lit, a sudden shock would have taken place and that particular one would pass on. The arched windows from the old reign still remained. In addition to that, the bedspread was changed from the generic colors of green and yellow to the new colors of the Starmos flag. The old armoire was replaced with a new, ultra- modern closet. The anachronistic T.V. was replaced by an ostentatious, 4-D television. Furniture changed tremendously in the Royal Quarters of the Alien Estate.

On one of the nightstands was a generic, analog alarm clock. This was the only item used by Cornelius Von Alien. In front of the bed was a dresser that didn't have any mirror. Featured on the top of the dresser were gifts from some of the loyal aliens. Among them were fruit baskets, jewelry, and items that belong in a haberdashery. The alarm clock started making a noise that sounds similar to the EAS (Emergency Alert System) used on earth. Will was sound asleep in the regal bed. All of a sudden, he heard a noise and he sprung out of the bed from the long sleep. He walked around the room.

The alarm clock showed the time of half past five in the morning. He fell back asleep. A half hour later, the new alien leader heard soft spoken words that had the voice of a female. "What's going on?" asked the mysterious voice. The room was as quiet as a church. The new alien leader started to shiver in the bed. He pulled the blanket over his head. This mysterious noise started talking again. "Who's here? Who is sleeping?" she asked. The new alien leader was so nervous that he bit the blanket. He sprung right out of the bed. "What do you want?" he shouted. The mysterious voice stopped talking. After two minutes of silence, he fell asleep again. Loud thuds were heard from the walls of the bedroom. Now these noises kept him up. It is now 6:45 in the morning and the thuds are dying down.

At 7:00, the sun's rays beamed in the room. It is now sunrise. Will woke up from the crazy last hours of his sleep. He walked up to the window and opened the tall, maroon curtains. His aqua, blue eyes started to tear, when he opened the curtain. He suddenly turned around and walked away from the windows. he left the bedroom. The chandelier lights in the hallway were still on. The new alien leader walked down the hallway in blue and grey striped pajamas. he knocked on the guest room door. Tom Jackson emerged from the door in a running suit. He was jogging in place. "Hey, good morning," said Tom.

"Why are you so jumpy?" asked Will. "I guess when I am in a new place, I act so jumpy," answered Tom. He started to run down the hallway. "What are you doing?" shouted Will. Tom turned his head around. "I'm running," he answered. He dashed and crashed into the wall. He fainted and Z's started coming up from his head like a cartoon. The new alien leader was laughing. Will walked to Tom, still chuckling, and helped him up. "I think you did such a good job running," he said sarcastically. "I know," replied Tom. "What is wrong with you?" asked Will. "What do you mean?" asked Tom. "Well, gee, you ran into the wall like a fool at the..." answered Will. "What are you going to say?" Tom interrupted. "Never mind," replied Will happily. "Were you going to say that I ran like a fool at the Circus?" asked the foolish guest. "Yes," answered the new alien leader. "Ha, ha, ha real funny," replied Tom. He walked down to the new kitchen.

"Oh my God, what happened here?" asked Will. His eyes were open in shock, and his mouth was gaping in disbelief. The kitchen looked totally new. The floors were made of marble stone. The chandelier had candle lights that glimmered in the kitchen. The curtains were removed from the window, and WVA (Will Von Alien) Boulevard was able to be seen in clear view. The wall that obscured the cooking area was destroyed, and now one can see the activities in the cooking area.

The wall featured a burly wood murphy table. The gas lines were removed and cooking would depend on electricity. The retro refrigerator was replaced with a stainless steel fridge. The tiled floor was replaced with wood. "Say, why are you so surprised to see the kitchen looking like this?" asked Tom. "Yes, I am," answered Will. "In a good way or bad way?" he asked. "Are you kidding me? I love this place. It is like heaven in here," answered Will. "Say, are you still going to cook in here?" asked Tom. "Of course," answered the new alien leader. He walked up to the fridge. "You going to cook?" asked Tom.

"Of course, I am. Just give me a chance," answered Will happily. He pulled out a carton of eggs, cream flavoring, and a small kitchen torch. He walked up to the kitchen counter. He spun three of the eggs and cracked them. He tapped on the garbage and tossed the shells into the garbage. He mixed the egg and the cream and he placed the delectable breakfast in the oven. "What are you making?" asked Tom. "A surprise," answered Will. "I hope it doesn't contain any poison," replied Tom.

"Why do you think it would contain poison?" asked the new alien leader. "Because you were the chef that worked for that last brute, Cornelius," answered Tom.

"Well, Cornelius is dead and that disgrace is not worthy enough to have an unmarked grave," replied Will. "Hey, that's not nice to say," said Tom. "You're saying what I am saying is not nice when that brute tried to poison you and kill you?!" replied Will.

"Well, good point, I forgot about that. My amnesia must be kicking in," said Tom jokingly. "You are only twenty one years old. How could you have amnesia at such a young age?" asked Will. "You're right, I don't have amnesia. I was just playing with you," answered Tom. "Ha, ha, ha, real funny," replied the incumbent alien leader. Will continued to cook the delicious meal. After fifteen minutes of preparation, the meal was ready to be hit with a blow torch. Will hit the igniter for the blow torch and not a single spark came flying out. "What is going on? What is happening?" he asked himself.

He stared into space and started to have a flashback. Twenty five years ago on the same morning, Will accepted the job as the chef at the Alien Estate. The first meal he made was a creme brulée. Cornelius was sitting at the old nook table waiting for his meal to be served, and this was the 20th anniversary meal of Starmos City. "So, what do you think of the crème brulée?" asked the young chef. "I hate it. Can't you make anything better?" asked Cornelius. "No, this is the best thing I have ever made," answered the young Will. "Well, I am banning crème brulée from this city," replied Cornelius. "You're not going to stop me," said Will.

"Oh, really, we'll see about that," replied Cornelius. The Alien dictator dumped the blow torch in the hills of Starmos City. The day dream just ended. "So, now I know where that thing is," said the new alien leader. Tom walked up to Will. "What are you doing talking to yourself?" he asked. He grabbed Will and spun him around. He smacked the new alien leader in the face. "Have you lost your mind?" asked Will. "No, I haven't. Just stop talking to yourself." answered Tom. "I was so not talking to myself," replied Will. "You were too," said Tom. "Whatever." replied Will. The incumbent alien leader opened one of the drawers and he discovered a blow torch.

"Hey, Tom, miracles do happen!" he said. "You're delusional. What miracles are you talking 'bout? There are no miracles going on around here," Tom replied. "Oh, shut the hell up," said Will angrily. He pointed the blow torch toward the delectable breakfast. A couple of minutes later, the breakfast was ready. "Come over here, please," said Will. "What do you want?" asked Tom. "Unfold the murphy table," replied the incumbent alien leader. Tom walked to the murphy table. It was a struggle for him to open it up.

KABOOM! The table had all of a sudden fallen on him. Will started laughing in a vociferous manner. "Shut up," said Tom. Will continued laughing. "Instead of your name being Tom, it should be Donkey head," replied Will. "Shut up," said Tom angrily. He managed to pull himself up from under the table. The alien leader placed the breakfast on the table as well as the beverages. "Sorry for laughing at you," he said. "Okay, I'll forgive you," replied the foolish Tom. "Now, I have another question." "And what would that be?" asked Will. "What are we going to eat with?" asked Tom. "You figure a way to eat it," answered Will. "Well, don't we need a spoon?" asked a perplexed Tom. "You know, man didn't always have silverware," answered Will. "What's silverware?" asked Tom.

The new alien leader had fallen into a moment of laughter. "How could you not know what silverware is?" he asked. "I seriously don't know what silverware is," answered Tom. "Well, guess what, I am not telling you what it is. I guess you have to figure out some way to eat it yourself," replied Will. Tom shoved his face into the small dessert dish. He ate the breakfast like it was a Banana Cream Pie. The alien leader had once again fallen into laughter.

He was chuckling heavily at Tom's foolish antics. Will retrieved his aPhone and he started to record Tom eating the crème bruleé like a fool. Tom looked up. "What are you doing?" he asked, with the breakfast stuck to his face. "Oh nothing. I am just filming you acting like a complete and total fool," answered Will. "Real funny." replied Tom. "Now we'll get some Banana Cream Pies and start eating them," said Will. "I think I am full," replied Tom. "Oh, yeah, you're full?" asked Will. "Yes, I am. I need to go outside to get a sarsaparilla," answered Tom. He left the kitchen. Meanwhile, Will walked into the pantry in the rear of the kitchen which contained fifty banana cream pies. Each pie had its own box. He opened the boxes and organized two forts. He folded up the murphy table, and he got into his position, ready to fire the first pie at Tom. The kitchen door opened and Tom Jackson emerged from the door not knowing what's going to hit him. He turned around. SPLAT! A pie hit his face. "What are you doing!?" he asked. "Well, have you ever heard of such a thing as a food fight?" asked Will. "Yeah," answered Tom. "I am going to give you about twenty seconds to get to your side and mobilize.

Tom opened the first box and squinted his eyes at Will. "Bring it on!" said the new, incumbent, alien leader. Tom fired the first pie at Will at blazing speed. The new leader didn't know what hit him. He flew all the way to the back of the kitchen hitting the fridge and falling. "It's war time!" he shouted. The two of them started tossing pies at one another. After ten minutes of the food fight, the kitchen looked like it was hit with a tornado. The walls were now painted with food. "Who's going to clean the mess?" asked Will. "You are," answered Tom. "Wrong answer! Looks like *you're* going to do it." said Will.

"Hey! What the hell? I shouldn't have to clean up your mess," replied Tom angrily. "You know that I can throw you in the dungeon, so you better be careful with yourself and your behavior over here," said Will. "Who are you to tell me that, when you hated the ruler who said the same things as you're saying right now?" asked Tom. "Good point, Tom, we'll have the maid clean it up." It is now 8 in the morning and the breakfast and clowning around is complete. Tom opened the door. "Have you forgotten something?" asked the new, incumbent, alien leader. "What?" asked Tom. "Your APhone," answered Will. He held Tom's aPhone in his hand and Tom tried to grab the phone out of Will's hand. "Cut it out," said Tom. "Oh, yeah, I will," replied the alien leader sarcastically. As Will's smugness started to show on his face, Tom's eye brows started to crinkle on his face. "Hey, fool, give me the phone!" he said. "Who you callin' fool?" asked Will.

"You the fool! Gimme the phone!" answered Tom. The alien leader stood on his tippy-toes and he reached his arm all the way up to the bottom of the chandelier. Tom jumped up to retrieve his APhone like a kid wanting to get their toy from their older brother. "I will give you the phone only under this one condition," said Will. "What in the world are you talkin' about?" asked Tom. "I will give you the device as long as you say, 'please'," answered Will. Tom angrily crossed his elbows, tightened his fists, and started to kick Will. He kicked him in his right knee. The alien leader had fallen to the ground, and a loud thud had been heard. BANG! "Hey, what the hell?" asked Will.

"You are causing all of the trouble by blazoning the aPhone in my face and then standing up tall on purpose so that way I can't get it. People like you are what I like to call big bullies," answered Tom. "First of all, I am not a person. I am an alien who rules an alien city. In addition to that, you shouldn't be calling me a bully because I was the one who rescued you and a lot of other folks from that ol' brute," replied the alien leader. "Shut up," said Tom nonchalantly.

He walked out of the room. Will swooped his webbed hand towards Tom's left leg. A loud thud was heard on the ground. "So, we want to play it that way?" said Tom sarcastically. "Yeah, sure," replied Will. Tom got up from the ground immediately after he had fallen. The alien leader then stood up. "Why don't we stop this fight and be nice to each other?" he asked. "No, I want to continue fighting," answered Tom.

"Okay," replied Will. The alien leader grabbed Tom by the shirt. "What are you doing?" he (Tom) asked. "Oh, I am going to throw you in the window," answered the alien leader. "No!" shouted Tom nervously. "Yes," replied an exuberant Will. He carried Tom, who was screaming, and started running toward the arch window. He suddenly stopped, and was getting ready to toss him out the window. "Any last words?" he asked. "I surrender," answered Tom.

Will showed a face of disbelief with his eyes wide opened. "Let me put you down," he said in shock. He put Tom down. "I am in such shock," Will said. "Well, I am putting up my white flag," replied Tom. "Okay, that's a good thing," said the elated alien leader. "Say, where's

Light?" asked Tom. "Oh my God, you've just reminded me. I forgot that he was here. He is very quiet," answered Will. The alien leader and the foolish Tom left the kitchen and walked down the hallway. "Where do you think he is?" asked Will. "Oh my God.

Maybe he had six dozen martinis at the party last night and he stayed up all night because of that." answered Tom. "That is the stupidest answer I have ever heard. Can't you come up with any better answers?" asked Will. "No, I guess not, because I am a dope and dopes like me know nothin'." answered Tom. "Tom, I have no idea as to why you are constantly with me. It is like annoying as hell. You don't even put an effort to answer a single question that I ask you in an intelligent way. And if you did, put a whole lot of effort and made those rusty wheels in your head turn, your answers to my questions would still be erroneous," replied Will.

"I really don't care," said Tom. "Well, maybe if you gave a hoot, the world would have been different," replied the alien leader. Tom and Will kept walking down the hallway in silence, and they were stopped by the slightly opened guest room door. The room consists of a cherry wood platform bed with a mattress that required water. The television was built into the burly wood dresser's mirror. The windows were in the shape of an arch, and the curtains were half transparent.

The room had the featured view of the Front lawn. "This room looks really nice," said Tom. "Well, thank you," replied Will. "But, more importantly, we have to find Light." Tom remained by the door, while the alien leader started to inspect the bed. "The covers look like they've been used. But, yet no one is lying there," he said. Tom walked up to Will. "What do you think might have happened?" he asked. "I believe that somebody broke in, during the early morning hours," answered Will.

"Check those lumps right here on the..," said Tom. "Splurt it out," shouted Will. "Check out those lumps on the foot of the bed," Tom said quite quickly. The alien leader pulled the sheets and comforter down to the foot of the bed. A lifeless body that had the appearance of a robot was found on the foot of the bed. Tom gasped. "What's going on 'round here?" he asked. "Looks like Light is dead," Will answered slowly. There was a precise physical resemblance of Light in the dead body.

"What shall we do with him?" asked Tom. "Put him in front of the fountain on the front lawn," answered Will abruptly. Tom did as he was told. Meanwhile, Will investigated what happened. He opened all of the sixteen drawers in the room including the drawers in the powder room. He finally finished opening the last drawer, which was on the dresser. He noticed that all of the clothes were stuck in this particular drawer. He threw all of the clothes out of there, and he noticed an envelope. He hesitated, and he looked in the direction of the front lawn. Tom was seen in view putting the body in front of the fountain. "Come in here," shouted Will. Tom placed the body on the blue grass and returned back into the bedroom.

"What's wrong?" he asked. "I found a note right here. Why don't you open it up," replied Will. Tom opened up the envelope. The letter started to illuminate and flow in midair. It started talking very loudly and it had a female tone. *"To whom it may concern. If you are wondering what happened to Light, I kidnapped him. If you want to know where he is go to California County. I will tell you why I abducted him when you come see me, if you even care about him. If you don't come to him within thirty six hours, he will be officially dead. This letter was written by me, Jacqueline Langyaw. By the way, I am going to kill Will Von Alien and Tom Jackson next. So, come and get me, whoever you are. In addition to that, if you are wondering why that body is in the bed, it is really a hoax. See, I can fool you."*

"Who do you think did it?" asked Tom. "I am not too sure. But, we must make some sort of immediate investigation," answered Will. "Well, when are you going to make this doohickey thing?" asked Tom. "Did you just call this investigation of import a 'doohickey thing'?" asked Will. "Yes, I don't know what an investigation is," answered Tom. "Well, you're going to find out now," replied Will. "I ain't goin'," said Tom. "Okay, you have a choice. The first choice is you come along, help me, and be hailed as a hero. Or, the second choice is that you act like an uncooperative moron, you don't do anything, and I sentence you to life in the hole without parole. It is your choice," replied Will.

"I'll take the first choice for 200," said Tom nervously in a high pitched. "Yeah, I think that is more like it. So get ready to go to the train station over here in the North block of the city," replied Will. "Okay," said Tom. "How long do we have to get ready?" he asked. "About a half hour," answered Will. The intelligent alien leader and the foolish man left the tragic and gruesome scene. This scene was really a fallacious hoax. Will walked into the royal quarters and Tom walked into the guest quarters. Fifteen minutes later, they returned into the hallway wearing black tuxedos.

Their hair was slicked back and they looked like agents. "Are you ready?" asked Will. "Yes," answered Tom. Will took out his yellow, digital watch. The watch had shown 9:00 A.M. We have about 32 more hours to rescue him. Both disguised agents positioned themselves as runners getting ready for a lap. They started to run down the hallway. As they were running, Tom ripped his pant on his knee.

He suddenly stopped. Will continued to run and he arrived at the door. He noticed Tom a distance away bent over in the hallway. "What are you doing?" he shouted. "Oh, nothing," answered Tom. "Why are you bent over if there's nothing wrong?" asked Will. "Because I ripped my pants," answered Tom." "And where is the rip?" asked the alien leader. "It is on the knee part," answered Tom. "Okay, who cares about that! Besides, we have a mission to complete," replied Will. "Good," said Tom. One second later, he dashed down the hallway, right up to the door way. "You run like a speed demon," said Will. "I know. Everybody says that about me," replied Tom. "Now, I hope you won't be the speed demon when you are interviewing the witnesses," said Will. "Oh, no. Why would I do such a thing?" asked Tom. "You *would* do such thing," answered Will. "Oh. Shut up," said Tom. The alien leader opened the thirty foot tall door leading into the Alien Estate. This door featured ornate decor. There were swirls of gold and silver, and there were hundreds of wooden panels. A tall, goliath-sized alien officer ran up to both disguised agents. "Who are you?" he asked. His voice was monstrously loud. "I am Will Von Alien and this guy is Tom Jackson," answered the alien leader. "What are you two doing here as freed men when you two are fugitives?" asked the officer. "We are not fugitives," yelled Tom. "Have you ever heard of the phrase of 'Earthlings should be seen and not heard'?" asked the officer. "No, I haven't and what gives you the right to say such a thing?" asked Tom. "Who are *you* to tell *me* which rights I have and which rights I don't have?" asked the officer angrily. "Don't you dare tell me that," answered Tom. "I just did. In fact, I hereby sentence you to life in the hole without parole," replied the officer. The officer shoved Tom into the hole. Meanwhile, Will left the estate and he waited at the gate. Tom never arrived. "See you later Brutis." he shouted. Brutis ran up to the gate. He started banging on the gate. "Will, I am going to kill you," he said.

"Looks like it is too late," replied the alien leader. The goliath sized officer turned around. There wasn't anything there. "See ya' sucker," said Will. He ran down WVA Boulevard to the Starmos Train Station. This was the only place that one can see visitors coming and going by train over here. Will arrived at Orange Circle. In the center of the circle was the toppled statue of Cornelius Von Alien. The circle was lined with fountains.

The station had an old-fashioned appearance. The building was a vintage brick building with four arched windows on its front facade. Hovercraft buses, that each accommodated 60 folks, were lined on the ground perfectly. Right outside the revolving door was a man in a blue uniform. The alien leader approached the properly dressed man. "Who are you?" Will asked. "I am Howard Carterson," he answered. "What are you doing here?" asked Will. "I work as a chauffeur," he answered. ", and who do you work for?" asked the alien leader.

"Jacqueline Langyaw," he answered. "What!?" shouted Will. "Yeah, Jacqueline Langyaw, the former prosecutor. Why are you asking me such a thing?" he asked. "I would like to know her whereabouts. I heard she has committed a serious crime. So, I want to know where her present location is," answered Will. "What business is it of yours about her present location?" asked Howard. The chauffeur crinkled his bushy, brown eyebrows and tightened his lips. His jade, green skin changed to the color of fiery, red cinnamon.

"Why the hell are you asking about this innocent woman's location?" he angrily asked. "Don't you dare take that tone with me young man!" said Will. "Oh, now, *you're* saying that *I am* taking a tone with you when you are having a malicious attitude with me? Who the hell do you think you are?" asked the angry chauffeur. "I am Will Von Alien," answered the alien leader. "Which Will Von Alien are you?" asked Howard. "I am Will Von Alien," answered the alien leader, once again. "Well, there are two Will Von Aliens. There is the Will Von Alien that is the fugitive and the Will Von Alien that is the successor of Cornelius Von Alien," replied the chauffeur. "Okay. Well, I guess that I am the successor of Cornelius," said Will.

"Oh! Well what would you want me to do?" asked Howard. His attitude toward Will suddenly changed. "Two things. The first thing is that you are not going to talk to me like I am some sort of king. I am your president. You should have some respect for me. But, don't treat me like I am royalty because I am not. In addition to that, I want to get some more information out of you regarding Jacqueline Langyaw," answered Will.

"Okay, well, where do you want to meet?" asked the chauffeur. "I want you to come with me," answered Will. "Well, I suppose I can come with you for 'bout forty eight hours. Because that is when she is supposedly coming here," replied Howard. "Well, that's a good thing. We only need about thirty hours of your time. So, why don't you come with me to a couple of places. Before anything, I must pay for my train ticket," said Will. "Well, I'll come with you to do that too. Besides, I also need to purchase a train ticket," replied the chauffeur. "I thought you're allowed to go on the mass transit for free," replied the alien leader.

"Because, Jacqueline Langyaw is a selfish pig," said Howard. "I thought you liked her, and I thought she was your best friend?" asked Will. "Well, guess what? She's not," said Howard. "But you quickly and angrily defended her when you totally despise her?" asked Will. "Because that's what she requires," answered Howard. "How could she require you to do anything?" asked Will. "Because she is the prosecutor. She could do whatever she wants. She has unlimited prerogatives," answered Howard. "I don't know about that," replied Will.

"Why would you say such a thing?" asked the chauffeur. "She had her license revoked," answered the alien leader. "How did her license get revoked?" asked Howard. "She made a plea deal that stated that she would testify against her co-defendants in exchange for revocation of her prosecuting license," answered Will. "Well, I don't know about that," replied Howard. "And now why would *you* say such a thing?" asked Will. "Because it is true," answered the chauffeur.

"Okay, we will get more into this later. For now, we must get ourselves ready to get out of here. Remember, we don't have unlimited time. I only have thirty two hours. So, let's cut out the discussion and start getting ready for departure from this place," replied Will. "That sounds very good and intelligent with me. You are probably one of the smartest folks that I ever know, and there's a high probability that you'll go down in history in Starmos City," said Howard. "Oh, don't say such a thing. I am not the most intelligent fella in the universe. And I am probably not going to go down in history for my smarts," replied Will.

Chapter II: Starmos Station and the Orange Liner

It is now half past ten in the morning and Will Von Alien meets Howard Carterson, Jacqueline Langyaw's chauffeur. The alien leader walked up to the motorized revolving door at the Starmos Train Station. This revolving door was a solid, glimmering gold color. Howard followed Will. They goofed around in the door. Howard started to hang on the rail in the door than they started bouncing up and down. A couple of minutes later, the door stopped. "What happened?" asked Will. "I have no idea," answered the former prosecutor's chauffeur. A couple of minutes later, the security guard walked over.

He turned the revolving door back on and made Will and Howard come into the Main Hall of the train station. This security guard had a slender appearance. He stood at six feet tall and looked like he weighed around one hundred and thirty pounds. "What are you two doing acting like two clowns?" he asked. "You see the door got stuck, and so in order to make it "unstuck," we started to bounce up and down. Suddenly the door became more stuck, and here we are today," answered Howard. "Okay, this sounds quite believable to me. I think that this story can go through. I won't arrest you," replied the officer. "It is not against the law to bounce and clown around on public property," said Will. "That's true. Good point," replied the officer.

This officer had a raspy voice with a Latino Dialect. "Now, what do you want?" he asked. "I need to know where the Ticket Purchase Center is," answered Howard. "Over down there," he pointed toward the Ticket Purchase Area. "What is your name?" asked Will. "Officer Valencia," the officer answered. "Can you escort us to the area?" asked the chauffeur. "Why do you want me to escort you when the purchase center is right over there?" asked Officer Valencia. "Because this place might be a shady place," answered Will.

"How do you know that? Have you ever been here?" asked the officer. "No, I haven't. But, I suspect it is shady because the statues of Cornelius Von Alien are "looking" at me in a creepy way," answered Will. "You didn't answer my question," replied the officer. "Did I not answer your question properly in your eyes?" asked Will. Officer Valencia replied "Because I asked you as to why this place is so shady and quirky in your eyes."

Will had to explain. "Okay, the real reason is because there are a ton of officers in this place, and they may think that I am still a fugitive." Officer Valencia drew his gun toward Will. "Don't you dare move a muscle," he said sternly. "I don't have any weapons on me," replied Will. The officer lowered his nine millimeter hand gun. "Why were you a fugitive?" the officer asked. "Because when Cornelius Von Alien was ruling this city, I was the chef. This beastly dictator tried to poison his guests for some nasty reason. So, the plan backfired on him. I was apprehended. I managed to escape imprisonment.

That was when I became a fugitive," answered Will. "Were you innocent or guilty?" asked the officer. "Well, it depends on how you look at things. If you were Cornelius Von Alien and his malicious guards, you would think that I am a guilty traitor. If you were me and my friends, you would think that I am completely innocent. Truth of the matter is that I am totally innocent, and those allegations are so fallacious," answered the new alien leader. "Most fugitives say their innocent. Are you truthfully innocent?" asked Officer Valencia.

"Yes. Can we get into this later? I have to purchase my ticket" answered Will. They walked down the stone tile floor to the train booking desk. There was a Cheshire clock in the center of the train station. Adjacent to the clock was a waiting area of wooden benches. About fifty feet from the waiting area was the train ticket purchase center. The alien leader, the chauffeur, and the officer arrived at the waiting area. "Who do you want to buy the tickets?" asked Will. Not a single answer of yes or no left the officer or the chauffeur's lips.

"I guess I will do it," said Will. Officer Valencia and Howard sat down on the wooden chairs while Will waited on the line. "Next one to board," said the purchase center lady. "She had blonde hair, aqua blue eyes, and blue skin. She looked at Will. "Who is this?" she asked with a wink. "Will Von Alien," He answered. "Were you the fugitive that stayed at the Star Hotel a while back?" she asked. "Yes, what happened to your job over there?" asked Will. "Oh, the place went out of business," she answered." "And what was the reason for that?" asked the alien leader. "Because Cornelius didn't like it that you escaped," she answered. "I guess that's what happens when there's such thing like communism," replied Will.

"Shhh! don't mention that word," said the ticket purchase lady. "Why?" asked the alien leader. "Because if you call Cornelius a communist then you get executed immediately!" she answered. "Cornelius is dead," replied Will. She was surprised to hear this. "How can he be dead?" she asked. "Because I killed him," Will replied. "I don't know about that," she replied. "Why?" asked Will. "Because there's a mysterious effect that takes place in the statues once in a while," she explained.

"I don't believe that in any way, shape, or form. There's no way that can happen. Now I want to know your name again," said Will. "I am Rubi," replied the former hotel clerk. "Are you Ruby?" asked Will. "No, I am Rubi, the Russian former hotel clerk," she answered. "Oh! You were the one that helped me in the rescue for my friends who were imprisoned at the Alien Estate!" replied Will. "Yes," said Rubi. "Well, it's nice to see you," replied the alien leader. "Would you like to buy a ticket?" asked Rubi. "Yes. I actually need to buy three tickets to California Station," answered Will. "

There are ten California Stations," Rubi replied. "And where are they?" asked Will. "Well, there are eight in the state of California, one in the state of Delaware, and one in upstate New York," answered the train station clerk. "I need the one in New York." "Okay, three tickets for New York. That will come out to three hundred Starmos Bucks," she said. "That's not bad. That's actually quite cheap." replied Will. "Oh yeah - I need some other payment," she said. "And what would that be?" asked the alien leader. "I need you to give me a smooch," she replied. She grabbed Will's head and kissed him. The folks waiting behind him were complaining.

"Get moving, 'lady's man'" shouted one of the people waiting on line. She gave Will the tickets for the noon departure. He waved to his "girlfriend" and returned to the seat where the officer and the chauffeur were waiting. "I saw you schmoozing with your "girlfriend" said Officer Valencia "Yeah. So what does that mean?" asked Will. "I thought you were there to purchase the tickets," answered the chauffeur. "Yeah, and I have the tickets, and you better not loose yours," replied Will.

He presented two tickets, one he gave to the chauffeur, and the other to the officer. .An announcement came over the PA system "Boarding will be in a half hour for the train to California County, New York. Once again, boarding will be in a half hour for the train heading to California County, New York," "We have to go get something to eat," said Will. "Well, we only have one restaurant here," replied Howard. "Okay, we'll start heading there right now but run.

We don't have much time." said the alien leader. He started to run to the restaurant and the officer and the chauffeur followed. The only restaurant at the train station was the Randall Grill. The front facade of the restaurant was made of antique bricks, and featured a fancy marquis that displayed the name of the restaurant. The trio of gentlemen entered the restaurant. Will and Howard sat down, and Officer Valencia walked up to the counter. In front of this counter was an aPad.

This aPad contained the menu of the restaurant. Officer Valencia ordered three Strawberry Smoothies. He paid through the Star Card. A vending machine dispensed three large smoothies. He returned to the table. "What time is it?" Howard asked. "Three quarters past the hour," answered Will. "Don't you mean 11:45?" asked Howard.

"You know what I mean," replied the alien leader. The motley trio started to drink their smoothies. Five minutes later, a loud noise was heard. "Ladies and Gentlemen, it is the final boarding call for train departure heading to California County, New York.

Once again, this is the final boarding call for the departure heading to California County, New York," said the PA system. "We have to get going," said Howard abruptly. He started to run out of the restaurant with his smoothie. The rest of the group followed. They arrived at the gate to the platform. Their tickets were accounted for. When Will passed through the gate, a green, luminous light that were in the eyes of the statues of Cornelius Von Alien started to blink, and the ground started to rumble. The train was at the platform. This train looked like a View liner. There were two levels on this train.

The first level featured sleeping quarters, and the top level featured seats and the dining car. This train also featured a conference center. The top of the train had an orange color. The motley trio boarded the train. They were greeted by the train attendant. "Is this the train to California County?" asked Will. "Yes," answered the train attendant. "What do you need?" she asked. "I need to know where I sit," answered Will. "You can sit anywhere for now. You can even go up to the dining cabin," replied the train attendant. This train attendant wore a cap. She had a Russian accent, blonde hair, and blue eyes.

Also, she had blue skin. "Do you happen to know where the cabin is?" asked Will. "Follow me," she said. She ran up two flights of stairs. The motley trio followed. Howard stopped. "Do you think this lady is the same lady who you dealt with earlier?" he asked. "Probably not," answered Will, although he knew exactly. "Why would you think that?" asked the chauffeur. "Because it is physically impossible to have two completely different jobs," replied the alien leader. "And why would you think that?" asked Howard. "Because, it is not possible," replied Will.

"Well, I saw that she had the same accent, same voice, same skin color, and same hair color. This is definitely your girlfriend," said Howard. "Yeah, you're probably wrong," replied Will trying not to show he knew it was Rubi. "I don't know about that," said the chauffeur. "Well, I am pretty sure that this woman is not Rubi. So, stop saying that," replied the alien leader. "Hey, find out for yourself," said Jacqueline's chauffeur. They walked up the stairs to the second level in the train.

They were greeted by a long, narrow, gray hallway. Will arrived at the top of the stairs landing. "Say where is the dining cabin?" he asked. "I have no idea," answered Officer Valencia. "Which way shall we go? To the right or to the left?" the alien leader asked. "I don't know again." answered Howard. "Well, usually when you go to the right you are going the Conservative Route. But when you go to the left you are usually going to the Liberal Democratic Route," said Officer Valencia. "Yeah, that's just politics," replied Will.

"Well, then if you go to the right, you are going in the correct or, simply right direction. But, when you go to the left, you are going to the bad and incorrect direction. So, I'd recommend you go to the right," said the officer. The motley trio walked down the long, narrow, gray, windowless hallway hoping they will get to the dining car. Two hundred feet later, the alien leader arrived at the door. There was a chain bridge that kept the walkway of the train together. Will walked down the hall, and he opened the door. The wind hit his face.

"Guys, come here," he shouted. The fellow gentlemen ran to Will's location. "What's wrong?" asked Howard. "I found a major hoop," answered the alien leader. "Oh, give me a chance to jump through the hoop," replied Officer Valencia. "It's not really a hoop. It's actually a narrow chain. But, we have to cross it," said Will. "Well, I'll wish you some good luck," replied the chauffeur. "Here goes," said the alien leader. He placed his right foot on the chain. His left foot followed. Every move he made was a life or death scenario.

Crossing the chain was like crossing the widest part of the Grand Canyon. Three feet to the ground seemed like three thousand feet. Seconds felt like minutes, and minutes felt like hours. Within two minutes, Will made it from one car to the other car. Howard followed. He prayed to God before he started to move. Left, right, left, and right. His feet moved in that pattern. After, two seconds of crossing the chain, he stopped, and remained in the middle of the chain. His right foot slipped, he screamed. "What's wrong?" asked Will. "No time for questions! Help me!" Howard answered abruptly. Will slowly reached out with his arm. "Faster!" shouted the chauffeur. The alien leader grabbed the chauffer's hand and pulled him back up onto the chain. He continued crossing, and finally, he made it onto the other car. Lastly, Officer Valencia had to cross the terrifying, teeth chattering chain. The officer leapt across from one car to another. "How did you do that!?" asked Will, in disbelief by that move. "I just had to run and jump. It doesn't take a rocket scientist to do that," answered the officer. They had arrived at the Dining Car.

The Dining Car door mysteriously opened. "What just happened?" asked Will. "Nothing that I know of," answered Officer Valencia. "Maybe it was some sort of an occult effect," answered Howard. Will walked into that particular train car. There were a lot of aliens talking. The ones that were seated at the bar were considered to be the affluent ones. Those individuals refused to talk to the bar tender. Will walked up to the bar stool. This bar was an antique wooden bar with granite countertops. The five chandeliers are made of wine drinking glasses.

The train car looked like a parlor room. The windows were covered with fully translucent curtains with ornate floral patterns and designs. The bar tender was a tall, college gentleman serving drinks to the patrons on board the train. The affluent talked to one another on political affairs. They spoke with such a strong command of the English language. But, yet, when they talked to the bar tender, they use questionable words. "Hey, M-F'er! I want more ale!" said one of the affluent folks. The bar tender willingly served that particular one with beer. He disregarded what that affluent, "high class" mouth said.

A loud noise was just heard. An announcement was coming over a speaker. "Ladies and Gentlemen, welcome on board the Sun Star Railroad. Before we make our route to California County, we must go through the following rules. At around 2:00, you will come on down to rest. But, for now, you are free to move about the cabins. Secondly, looking out the window is prohibited when we get closer to the portal to Planet Earth. Arrival is scheduled for 5:00 in the afternoon. I hope you all have a safe and enjoyable train ride to California County," said the train attendant on the PA system. The bar tender walked up to Will.

"I noticed you looked at me in a funny way," he said. "Oh, it was because I felt bad for you," replied the alien leader. "Why would you feel bad for me when you look like all the other rich folks?" asked the bar tender.

"Because, I could assure you that I am rich, but I am *not* like all of the other rich folks." answered Will. "How could you say you are *not* like all of the other rich folks when you are rich?" asked the bar tender. "Because I am not monetarily rich. I am emotionally rich," answered Will. "I only thought that people who are rich have a lot of money," replied the college bar tender.

"That's not the full definition of rich. To be emotionally rich means that you are happy and you remain fortuitous when going through trouble and strife," said the alien leader. "Interesting," replied the bar tender. "Now, can you do me a favor please?" asked Will. "What would that be?" the bar tender asked. "I would like to have a couple of drinks. Can you do that?" asked Will. "What kind of drinks?" asked the bar tender. "I would like to have lemon lime carbonated drinks," answered the alien leader. "Okay, that won't take much," replied the bar tender. He returned to the back of the bar, and retrieved three glasses that were hanging from the ceiling. As he was taking them down, the other glasses started to cling together. CLANG, CLANG, CLANG! The noise was ear piercing to the affluent folks. "Does it take a rocket scientist to take down some glasses?" asked one of the rich folks. "Hey, shut the hell up!" shouted Will angrily. "Who are you to tell me to 'shut the hell up'?" asked the disrespectful affluent pig.

"I just did. You are totally not nice to this innocent college kid who is learning to be on your social class level. You claim and tout yourself to be so well mannered and straight-laced. But, yet, you act like a total fool. You tell this gentleman that he is an M-F'er, when he is a college student learning his way toward your monetary level. Just because his monetary status is nowhere near yours, yet, his personality status is much higher than yours," replied Will angrily. The affluent brute stared at Will with his eyes opening wide. "I even know who you are but I don't know why you're here when you are the biggest fugitive in Starmos City right now. You are Will Von Alien, the fugitive," said the disrespectful affluent pig. Everybody in that particular train car stared at Will. "Will Von Alien," they shouted.

"Yes, indeed. This is definitely Will Von Alien, the beastly fugitive. He was the one who tried to kill our idol, Cornelius. He probably had jealousy over the way Cornelius ran our beautiful city. now that we rich guys caught him, he is going to be cooked!" said the affluent pig. "For your information, I am no longer a fugitive. And by the way, Cornelius is dead. In addition to that, I am now the president of Starmos City. So, you better not assume that I am a fugitive because I can be arbitrary like Cornelius, and make whoever I want to become fugitives," replied Will angrily. The affluent pig mockingly said to Will "Yeah, you do that.

Remember, we rich folks pay taxes, and give donations to keep you in your residence. We can easily make you poor, and we'll do that if we feel you're going to be a horrible leader!" Will shook his head. "Why do you act the way you do?" asked the alien leader. "Well, that's the way everybody else acts," answered the affluent pig. "Be the leader. Not the follower," replied Will. "What does that even mean?" asked the affluent alien. "It means that if the whole entire crowd causes trouble or does anything that you feel is considered to be wrong you shouldn't go along with that crowd. Essentially, what I am saying is to be yourself," answered Will. "Okay, my conscience is going over to your side," replied the affluent alien.

"What is your name?" asked Will. "Sir Anders Johnson," replied the affluent alien. He wore a black tuxedo and a red bowtie. He stood a staggering six feet six inches tall. "Now may I talk to you for a little bit?" asked the alien leader. "Sure," answered Sir Anders. "What is it that you need to talk to me about?" "I need your help. My friend has been kidnapped by this nit-picky prosecutor who has a vendetta for me and my friends. She dated Cornelius, who was an evil dictator, and also my distant cousin. Now, I need your help with my situation. My friend got abducted by her, and I am on a hunt to rescue him, and to bring this bitch-excuse the language- to justice," answered Will.

"I'd be willing to help you. So, come on with me, and we shall hunt this one down," replied Sir Anders. "Great! So you will help me in my fight to bring her to justice," said the alien leader. "Can you hold on for a second?" he asked. "Sure," answered the affluent alien. The alien leader walked away from the affluent alien for a short time to meet up with his acquaintances. "Was the lemon lime soda brought over here yet?" asked Will.

"No," answered Howard. "What do you mean?" asked the alien leader. "That busy bar tender was ignoring us because of the rich pig heads trying to bribe him from going to us," answered Howard. "I ought to arrest them," replied Officer Valencia. "You can't arrest them without a court ordered warrant," said Will. "Well, you're the leader of Starmos City. Can't you issue a warrant?" asked the officer. "No, that would be a troublesome abuse of my power as the leader of Starmos City," answered Will. "Good point," replied Howard. "Let me know when the drinks come," said the alien leader. He returned back to Sir Anders Johnson. "So, who are those two?" asked the affluent gentleman.

"Howard and Officer Valencia," answered Will. "That is quite a bizarre name, Officer Valencia. He must've been named after two cities," replied Sir Anders. "What cities would that be?" asked Will. "You probably don't know this because you probably have never been to Planet Earth. But, the cities that I am talking about are in Spain and the state of California," answered the affluent gentleman. "Interesting, we are going to a county named California County," replied Will. The bar tender approached the alien leader.

"Sir, you ordered drinks?" he asked. "Yes," answered Will, " and was your drink a lemon lime soda?" the bar tender asked. "Yes," answered the alien leader. The college bar tender presented Will with his drink. Eventually, the bar tender reached the rest of the motley trio. After receiving his drink, the chauffeur walked up to the alien leader. "Did you get the drink?" Howard asked. "Yes," answered Will. "Now, what is it that you need?" "Nothing," answered the chauffeur. He walked back to Officer Valencia. Returning his attention to Sir Anders "Where are you sitting?" asked the alien leader. "Over on Level One, Car #5, Row 7, Seat 5," answered Sir Anders.

"Wow, you're only two seats away from me," replied Will. Everyone present on the train car stopped talking. The clicking of the PA system started to be heard. Then somebody started talking. "Ladies and Gentlemen, I would like it if everybody would start heading to their seats because in about five minutes we will be departing from the Starmos City Station. It is mandatory that everyone remains in their seats for the first forty five minutes after departure," said the train attendant. Like a mob, everyone started to cram their way through the narrow door crossing the chain and trampling each other down the stairs to head over to their seats.

Meanwhile, the motley trio and the now apparently, aristocratic gentleman, Sir Anders Johnson, remained on board the dining car. "To all of the folks who didn't get down to their seats, this is your final call before I throw you off of this train," said the train attendant over the PA system. The motley trio and the affluent gentleman have thirty seconds to get to their seats. For the first five seconds, they all leapt across a long chain connection.

With twenty five seconds left, they ran down the narrow hallway, and jumped down the two flights of stairs, which were used as the dumping grounds for the beverage glasses. As the motley trio and the affluent gentleman jumped down the stairs, the glasses started to shake, and some of them broke. Fortunately, not a single fellow was injured jumping down the stairs. Finally they and Sir Anders arrived at their seats. Sir Anders Johnson sat in the opposite seat of where the trio sat.

Will sat by the window, Officer Valencia sat in the middle and Howard sat on the aisle. "What do you think of these seats?" asked the chauffeur. "They are probably one of the best seats I've ever sat in. They are extremely comfortable," answered Officer Valencia. "Do you have anything to say, Will?" asked Howard. "Who me?" asked the alien leader. "Yes, you," answered the chauffeur. "Can you please reiterate your question for me?" asked Will. "Sure, I asked you if you like the seats or not," answered Howard. "Oh, I think these seats are the most comfortable seats I've ever sat in of my life. Plus, they have recliners. That is a double plus," replied the alien leader.

He reclined all the way back. "Well, thank you for those comments. By the way, before I was that prosecutor's chauffeur, I used to be the one who designed and built these beautiful seats," said Howard. "Well, that must've been some interesting career especially before being a chauffeur to a nasty witch," replied Will. Howard suddenly turned on the alien leader. "Hey! Who are you to call one of my buddies a witch?" asked the chauffeur. "Are you on our side or are you against us? Are you going to join or die?" asked Will. "I will not take your side if you're going to call my buddy a witch," answered Howard. "Well, your buddy is a nit-picky, conniving prosecutor," replied Will. "No, she is not," shouted the chauffeur. "Yes, she is. Look what she did to me and my friends," replied Will angrily. "Oh, she might have tried to prosecute you and your demonic and heretic friends. But, that is because you tried to revolt and kill Cornelius Von Alien. In fact, you don't deserve to be the leader of this alien city. You should be in the hole right now, if not dead. Shame on you because you are disgusting in your attitude; a liar in your words; and the bottom of the social class structure in my eyes," shouted the chauffeur. Will is now confused and angry. "Who are you to tell me that?!" "I am the prosecutor's chauffeur. I could tell her what you're doing, and you can be criminally charged and put to trial. Do you want that to happen?" asked the chauffeur.

"Sure. And any jury will believe my innocence. In fact, I will give Ms. Langyaw back her prosecuting license," answered Will. The train car remained silent. All of a sudden, a loud grunt was heard. The alien leader punched the chauffeur in the stomach. "What the hell?" shouted Howard. "You are just as guilty as she is," replied Will angrily. He grabbed the chauffeur by his shirt, and started shaking him. The chauffeur squeezed the alien leader's muscular arms. that didn't stop Will from shaking him. Howard stopped squeezing Will's arms, and he smacked him in the face.

Two teeth came flying out of the alien leader's mouth. "So, you think you're so tough?" asked the prosecutor's chauffeur. "Yes, I am, and good will always win. You're the evil one and I am the good one. So, evil shall never mess around with the good," answered Will. "I am not scared of you," replied Howard. The alien leader moved his hands up toward the prosecutor's chauffeur's neck. Howard's head started to change colors. He changed from his normal pigment to the color of red. As Will's choke hold increased, the chauffeur's head started to turn purple. After one minute of choking Howard, the alien leader had withdrawn his hands from the chauffeur's neck. Howard started to cough and catch his breath. "Okay, I give up. I am going to jump off of this train," he said. "Good, I hope to never see you again," replied Will.

"Oh, you won't," said Howard. He started to walk to the exit door. As he was walking up to the exit door, an alarm was heard. All of a sudden, the train attendant rushed down the stairs. "Who dares to stand up when we are getting ready for departure?" she asked. "It is I, Howard Carterson. I hereby want to depart this crummy vehicle, and have nothing to do with you or these idiots in the front row over here," he answered. "Guess what? I don't care because you shouldn't be standing up when the train is right on its way for departure.

Now, I had to stop the train because of that stupid and ridiculous antic that you just pulled with me. I have a special place for insolent, ignorant imbeciles like you," she replied. "Ooh, I'm scared," he said. "Don't you dare to mess with me because I will beat the hell out of you," she replied. "Oh really," he said. She turned around. All of a sudden he smacked her. "So, do you like smacking?" she asked. "Yes, it is a very delightful and mind satisfying activity," he answered. "Can you hold on for a second?" she asked. Rubi, who was indeed the train attendant, walked over to the red security button.

She slammed her hand on the button and then she returned back over to Howard. "There are some guys coming over to you to escort you off of this train," she said. "Ooh, I am so scared," he again replied. Loud pounds in the ground were heard. There were five security guards wearing yellow shirts coming after Howard. They shackled him and carried him to the back of the train. There, he was confined in a holding cell until the train journey was officially ended. Rubi walked up to Will. "So, how's everything going?" she asked. "Very good," he answered. "How about you?" "I'm doing okay," she replied. "Did anything happen to you while I was gone?" she asked.

"There were many things that actually happened," answered Will. "Okay, will you please tell me the most important thing that has happened so far on this train?" she asked. "Well, right before you came down, I ended up in a huge fight with the same one that you just fought with," answered Will. "Say, do you want to see the Security surveillance room?" she asked. "Sure," answered the alien leader. She escorted him up the stairs and they ran past the dining car.

They entered the main car. On the second level, the main car featured the security surveillance area. In this area, were one hundred and fifty closed circuit televisions. The first fifty C.C.T.V. systems were used to record all of the events that are or have been occurring on the platform. Followed by that, the next ten cameras recorded the dining car and the kitchen. The next twenty cameras recorded the cabin cars and seating cars. The rest of the cameras were not in use. "So, what do you think of this area?" asked Rubi. "I have never been in a place with this much complex technology.

There must be a copious amount documents of recorded film," answered Will. "I love it that you like this place. If you were to choose another profession besides being a chef, what would you choose?" she asked. "I would probably be a security guard because I am very muscular," answered the alien leader. "How do you like your job now?" she asked. "It is the best job I ever had. I would never expect in my one quarter century old life to be a leader of a beautiful city. I love this place, and as leader I will undo all the evil Cornelius did, and I will improve this place tremendously," he answered. "That's my leader," replied Rubi.

"Thank you," replied Will. "If you were to make some changes on this train, what would you do?" asked the train attendant. "Well, there would be many things that I would have done. First, I would have placed railings along the edge by the tracks because I don't want anybody getting hurt. In addition to that, I would put a fountain in the center of this train station. The tertiary thing that I would do is expand the menu because folks get bored of the same menu. We have a demanding society, and so we must accommodate and acclimate ourselves to the society that we live in.

We must even go beyond the societal demands. We must serve our customers with meals instead of insubstantial drinks and snacks. We don't live in the 1970s or 1980s. We live in the 2040s. We live in a society where everyone is constantly craving gourmet and delectable meals," answered the alien leader. "Do you have any questions for me?" asked Rubi. "Yes," answered Will. "Are you a native of Starmos City?"

"No, I am not. I am of Russian origin. You can clearly tell by my accent. I look like an alien because I was placed in the Alien Maker 4000," answered Rubi. "That is quite interesting. I can't believe that I didn't know that, and the Grand Fromage of an alien city should know everything. I must learn how to get myself more involved with this place," replied Will. The train started moving, and it is now on its way to California County, New York. It is now 2:00 in the afternoon. The train moved at Mach ten speed. It left the sandy dunes of Starmos City, and it will be officially out of the alien city when it travels past the gigantic, three hundred foot tall orb.

Chapter III: The First "real" Ordeal: The Voyage on the Train

The train finally departed from the Starmos City station. Now, everyone is on their way to California County Station. Will and Rubi were on the upper level in the Security Camera Room. "How do you like this train ride so far?" she asked. "It is amazing in terms of the security operations," answered the alien leader. "Well, you ain't seen nothing yet. We have more to explore on this impressive train," she replied.

Will started to jump up and down like an excited child, and he started to run in place. "Where are we going to next?" he exuberantly asked. "Easy there, tiger," replied the female train attendant. "It is a surprise." "Well, I demand to see it," he replied. "Well, I suggest you stop demanding from me because what you're doing is going to cause some trouble, this is me remember." said Will's girlfriend. "And what trouble would that be?" the alien leader asked. "Trouble for yourself and trouble in your head. So stop being so demanding, and you won't have to worry about trouble coming your way," replied Rubi. "Come with me." She left the Security Camera Car unattended and she opened the door. Suddenly, she vanished.

Will walked out of the door while the train was moving at Mach four hundred speed. "Rubi? he shouted. "Rubi! Where are you?" The noise of the loud train engine was heard. All of a sudden footsteps were heard. These footsteps sounded very low in volume. "Rubi, where are you?" he shouted again. "I'm up here," she said. "How will I get up there," the alien leader said to himself. He glanced at the next car over. On the rear of the next car over was a bar ladder. Now, he thinks he is in a double life or death situation. This will be the biggest decision of his entire life.

He has to first cross the perilous chain. Now, that the train is moving, double trouble is going to take place. One wrong move, he could die within a matter of seconds. He carefully crossed this chain. His heart was racing at two hundred beats per second. The alien leader feels like he is already in a detrimental situation. This is an additional stress to this situation. He looked down at the perilous track. The fear of being pulverized by the train was t instilled in his mind. He continued to cross the chain until finally, he made it across.

A sigh of relief left his mouth. Now, the train has started to increase its speed from Mach two hundred miles per hour to Mach six hundred mph. He tip toed up to the metallic bar ladder. There are eight bars to climb. The first four bars he started to climb were safe and comfortable. As he made it up to the next two bars, he started to have a feeling of discomfort. Now, climbing this bar ladder is beyond uncomfortable. It is treacherous and deadly. The two hundred mph wind from the train's swift speed started to blow into Will's face. His long blonde hair started to flap in the wind, and his watery blue eyes started to dry.

His eyes started to tear. Finally, he made it up to the roof top of the train car. This rooftop had the appearance of any mundane train rooftop. It was the boring color of grey. But it wasn't made of metallic components. Instead, it was made of fiberglass and plastic. Another bizarre feature of this mundane rooftop is that it is soft. Every step that one made, there would be a small, temporary scar that would be created. Rubi walked up to the alien leader. "Why did it take you so long to get up here?" she asked. "Well, gee, when you've never been on board a train in your life, expect that to happen," answered the alien leader, who was out of breath at the moment.

"By the way, we have to continue crossing," replied the female train attendant. "What do you mean?" asked Will. "I mean that we have to go to the back of the train. That is where the secret spot is located," answered Rubi. "What secret area are you talking about?" asked the alien leader. "I am talking about a secret area. I'm not going to tell you about the area that is in the back of the train until we get to that particular area," she answered. "You go first," replied the alien leader.

"Okay," she replied. Rubi started to build up speed by running on the rooftop of the train. She leapt across the seven foot gap between the first and second car. "Come on, Will. Do it," she shouted. "Okay. This is going to be nerve wracking. But I will try. Don't be surprised if I don't make it," the alien leader replied. "Don't say such a thing. If I am shorter than you and I can do it so can you. Do not be terrified and do not be nervous," replied Rubi. "Okay, I'll try," said Will. He positioned himself like a runner three seconds before the race. He dashed up the rooftop and made a daring leap across the seven to eight foot gap. His leap lasted about three seconds. to him, it felt like a three minute daring leap.

His girlfriend was waiting on the midpoint of the rooftop on this particular car. He ran up to her. She hugged him. "How's everything going?" she asked. "Great. That pessimistic attitude should have never been in my personality," he answered. He started to run and jump over again. He realized it was easy for him to leap across train cars like a frog leaping from one lily pad to another. He finally made it to the caboose of the train. Rubi was still moving. A couple of minutes later, she had arrived. He was elated.

"You see, it is much easier for you to do this than myself because you're much taller than I am. After all, I am only five feet nine inches, and you are six feet seven inches tall. Like the other car, this caboose was not ordinary. This rear end of the train was adorned like an urban style subway car. It featured an abundance of colorful urban art. The citizens' graffiti signatures were prominent on the sides of the caboose. The rooftop had an anamorphic art style painting of an iceberg waterfall. It did not have any windows, and at one time, this caboose was used as a boxcar.

On the rooftop was a white hatch. Rubi was standing next to the alien leader. "I think this is the best painting I've ever seen. I am quite skeptical as to what kind of art this is," said the alien leader. "It's anamorphic art," replied Rubi. "What's that?" asked Will. "It's art or a portrayal that is made to look like one is falling into a hole, abyss, or even a waterfall, when they are really on the ground. It is made to look real when it is really fake. They often use this type of art in the movies. On a rare occasion, they use this artistic style as a form of street art," answered the female train attendant. "Can you tell me what's below that hatch?" asked the alien leader. "I can. But will I do it is the question," answered Rubi.

"Ha, ha, ha, real funny," replied Will sarcastically. "I know," said the alien attendant. "Would you please open the hatch for me?" asked the alien leader. "No," she answered. "So, did you make me leap from one train car to another just for some sort of meaningless reason?" asked Will. "No," answered Rubi. The alien leader turned around. A clicking noise was heard. "What was that?" asked Will abruptly. "Oh, you said you wanted to go down in my secret train car. So, I have a little surprise for you," answered Rubi.

"Really, you did that?" asked the alien leader. "Well, what would you think that clicking noise was for?" asked the train attendant. "I guess it was for that," answered Will. "Do you want to go down first?" asked Rubi. "No, ladies first. You must go down first. After all, you're a lady. You deserve the utmost respect," answered Will. "Well, because this is your first time doing this, I insist that you go down," replied Rubi. "Really?" asked the alien leader.

"Do you think I'd be lying to you?" she asked. "Well, you have been a little sarcastic to me today, and sarcastic words are usually little fibs," Will. "Just go down," replied Rubi. He started to climb down the hatch into the caboose. The alien leader's girlfriend followed. The place looked like a club for teens. There was a huge stage. This stage highlighted a marquis that showed the title Pop Town Starmos. The marquis was made of golden light bulbs. There was a vintage brick background behind the stage. There were seven bean bags in front of the stage. Each bean bag had its own individual color from the rainbow. The first bean bag was a fiery red color and the last one was violet color.

The stage was made of burly wood. The two side walls of this train car were both crimson colored. In the back of the train was a retro Bar. The bar was comprised of a huge soda fountain with over thirty flavors of soda; a malt maker; and a frozen yogurt machine. Adjacent to three dessert machines were two ovens, and a french fry maker. The countertop on the bar is made of granite. The most interesting feature about this bar is the "Don't Cry Over Spilled Drink System" (DCOSDS.) If someone were to spill his or her drink by accident, no one would have to clean the mess up.

The table top was made slightly slanted so the spilled liquid would go down the drain. There were sprayers hidden on the sides of the table top. These sprayers would make sure that the mess would be gone forever. The floor is comprised of blue and white checkerboard tiles. At night these tiles would change color. "This place has surely changed," said Rubi. "I thought this place was always like this," replied Will happily. "No, it was once a box car. This was the car that we lived in," said the female train attendant. "Really. I can see that this train car can be an excellent, secret club, and an entertaining area. But I can never see it as a living space for anyone," replied the alien leader.

"Well, it was a living space for my family and I." she said. "What do you mean?" asked Will. "You know, this place wasn't always like this," she answered. "What in the world are you talking about?" the alien leader asked. "This place didn't always look like this. It was an old, dilapidated boxcar. Imagine living with zero windows or doors. Imagine having to climb down in a residence instead of walking through a normal doorway system, and finally, you should imagine what it is like to live uncomfortably." Rubi answered in a melancholy tone. "Well, I feel bad for you. But I've gone through much worse. Believe me," replied Will. "You didn't go through worse.

For God sakes, you were raised by a royal family, and I was far from royalty anywhere," said the alien leader's girlfriend. "I felt like I was treated like a peasant all my life at the Alien Estate. Just because I lived with a distant cousin, who was a ruler doesn't mean that I lived the sweet life. Instead, I've been to a gruesome, mind-crushing dungeon. I've been to a hell hole, which I hope you or anybody else will never encounter," replied Will. "Can I tell my story first?" asked Rubi. "Sure," answered Will.

"I was born in Oktosk, Russia in the year 2022 to two parents. I was the second child of eight children. I have four brothers and three sisters. My first sister, Gladys, was born in 2019. My younger brother, a twin, Ivan, was born in 2023, after me. My nameless younger twin sister was born in 2023. The rest are not important. But, I will tell you about my life in Russia. I am sure you very well know that Russia was ruled by a Communist leadership from 1920-1991. The Communist government was restored in 2013, when that President who belonged to Red Army took over. Ma was born in the capital, Moscow. She left Moscow in 2016 and she escaped to Siberia.

That's where she met my Eskimo father. She gave birth to eight children over there, one of them being myself. Due to the fact that she had eight children, she had to move out of the cold, harsh wilderness. She discovered Starmos City was a good horizon, not realizing that Cornelius Von Alien was the tyrant. That dictator rejected all immigrants from living in this city. So, he made my family move into a boxcar on the outskirts of the city.

This was where I grew up. My parents got jobs as LSC drivers. They made enough capital that they can sell the boxcar to the Orange Train Line Company. Now they live back in Russia. After they moved out of Russia, this Boxcar was renovated to be used as an employee hangout area. Guests are never supposed to know about this area because they will try and intrude. So, keep it a secret," replied Rubi.

"What an interesting story", said Will. "Were you able to eat every night?" "No. In fact, every night we had to worry as to whether or not there is going to be food on our table. We didn't even have a real table. We had to eat in the train station. We never had three meals per day; we only had one meal, and that was dinner," answered Rubi. "That must have been a very uncomfortable lifestyle," replied Will. "Yes. Now, please, tell me about what happened in your life," said Rubi. "Sure, I am a native of Starmos City. I lived in a high class apartment up until I was 15 years old. That was when my parents died.

I moved to the Alien Estate because I was homeless. So, I learned how to be a chef. For ten years, I worked as a chef for Cornelius. As Cornelius's leadership increased, my say in the Alien Estate decreased. I ended up at my boiling point when he tried to poison two of his guests. That was when I poisoned him instead. His guards apprehended me and the two guests. I was sentenced to life in the hole without parole. Fortunately, I managed to escape the hole and I eventually killed Cornelius; I became leader. Some folks have a problem with my leadership. One of them is Jacqueline Langyaw," replied Will. "I am sorry to hear that," said the female train attendant.

"And I, too, am sorry to hear your story," said the alien leader. "Thank you," replied Rubi. "Say, is there any way that we can get some of these things down here working?" asked Will. "Sure," answered the female train attendant. "What do you want to use?" "Well, I'd like to use all of the things over here," answered Will. "Which one would you want to use first?" asked Rubi. "Oh God, I want to use the 50s bar first. Then, the show theater, and the movie theater," answered the alien leader. "Okay," replied Will's girlfriend. She walked over behind the bar, and placed her hand behind the Malt Maker Machine. She hit a button.

All of a sudden, the wall started to open up. A yellow slide appeared. Three maids wore aquamarine striped shirts. They started to sing. They started to dance on the bar. One of them had blonde hair and fair skin; another, had red hair and freckles; the third woman had brown hair and dark skin. The brown haired woman remained at the bar. "What do you want?" she asked. "A vanilla malt, strawberry short cake and a root beer float," answered the alien leader. "What do you want, Rubi?" asked the 50s style waitress. "Same as my friend without the strawberry shortcake," answered the female train attendant. About thirty seconds later, she served the boyfriend leader and the Russian girlfriend. They ate their delectable dessert. "So? What do you think of the meal?" Rubi asked. "It's terrific! In fact, this is the best strawberry shortcake and malt I have ever had!" answered the alien leader. "Goodbye," replied the brown haired woman.

She climbed back up the yellow slide and the sliding door closed. "Are you looking forward to the entertainment that is coming right now?" asked Rubi. "Of course, I am. Granted, I didn't finish my dessert. But, hey, food and entertainment is the perfect couple," answered the alien leader. The female train attendant clapped twice. All of a sudden, a fireman's pole started to come down. Three men in tuxedos started to slide down that pole from the ceiling. They walked up on the stage. They sang popular songs in a Barbershop Quartet Style.

They then sang some American patriotic songs like the Armed Forces songs medley, and *Stars and Stripes Forever*. A mysterious effect started to take place whereas musical instruments started to pop into the singers' hands. The left musician had a drum set. The middle musicians had trumpets, and the right musician had a tambourine. They played *Seventy Six Trombones* and *Strike up the Band*. Than they floated to the top of the ceiling and disappeared as soon as their heads hit the top. "This was excellent entertainment," said Will. He clapped and whistled as the entertainers started to float up to the ceiling. "So, obviously you did enjoy the entertainment that I provided you?" asked the female train attendant.

"These were probably the best shows I've ever seen. We need to have these bands come to the streets more often," answered Will happily. "Are you ready to return back to your seat?" asked Rubi. "Yeah, sure," answered the alien leader. She climbed up to open the hatch. He followed up the ladder out of the caboose, and closed the hatch. They started to run at a synchronous pace on top of the train like a boyfriend and girlfriend racing each other in the park. They leapt from train car to train car. Finally, Will returned back to his seat with Rubi. It was now 3:00 in the afternoon. Officer Valencia is asleep. Will walked to the window seat and admired the Lord's creation seen through the window. Natural sandy dunes surrounded a beautiful river. The river shined in the Starmos Sun.

This river is the Gold River, which is the marking for the border of the alien city. The train crossed the Trestle Bridge, which was made of wood. Seen within this river are kayakers, who were moving their oars, left to right, forwards and backwards with the quick current. Within these dunes were giant cobras and Gila monitor lizards. Seen within the orange dunes were two black eyes and a giant green head. A hissing noise was heard from a distance. "I'll get you, Will, and your friends too. I am coming after you." said the beast. After thirty seconds, the beast disappeared in the dust.

It was just a spiritual mirage. This beast had the voice of Cornelius Von Alien. Fortunately, the beast's presence was transient. It is now half past three in the afternoon. Officer Valencia started to wake up. His eye twitched. "What's wrong?" asked Will. "What?" asked the officer. "Why is your eye twitching?" Will repeated. The officer sat up from his long sleep. "Oh, that's a long story," answered the officer. "Well, tell me the story," replied the alien leader. "Okay, when I was young, I came from Ford City. This was a city that was sort of like the predecessor of Starmos City. Ford City was underdeveloped as compared to Starmos City.

When I was in my twenties, I worked on a construction site for the Alien Estate over there. The Alien Estate in Ford City had a modest, yet ostentatious appearance. This was Cornelius Von Alien's birthplace. In 2020, there was a sandstorm that had taken place over there. It blinded me in the right eye. Also, it made my ocular nerves twitch whenever I woke up. That storm was the worst ordeal of my life. That event keeps playing over and over again in my head," said Officer Valencia. "When did you become a cop?" asked the alien leader.

"Oh, that's a long time ago, and by the way, that's police officer to you, young man. Don't call your protector a cop," answered the alien officer. "You didn't answer my question. I want to know when you become a cop," replied Will. "I became a police officer about fifteen years ago, five years before I moved over to here," said Officer Valencia. A stewardess on the train started to walk down the narrow aisle with a metallic cart. This cart contained refreshments and snacks. This cart featured beverages from all over the world and snacks from every nation.

The stewardess was a brunette. She wore a navy blue dress, cap, and shirt. The shirt had light blue stripes and gold buttons. The cap she wore had the appearance of a beret. She walked to every passenger and patron and offered them free drinks. Eventually, she reached the duo. "What would you like, sir?" she asked. "Oh, you don't have to call me, 'sir.' My name is Will," answered the alien leader. "Are you Will Von Alien, the new ruler of Starmos City?" she asked. "Yes," answered Will. "Well, you saved me from hell," she replied. "Are you the soft spoken lady that my friends told me about?" asked the alien leader. "Oh my God, yes. I was the one who ended up in the hole. In fact, I was Cornelius's ex-wife," she answered. "What's your name again?" asked Will.

"Nova," she answered. "Your name sounds beautiful," replied the alien leader. "What drinks do you want?" she asked. "Oh, I am not thirsty," answered Will. He smiled. "So, what was it like to be married to Cornelius Von Alien?" "If you want to know the definition of the worst husband on the face of the Universe, then it was that guy. Cornelius was an evil brute. He was so extreme that he threatened to throw me into the hole because I would eat differently than he did. He would threaten to exile me from the alien city because I talked to my friends on the phone. About eight years ago, I talked to another co-worker.

That was when that beast snapped. He accused me of cheating, or in legal terms, adultery. I never even cheated. A few years ago he sentenced me to life in the hole without parole for no reason. If you want to know the epitome of evil, the true definition of evil, and the worst husband? That was him. Thank God, that cold alien dictator is dead," she answered. She served him the drinks. The train's gray first floor started to turn the color red. All of a sudden hissing noises were once again heard.

Envy, green pythons and cobras began to emerge from the ground. Tarantulas also started crawl down the walls and windows. Will's eyes opened wide in shock. He climbed up into the luggage shaft. He was cowering in fear and nervousness. Officer Valencia was completely asleep and in a state of oblivion. Spiders started to crawl up his legs, above his shorts. He started to scratch the top of his head. He started to open his eyes. He rolled his eyes to point upward. A scream was heard on the quiet, animal infested train. He started to scream in panic.

He jumped out of his seat like a grasshopper and ran up the stairs, and retrieved the red Emergency Ladder. He climbed up this ladder onto the rooftop of the train. Rubi was on the top of the train. "Who are you?" she asked. "I am Officer Valencia," he answered. "Are you going to arrest me?" she asked. "Why?" asked the officer. "Because I am an illegal immigrant," she answered. "I can arrest you. But because you are hardworking, I'm not going to put you away," he replied. "Thank you," said the female train attendant. "Now, what exactly do you do on this train?" he asked. "Pretty much everything. I book tickets for clients who request to book, serve drinks, manage the secret boxcar in the back, clean the train of messes and evil ones, and I do much more," answered the train attendant.

"Now, I want to make you aware of something quirky that is happening that caused me to wake up from my long sleep," replied Officer Valencia. "What would that be?" asked Rubi. "There are crazy tarantulas, cobras, and pythons down in the car! This is an important lesson that I learned never to sleep while on a moving vehicle," the officer answered. "You brought up a pretty good point. Stay up here and walk down to the edges of the railing on the rear part of this car. I'm going to go back into the train, and calm everyone's worst fears," replied Rubi. She carefully climbed down. On the top level, not a single noise was heard. Meanwhile, it is a zoo below. She walked down the stairs. Her blue eyes widened.

She was in disbelief and dismay. Everyone was calm in their own mind, not caring about their surrounding their environment. Some passengers are listening to their ear phones, while others are immersed in a book. Many fell asleep like Officer Valencia. "Wake up, everybody!" she screamed. "Stop listening to your music, reading, or even sleeping. Bring your children, and your important valuables, and follow me up." Every alien and human passenger heard her speech. They moved their eyes left and right. "Now," she screamed. Still, every passenger remained in his or her seat. "What are you doing!?" she shouted. Everyone all of a sudden sprung out of their seats like a jack in the box.

They followed Rubi up the stairs to the second level. She opened the rooftop hatch and all of the passengers in Car #5 climbed up onto the top. The wind from the train's speed blew into the faces of the passengers. Seen in the distance was a gigantic orb. It had the appearance of the Milky Way Galaxy. Rubi also noticed the orb. "Stay right here. I will return back up in a couple of minutes," she said. She ran down the stairs to the passenger seating area. Still, the disgusting and malevolent creatures were present. They increased in size.

Now, they're lethal. Not a mortal human or alien could defeat them. The magic of Will Von Alien could defeat them. But, where's Will? He must be hiding. Rubi screamed in nervousness. "Will! Come out where ever you are," she shouted. He jumped down from the luggage storage area. He stepped on the rattler of the giant cobra.

The evil beast turned around. "Who are you?" he asked. The red eyes glared at the alien leader. "I am your worst nightmare," the alien leader said. "Ooh, I am scared," replied the devil serpent. The serpent showed his tongue towards Will. Will grabbed the snake by its rattler and pushed him to the side. "What are you doing?" he asked. "Oh nothing. I am waiting for you to make your next move. I just have to get this dagger," answered the alien leader. Will opened a cabinet in the train car, and he retrieved a twelve inch long dagger. He positioned himself like a valiant fighter.

The snake showed its fangs in an intimidating manner to the alien leader. "Bring it on," the serpent said. "Sure," replied Will. He suddenly moved the dagger on the left side of the snake. Thus, the snake turned around. He grabbed the serpent's tail and twisted it into a knot. The snake whimpered like a sick, sad dog. Will pointed his eyebrows downward. "I'll cut off your head if you mess around with me or any of the passengers on this train. Now, who are you?" he asked. "I am Korbian," the serpent answered. "Okay, what has brought you onto this train?" he asked. "I came here because..," Korbian began to answer.

Will interrupted. "Well, what did you come here for!?" he asked. "I came here to stop your evilness as the alien leader of Starmos City. You are a malicious, evil leader for forcing Cornelius Von Alien off of the throne," answered the sinister serpent.

"Yes, I did, because he tried to kill my friends, and his sick beliefs unfortunately live within this city. So, why not destroy him? More importantly, you did not answer my questions. I will untwist you and toss you off of this train," replied the alien leader. He grabbed Korbian, and tossed him off of the train. "Who's next?" he asked. "It is I, Serpianto," answered the second creature. This particular creature's origin is Spain. He is a bilingual beast. This creature is a giant green python. "You shall come over here now," it said. "And what if I don't?" asked the alien leader. "I'll figure out a way to make you come over," answered Serpianto. "Oh, I am so scared," replied Will sarcastically. "You *will* be scared," said the malevolent serpent. The foul beast swung his tail like a Roman swinging his whip.

He grabbed the alien leader's legs and constricted them. He attempted to suffocate him. While he was suffocating the alien leader, he didn't know what was coming at him. The alien leader started to gnaw on Serpianto's tail. Finally, he bit the tail. The serpent started to change different colors. His eyes rolled back, and this beast slithered out the window and into the Starmos Canyon. The last beast retreated also. Finally, the ordeal with the serpents is over but the tarantulas were still present in the train car.

The alien leader ran to the back of the train car. He ransacked the mini fridge. This fridge contained many spices. The tarantulas surrounded him in a 270 degree semicircle. The alien leader tossed mint leaves on top of those beasts. That method didn't kill those disgusting creatures. Will walked to the back of the spice closet. Inside of this spice closet were rose petals. The spiders crawled closer to the alien leader. "Die beasts!" he said.

He tossed the petals on top of the spiders. Immediately, those beasts disintegrated and vaporized. He then ran back up the stairs to the rooftop of the train car. "You can come down now. The coast is clear," he shouted. Everybody returned back to their seats in a quick, orderly manner. Rubi closed the hatch. Nova returned to the rear of the car to clean up the mess made by the alien leader. The train had officially passed through the orb. As the train passed through the orb, all of the passengers were blinded by the ephemeral sunlight. "What is going on?" asked Will. "It's nothing. Just the usual sunlight," answered Nova. "This is usual to you," the alien leader asked. "Oh, yes. Granted, I've been stuck in a dungeon for almost a decade. But, I would probably give yes as my answer," replied the stewardess. She walked up to the microphone. "Ladies and gentlemen, if you are sitting by a window seat, I would recommend you look the other way or close your eyes.

If you can't do either one of those things, you will receive sunglasses that you are to return after the train ride," she announced. Sunglasses were in one of the cabinets. She put them on the cart and moved up and down the aisle distributing the sunglasses to each and every passenger. Some passengers thanked her, while others were in their own world on their headphones. The blinding sunlight had ended. The next ordeal is now about to take place. Will noticed the train was off track.

The train is traveling at zero gravity speed, swerving out of control, left to right. The human passengers were looking out the windows at the surrounding planets.

Oohs and ahhs were heard from the human kids. The aliens opened their eyes wide in surprise and awe. Seen in the distance was a little, circular spec, which was as blue as the ocean. As the train drew closer to this spec, green dots were seen. The train was only one hundred miles from the planet. That was when those green dots started to look like shapes. "It is Planet Earth!" shouted Will.

The train passed the stratosphere, passed the mesosphere, and entered the atmosphere. The United States of America was able to be seen. As the train drew closer to the ground, train tracks were visible. Will turned on his aPhone, and opened up the GPS application. This application showed their location. If the one who was viewing the GPS app couldn't see the location clearly, the voice control on the aPhone would read the location.

"You are 1/4 of a kilometer above sea level in Charleston, South Carolina," the GPS read. All of a sudden, the train landed on the tracks like an airplane landing on the runway. This landing was abrupt and sudden. The train moved on the tracks at three thousand kilometers per half hour. The train passed through all of the states on the Eastern seaboard until it reached the state of New York. It passed through Bayonne, New Jersey, and entered a lengthy tunnel into Manhattan.

All of a sudden one of the track switches went on. The train accidentally switched onto another track. It ended up at the 90th Street Station and the train derailed. The train climbed up the eighteen tracks to the street. The passengers on the train were quiet as church mice. Will was starting to feel of nervous. His eyes were squinted to the point where they were almost closed. He started to shake. Rubi walked up to him. "Why are you so nervous?" she asked. The alien leader appeared to be as stiff as a board. "Answer me!" she (the female train attendant) shouted.

"Okay, I am panicking over the fact that we are stuck in an unknown place, and this train derailed," the alien leader replied clearly nervous. "Never panic in a situation like this. Panicking will only make the situation much worse. Remain confident and be strong. Granted, I've never been in a situation like this. But things can be much worse. I've seen worse," she said. "Okay," replied Will. He calmed down. The train climbed up the stairs, and ended in the middle of a busy intersection.

Chapter IV: The Ordeal in Manhattan and the Drive to Corona Park

This crazy train is now in the middle of a busy intersection on 90th Street and 20th Avenue in Manhattan. Cars are driving by the train and Will and the passengers are stuck on board the train. The street lights turned red and every car stopped. "What's going on?" asked Will. "The cars are stopped because the lights are red," one of the human passengers answered. "Why don't you know that?" she asked. "Because I'm not familiar with a busy city," the alien leader answered. "Well, get familiar because this is your new home," she replied.

This passenger has black hair and brown eyes. She has an arrogant and snooty personality. Fortunately, she is not in coalition with the malevolent aliens. She is a native of Manhattan though. She tried to open the door of the train. All of the cars were stopped and traffic started to accumulate at the intersection. Horns are honking and sirens are whaling. It is 5:00 in the afternoon. This is typical of rush hour; but it is not typical of a train to be in the middle of an intersection. The alien leader looked out the window observing his surroundings. The driver in a red Buick called the police. It is the day before Labor Day and the police are wrapping up their hard day's work. This woman wore typical, white collar work clothing. She had a brown striped dress and high heels. She had red hair and sea green eyes. She is wearing transparent sunglasses to cover her eyes. She picked up her ancient flip phone to call the police. The police operator was a male operator from the 700th precinct. "Who is this?" the dispatcher asked. "It is Ms. Luntsford calling," the white collar worker answered. "Okay, what seems to be the issue?" the dispatcher asked. "I see some unfamiliar double decker train in the middle of 90th Street and 20th Avenue," Mrs. Luntsford answered. "I'm sending some guys down," the dispatcher replied. The female hung up the phone.

The cars are still in the intersection. Meanwhile, on the train, all the passengers are looking out the windows. Seen in the distance are red flashing lights on the tops of white cars. The squad cars are being driven on the sidewalks due to the traffic on the streets. A couple of minutes later, eight police cars surrounded the train. "Remain on board; we will rescue you," the police commissioner shouted through his megaphone. The jet black hair of the police commissioner shined in the September sun.

He stood a staggering seven feet tall and had blue eyes. He retrieved his crowbar, and opened the doors of the train. He entered the train. "Ladies and gentlemen, everything is going to be okay," he said. The alien leader walked up to him. The officer showed an appearance of perplexity and skepticism towards the alien leader. The humans and the aliens were sitting down comfortable on the train. The police commissioner was in shock. he shook Will's hand. "What is your name?" the police commissioner asked. "Will Von Alien. I am the leader of Starmos City," answered the alien leader. "Interesting, where is that?" the commissioner asked. "In a dimension far, far away," answered Will.

"Okay," the officer replied. He widened his eyes in disbelief. The officer hesitated. "Can you excuse me?" he asked. "Sure," the alien leader answered. The officer walked down the aisle of the train car. In the back of the car, was Rubi. She was turned around talking to her colleague. The officer tapped on her shoulder. She turned around. "Are you the train attendant?" he asked. "Yes, I am," she answered. "What is the problem?" "We need to evacuate all of you and investigate the train," the officer answered. "Okay, I'll help you open the doors," she replied. She opened the doors on the rear of the car and the officer opened the doors on the front. As the doors were being open on every train car, the passengers evacuated. The passengers were moved over to the sidewalks at the intersection.

They were taken in squad cars to the precinct as the train was removed by a tow truck and taken to a secluded area for further investigation. The squad cars arrived at the 700th precinct. This precinct's front facade was made of window panes. The sides of the building were made of metal to contain the detainees. Squad cars were parked in front of the building, and ATF vehicles were parked on the sides. The rooftop is used for the helicopter landing.

Every officer from every squad car brought all of the passengers into the building. Once there the passengers were accounted for. The aliens remained in the custody of the officers. Will, Rubi, and Officer Valencia remained in the waiting room, sitting on the silver benches. Most of the alien passengers were interviewed. The Police Commissioner walked up to the motley group. "I want all of you to come with me," he said. The Police Commissioner escorted them down the hallway to the interrogation room "area."

"What's going on?" asked Rubi. "I don't know." answered Will. The area had a window and metallic chairs. "I will interrogate Will before I interrogate all of you. But, for now, you will sit down in this waiting area and wait your turn to be interrogated. So you can't escape, one of your hands shall be shackled to the bench," the commissioner. "Just wondering, what is your name?" asked Officer Valencia. "Commissioner Clayton," answered the commissioner. Clayton escorted Will into the interrogation room. The room had no features; just gray walls and a wooden table. At this table are two chairs and a camera. While the alien leader waited in the interrogation room, the officer shackled the rest of them to the benches. He finished that task then walked back to the interrogation room. He pointed a bright light at Will. "You're blinding me. Can you remove that?" Will asked. The officer dimmed the light. "Now, where do you come from?" he asked. "Starmos City," the alien leader answered.

"Where's that?" asked Commissioner Clayton. "It is a couple of dimensions away from here. It is two days ahead of our time," answered Will. "Would it be possible to get to this place from over here?" he asked. "It would only be possible by a Light Speed Cycle and Light Speed Train. Otherwise, you can't get over there from here," the alien leader answered. "Okay, I've never heard of those modes of transportation. But I guess we live in a world on the move," the commissioner replied. "Now, who are the ones accompanying you?" Clayton asked. "The ones that are waiting outside the window over here?" answered Will.

"Yes. Who are they?" the police commissioner asked. "They're my friends," the alien leader answered.

"Where was this vehicle coming from?" asked Clayton. "Starmos Station," answered Will. "Where's that?" the commissioner asked abruptly. "It's all the way up on the Northwest Corridor of Starmos City," the alien leader answered. "What year were you born?" the police commissioner asked. "2022," answered Will. "Now, what brings you to Manhattan today?" asked Clayton. "The train accidentally arrived here," the alien leader answered. "What do you mean?" the commissioner asked. "The train was supposed to be heading to California County; but it accidentally arrived here due to a malfunction in one of the track switchers," answered Will.

"Okay, what was the train's speed?" asked Clayton. "To be honest, I really don't know. It seemed like it was traveling at 3,000 miles per hour. But I wasn't really sure," answered Will. "Is that the maximum speed for the train?" the commissioner asked. "I believe so," the alien leader answered. "Now, do you have a criminal history?" asked Clayton. "No. Not on Planet Earth. But I was apprehended in Starmos City," answered Will. "For what?" the commissioner asked.

"Attempted murder and treason," the alien leader answered. "Those sound like pretty heinous crimes. Please tell me about them." the officer replied. "This is what happened. Before I became leader of the alien city, there was this tyrant named Cornelius Von Alien. He was my distant cousin. I worked in the Alien Estate as the chef. Last week, Cornelius invited a couple of guests to come over. Their names were Tom Jackson and Light S. Cycle. Cornelius didn't like those two for some crazy reason, so he told me to poison them by putting arsenic in their food. I decided that this leader was a psychopath.

So I made his plan backfire when I made his dessert. As a result, he fell into an unconscious state. The two guests and I walked down the hallway, and we were about to exit the estate. Twenty-five officers came swooping down from the ceiling, and they shackled us three. We were forced into a sensory deprivation room. This room was pitch black. The officers pulled us out of the room and brought us over to Cornelius. Cornelius read the "charges" and sentenced us three to life in the hole without parole. I managed to escape as I was being escorted. But, unfortunately, my friends didn't escape. Later that night I rescued them. At that point all three of us were fugitives. Eventually, Cornelius and his brutes invaded California County. I became a bounty hunter and arrested him and Jacqueline Langyaw to bring them to Starmos City to stand trial. Jacqueline Langyaw pled guilty in exchange for immunity and Cornelius was convicted, and he faced a death sentence. He gave up his leadership license. I still cooked for him. The next morning after he was convicted I poisoned him to death and I proudly showed his lifeless body. Later, that day, all of the citizens and I had a huge jubilation. That was when I officially became the leader. Early this morning Jacqueline Langyaw abducted Light, and that was when I was how I came to be on my way back to California County." said Will.

"That was a terrible ordeal," replied Clayton. "I know," the alien leader said. "Tell me, who is Jacqueline Langyaw?" the commissioner asked. "She is simply a nasty bitch. She is the prosecutor of Starmos City, and she was the one that brought further charges against my friends and I when we escaped. She was in cahoots with Cornelius though. Later, I found out that she was Cornelius's girlfriend. She is a woman of malice, and she abducted Light because she has a vendetta for me." the alien leader answered. "Well, I got enough information out of you that seems to be believable. I am happy that you are the leader of Starmos City, and I want you to call the next one to come in here," replied Clayton.

"Okay," said Will. He walked out of the interrogation room, and sat in one of the chairs right outside of the window. "Rubi, the commissioner wants you to come into the interrogation room," he said. "For what?" she asked. "He needs to interrogate you," he answered. "Did I do anything wrong?" she asked. "Absolutely not. I don't believe so. I suggest that you answer his questions properly, and then you won't be suspected as a criminal," the alien leader answered. "Why were you not suspected to be a criminal?" she asked.

"Because I told the whole truth and nothing but the truth, so help me God," answered Will. "Okay, here it goes," she said. The alien leader knocked on the window. The commissioner emerged from the interrogation room. "What's wrong?" he asked. "I need you to remove the cuff from this woman. You needed to interview her," the alien leader answered. "Yes, of course." the commissioner replied. Clayton un-cuffed Rubi, and he escorted her into the interrogation room. Both the commissioner and the detainee sat down in the seats. The commissioner walked to the corner of the room. He retrieved two cups of water. "Do you want a drink?" he asked. "Sure," she answered. The commissioner presented Rubi with a cup of water. "Drink this," he said. She pressed her lips up to the cup. She gulped the drink down her esophagus, and tossed the drink into the wire trash can. "Why did you gulp the drink so quickly?" the commissioner asked. "Because I was thirsty," she answered. "Okay, let's get to the interrogating. What is your name?" asked Clayton. "Rubi Woschinskiwitz," she answered.

"Okay, Miss Woschinskiwitz, where do you come from?" Commissioner Clayton asked. "Russia. That was my birthplace. But I lived most of my life in Starmos City," she answered. "Now, what brings you here?" asked Clayton. "Because my train accidentally derailed due to a malfunction in the track switcher, I am here today. It would have gone smoother if that track switcher would've worked. But, what can I say?" she answered. "Why are you coming to California County?" the commissioner asked. "Two reasons.

First of all, I am the train attendant. So, I am obliged to obviously take control of the employee to guest operations on board this train. Also, I am here to help my boyfriend, Will, who was in a horrible situation because one of his friends got abducted by his mortal enemy, Jacqueline Langyaw," answered Rubi. "Did you have any other jobs before you worked for the train company?" the commissioner asked. "Yes, I worked at hotel as a concierge woman," she answered. "What is or what was the name of the hotel you worked at?" Clayton asked.

"The Star Hotel. It is now defunct. When it closed down, I was laid off. I had to search for another job at another place," answered Rubi. "Now, how did you meet Will?" the commissioner asked. "Let's have a flashback from a couple of days ago. That was when I worked at the Star Hotel. Throughout my career over there, I came across many guests. But, this is probably the most important guest I've encountered. That's why he's my boyfriend. He escaped from the Alien Estate, and I got him a free room. He returned back down to me because he discovered that one of the guards at the Alien Estate saw him in his room. I let him "steal" from the store in the hotel.

He retrieved clothing that would make him blend in with the crowd. He then arrived at the restaurant in the hotel. That was when Cornelius paid a visit. As a result, I aided him on his escape. He returned back to the Alien Estate to rescue his friends," she answered. "Interesting story," replied Clayton. "I will dismiss you. Thank you for being compliant with me on the interview. Wait outside," he said. She returned to the hallway and sat down on the bench. She is no longer shackled. "So, how did the interview go?" asked Will. "You were right on the advice. You must have a lot of wisdom in your soul," answered Rubi. "So, it went good," the alien leader said.

"Yes, hopefully after Officer Valencia's interview, we will be on our way to rescue Light," replied Rubi. The commissioner emerged from the interrogation room. He un-cuffed Officer Valencia and escorted him into the room. "Who are you?" the commissioner asked. "Officer Valencia," answered the police officer. "Where do you come from?" asked Clayton. "Tijuana, Mexico," answered Officer Valencia. "Okay, did you live anywhere else besides Tijuana?" asked the commissioner.

"Yes, Starmos City," the officer answered. "Did you have any careers or jobs in Starmos City?" asked Clayton. "Yes, I have a job at the Starmos Station as an alien Police Officer," the officer answered. "How did you become an alien if you were a human at one time? How is that physically possible?" the commissioner asked. "Before I became a Police Officer, I was an astronaut. My shuttle unfortunately crashed into the Milky Way Galaxy, which was also known as Highway D.

Somehow, I arrived in this desert of dunes. I climbed through these dunes and I discovered a spec. As I drew closer to this spec, it started to get bigger in size. It looked like a city, particularly a city from the retro-future. I crossed the border into the city and was turned into an alien in a machine called the Alienater 3000. Once I was there I applied for a job at the Starmos Station to become a police officer and here I am today," the officer answered. "Interesting," replied Clayton. "How many years were you an officer for?" "Oh, gosh. Four Decades," the officer answered. "How did you start to associate with Will and Rubi?" asked Clayton.

"I was doing my usual activity as a police officer in the train station, when one guy came up to me to ask me where the Ticket Purchase Center is located. I directed him to the purchase center. But then he wanted me to take the train with him. Fortunately, today was my day off, so I decided to take the train with him to make him feel safe because I heard that he was a target of a witch, Jacqueline Langyaw. So, I came with him for his protection. Rubi, apparently is his girlfriend. So that is how I associated with her," answered Officer Valencia. "Interesting. Did you associate with anyone else besides these two?" the commissioner asked. "Yes," answered Officer Valencia. "Who would that be?" asked Clayton.

"Howard Carterson," answered the officer. "Who is that?" the police commissioner asked. "He *was* one of Will's confidantes. He worked as the one who opened the tall doors at the train station. He was supposedly helping Will until I found out that he actually attempted to beat the heck out of him. That was when I disassociated myself with Mr. Carterson. This guy was nasty and filled with malice. I suspect that he is working for Jacqueline Langyaw. He is probably in cahoots with her. I also heard that he might be her chauffeur. This might be dangerous," answered Officer Valencia. "Okay, I think I got enough information from you," replied the police commissioner.

"Thank You," said the alien officer. Commissioner Clayton escorted Officer Valencia out of the interrogation room. Officer Valencia sat down with the others. The N.Y.P.D. Commissioner Clayton stood up in front of the motley group. "None of you guys seem to be suspects. So, I will set you all free. But I need you guys to do one important thing," said the commissioner. "And what would that be?" asked Will. "Come over to the booking desk, and I will give you three passes to the American Consulate in Manhattan," answered Clayton.

The police commissioner escorted them down the hallway by the booking area. They walked into a room that had the similar appearance of a generic recording studio room. The only difference is that there isn't a recording device or fancy technology. Also, the room is not soundproof. The room has a camera facing the mugshot wall. It had markings for individuals' heights. The commissioner made the motley group stand by the door as he opened one of the file drawers. In this drawer were a bunch of papers. He reached all the way in the rear of the drawer and placed his hand inside of the pit of papers; he retrieved a couple of tickets to the American consulate in Manhattan. "What are you getting these for?" asked Officer Valencia. "Your gateway to citizenship in America," answered Clayton.

The police commissioner presented the motley group with the tickets to the American Consulate. He escorted them into the waiting area outside of the precinct. "What's next?" asked the alien leader. "You're coming with me," answered the police commissioner. Clayton placed the motley group inside the squad car and drove them over to the American Consulate in Columbus Circle. The American Consulate was made of vintage, brown bricks. In the front of the consulate were two windows. These windows were made of four panes. On the top of the consulate was a gigantic American flag from 1959.

Commissioner Clayton parked the squad car in front of the place. Will opened the door and followed the commissioner into the consulate. Officer Valencia and Rubi followed. Two, tall doors greeted them and the police commissioner. These doors were made of windows and gold bars. Clayton opened the double doors, and he entered a dim room. This room has a similar appearance to an old fashioned, generic bank. The staff members that distribute passports, green cards, and visas work behind a glass window. The offices are separated by wooden walls.

Sitting behind the glass window were three employees who belonged to the consulate. Each employee wore a suit and a tie. Commissioner Clayton walked up to an employee, who wore large specs. He had brown hair and a beard, and he was heavy set. "Who are you?" he asked. "I am Commissioner Jackson Clayton," the police commissioner answered. "Now who are your confidantes behind you?" asked the consulate employee. "Fellas, introduce yourselves," said Clayton. Each individual of the motley group introduced themselves.

The American Consulate presented an interesting environment. On the walls were blinking portraits of our founding fathers. These portraits were portrayals of Alexander Hamilton, George Washington, John Adams, Thomas Jefferson, Aaron Burr, James Madison, James Monroe, John Quincy Adams, and Benjamin Franklin.

"What's this?" the alien leader asked the consulate employee. "Those are blinking pictures of the founding fathers of our nation. I'm sure you don't know who they are but you'll find out later in life, when you take the test for citizenship," the condescending consulate employee replied. Officer Valencia defensively told him "Oh! Shut the hell up!"

"Okay." the consulate employee replied. He walked away from his desk and he grabbed Commissioner Clayton, for some reason, by his shirt. "What do you think you are doing!?" the NYPD commissioner asked. "I am going to beat the living crap out of you," the consulate employee answered. Clayton pointed his Taser at the disrespectable consulate employee. "Tell me your name, and we won't have to go through a fight," the commissioner said as he nodded toward the trio to head out. The motley group walked out of the consulate. "What do you mean?!" the consulate staff member asked. "Just tell me your name." answered Commissioner Clayton. "Okay, my name is Mitchell Taft," replied the consulate employee.

The police commissioner withdrew his weapon. "Now tell me why were you being violent with my confidantes and I?" he asked. "Because your confidantes acted like complete assholes!" answered Mitchell. "And where do you come from?" asked Clayton. "Staten Island, New York," the consulate employee answered. "Who is your employer?" the police commissioner asked. "The government," answered Mitchell sarcastically. "Fine!," replied Clayton. Rather than causing a ruckus, the police commissioner walked out of the consulate. His eyebrows were crinkled, and his lips were tightened. His face was red, and filled with anger and disgust.

The Starmos trio were waiting outside. "What happened?" asked Rubi. "Nothing important. This man just annoyed the living crap out of me. So, I left, rather than make a ruckus" answered the commissioner. "Did anything happen to you while you were still in the consulate?" asked Will. "Yes, the man attempted to beat me up. I drew my Taser in front of him. I made him answer questions," answered Clayton. The motley group and the commissioner returned to the squad car. "How was his demeanor?" asked Rubi. "This man was haughty pig. He thought he was above everybody else, and he showed great animosity towards me," answered the commissioner. The squad car made its departure from the consulate.

Meanwhile, Mitchell was still in the hallway of the consulate. He was standing on the marble floor with a sinister smirk on his face. His boss emerged. "You're fired," said his employer. "For what!?" asked the consulate employee. "Because you tried to start a fight with my friend, Commissioner Clayton," answered his boss. Mitchell threw an angry temper tantrum. He started to pull some of his hair out of his head. "Get out of here!" his employer yelled. The ex-consulate employee angrily walked out of the American Consulate. "We'll see about that!" he said. He reached his hand into his pocket to retrieve his obsolete flip phone. He called Jacqueline Langyaw.

Ms. Langyaw answered the phone. "Hello." "It's me, Mitchell. Where's Light?" he asked. "With me at the dumpy island" answered the former prosecutor. "Did you try and kill them?" she asked. "No," answered Mitchell "Why?" asked Jacqueline. "Because I didn't have an opportunity." the ex-consulate employee answered. "Why didn't you kill him?" the disrespectable prosecutor asked.

"Because, he drew his weapon at me," answered Mitchell. "And who is "he"?" asked Ms. Langyaw. "Commissioner Clayton," answered the ex-consulate employee. "Oh! That bastard! There's no way I can kill Will. There's going to be some tough luck. Say, where's Howard?" asked the evil former prosecutor. "Oh, I don't really know," answered Mitchell. "Never mind that, I just received a text message from him stating that he just arrived at some sort of train yard," replied Jacqueline. "Okay. What do you want me to do?" asked Mitchell. "I'll meet you at Swinburne Island" answered Ms. Langyaw.

"Okay. Good bye." Mitchell hung up, jumped into his white vehicle and started to head over to Staten Island to get to Swinburne Island.

Meanwhile, the motley group and the police commissioner were on their way to the residence of Clayton. Rubi looked out the open window. She was impressed by the sights, smells, and tastes of Manhattan. She savored every moment of that car ride. Will was texting on his aPhone, and Officer Valencia was sleeping as usual not giving a care about his surrounding environment.

He was in a state of oblivion. Commissioner Clayton was driving at normal speeds in his Chevrolet squad car. "Where are we going?" the alien leader asked. "My house," the commissioner answered. They were heading past One Police Plaza, and were on their way, crossing the beautiful Brooklyn Bridge. Adjacent to them were bike riders that were racing. These bike riders moved just as fast as the cars. Traffic was seen in the distance. "I'm not dealing with this," he said. The commissioner increased his speed. He moved at speeds of two hundred miles per hour. All of a sudden, he hit a speed bump.

The squad car flew over the other cars. "What's happening?" asked Rubi. "We're traveling at high speeds," answered Clayton. The commissioner removed the heavy foot on the petal, and returned back to normal speeds after that daring jump. He drove the squad car onto the exit ramp for the Brooklyn Queens Expressway into Queens and Long Island. The oblivious alien officer was awakened by the sunlight. The Labor Day Weekend Sun was present. "Where are we now?" asked Officer Valencia.

"Queens," answered the police commissioner. "Finally, you woke up," said Rubi. "I know, I have a sleeping disorder where in some points of the day, I'll just fall into some sort of a deep sleep," replied the officer. The officer placed his elbow on the door by the window. He was impressed by the obsolete structures that were featured in the area. Many old, abandoned, defunct factories were seen in the distance. The commissioner reduced the speed in the squad car as it had drawn closer to the inoperable factories. "I am not only a police commissioner; but also a tour guide to some folks who have never visited this city before. These factories right here are what I like to call 'the boondocks'.

They became derelict when they ceased their operations in the 1990s, and now they are defunct. The factories used to remove their wastes by dumping it into the canal over here. In fact, when I was raised, the water over here was green due to the sludge. The wastes from the factories destroyed the ecosystem and killed the innocent fish. In fact, it caused some mutations in the animals. Now, the fish that are born in this canal do not have fins because of this trouble from the factories. The fish are mutants. Fortunately the canal over here has now been cleaned and purified and the natural ecosystem is coming back.

Soon, the factories will be destroyed. the only problem that exists is that the Parks Department wants to keep them and does not let a bulldozer or crane come onto their land. To me, that is just sheer ignorance. The city government wants to build a nice ecosystem and wildlife reserve, but the world class idiots in the Parks Department do not want to do anything like that. This is just another feature of bureaucracy. The Parks Department just wants to let the plants take over and that is wrong." said Clayton. "Well what would you do with this area?" the female train attendant asked. "Oh, I would probably change this area tremendously. First I would destroy the factories and tear them down. Than I would remove all of the scraps and garbage from the area. Finally, I would plant beautiful plants here and turn this place into a nice, green, ecologically friendly park. In addition to that I would put windmills and solar panels over here to power the neighborhoods surrounding this place," the commissioner answered. "Interesting." replied Rubi.

The trio and the police commissioner drove past the boondocks, and they are now passing the former site of the 1964-1965 World's Fair. "Look what we have here, the World's Fair Grounds. This was the place where Joseph Salvatore Pidoriano designed an incredible theme park resort. But, unfortunately, he was advised not to talk to the Parks Department. So, he had to build his resort upstate," the police commissioner said. "May I see the World's Fair Property?" Will asked. "Sure," answered Clayton. He merged onto the exit and he traveled down Industry Avenue. Fountains lined this beautiful gateway to the Unisphere.

Some of the jets on these fountains were two hundred feet tall. Usually there are people standing all over

Corona Park, but everyone was chilling out by the Unisphere. Some of the people sat on the benches that surrounded it while others, picnicked on the grass. Then, there were the batty ones, who jumped into the reflecting pool by the Unisphere because they thought that it would let them live forever. Standing by the fountain were police horses who tried to stop the insane people from jumping into the fountain. "What is this place?" asked Will. "The place of the World's Fair," answered the commissioner. "Why are there so many people that are sitting by the fountain?" the alien leader asked. "Because this week travelers from all over the world are coming here. Some of them are staying at local hotels in the neighborhood while others are staying in Manhattan. There are some locals that are coming here also. Tomorrow is the U.S. Open. So there'll be tons of people seeing this event," answered Clayton. "What is the U.S. Open?" asked Rubi. "It's the World's Largest Tennis Tournament that only takes place here a few days in the year. It is always around Labor Day," answered the commissioner. "What is tennis?" asked Officer Valencia.

"Oh, that is right – you do not know. It is a sport that requires two paddles or sometimes four. That's if you have two players on a team or as they say on one 'side'," the commissioner answered. "Do you think I'd be an excellent tennis player?" Rubi asked. "Let me think. Of course, you would be. I'd think you'd win against the most recent winner," Clayton answered in a sarcastic manner. "Are you serious?" asked Rubi, not knowing who he was referring to. "Why, of course I am," the commissioner answered sarcastically. The commissioner drove the squad car around the Unisphere and then headed to Industry Pond.

"Where are we going now?" asked Will. "To the ultimate reflecting pool in the World - Industry Pond. This was built in 1939, when the World's Fair took place," answered Clayton. "I thought the World's Fair took place in 1964-1965," the alien leader replied. "There was another one that took place in 1939. But it wasn't as great as the one in 1964-1965. The 1939 Expo took place slightly before the start of World War II," said Clayton. The trio and the commissioner pulled up to the cobblestones at Industry Pond. Officer Valencia jumped out of the car. Will and Rubi followed him. The commissioner walked behind the group. They walked up to the railing. "This *is* a beautiful sight," said Rubi. "Well, thank you. This is just one of the many unique and beautiful things in New York City," replied the police commissioner.

Chapter V: The Third Ordeal: Meeting the Homeless Man

It is now 6:00 in the evening, and the sun set is taking place in Corona Park. The motley group and the police commissioner are viewing and admiring Industry Pond. The fireflies emerged and they started to glow in the dark evening. "What are these?" asked Officer Valencia. "We call them "lightning bugs" answered Clayton. The bright LED lights that surrounded the pond had came on. A man on the Italian Gondola traveled around the lake to a derelict, wooden dock.

He tied the boat up to the dock. The back of his body faced the motley group and the police commissioner. "What's going on?" asked Will. "This man is just one of those introverts who is some sort of a non-entity to society. Some consider people like that enigmatic. Due to his size, he might be even questionable," answered Commissioner Clayton. This mysterious man kept waving his arm at the motley group and the police commissioner. "Should we see what this man wants?" asked Rubi.

"No, the man is just a shady introvert," the commissioner answered. "I don't know about that. He keeps flagging us down almost like to come o'er to where he is," the alien leader replied. "Do you have anything to say about this, Officer Valencia?" asked Clayton. "I don't really care," the lazy alien officer answered.

"Rubi, do you want to come with us to investigate this guy?" the commissioner asked. "Sure, I'll come," she answered. Will started to run down to him; Clayton followed and Rubi tried to keep up with them. Officer Valencia remained by the railing. The commissioner, the alien leader, and the female train attendant arrived at the secluded area. Will dashed down the twelve wooden steps leading to the derelict dock. Rubi and Clayton followed the alien leader. Adjacent to these wooden steps were two tall oak trees. The introvert on the dock turned around. He stood at a shocking seven feet eight inches tall, and had black hair and a large mustache. He weighed about two hundred and fifty pounds and had a muscular physique. Yet, he had the appearance of a homeless man. He wore ripped gloves and had an unkempt beard. He had a terrible body odor and a scowl on his face. His eyes were as black as a tire. He wore ripped jeans and a wrinkled hat. His voice was raspy due to the change in the season.

"Who are you?" he asked. Rubi, Will, and Clayton introduced themselves. "Where do you come from?" the alien leader asked the man. "Right here in Queens. In fact, I was born in Flushing Meadows Corona Park. My parents were homeless and even my grandparents. Once a homeless one, always a homeless one. It is hard to get out of poverty," the mysterious homeless man answered.

"That's unfortunate," Will replied. "I know. I guess that's what happens when rich folks like you disregard us homeless men. We have to eat our dinners from trash pails, and use the dirt as our playgrounds. We can't do anything. People are always telling us homeless men to get out of here. The government closes the doors on us. We are even considered parasites by some because we can't find jobs. Some of us do find jobs.

Sometimes, we have to steal to live. That is when we're considered scoundrels and street rats," the homeless man said. "I feel sorry for you," the female train attendant replied. "You know, if you really felt sorry for me, you would pay about five bucks to ride my gondola with me. I stole this from a boat fair in Knoxville. Then I rode the rails back to New York so that way I wouldn't get caught," the homeless man said. "Would you take some Starmos bucks?" the alien leader asked. "What are Starmos bucks?" the homeless man asked. "It's a currency from another dimension," answered Will.

"I think the man wants U.S. dollars," replied Clayton. "How much do you want?" asked Rubi. "Five dollars per person," the homeless man answered. "My girlfriend and I are not people. We're aliens," replied Will. "You're aliens," the homeless man shouted. "Yes, we're aliens. We came from another dimension far, far away," the alien leader said. The homeless man jumped onto the gondola. "Don't touch me! You might give me some sort of sickness!" he said nervously.

"We treat you as an equal. Why don't you treat us as equals?" asked Will. "Because, you're aliens," the homeless man answered abruptly. "Those are just a bunch of phony stories. Don't believe what you see on T.V. or, what you read in books," the alien leader replied. "Oh, I never read a book in my life and I could tell you that I don't know what a T.V. is," the homeless man said. "Well I'll tell you about that later," replied Will. Calming down the homeless man again asked "Okay. Now, do you want to go for a boat ride?" "Sure," answered Rubi. She jumped into the gondola. Will followed her; and the commissioner jumped in last. Being the only human with U.S dollars, he handed the fifteen dollars to the homeless man as soon as he jumped in.

They pushed the boat off of the dock. "What's your name?" asked Rubi. "It's Buck. My people just call me Brutis because I am deemed as the toughest and smartest one," Brutis said. He paddled his gondola around Industry Pond. He started to head east bound. "Please tell me your story," said Will. "What story?" asked Buck. "The history of your life. I am very interested to know," the alien leader answered. "Well, my grandparents were very successful entrepreneurs; but they put their eggs in one basket, if you know what I mean by that. That basket is what is known as the Stock Market. It was a way for people to invest money to make a lot more money. From 2008-2009 the Stock Market crashed. 2008 was the year I was born. My parents lived off the land of my grandparents because they received constant trust funds from them. When the Stock Market crashed, they became poor, and I became poor. I was born in this park over by those two trees over there. I didn't attend school in my youth, but I learned certain things from many "laid-off" public school teachers. I eventually went to night school. That's also why I know a lot about politics. Now, when I was ten years old, my parents died of different diseases. That was when I moved to a homeless shelter. Unfortunately, I had to move out because somebody discovered that I smuggled in some alcoholic beverage. To be precise, it was beer. That was when I officially became homeless. Now there's no way I can move back into a shelter and I've been living on the streets," said Buck. "This would probably be a stupid question for me to ask. But, can I ask it?" asked Rubi.

"Sure," the homeless man answered. "Now, how did you vacation?" she asked. "Normally, you would think being homeless, you never have a vacation. But, in some way, you live a vacation. As a vagabond, I could decide at the spur of the moment whether or not I vacation that day or not. It's called riding the rails. I walk for miles and miles to the nearest train yard, and I ride on the Boxcars of freight trains. I've been to places that some have never been to. I've been in almost every state in this country except for Hawaii, and I've been to most of the countries in North America.

Maybe, I didn't stay at luxury resorts or fly on luxury jets. But, I've been to these places. Yet people think that we homeless men never vacation, but some of us in some cases, we practically live a vacation. Anybody can vacation, whether you're rich or poor, smart or dumb, weak or strong, challenged or able, or docile or rebellious. As a homeless man, I can do anything I want," answered Buck. "Now, this would be considered a controversial question, maybe even absurd, but would you prefer to be homeless or in jail?" asked Clayton. "Yes, that is a crazy question. But, I'd rather be homeless. Remember, I can go anywhere I want without having to worry about being watched by cops. Somebody in jail can't go anywhere they want." answered the homeless man. "Good point," replied the commissioner.

"I have a secret area in the back of this place. So let's go back there," said Buck. He paddled the gondola boat to a dark cave. This cave is darker than the moonlight. You could just make out the outlines of stalagmites and stalactites in this pitch black place. Droplets of water hit the motley group, the commissioner, and Buck. "What is this place?" asked Will.

"This is what we homeless men like to call Serenity Alley. This is the underworld in the average man's eye, but the homeless men and the drifters take a different standpoint." A large light was seen in the back of this cave. It was not necessarily a light; it was more of an illumination. It looked sort of like the end of the cave, and the gateway to a Celestial Palace. As it turned out, it was a far cry from that. As they drew closer to this large radiance, Will's eyes started to burn.

"Buck, you know, I don't want to be rude. In fact, I think this place is a one of a kind, but my eyes are burning. I would appreciate it if you left the cave," he said. "Too bad for you," the homeless man replied. "Listen, I can easily arrest you, and I'll put you away for long time," the police commissioner said. "Who died and left you in charge!?" asked Buck. He was feeling confident in his element. "I am the police commissioner. I can arrest you because I caught you doing a violent crime," answered Clayton. "There's no way you can take me down. First of all, I have buddies that can beat the living hell out of you. Second of all, there's no way, no where, no how, that you can arrest me in this country because you don't have a warrant.

Thirdly, if you can take me down, you'll get in trouble by the justice department for violating Habeas Corpus," the homeless man replied. "Pretty smart for a hobo," said Clayton. "What did you just call me?" asked Buck angrily. "A kind gentleman," the commissioner answered sarcastically. "Yeah, I did not hear that. Besides, not a single soul ever called me a kind gentleman," the homeless man replied. "No, I said the whole truth, and nothing but the truth," the commissioner said. He lied through his teeth in an attempt to save his own skin. "I don't believe you," Buck replied.

"Well, you better believe me because I am the commissioner. Always believe the commissioner. Don't believe the human or any other living creature," said Clayton. Will and Rubi looked at the police commissioner with an angry appearance. "What did I say?" the commissioner asked. "You knew what you said," Rubi answered. She and the alien leader nodded their heads up and down. "Yeah, what she said," Will agreed. "Okay, whatever she says," the confused commissioner replied.

The illumination in the distance started to wane. As they drew closer, the light started to disappear. Fortunately, for the alien leader, the light was fleeting. A loud noise that sounded like a waterfall is now being heard. The alien leader panicked, "What's happening over here?" He sighed, inhaled and exhaled quite quickly. He started panting like a dog. However it was in nervousness. Rubi also showed a nervous appearance on her face. Her eyes widened. She froze like a sculpture. Her lips narrowed, and she took deep breaths. She turned her head around, and waved "Goodbye" to the real world. The commissioner showed an appearance of confidence.

He stood up in the small gondola, and stared down the homeless man. "Where do you think you're going?" he asked Buck in a bold and blunt manner. "How dare you ask me where I'm going, besides, I am the one that's driving this. Don't be a backseat driver," the homeless man answered. Trying to get Buck back to attention Clayton pursued a conversation. "Listen, I agree with your political views, but I totally disagree with your attitude. So, don't mess around with me. Granted, I don't have to do this but regardless what you think, I *can* easily beat the living crap out of you. I worked for the police department for over 35 years. I think I know what I'm doing.

Granted, I'm almost 70 years old but despite my appearance, I am much stronger than you, and I have much more wisdom than you," replied Clayton. "I don't believe you for more than one second when it comes to this especially when you call me names. So, you might as well admit that you're a pathetic, pathological liar. Everything you say is nothing but a phony lie. You are stupid, dumb, and useless to society. All you do is bark orders at your employees below you and arrest criminals who commit predominantly little Robin Hood crimes. You like holding others accountable for their actions. Yet you never hold yourself accountable for your actions. So, don't lie to me! You can never fool us homeless men!" said Buck. This was not working like Clayton planned so he started to rave himself. "What the hell in the world are you talking about? I got some of what you're talking about but then the rest sounded like some absurd foreign language. What you said was not explicit enough! Maybe you should learn how to speak explicitly, then I will be able to hear you but that'll never come true. You are not as intelligent as you think you are! All you do is splurge out words. You hear words from your fellow street rats and scoundrels. Now you are going in the wrong direction by keeping your mouth open. So, I'd simply recommend that you keep your mouth shut. Maybe if you kept your mouth shut you would learn! Maybe if you would stop being a smart ass you would learn, and stop calling me a pathological liar because it takes one to know one!" the commissioner replied. "Oh, he just owned you right here and now. So, what are you going to say back?" asked Rubi. "I have some good news in store for you," the homeless man answered sarcastically. "What do you mean?" asked Will.

"Oh, you know exactly what I mean. Besides, in life, there are always good things in store for everyone. Try my patience if you dare," answered Buck. "What in the world are you talking about?" asked Will. "You've clearly heard exactly what I'm saying. You will be heading to the pits of doom," the homeless man answered. "Again, what the hell are you talking about?" the alien leader asked. "I am talking about the fact that hell is within a short distance. No worries shall poison your mind though because people like you are going to heaven. You believe in God. You're a Christian; I'm not. You'll be saved from Hell. So, what do you have to worry about? You can die right now, and the Lord will take you up to Heaven. Hell on Earth is going to be coming to you, but your soul will be stuck in Heaven for eternity," the homeless man continued. Now thoroughly confused Rubi asked "What are you talking about?" "You'll see it in less than a couple of minutes," answered Buck. He seemed crazed. The gondola started to approach the treacherous waterfall.

Everyone in the boat relaxed, and didn't seem to care about what was about to happen next. The boat struck a boulder. "What's this?" the alien leader asked. "Oh, just your typical, classic boulder. I've been in this cave before. In fact, this is probably one of the most unique places I have ever been inside; but never this far back," the homeless man answered. "What do you think is back here?" asked Clayton. "I have no idea, but first, I must dislodge this boat from the boulder," answered Buck. He jumped into the water inside the cave. He dislodged the gondola from the heavy rock then he jumped back on board. The gondola started move closer to the treacherous part of the cave. Suddenly, it started to tip forward. As though he didn't bring them to it they heard "Push your weight to the stern of the boat," the homeless man said. Everyone followed his direction including the police commissioner. They suddenly noticed a gigantic waterfall that entered an abyss. "Oh my God!" shouted Rubi. "What's wrong?" asked Will.

"Look ahead, we're going down a waterfall," she answered. "Each one of us must jump out of this boat because there's no way out. Death will do its part if you refuse to jump," Buck replied. "Okay, here it goes," the alien leader said. He jumped out of the boat, feet first. Rubi followed. Then, the commissioner came down, and the homeless man last. "Where does this place lead to?" asked Rubi. "I have no idea. This is my first time in this pond. Frankly, I didn't even know we had any caves in New York City," the commissioner answered. "Haven't you all realized that you have fallen into a trap?" asked Buck. "No. What do you mean?" said Rubi. "I am not here to help you. I am here to take your lives and take your money. I am here to kill you. I killed so many, and you are my next prey. So, this is going to be your last night alive," answered Buck. "Then, why did you take us for a ride in the gondola?" asked Will. "That's the stupidest question you can ask.

I took you away to kill you and your friends. Face it, you deserve to die. After all, you are the alien leader of Starmos City," the homeless man answered. "How the hell did you know that when I never told you such a thing?" the alien leader asked. "Because I have telepathic powers. I see into an individual's mind. I know exactly what everyone is doing. It's like I have Closed Circuit Cameras built into my system. I am a stalker. For decades, the police were on a manhunt for a serial killer in this park. In fact, they were wondering why so many bodies disappeared. After wondering, for decades, they gave up on the case.

So, I've been a free man and a murderer all along. I hold individuals hostage. Most don't make it out alive. Fortunately, they still have the opportunity to reopen the investigation, and they can still go after me. That's if I come out of hiding," answered Buck. "Don't you have to come out of hiding in order to survive?" asked Clayton. "No, I survive off the flesh of human bodies. Unfortunately, because your alien friends aren't human, they will be burnt at stake, and killed. Then, I will skin them, and I will turn them into clothing," the homeless man answered. "You're sick and disgusting. If one of the district attorneys find out what you've been doing, you will end up in the electric chair," the commissioner replied. "What do you mean?" asked Buck. "Over the course of the past couple of years, the murder rates have increased in this state. So, I decided to talk to the legislature about bringing back the death penalty. The legislature agreed with me about bringing back the death penalty for capital murderers or serial killers, and the death penalty applies to the ones who commit over five felony murders," answered Clayton. "What's a felony murder?" asked the homeless man. "It's when you commit murder in the commission of a kidnapping, robbery, or burglary," the N.Y.P.D. commissioner answered. "Looks like if I get caught, I will end up on death row. I must cover my tracks!" replied Buck. "Well, why do you do these crimes?" asked Will. "Because I am sick in the head," the homeless man answered. "How many more feet do we have to go before we hit the bottom?" asked Rubi. "About five hundred more feet," answered Buck.

They continued falling. A couple of seconds later they landed in a small pond. Somehow and fortunately not a single man or woman was injured from this fall. Rubi's beautiful blonde hair was drenched in the pond. Will's blue skin remained blue. Commissioner Clayton swam up to the rocky shore. The cave had high ceilings. The stalactites were at the bottom of the cave. The floor was made of ground rocks that came in all shapes and sizes. Buck suddenly emerged from the body of water inside of the cave. "I hope you creatures did not escape," he said. "And what if we did?" asked Will. "Then, there would be hell to pay," answered the homeless man. "Just what would that be?" the alien leader asked. "Oh, my God. Just shut the hell up," answered Buck. He was drenched in his clothing and now was getting confused. "Is this where you live?" asked Clayton. "Yes. In fact, there's a comfortable white couch over there," the homeless man answered. Will sat on the couch. He leaned back and heard crackling noises. These noises sounded live bones snapping. "What is this?" he asked. "Oh, it's just some human bones and cartilage. I hope you enjoy because you'll be part of this couch," answered Buck. The homeless man walked across the rocky floor. He walked up to a cauldron. "Fellas, did you know that this is going to be your last meal?" he asked. "What do you mean?" the alien leader asked. "I mean that this is going to be the last thing or last meal that you eat or drink before I kill all of you," answered Buck.

"Am I on your hit list?" the commissioner asked. "Let me look at my written out list to see who I am going to kill today," the homeless man answered. Adjacent to the cauldron, is a sheet of paper. This sheet featured the names of random people. Commissioner Clayton's name was the first to be shown on the list for September 1st, 2047. "Your name is on the list. In fact, you're the first one that is supposed to be killed today. I'll kill the rest of you along with killing Commissioner Clayton," the homeless man said. "Why would you want to kill all of us? What have we done to you?" asked Rubi.

"You've done a lot. First of all, you all were going to rat on me because I've been killing so many individuals. Second of all, you all demean me and treat me like I'm not a human, and that I'm a street rat. Third of all, you and everybody else in this world judges me because I am some sort of vagabond, or hobo. I say no more," he answered. "Well, I didn't do all of those things. Would you kill me?" the female train attendant asked. "Of course, I would kill you. You would be a witness who would rat on me, and send me straight to the electric chair. I am sure you think that I deserve death," the homeless man answered. "Oh, no. You don't deserve death. You are a very nice man. You've killed so many. That's what makes you nice," the police commissioner replied in a sarcastic manner.

"Really?" the homeless man asked. "Oh, yes," answered Clayton sarcastically. "You do realize that I am not your ordinary hobo or homeless man?" asked Buck. "Of course," the police commissioner answered with a snicker. "Now, sit down at my table over there because, you will be spending a long night over here," the homeless man said. While the homeless man cooked up a delectable dinner, the alien leader, his girlfriend, and the commissioner walked down to the table. This is made of shale stone. "What do you want us here, for?" asked Rubi. "What are you, stupid? You are going to have your last meal before I kill you and all of your friends," answered Buck.

Adjacent to the cauldron are the ingredients needed for the stew that he'll serve the "guests." The following ingredients he included in this meal were chicken bones, fish bones, fish oil, chicken crumbs, bread crumbs, cow excrement, and garbage scraps. While he stirred the stew in

the cauldron, the "guests" started to move closer to each
other at the table, and they huddled. They started to discuss
an escape plan. "I want each one of you guys to tell me
what your plan is," said Clayton. "Okay, now, the first thing
that I would do is sneak out now; so, that way that
malicious beast doesn't kill us. Sneak out while he is
preoccupied. Think of it, we have the sound of the waterfall
crashing to protect us.

     The only problem is that we have two tunnels to
escape from. We unfortunately don't know which tunnel
leads to what place. Besides, this is our first time being in
New York City. So, how would we know where we're
going? That's not the only problem. We can't swim under
the water because it is so murky. That's also another
problem, and that will prevent us from seeing where we're
going, and we might end up in some trap. Besides, I'm sure
that this nut premeditated this crime to take place. This is
my plan," the alien leader replied. "Now, Rubi, I want to
know your plan. I want to see what you would do to rescue
us from this situation with that bastard," the commissioner
said. "Well, the first thing that I would do is try to beat him
up, and debilitate him. I would make sure that he is so weak
to the point where there's zero chance of him trying to hurt
us or hinder us from the escape.

     Then, I would enter the tunnel by the water fall
because I know the waterfall is on the western part of this
cave and the western part is usually the good part of the
world according to folklore and the western part is more
advanced than the eastern part. Also, the western part of the
world has less trouble than the eastern part of the world.
Oh, you get what I'm saying," replied the alien leader's
girlfriend. "Now, what you've said made a lot of sense. I
mean both of your suggestions make a lot of sense. In fact,

I can very well understand them. They're very intelligent. Now, I will take both of your decisions, and kind of combine them to make one ultimate decision which is very important," said Clayton. "What kind of decision would you make?" asked Will.

"I don't really know. I was going to take both of your ideas. Personally, there wouldn't be any way for me to escape here. I am not that bright, but, I am able to fight. That's why I became police commissioner. I also caught the most amounts of criminals because of my agility. You aliens are intellectually superior than we humans are. You are able to easily analyze situations, and make a decision that is brilliant based on these situations. Not to sound like I am playing the game of favoritism, but Rubi, I like your decision much better than Will's decision. Now, Will, don't be offended by this statement that I am going to say about your decision."

He paused. "I think that your decision is quite erroneous and stupid. First of all, you're extremely pessimistic. You show very little optimism, and you're supposed to be the leader of a retro futuristic alien city. That is a little unfortunate because your decision making is terrible. You can't make a good decision, and by the way, I was lying when I said that your plan was excellent. It was not even a plan. It was just a sermon of negativity about the escape plan. Listen, we must escape. Now, this is what we're really going to do," the commissioner said. "And what would that be?" the alien leader's girlfriend asked. "Okay, so that way no one gets confused, I'll describe this plan precisely in chronological order. First, we will eat with this fool, and have his crappy dinner. Next, right when he's about to get up from the chair, Will shall lunge at him and drown him in the pond over in this cave. Then, when he's unconscious, you, Will, shall pull him out of the pond, and place him onto the shore.

Now Rubi, that is when you come into play. You will find a movable boulder to turn off the waterfall, and we'll head down the dark tunnel over to Staten Island. I don't want to kill Buck but I want to be able to stop him to the point where we can escape without having to worry about a nut-job coming after us. This man is totally nuts. He is a serial killer and then we'll tell the District Attorney," answered Clayton.

"Now, why would you try and be so condescending and mock my plan?" asked Will angrily. "Excuse me but I think that you're being disrespectful to me. You should never be disrespectful because I am a police officer. Actually, I am higher in ranking than a police officer. I am the Grand Fromage of the police force. So, I have full control, but, anyway, you should never be disrespectful to the police commissioner or a police officer. These people are out here saving your life from idiots and low lives like these men, and you disrespect them. Shame on you," the commissioner replied.

"Well, let me just tell you this. I am so pissed off at you because you're so patronizing to me and that homeless guy, Buck. You shouldn't be nasty and judge a book by looking at its cover. You think that I'm unintelligent, but I am probably way smarter than you. One thing that we Starmos aliens instill in our students is reading and writing unlike you Earthlings. All you Earthlings do is prepare your students for standardized testing, which is just wrong as could be, but then again, to you Bureaucrats, everything that is bad is okay, and oh yeah, you preach that Bureaucrats are bad, when you're a Bureaucrat, yourself. Hey buddy, I suggest you stop being a Bureaucrat. You are so damn disrespectable. All you politicians are dishonest and selfish. Your basic belief is what I like to call 'Social Darwinism', which is essentially being prejudice and being bias. You should never be like that because we aliens were never racist to you humans.

In fact, we rescued your kind from the hell hole of our old leader Cornelius Von Alien. I could've remained with Cornelius and had taken his side because I am an alien, but, I do what is known as the right choice and your choice is the extremely wrong choice. Right now, one thing that we must agree with is that Buck is a sick, twisted, nutty serial killer," the alien leader said. "I guess you are right. I am so sorry that I talked to you like that. Maybe I shouldn't be so condescending with you. I am totally sorry," the police commissioner replied remorsefully. Now, Buck is finished making his meal.

"So, are you all ready for tonight's dinner?" he asked ecstatically. "Yes" Will answered sarcastically. He jumped up five feet in the air with the pot of soup in his hand. None of the disgusting soup splashed out of the pot. He then walked to the shale stone table, and gently placed the last meal on the table. He than retrieved three bowls from the closet. "This is where you all will be eating from, and if I get any complaints, I shall kill you immediately," he said. "Aren't you already going to kill us to begin with?" asked Rubi. "Of course, at some point tonight, I'll kill you. I am nice enough to give you all a last meal before killing all of you. So, be grateful for what you get. Then after your meal, death shall do its part," answered Buck.

"What happens if we don't eat our meal?" asked Clayton. "Then, you die without a last meal, and we don't want that to happen," the homeless man answered. "I really don't want to eat this disgusting crap," Will said brusquely.

"Well, it's too bad. It's your problem. I don't think that you want to be killed without a last meal," the homeless man replied. "Fine. Then, I'll do it to shut you the hell up," the alien leader said angrily."

"What if I kill you before you kill me or any of us?" asked Rubi. "There's no way that you can kill me. First of all, you are blonde so that means that you're stupid, and you wouldn't know how to kill a single soul. So, don't try me. Secondly, your arms are so weak as compared to my muscular arms. In fact, throughout my life, I've been working out on trees doing pull ups, push-ups, and sit ups. I bet where you came from, there is no such thing as a single tree. Thirdly, I can crush you like a grape. Granted, I am a little bit taller than you but I am also much heavier than you. As compared to my weight, you would be considered anorexic," answered Buck scornfully.

She ignored the homeless beast and turned her head to her boyfriend. "Let me just tell you this, honey. This man is more bigoted and chauvinistic than Commissioner Clayton. He called me stupid because I have blonde hair. He told me that I was weak because I am a woman, and he is very disrespectful towards me and other women. I don't see you doing anything to protect me from this foul beast," she said angrily. "What do you expect me to do?" Will asked. "I want you to tell that Son of a Bitch off, and basically, destroy him! He is nothing but a wise guy, and he is an arrogant smart aleck, and don't fight with Clayton over the Social Darwinism thing because this homeless man is more of a Social Darwinist than Clayton. This man is the most bias soul towards us aliens. He thinks he knows everything, when he really doesn't. He might know some political nonsense but he is not the most intelligent man in the world or even in this universe like he touts himself to be. This man is a braggart!" answered Rubi.

Chapter VI: The Escape

It is now 7:00 in the evening at Buck's cave abode. This is not a typical dwelling for a homeless man, but then again, this man is not a typical homeless person. He is really a serial killer. The "delectable" dinner is now present at the shale stone table. "What is this?" asked Will. "For the three hundred and fiftieth time, it is your last meal. You know, everybody has to have a last meal before dying. You must have a last meal too and this meal is going to be so gourmet, once you try it. Come on, try it," answered Buck. He got up from his seat and started to walk over to the cauldron. Right before his eyes, a stalagmite suddenly fell to the ground. Yet, he didn't realize that this happened. He continued walking and tripped on a large piece of the stone.

"What's this?" he asked rhetorically. He turned his head around and saw the alien leader texting on his aPhone. "You must've done this to me. Shame on you! I ought to shank you," Buck said. "Excuse me. What did you just say?" asked Will. "Nothing," the homeless man answered. He continued walking down to the cauldron. The commissioner crept up behind him, and grabbed a rock from the floor. The homeless man didn't know what was about to strike him. Clayton retrieved a rock and tossed it to the top of the cave ceiling.

The rock started to fall back from the ceiling. After three seconds of falling, it landed adjacent to the homeless man. BANG! The rock falling caused a loud vibration. The homeless man turned around. "Who threw that rock!?" he asked. "I did," answered Clayton. Buck lunged at the commissioner, and grabbed him by his neck and started to choke him. Despite the commissioner being placed in a choke hold, he managed to kick the homeless man in the stomach.

Buck released his hands and the strong grip on Clayton's neck, and bounced backward. The commissioner started to cough for air. Fortunately, his windpipe was not crushed from the strong hands of the homeless beast. Buck looked at the commissioner in an arrogant manner with his eyes squinted and his eyebrows slanted down. His face is now inflamed in anger. He turned around and retrieved a wooden spoon which was adjacent to the Cauldron. He pulled the commissioner up from the rocky floor and walked over to the shale stone table. "So, why did you kill my friend?" asked Will. "I didn't kill your friend. I attempted to kill him. I don't think you would like somebody to throw rocks at you. I am sure if somebody threw rocks at you, you'd try and kill them yourself," answered Buck.

"No, I wouldn't kill somebody if he or she threw a rock at me. I'd have them arrested if I was injured but otherwise, I wouldn't have anyone do anything about it," the alien leader replied. "Well, that's stupid on your part. Besides, I bet that you have secret service protecting you at all costs, even if you don't want them to be with you. You are this rich, aristocratic leader, and you can afford a body guard. I am this penniless person. I have to constantly defend myself, worrying whether or not I am going to have the crap beat out of me. We homeless men have to fend for ourselves," said Buck.

"*You* are *not* poor." Will yelled at him. "In fact, you only let yourself be poor. You are really rich. Also you can't...," the alien leader was rudely interrupted by the homeless man. "How can I be rich when I don't have a penny to spend!? I can't get a job in this government controlled economy. Besides, ever since that idiot took over thirty nine years ago, this country went down the tubes. The taxes kept going up, and everybody became poor. More people are becoming homeless because of that idiot's reign. Eventually, the American population will go homeless because of these stupid democrats and republicans ruining this country!" the homeless man yelled.

"What I was trying to say is that you are rich in a different way. You are rich in a happy and energetic way. You can be rich by choice. You choose to be happy or you choose to be a miserable bastard. Often, in life, you make choices. You choose to kill, do drugs, commit criminal acts, or do anything with malicious intent," replied Will. The homeless man disregarded Will's commentary about choices, and placed three clay bowls in front of the "guests." He set the dirty spoons on the table in front of the bowls. The soup is now being served.

"What kind of meal is this?" asked Clayton. "It is what I like to call Cauldron Sink Soup. It is a soup with some ingredients that I don't want to mention," answered Buck. He had a sinister smirk on his face as he answered the question. "What ingredients do you have in this soup?" the alien leader asked. "First of all, it's not a soup; it's a stew. This is a delicious meal. Now, I used many ingredients, and I have to try to remember them. I used paprika, curry, cloves, mint, and other delicious ingredients," answered Buck, who was lying through his teeth. "I don't believe that. I don't even know where you can get all of these delicious ingredients from," replied Rubi.

"Okay, maybe I didn't tell you the truth earlier; but I used to work at a restaurant that featured spices. Unfortunately, I was laid off during the second recession. After my termination from the job, I started stealing things and riding the rails. That's how I really got those spices. When paprika was rationed, it was considered a federal crime to steal that particular spice, and I was posted on the U.S. Marshall's Most Wanted Criminal's List. For ten years, I remained on that list. Because the statute of limitations ran out, the case against me was dismissed and I didn't have to worry about arrest. Eventually, I started to eat paprika as a meal. Somehow, my mind became warped, and people started disappearing from Industry Pond. That was because I was killing them off. Throughout my life, I have killed over six hundred people. That means that I will probably be serving life in prison without the possibility of parole or get the death penalty now, but then again, the cops won't know that it's me causing the mysterious deaths of over six hundred people," the homeless man said.

"Okay. That's a pretty interesting story," replied Rubi. "Well, thank you. I know I tell very interesting stories. Unfortunately, none of them are ever told to anyone," said Buck. This homeless man just found out another way to aggrandize himself, and make himself look excellent. "You know that you're very egocentric," replied Clayton. "Well, thank you," the homeless man said. "And you're also very talented," the commissioner replied in a sarcastic manner.

"Now, when are you guys going to try this delicious meal I made?" asked Buck. "I don't know - about now. Perhaps, we shall try it in a little bit," the alien leader answered. "Well, I need somebody to eat it now," the homeless man said. "What happens if we don't have it?" the police commissioner asked. "Then, like I said earlier, death will do its part immediately, instead of after the last meal," answered Buck. "Fine. I'll have it now," replied Clayton brusquely. The homeless man stared at the police commissioner's bowl. The commissioner reached his hand toward the spoon adjacent to the bowl. He was about to taste the "delectable" soup.

He placed the soup to his tongue. All of a sudden, he spit the soup out on the homeless man. "What ingredients are in this soup!?" he yelled "Oh, the ingredients that I said earlier. All of the delicious spices," answered Buck. "This meal tastes totally different from those spices. It tastes more like garbage to me. In fact, it tastes like cow excrement, dirty sweat socks, and salt, combined into one meal! It is disgusting what you served me! Shame on you! You did this on purpose so that way we can die before we finish our last meal. You're sick in the head!" yelled Clayton.

The homeless introvert objected to the police commissioner's statement. The alien leader and his girlfriend tossed the bowls of the foul soup on the stone floor. "What are you doing?" asked Buck. "We're objecting to your so called 'good' meal. We think this meal is disgusting, and we totally agree with Clayton's idea. I think you're trying to cause us a slow death by giving us cow excrement! You're trying to cause E.coli! You're trying to ruin our stomachs to cause our demise," the alien leader answered angrily.

"Yes, I am even proud of the fact that you were going to say that! You know that I have a vendetta for you because you're the leader of an alien city, and you are out to harm so many people, and so many innocent Earthlings like myself. Aliens are out to hurt innocent people! So, since, you, your alien girlfriend, and that stupid police commissioner fell into my trap, now, you're going to get killed! You aliens also set high standards for yourselves unlike us Earthlings. Shame on you," the lunacy spewing from Buck continued."First of all, you shouldn't make me feel ashamed. I am the harmless person, alien rather. I didn't kill six hundred people; I saved one hundred and fifty from a raid from a beastly army. Second of all, I loathe evil brutes who cause damage toward innocent lives like myself, and third of all, you make yourself to be the victim when you're not a victim. In fact, you're far from a victim. You are a disgusting, malicious, cruel, cold-hearted, malevolent, deleterious, sick, twisted, mind-crushing bully!" Will said angrily.

"Are there any other names you can call me?" Buck asked in a smart aleck manner. "Oh yeah! But, I don't want to mention them," the alien leader answered. "Well, bring it the hell on. I want to fight and take your life away from this Earth. After all, you're the only strong one of the group. Your girlfriend doesn't stand a chance messing with me, nor does that old Neanderthal of a police commissioner. I will fight all of you but I am going to fight you first," replied the belligerent homeless man. The alien leader's lips tightened and his hands became clenched into fists. He lifted up his arms and positioned his legs into a war-like stance. The homeless man lunged at him again. As he lunged at him Will grabbed his neck and started choking him. The alien leader smirked. "Looks like you're going to be destroyed because I totally own you this time. You think you can mess with me when you really can't. You think you're so strong when you're really weak. You think you're so bright when you're really dumb. You are worse than Manson with that brutal, cold-blooded, sick, twisted attitude. You think that you rule the world when you really don't, and finally, you make like you're the victim when you are the total opposite. You think that you're stronger than everybody else when you are not stronger than me. Now *you* don't mess around with me!" he said.

The homeless man's head was turning red like fire. Some of his unkempt, brown hair started to fall out of his head. The alien leader tossed him inside of the pond. His body appeared to be lifeless. Bubbles from his mouth started to come up to the top of the water. He was unconsciously floating on the top of the pond.

"Guys, it is time to make the escape. We must get out of here now and leave while this nut is unconscious. If he is wakes up and he sees us trying to escape from the cave, we'll be dead. Now I don't know about you guys but, I don't want to die. I want to live to see my children, grandchildren, and even my great grandchildren. So, let's find the stone to escape from here. Once we find the stone, we'll be perfectly okay and we'll be free, and head over to Staten Island the safe haven," said Will. Rubi started to turn over all of the stones. Some of the stones she turned over were mossy. While others, were perfectly pure and amorphous. Some of the stones had spiders underneath. Others contained salamanders. She then noticed a stone that wouldn't budge. This stone looked similar to an eight banded Armadillo. This peculiar stone was the color of yellow and felt like a shell rather than a stone.

It was so amorphous like a stone and it had moss. This peculiar stone stood up and blinked with two eyes. Rubi stepped back. "Hey, Will, check this out. This stone is actually moving and standing up." "What do you mean?" he asked. "It just stood up, but it returned to its normal position as a stone," she answered. The peculiar stone stood up tall. It had a face that was as grey as an elephant but the "skin" was as yellow as an armadillo. This bizarre stone featured a horn like a rhinoceros. He wore a gigantic green, mossy cloak. "What is your name?" asked Rubi.

"Stein Weidon," the unique stone answered. "For thousands of years, I've been stuck between all of these stones because of that smart aleck cave man who occupied this place for decades. This caveman I heard was nothing but, a homeless, dangerous introvert, and I also heard you talking to him and that he just confessed to killing over 600 people. That's a hell- hole number. But, for decades I've been stuck by these stones, which was very unfortunate for me. I need to stretch now."

"Okay, nice sermon. Now, can you come with me?" the alien leader's girlfriend asked. "Sure, where do you have to go to?" the stone asked. "Staten Island" answered Rubi. "Oh, Staten Island the place that used to have the old dump, which is now, a big, beautiful park. This was the place where the old loop was supposed to be built. In fact, this loop was supposed to be heading to New Jersey," replied Stein. "Okay, you can stop talking," said Will. "Who are you?" asked Weidon. "I am the alien leader of Starmos City. I am also a big hero on Earth. I am Will Von Alien," the alien leader answered. "Okay, that's a good answer. What three wishes do you want?" the stone asked. "Oh, I don't want too many wishes.

All I want is to get the hell out of here. Besides, it is important that we are given freedom. After all, I have to head back to Starmos City to govern my people and help take care of my people," answered Will. "Gentlemen, enough with the clowning around and the chitter chatter. We have to get the hell out of here," the commissioner said. The alien leader jumped into the pond and started to swim

in the pond across the cave. "What are you doing?" asked
Rubi. "I am swimming eastward," answered Will. "What do
you mean you're swimming 'Eastward' when the third
largest borough is westward?" asked Clayton.

"Okay, smart guy, I meant westward to the island
"Does anybody need me for anything?" asked the stone.
"Yes, I need you to block the waterfall," answered Rubi.
"How would you expect me to do that?" asked Stein. "You
are going to remove some more stones right there,"
answered Commissioner Clayton. "While I do that, you and
Rubi start swimming to the area of the waterfall," the
talking stone replied. He started to remove all of the other
nonliving stones. While he was doing that, Rubi and the
police commissioner cannonballed into the pond. They
started to swim briskly to the waterfall. "Stein," shouted to
Will, "What do you want?" he asked.

"My two other confidantes just came over to the
waterfall. Did you remove all of the stones?" the alien
leader asked. "Of course. In a second, I'm going to pull the
lever," answered Stein. The waterfall started to disappear.
Will started to stare into space with his eyes wide open. He
started to have another flashback. When he was a toddler in
Starmos City, he lived by a dam because his parents
worked near there.

As a lad, in his apartment, he would always see a
big reservoir in view, which supplied water to the alien city.
Cornelius came over to visit because he was Will's distant
cousin. Cornelius was about 30 at the time. He was
babysitting young Will. He walked up to the balcony. "Hey,
Will do you notice that lake right there?" he asked. "Yeah,"
the young alien answered. "Well, that's going to disappear
today because I am going to build the Alien Estate over
there. I will cut off all of your drinking supply, and you'll

have to get water from Planet Earth," replied Cornelius. "Where's that?" asked the young Will.

"Oh, you don't need to know. Besides, you shouldn't even care. All you have to care about is Starmos City," the alien leader answered. Clayton yelled. "Will, what are you doing?" The flashback suddenly ended. "Why did you yell at me like that?" the alien leader asked. "Because I wanted you to snap out of your daydream, and get into reality. You need to get into the real world; we are trying to escape that evil man, Buck," the police commissioner shouted. "Okay, let's continue on our mission," replied Will. "Wait for me," the stone shouted. He started to walk on the stones that surrounded the pond. "Come on hurry up," the alien leader replied. "Well, how can a seven foot tall giant like me hurry up. I can't run. I am made of stone. Granted, I have the body of an armadillo, but I am not as agile as you are because I've been stuck for decades. it seemed like thousands of years," said Stein. He continued walking alongside the stones that surrounded the pond. He came across a gap between the gateway to Staten Island and the last stone. He stood on the last stone and remained there. "What are you doing?" asked Will. "I am thinking whether or not I should jump across this gap," answered Stein. "Just jump across it," replied Will. "Fine then, I'll do that to satisfy you, and shut you the hell up" said the talking stone. He made the daring leap of nine feet and he arrived in the cave to Staten Island. "You see, I knew that you were able to do it. After all, if you put your mind to anything, you can achieve it," said Will. "Good point," replied Stein.

He and Will walked side by side. Their shoulders didn't touch. The stone creature is much taller than the alien leader. The escapees continued to walk down into the Gateway to Staten Island. As they are walking, they encountered a swamp monster. Will crinkled his eyebrows, and he opened his mouth in disbelief. The monster kept approaching. "Who are you?" the alien leader asked. "Oh, I am your worst nightmare, Monstre. I have been on the hunt for you for the past twenty-five hours," the swamp monster answered. "What do you mean by that?" asked Will. "It means I have been on the loose for 25 hours!" answered Monstre. "Were you the one that I locked up?" the alien leader asked.

"Yes, I am your worst nightmare. I'm planning on killing you executioner's style. So, don't you dare ever mess with me again," the swamp monster answered angrily. "And what happens if I do mess with you?" asked Will. "The consequence that I just said to you a second ago," answered Monstre. "Tell me what happened after I arrested you," the alien leader replied.

"After my arrest, I was brought to the Starmos Court. That was when the judge ruled that I was competent for extradition to the Garden City, and when I was placed on trial for the crime of murder in the first degree. Specifically, felony murder. I was charged with four counts of kidnapping, one count of murder, and one count of false imprisonment. I didn't request to be tried by a jury. due to the fair government in the Garden City, I was placed on trial. After less than an hour of deliberation, I was convicted on all counts. I was sentenced to death plus twenty five years; twenty years for kidnapping; five years for false imprisonment. I was taken to death row, and I was supposed to die by drowning, but I filed an appeal, and I am waiting for that appeal. So, while I am on appeal, I escaped. When the guards weren't looking or standing the guard down, I got a newspaper and stuffed a plastic bag thinking that the guards would've thought that there was somebody in the cot. I slipped out, stole Light, brought him over to Jacqueline Langyaw, and then returned back to my land of Garden City so I could kidnap Gairdon. I kidnapped him, and he's now with Light and Langyaw," said Monstre. "Well, you should be ashamed of yourself because you kidnapped probably one of the greatest emperors of all time. You also kidnapped one of the greatest, most quiet souls of all time. It is disgusting why you kidnapped Light. You are nothing but an atrocity to society," the alien leader replied.

"Monstre, why would you commit such a wicked act?" asked Rubi. "Don't you remember that I am the activist of the underworld monsters? I support the underworld. That's where I came from," the swamp beast answered, "Where? Where did you come from?" asked Will. "The land of Hades. Hell. I came from a land that was gray and gloomy. This is the land where I learned to be evil. When I was born, I started off as a spirit. Eventually, I became a real creature. I had many jobs as a real creature. My very first duty was to kill a couple of hundred animals in the wilderness. So, I traveled to Britain and I discovered that there weren't any animals over there. Therefore, I consulted Hades, and I talked to him about making a deal for citizenship in the Under World. In exchange for the citizenship, I had to kill many people in the United Kingdom in the late 1800s. The classic way for not being captured is making an alias name. So, I decided to change my name in the United Kingdom to Jack the Ripper. The British police were on national manhunts for me. They falsely accused other people of being Jack the Ripper. I moved up to the hills of Scotland way past Edinburg. That was where I met Hades and he put some magical power into my system. He turned me into a Swamp Monster, and that was when people started to mysteriously disappear in the Loch Ness Lake. A couple of times, some hunters spotted me. They tried to shoot me, but I swallowed them up. In the year 1900, I departed from Planet Earth and returned to the Underworld. There I learned how to read and write, and speak all of the languages of the world, including Old English and Gallic. I learned chemistry, and how to dimension travel from one place to another. Now, I took the test, where I had presented Hades with my magical powers. Unfortunately, I failed," answered Monstre.

"Besides killing people - because you couldn't kill animals - what are the other sick, twisted reasons why you kill people?" asked Clayton.

"Well, first of all, throughout my entire life I've been bullied. When I attended primary school, I was bullied the most. I was too smart for my class, and I am also an introvert. I didn't fit in with the crowd because of the pale color of my skin. That was when I grew closer to the Underworld. They influenced me into thinking that stealing lives is acceptable. In addition to that, I don't kill just people, I kill all creatures. I've killed many animals, bugs, aliens, and giant insects. You Earthlings and you aliens think that killing is unacceptable; but we creatures in Garden City absolutely condone killing. It is okay to kill in Garden City. I also realized that I can make a lot of money from committing acts that you call wicked and heinous. When I became a citizen of Garden City, the inhabitants knew about my strength and my height, and they also knew that I can use it for all of the 'right' reasons. Throughout my killing career, I've made hundreds of millions of Dronkas, the currency in the Garden City. This money is the equivalent to the money in Starmos City. Spazerstock, a longtime friend of mine, decided that he had enough of one of his guests, Tom Jackson, a human being. That was when I was apprehended by you, the alien, beastly leader," answered the beastly swamp monster.

Will showed a facial expression of sheer anger. He ran up to Monstre and started to kick him in the stomach. "Do you think you're wise?" Will asked angrily. The swamp monster snickered in a nasty, demonic manner. "What do you mean by that?" he asked. "Well, when you slandered me and ridiculed me for rescuing innocent lives, you infuriated me. You caused my brain to go insane. You are a piece of junk. You are a low life and you belong in the lowest place in the world, the foulest place in the universe, and the most securely, confined place of all dimensions. Unfortunately, you're out. Your arrogant attitude is out in society. You and Buck are here to ruin all living creatures around the world. Now, you will die. This is whether you die in prison or whether you die at somebody else's or your own stone, you shall be gone. You are not a sane soul. You are brilliant in your knowledge; but you use your knowledge for the wrong things! With your brilliance comes ignorance. Your rank ignorance is clearly shown because of the fact that you are willing to learn the skill of bringing violence towards others. However you are not willing to learn the skill of bringing love and kindness into the world, and maybe, I am kind of condescending, but at least I am here to help the world, heal the problems in the world, and help all of the cities that I've been to, and help the dimension that I lead," the alien leader answered. The violent swamp monster continued walking. Within a matter of seconds, he vanished into the cave.

"Thank God, that thing is gone," the police commissioner said. "Why are you saying such a thing?" asked Will. He looked at the alien leader incredulously.

"Because, look what he did to you. He tried to ruin your life. For God sakes, he tried to kill you years ago! Instead, he killed your friend, Tom. You should've killed him before he could kill somebody else. Capturing him means nothing. Killing them is something important. This swamp monster is a low life. He comes from the bottom of the Earth. The bottom of the Universe. He even comes from the bottom of the abyss. This soul is more evil than Lucifer himself. In fact, he is the epitome of evil," answered Clayton. Will replied "Don't think that I am condoning what this foul beast does. In fact, I think he's evil. I think what he did is atrocious, and he definitely deserves to be flogged with the Cat O' Nine tails and hit with a twenty two caliber. But you said two untrue statements that you believed. Tom was never killed. This beast *tried* to kill him. Also, his mind might come from the Bottom of the Earth, if not the bottom of the Universe, but he physically never came from the Bottom of the Earth nor the Universe.

He came from a place where the evil deities originated. If you were listening, he said he came to Earth and took the form of Jack the Ripper, and then took the form of the swamp creature known as the Loch Ness Monster in the Hills of Edinburg. He is extremely evil and malicious, and we will hunt him down. When we capture him we will not take him to trial, and he shall be hurt but he is totally not worthy of trial," replied the alien leader.

"Why are you so condescending towards me?" the commissioner asked. Will answered, "Because I feel like it. Don't comment on what I say. Besides, I thought you were on my side. I thought you were here to help my cause. I thought you were here to help me rescue..." The alien officer started to speed walk. "Why are you walking so briskly?" asked Clayton. "Because I want to get to Staten

Island" answered Will. "What do you think, Staten Island will be the light at the end of the tunnel for you?" asked the commissioner. "Yes, because Staten Island is what I'd like to call the 'Ultimate Safe Haven' of the World. This place is going to bring me a lot of comfort. It is almost like the Celestial City of God," the alien leader answered. "That's totally stupid and bogus to say because there's no place on Earth that is even comparable to a Celestial City that is especially under God. The only place that is a Celestial City under God is Heaven, and if you believe in the Lord Jesus, that's the place that you'll be heading to," replied the police commissioner.

"Who is Jesus? Who is God?" asked Will. "It depends on how you look at the concept. Every religion or philosophy with a theistic belief, particularly a monotheistic one, has its own God or version of God. God is the Creator of mankind. He is the one that makes the guidelines for the followers of a philosophy. God is a spiritual figure that is universally accepted by all religions with a theistic belief. He created the world around you. He created you, your parents, and even your ancestors. He is the Creator of all Heavens and Earth," answered Clayton.

"Now, I get updates from the news that violence is always prevalent due to religion. Is this totally true?" asked Will. "Unfortunately, yes. Religion often plays a key role in the wars and battles of the modern day. People like to impose one's religion on another religion or group, and they try doing it every way possible. And we live in a world that is filled with bigotry. Aside from being the police commissioner of New York City, I have also worked for the Peace Corp. I would often have to come in to help settle certain conflicts and disputes between religions and cults. I believe that there's one God, and he is the ultimate Creator of mankind, and he will be the one who shall be the light at the end of the tunnel. He will be the one who will help you in a horrible situation," answered Commissioner Clayton.

"Granted, I don't believe in any religion. I do believe in God. I believe that he is my ultimate Creator, and he is the one that brought me to this World, this Universe, all Dimensions, and beyond," the alien leader replied. The alien leader, the commissioner, and Rubi continued walking. Seen in the distance of the dark cave is a green, luminous glow. As they continued, the glow kept increasing in brightness. "What's this?" asked Rubi. "I have no idea. It looks like an emerald to me. I've seen plenty of emeralds in my life, But this is the most unique emerald I've ever seen. I don't even know what it is. It must sound so much like *Botana Curus,*" the alien leader answered.

"First of all, you shouldn't be talking to me and being so demeaning to me by correcting me because you think that you're so smart and ingenious, when you are far from that. This time, I will correct you. First of all, *Botana Curus* is a specimen of plant life, and what you are seeing in here is not a life form at all. You're looking at some sort of bizarre rock or mineral that is from the Earth. It is almost like a geode. Second of all, I want to take your side. But, there are some things that get me pissed off like your patronizing attitude. Unlike you, I've disregarded this and I am not the type to point out everything that you do. So, don't be a smart aleck to me, and we shall move on with this," replied Commissioner Clayton.

The alien leader started to stare into the luminous light. His eyes are wide open and his eyebrows are falling off. The light became brighter. Within a matter of seconds, the emerald started to change different colors. After a time the emerald started to shake. Suddenly, it exploded. Smoke started to emerge from the spot of the emerald. "What's going on?" asked Rubi. The commissioner is now staring in the spot of the smoke. Rubi turned her head around. That was when the Will fainted. "Rubi, I think you should turn around," the commissioner said. "Why?" she asked. "Because of this," answered Clayton. "What's 'this'?" the alien leader's girlfriend asked.

"This is that; and that is this," the police commissioner answered. "I frankly think that your answer is one of the stupidest answers that I've ever heard. I never heard of the lamest, most stupid answer in my life like that one. On second thought, your answer is not so stupid. It is actually more of an entertaining answer than a stupid answer," replied Rubi. "Hey, that's not nice to say," said Clayton. She turned around with her hands on her hips. "I'm so sorry for being a smart aleck toward you because..." She paused. A dramatic gasp left her mouth. She screamed loudly. She leapt at the alien leader lying on the floor. "What happened to my boyfriend?! Did you murder him?" she asked angrily. "Stop accusing me of murder! I would never kill your boyfriend," the police commissioner answered. "Well, tell me exactly what happened," said Rubi. She stared at him. "Your boyfriend started to stare into the bright emerald. It seems a supernatural effect took place. The emerald started to shine brighter and changed colors. It exploded and was smoking and when he was staring at the smoke he suddenly fainted, and lost his consciousness. Now, I don't know if he is dead or not but I'll check to see if he is alive and breathing. I can't make any guarantees," replied Clayton. Rubi was distressed. "I could totally understand. If my boyfriend is deceased I will not be able to live with myself. Besides, he's the only one that I have as a loving boyfriend,"

Chapter VII: The "Garden of Eden": Lesson One

The alien leader fell into a long coma. He started having an important dream, a long dream that is starting to take place in his head. "Where am I? Where is this place?" he asked himself. "You're on the trail of goodness and joy," a loud, audible voice answered from above. "Who are you?" the alien leader asked. "I am the Eternal father, the Creator of all heavens and Earth," the audible voice answered. "Be very specific with your name?" asked Will. "I am God," the audible voice answered. "You are so not God," the alien leader answered. "Yes, I am," replied God. "Well, prove to me that you're this Creator," said Will. All of a sudden a bunch of seeds had fallen from the sky. "Do you think I am God, now?" the spiritual audible voice asked. "No. All I saw were seeds falling from the sky and landing on the ground," the alien leader answered. "Do you think that the sky can rain seeds?" asked God. "Yes, it can rain seeds," answered Will. "How can that possibly be?" asked the Creator. "A flock of high flying birds can disperse seeds on the ground," the alien leader answered. "And where did those high flying birds come from?" asked God. "Canada," answered Will. "Let me rephrase the question. Where were they born?" the Creator asked. "They came from eggs in a nest," the alien leader answered.

"You are totally wrong," replied God. "Okay, show me that you're not some mysterious audible voice. Show me that you are God. I want to personally see it," said Will. "Okay," the Creator replied. Will continued walking down the open trail in the wilderness. This was when he discovered a small sheet of grass. "I don't see anything," he said. "You're standing on the spot where the seeds landed.

Now, I will show you something even more unique,"
replied God. The beautiful blue sky remained the same
color. The harmonious trees were perfectly standing. Not a
single black cloud was seen in the distance. A loud clap of
thunder was heard. The alien leader became fearful.
"What's that?" he nervously asked. "That noise is what I
like to call thunder. If you notice there isn't a single black
cloud in the sky but it shall rain on you," answered God.
"Let there be rain!" he shouted. It started drizzling on top
of the alien leader. Than in a matter of seconds, it started
pouring heavily. "What's this?" Will asked. "How can you
not know what it is? It is what I call rain," answered God.

"Well, first of all, I've never been to a place with
rain. I never seen rain. Second of all, don't you take that
tone with me," the alien leader replied in a snooty manner,
still not believing he was talking to God. "Excuse me but
don't talk to your heavenly Father like that. You are clearly
committing a huge sin against me. Thou should honor thy
mother and father," said God. "I did honor my parents," the
alien leader replied. "No, you didn't!" yelled God. "Oh, I
absolutely did. I didn't cause them any trouble. I gave them
the utmost respect. I was the perfect child. I never
disobeyed them. I would always do the chores that I was
assigned; ace all my subjects in school to satisfy them; not
get involved in their own adult conversations; never make a
mess in the house. I have never lied to them or even made
up a fib. I would always tell the truth. I never acted out of
line in front of them or in school. I was the perfect child,"
replied Will.

"I could see that you're a complete and pathological
liar," said God. "What do you mean?" the alien leader
asked. "You're making like you're so immaculate towards
your parents when you are a far cry from being sinless.

You've committed such serious acts against your father. I am not talking about your biological father. I am talking about your spiritual father. You've never believed in him. You never showed faith in your life. You zealously proclaimed you're an atheist. However I shall forgive you because that is the right path to travel on," the Creator answered. The rain stopped.

"What happened here?" asked Will. "Oh, I was just showing you the powers that I have. I have the power to create and destroy things, bring light or create darkness and I also have the power to *be* the light at the end of the tunnel. So, therefore, I have all power. I am the one who is omniscient and omnipresent. I see everything that goes on in all corners of the globe, every planet in the universe, and every dimension. I even see in every individual's mind, whether you have the simple mind of a bird, or the complex mind of a human, or the bizarre mind of an alien. I see what everyone's thinking on a 24 hour, 7 day basis. Individuals don't hear me; they don't see me until they reach heaven. Some will never see me because they never believe, show zero faith towards me, or don't even obey me," answered God. "Now, granted, I don't think that I am going to die. But what is the status of my going to heaven?" the alien leader asked.

"Negative one out of one hundred. The reason is because you never believed in me. You were never taught about my existence. More important, you never even cared about my existence and my power. I have the power to do anything," the Creator answered. "How will I be able to get into heaven?" asked Will. "This is going to be a lengthy process but I will teach you and make you aware of your sins, and I will teach you the right road up to heaven. You are responsible for every move you make on that road;

you're accountable for it. I will shackle you to a chain and a ball. It will initially be a struggle for you to move down the right path with this chain and this ball, but eventually this chain will become lighter under one condition," answered God. "And what condition would that be?" the alien leader asked. "You must follow the right path. If you don't follow that path, the chain will become much shorter. If you continue down the Path of Evil on this trek that you shall be assigned to, you will forever be in hell. But if you go up the Path of Goodness, you shall prosper." answered the Creator. "How long have I been going down the Path of Evil?" asked Will.

"Your whole life. It sounds physically impossible, but all of mankind, whether immortal or mortal has original sin. Not a single soul is born sinless. you are not predestined to hell. You shall be brought up to heaven if you are a loving and caring being on Earth or wherever you come from. You must also have faith in me because I am going to lead you, and take you into the good direction. Satan will never do such a thing," answered God. "Who is Satan?" the alien leader asked. "He is the spirit of all evil. He is the epitome of intimidation. He may look very nice, but watch out, the ones that are too nice are dishonest with you and will bring you the most amount of harm. The one who curses you does not abominate you. The one who claims he loves you is a liar and he is Satan. I am here to help you, Will. Have faith in me, and you shall be blessed. Don't have faith in me, and trouble shall do its part," the Creator answered. "Now, what shall I do that would keep me on the pathway to heaven?" asked Will. "Be obedient and be trustworthy towards me. Do those things, and you will be fine. Also, don't be a follower; be a leader. You will keep on going down the right road," answered God.

"Well, I am the leader of an alien city. I am the leader of Starmos City, and I am here to control and help my citizens at the same time. I am not here to be unfair," the alien leader objected. "Maybe you'll learn to be a leader when I do this to you," replied the Creator. "Oh, I am so scared" the alien leader sarcastically said. "You better be," replied God. Will ran down the trail away from the field. As he was running, he was struck and electrocuted by a bolt of lightning.

The shock was ephemeral, and only lasted for thirty-seconds within his body. "What did you do that for?" he asked. "Well, that's just my form of punishment. But, wait there's more!" answered God. "That's it! I am going to get out of here. I don't want to have anything to do with you," the alien leader replied. He started running down the trail. He made a leap, and he froze in the midair. "Why are you in such a rush to leave me?" the Creator asked. "Because you make me sick," answered Will.

"That's what you Atheists say about me," replied God. "I am *not* a nonbeliever. I absolutely believe in you. I don't believe in a religion," the alien leader yelled. "We'll see about that," replied the Creator. Will fell to the ground. He was lying there for a couple of minutes. "Will, when are you going to get up?" asked God. "Now." he answered. He stood up and tried to run. He turned around and noticed a chain that was five feet long. Behind the chain was a heavy metallic ball. The ball was black. The reason why it's this color is to represent sin and evil that has taken over Will's mind.

"God, why did you do this to me?" he asked. "Because, didn't I tell you that I was going to hook you up to a chain and a ball? I told you that it was going to be extremely short and it would become longer dragging you back to the area that you started? Now let me tell you about the trek that you shall embark on. This trek is going to test your strength and your wisdom. Most of all it is supposed to test your decision making as to whether or not you will commit sins." the Creator answered. "What if I do commit sins along the way?" the alien leader asked.

"Well, the ball will become heavier. Eventually there shall be chains around both of your ankles so you won't be able to move. I will impose the punishment of Quick Sand against you. Death will eventually do its part, and you won't be going up to Heaven with me. Instead, you will be going straight to Hell with Satan! This time I really mean it," God answered angrily. "I wonder what Hell is like," said Will. "Hell is a place you don't want to be heading to. Hell is the place where the heads of malice and evil are destined to be. This is where Cornelius Von Alien is rotting right now," replied the Creator.

"Still, I *want* to see it," said Will defiantly. "Well, let there be Hell," shouted God. The blue sky started to turn the color of orange-red. Multiple explosions of fire started to take place in the sky. Chunks of fire started to rain down from the sky. "Do you get the picture?" the almighty Creator asked. "Yes, I do," answered Will. "Very well. You shall have the ability to start your journey now. I'll help you as you continue down the trail. Hopefully, you will head down the right path. Remember the consequences if you don't." replied God. Will started to walk straight down the trail. He walked as slow as a Galapagos Tortoise. "God, why do I have to do this?" he asked. "Because I told you to. Now, if you want to continue questioning me, I will increase the mass of the ball and darken the color," answered the Creator. "Ooh, I am so scared," the alien leader replied. "Who do you think you are?" God asked him. "I am Will Von Alien, your worst nightmare," the alien leader answered.

"What do you mean?" asked God. "I am the leader of an alien city. If I don't believe in you, I won't see you or even be in the situation that I am currently involved in." "So, I guess you must fight your own battles," answered God. Will thought that would "free" him. "Okay! Can you reduce the weight of that heavy ball?" "Let me think about that one. Hmm. No! There's too much sin inside of you," answered God. "Tell you what, can I apologize for my sins?" the alien leader asked. "Sure, you can, but that doesn't mean that I am going to totally forgive you. You shall be forgiven when you prove that you have truthfully apologized," answered God. "Well, don't you forgive all the time?" asked Will. "I don't forgive nonbelievers. I don't forgive Atheists," answered the Creator. "Let me rephrase that question. Do you have unlimited forgiveness grants?" the alien leader asked. "I hope you don't think that I am a genie who grants unlimited wishes because I don't do that. I forgive people if they ask for forgiveness and they put forth some effort *not* to commit the same wrongdoing as they did previously," answered God.

"I don't think you're a genie. At least you don't look like one, but you might be. Some folks say that you grant wishes. I don't believe that's true," replied Will. "Since, when do I grant *wishes*?" asked the Creator. "Maybe you've granted wishes in the past," the alien leader answered. "'Wish granting' is not my way of life. I answer every individual's prayer, and I hear all of their prayers but I don't grant any wishes," replied God.

"Can you try and make those shackles a little lighter?" the alien leader asked. "I can make that chain and ball a little lighter but I want you to learn the hard way. In life, every man, woman, and child will have the natural tendency to take the easy way out but,that is not the way to go with me. You must travel down the hard road to become a failure," answered the Creator. "That's totally not fair!" replied Will angrily. He kicked the ground.

"How dare you kick and destroy my blessed and beloved ground!" God shouted. "I just did. What are you going to do about it?" asked Will. "Now death shall do its part against you. I would never think that I would have to use this weapon. But sadly I must," answered God. A gigantic eight by eleven feet razor blade came down from the sky. It was rushing down the trail towards Will. The alien leader jumped to the side of the trail and into the trees. The razor blade whooshed past him. It cut the chain in half. The alien leader jumped back onto the trail. He snickered. "Look, who outsmarted you, God. It looks like I did!" "I may be omniscient but sometimes I can't predict what one is going to do next," the Creator replied. "That's right," the alien leader replied.

He started to run up the trail into the deep wilderness. He didn't know what was going to happen to him next. There was a patch of leaves in the distance.. He continued dashing on the trail. While he is doing that, God is waiting to see what shall happen to him. The alien leader didn't notice the patch of leaves. When he landed on that patch, he fell right through that patch into a deep abyss. He screamed. "What's going on!?" he asked. "Oh, death is just doing its part," answered God. "What do you mean by that?" the alien leader asked. "You just fell into your trap. This is where you will be dying, and going straight to hell," the Creator answered. Will continued falling. "God, why are you doing this to me?" asked Will. "Because I feel like it," answered God. "No, give me a real reason," the alien leader said. "Fine. The reason why you're going here is so you learn a very valuable lesson. You've never learned a lesson in your life and now you shall," replied God. The alien leader landed on a tar surface. "I thought this was an abyss?" he said. "It is not an abyss; but this is hell," replied God. "How is this hell?" asked Will.

"You are inside of a world filled with darkness. Look at it. It may look like an infinite desert and a tarry surface but Hell is straight down the road," answered God. "How is the Satanic Lair down the road from over here?" the alien leader asked. "Just ease on down the road and you will see the lair of Satan. You will be arriving at Lucifer's Palace," the Creator answered. "That is physically impossible. The only thing that might look similar to Satan's Palace is the Grand Canyon in the distance over there," replied Will. "How dare you compare my creation to the Palace of Lucifer!" shouted God. A loud clap of thunder sounded. Seen at the top of the Grand Canyon were Hillbillies that came down from the Boondocks.

About five hundred unkempt men, women, and children came down from their residences. "Water," they screamed. The women were sobbing tears of joy. About one foot of rain started pouring down from the sky. The children started playing and enjoying themselves in the water. The adolescents and younger men started claiming land for their farming. The older men returned back to their houses to fetch wood for the fencing, and tools for the farming. "Do you see what's going on?" asked God. "Yes, I do, the people from the Grand Canyon are having a blast," answered Will. "Exactly. Do you know the reason why?" the Creator asked. "I have no idea," the alien leader answered.

"Because, that's what your people are going through," said God. "I don't have many inhabitants that are people. Most of my inhabitants are aliens," replied Will. "Okay, once again, your special talent is being a smart mouth," the Creator said in a sarcastic manner. "Shut your mouth!" the alien leader replied. "I want to tell you an important story. This story is about the people of the hills over here. They're not literally from hills but they are poor and indigent people. They do not have three, gourmet meals every night. Instead, they have to worry if they're going to get any meal at all. They don't have a single dime or quarter and they live uncomfortable lives because their parents were poor farmers. Now, there has been a long drought that has taken place, and this clearly influenced their lives. Why don't you go meet a family or two?" said God. "I don't know about meeting them because they might have gangrene," replied Will.

"Why would you think that any of them are plagued with an ailment like that?" the Creator asked. "Because some people that raise question marks in one's head may be plagued with a neurological, physical, or mental ailment," the alien leader answered. "Do you not accept people who have any ailments? Do you have something against those people?" asked God. "No, I don't. They don't belong in our society because they bring harm to the society." answered Will.

"Well, you are not in your cruel, alien society. You are in the American society. You are in a society that accepts all men, women, and children for who they are," replied the Creator. "Well, guess what? I will try to colonize this society and when I do so, I will exile all of the plagued ones from this society. I will exile both the mentally and physically challenged," the alien leader said. "Silence!

Retract what you said!" God commanded. "What happens if I don't?" the alien leader asked. "Then, I shall hurt you so badly that you're paralyzed forever," the Creator answered. The alien leader smirked. Once again he was struck by a bolt of lightning. All of the poor Hillbillies were preoccupied with the jubilation of the miracle of water that they didn't realize that a lightning strike had taken place. The lighting burnt a large hole and wrinkled the fabric in the alien leader's shirt. "Is that enough for you?" asked God. "Yes," answered Will. "Don't you have any other words to say?" the Creator asked. "You made my shirt look really nice by adding a large hole and a bunch of wrinkles," the alien leader answered sarcastically. "That's a good thing. You kind of needed that punishment," replied God. "That's real funny." "Oh, you want more?" the Creator asked. "Oh, sure. I am really scared," Will answered. "You better be scared" God replied. "Well, guess what? I am far from scared. Bring it on," the alien leader said.

The skies became even darker. Down the long, asphalt road was a huge, tornado cloud. It started off as a narrow funnel. as it drew closer to the alien leader, it started increasing in size. The Hillbillies remained in the desert. The all-powerful Creator managed to hide the tornado in plain site from the Hillbillies. The tornado funnel is now one football field away from the alien leader, and now it increased in diameter to thirty feet. Seconds later Will was carried into the tornado. He screamed. "God, why are you doing this to me?" he asked.

"Because you showed an attitude of belligerence towards your Lord. You showed zero acceptance to those with disabilities, and you are becoming a complete Social Darwinist," answered the Creator. "Well, that's not fair," replied Will. "Yes, life's not fair. Get used to it." said God.

"That's a very nice thing to say," the alien leader replied sarcastically. The tornado ended, and the alien leader fell straight down to the ground. The Hillbillies were staring at him falling. A family of four standing by the desert grassland adjacent to the Grand Canyon were looking at each other in disbelief. They wore rugged clothing. All of their clothing was made of sheer, white cotton and wool. The father's dirty, blonde hair shined in the sunlight. He had a lot of facial hair. He wore blue jean overalls, and a cowboy hat. The mother had light-brown hair and was around five feet two inches. She wore a blue and white gown. The kids wore rugged school uniforms. The father's name was Jobe. "Stay right there," he said.

"Why?" his wife asked. "Because I must see what's going on." he answered. He stormed through the dense crowd of Hillbillies to the injured alien leader. Finally, he arrived on the tar surface in front of the alien leader. "Do you need help?" Jobe asked. Will looked up. "Do you think I need your help, street rat?" he asked. "Well, I saw that you were falling from the sky. I would assume that you would be needing help. It kind of bothers me that you are declining my helping you because of my appearance. I might not be the most tidy person in the world but I am a very loving person, and I care about my fellow brethren. I am more than willing to help you," the compassionate hillbilly answered.

"What is wrong with you? Can't you see that I don't want your help?" the alien leader asked in a snooty manner. "Well, to me, I see that you totally need help. You just encountered a severely, traumatic event. It is very unfortunate what you've just went through, and I want to take you in my home. I am very willing to accept you at any time that is necessary. You are more than welcome. In fact, you're more than welcome to be a member in my family," answered Jobe. "Well, what makes you think that I want to be associated with your unworthy family or even be in their presence?" asked Will.

"I am more than willing to welcome you inside of my home. I am more than willing to help you, and take you," the benevolent hillbilly father answered. He started to walk back into the crowd. He stopped. "You can come with me if you want," he said. The alien leader struggled to stand up. "Wait for me. Wait for me!" Will shouted. He limped into the crowd of people. Questions are now being raised about the alien leader being present in front of the crowd. He struggled to catch up with Jobe, following him in the crowd. "Stop. Please sir. I am sorry for calling you such a nasty name. Those words I never meant," he said. The benevolent man stopped and turned around.

The crowd moved away from the alien leader. Jobe approached him. "Why is everybody alienating me?" asked Will. "Because people have always shown a great hatred to those who come from other planets. We live in a biased world. To me that is very unfortunate. It is too bad we live in a world like that," answered Jobe. "Thank you for being so nice to me. That is very chivalrous of you," the alien leader replied. "Thank you," said Jobe. "Do you need me to help you?" he asked. "Yes," answered Will. Jobe leaned the alien leader's arm around his neck. They continued moving until they reached "their" family. "What is your name?" Jobe's wife asked. "Will Von Alien. I am the honorable leader of Starmos City," he answered.

"Interesting. This is impressive that you're an alien. You must be an excellent leader," she replied. "Well, what's your name?" asked Will. "Oh, my name is Naomi. I was named after one of the Biblical folks," she answered. "And that is interesting also. What is the Bible?" asked Will. "Did you just ask that question?" asked Jobe. "Yes, I did. I don't even know what a 'Bible' is," the alien leader answered. "My kids have to memorize the Bible when they're seven years old, and you don't even know the significance or the definition of the Bible. That is totally ridiculous. Boy, you're going to learn with me about this book because it can and it will make a severe, lasting impact on your life. It might even change your life and your outlook on certain aspects in life," replied the religious gentleman.

"I really don't care to know what the Bible is," said Will. "Well, I am going to tell you about the Bible whether you like it or not. The Bible is a book that is used in different religions in the Christian philosophy. The most mundane versions used are the New American Standard Bible, the King James Version, and the New International Version. I know all of the stanzas in the Bible. In fact, I can tell you each one of them, one by one, but we will get into that much later in our journey together. I hope you are willing to learn," replied Jobe. "Well, guess what? I really don't care because I've never even heard of such a thing, because that book never caused any effects on my life. Nor do I intend for it to impact my life in any way, shape, or form. I've lived my life without the Bible and enjoyed it totally. Granted, there were some events of misfortune in my life. I learned how to be resilient and strong during this adversity in my life. I managed to overcome my problems without some crazy book dictating to me and telling me what to do, how to live my life, how to deal with my problems, and what to do with my life. I am a full-fledged, and am very proud of the fact, that I am a nonbeliever. Besides, being a believer in any religion or philosophy causes fights. What is the sense in being somebody who condones violence and enjoys confrontations? I think learning the Bible is totally ridiculous and stupid," said Will.

"Do you want to come with me?" the religious man asked in an angry manner. "The only reason why I want to come with you is because *I have* to come with you. Like I said, I think that learning the Bible is totally ridiculous and stupid," the alien leader answered. "Yeah, you say that but you might learn how to improve your own life," replied Jobe.

"Whatever," the alien leader said. "Now, let's talk about your life," the Hillbilly replied. "Can we talk about yours first?" asked Will. "Sure. First, we must head up to the wagon in order to get to our home on the prairie nearby. The family and the alien leader started to head up the hill. The hill had dried grass and dead wheat that was supposed to be used for farming. As they continued trekking up the hill, they noticed a tree that has been dead for a number of years.

This tree's bark is bone try that, so much that if one touches it, the bark will easily fall off. Also, the trunk of this particular tree is very narrow. Yet, this tree is stationery, and it doesn't blow with the Easterly winds. Hanging from the branches are Possums. They eventually reached the tree. "What are those things?" asked Will. "Those are just "Posies." Or the proper term is called a Possum," answered Jobe. The alien leader remained by the tree. "Can I touch one of them?" he asked. "Oh, sure. It won't be a big deal if you touch them," replied the Hillbilly father.

The family continued walking to their wagon while the alien leader touched the Possum. He hesitated, and reached his arm towards the rodent. He slowly pet this animal's head. As the seconds moved by, he pet the Possum harder. All of a sudden, the creature jumped off of the branch to the hard, sandy ground. This animal then turned into a snake. The fangs started to show and the tongue moved back and forth in its mouth. He had the head of a cobra, and the tail of Diamondback Rattler. This creature was the voice of deception. "This is what I looked for. A fool like you to pet me. Now I am ready to attack you!" he said. "Who are you!?" asked Will.

"Oh, I am your worst nightmare. I am your stalker. I've been stalking you ever since you've worked at the Alien Estate when you were just fifteen years old. I always kept silent making sure that you would never know that I was present. I was hired by Cornelius Von Alien to kill you a long time ago but you managed to slip away to some remote location, but today, when you were traveling on the train with your girlfriend, Rubi, who I can't stand you noticed me and a couple of my friends getting ready to hurt you. The reason why is because you tried to take over Starmos City, and you managed to do so by apprehending such a wonderful man for committing crimes against humanity and war crimes and then killing him. Now you're trying to apprehend his widowed girlfriend because you don't like her. It's almost like you have a vendetta for all of the ones in the old leadership. I bet you even have something against your elders or the elderly," answered the evil serpent angrily.

The alien leader took four slow steps back from this poisonous beast. Yet he stared at this serpent in a belligerent manner. "Let me just tell you this. I don't have any vendettas against anyone. Those folks have vendettas against me. They're basically out to get me and cause me trouble. The ones who have vendettas against me, that you like, were Cornelius Von Alien and Jacqueline Langyaw. I apprehended them because they were trying to falsely apprehend my friends, and they wrongly imprisoned them. Than they forced the people of a county in upstate New York intoTime Capsules so that way it would freeze their growth. That was when I stormed in and apprehended the two of them! Jacqueline pled guilty in exchange for immunity, and Cornelius was put on trial, was convicted, and faced a death sentence. Fortunately, his death sentence was early. That was when I became leader. We had a jubilation for the demise of the dictator. The next morning my buddy, Light, was kidnapped by the prosecutor Jacqueline Langyaw. That was when I boarded the train to California County, and unfortunately, we had a screw up in New York City. So, you were wrong on that. In addition to that, I had tremendous respect for my elders; and I still show a lot of respect. So, you're totally wrong on that also. I was never once disobedient, selfish, insolent, or disrespectful. So, all your facts are wrong and deceptive to suit yourself. You lie all the time. That's what you are! You're nothing but a pathological liar!" replied Will.

"I can't stand the way you turn me from this nice serpent into a beast with a heart of malevolence. How dare you do such a thing! Also, you think that I am out to get you when I am not. I am here to help you. I would be more than willing to go up a Cactus to give you a piece of an exotic fruit. Yet, you're not willing to anything for me. Instead, you are against me. Shame on you! Go to hell because that's where you belong," the foul serpent angrily said. "Before we continue with this argument, I want to ask you a question of importance. What is your name?" the alien leader asked.

"That's totally not a question of importance but I am more than willing to give it to you any way. Besides, I am a Christian and you're a Devil worshiper. My name is Serpianto. I came from the underworld but became a Christian to save myself from going to Hell because I was predestined for that place," answered the serpent.

"Thank you for giving me your name but you are far from a Christian. You are out to cause a tremendous amount of trouble. That is the second lie, you've told, and it's not even been two minutes. You disgust me with your attitude. I don't want to have anything to do with you. Everything that comes out of your mouth is a lie," the alien leader replied in an angry manner. Jobe noticed Will talking. He approached him from behind. "Who are you talking to?" he asked. The alien leader turned around, and smacked him in the face. Jobe started to bleed from the mouth. "I am so sorry!" Will said. Jobe was stunned."Why would you do such a thing to me?" he asked. "Because I thought that there was somebody behind me who was ready to start trouble. I'll tell you about what happened later," answered Will remorsefully. "You're forgiven. Let's head over to the Conestoga," replied the benevolent Hillbilly. "Are you a Hillbilly?" asked Will. "No, I am a man who comes from the plains over here. I was just visiting my parents who are kind of Hillbillies," answered Jobe.

Chapter VIII: The Mormon's Family

In Salt Lake City, Utah, the alien leader started to walk with Jobe all the way to the Conestoga wagon. The wagon was obscured by the steepness of the harsh, sandy hill. "So, who were you talking to?" asked Jobe. "I'll tell you about it later," the alien leader answered. "No, tell me now," the prairie man demanded. "Why are you being so demanding?" asked Will. "Just answer the question without giving me a problem," said Jobe. "Fine then, I was talking a serpent," the alien leader answered. "Were you talking to Satan?" asked the prairie man. "I guess you would call this particular creature Satan but his name is not Satan. His name is Serpianto," answered Will." and where does this creature originate?" asked Jobe.

"He comes from the most evil part of every universe, dimension, or any place in our thoughts. This snake comes from the Underworld. He was born to Hades," the alien leader answered. "What is this beast's career?" the prairie man asked. "I am not too sure about his career; but I think that he's a career criminal," answered Will. "Well, tell me what he looks like?" asked Jobe. "Well, he looks like a Cobra and a Diamondback rattler combined" the alien leader answered. "That's too short of an answer to suit me. Describe this thing's physical features some more," replied Jobe. "Okay. Well he has a head that looks like a Frisbee and a tongue that has the appearance of a two-pronged fork. He doesn't have any hair.

His scales are wet and slippery. They didn't appear filthy. This creature has the eyes of evil and the mouth of a poisonous vile snake, literally and figuratively. His voice is extremely soft spoken, which would make you think that he is here to help you. he is actually here to hurt and ruin your life forever. This creature clearly showed anger if I didn't fall into his malevolent and malicious trap. He has the heart of evil, and he is out to get me. He clearly shows that he has a vendetta for me," said Will. " And why does he have the vendetta for you?" asked the prairie man.

"I got over here in quite a bizarre way. To make the long story short, I traveled on a train because I had to rescue my friend who was abducted by this wench who is tremendously jealous of me. This serpent is here to help this lady because he also shows a tremendous amount of hatred and disdain towards me," the alien leader answered. "Granted, we Christians don't show any hatred towards anyone but, why does this guy regard you with disdain and hatred?" asked Jobe.

"Because he is jealous that I became the alien leader of Starmos City instead of Jacqueline Langyaw. Also, I fight for justice and this creature is the clear epitome of injustice. He is out to cause trouble and ruin the world. Now that Cornelius Von Alien is dead he became jealous. Apparently, the evil of that former, alien brute did not only affect myself, the folks in California County, and the citizens of Starmos City but he made a lasting effect on certain creatures in the city. Instead of requiring the Liberal Arts studies as a mandatory group of subjects for the generation after my generation, he condoned the belief of illiteracy and violence. You see, when he initially became leader, he was out to help us aliens. That was when we really liked him but, when Jacqueline Langyaw planned on being an attorney, he required that the Starmos population would never have to be intelligent. As a result, she received her license immediately the day after she wanted to become an attorney. Specifically, a prosecution attorney. After receiving her license, Cornelius realized that I had animosity and hatred against her at fifteen years of age, which was ten years ago," the alien leader answered. "Interesting story. Explain why are you hunting down Jacqueline Langyaw, right now?" the prairie man asked.

"Because she is the most mean, malicious, malevolent, sick, twisted, evil, satanic, barbaric, and cruel soul. She has the intent to ruin my life, if not take my life. That serpent was one of the many who she hired to kill me. On the train earlier today, I was sitting on the first level relaxing and comfortably sleeping. I looked through the side windows and started to notice some giant tarantulas climbing on board the train. These spiders intimidated the hell out of me. To add insult to injury, the serpents started to board the train. These serpents grew to be huge in size and vicious in attitude. Instead of being a hero or team player, I did the total opposite. I am sure you are very well aware of the luggage storage areas right above the seats in the trains or the planes? Well, I jumped into the luggage storage area. Up there, I was cowering in nervousness because Serpianto is out to cause trouble," answered Will. "Okay, that was enough I heard from you about this story. Now tell me about your life story," replied Jobe.

"I'm not going to tell you any stories right now because you should look in the distance," the alien leader said. The prairie man looked at him. "Why are you asking me to look in the distance?" he asked. "Look up ahead. Something important is parked over there," answered Will. "What's is it up there?" asked Jobe. "Are you going to be playing that game?" the alien leader asked. "I don't know what game you're talking about. I am not playing a game. I am serious," answered the prairie man.

The Conestoga wagon is seen one thousand feet in the distance. The snowy, white cover shined in the beautiful Utah sun. Two oxen are used to make this wagon move forward or backward, Eastbound or Westbound, or Northbound or Southbound. Both of these domesticated animals have thick skin due to the climate. Its hooves are very well kept because the role of the mother in the house - take care of the animals and tidy up the residence. The four wheels on the wagon are perfectly even in height, size, and weight. Seen in the back of the wagon were four barrels. Each barrel is individually labeled with the items that it contains.

The barrels are perfectly organized. The barrels contained various spices, goods, drinks, and jars of food. "What is this?" the alien leader asked. "It's my primary form of transportation," answered the prairie man. "That's an interesting lifestyle," replied Will. "This is actually not my full lifestyle. I have a home in the prairie region of the country. This is a significant form of transportation for us prairie folk," said Jobe. "Can you tell me what year this is over here," the alien leader replied. "Why are you asking such a question?" the prairie man asked. "Because this year doesn't seem like 2047. It seems more like 1647," answered Will. "What are you talking about?" asked Jobe. "I want to tell you an interesting story. I want to tell you something important that..," the alien leader was interrupted by the prairie man. "Tell me when we are ready to head on board the Conestoga."

"Well, I might forget about what I am going to say by the time we get there," replied Will. "I don't think you can forget in one hundred and fifty feet," said Jobe. "Hey, you never know," the alien leader replied. "Yeah, yeah, yeah," the prairie man said. They continued down to the

Conestoga. Finally, they arrived. "My feet are very tired after all of this walking," the alien leader replied. "Well, you'll be fine. You only have to remain in this spot for a couple of minutes. Granted, the desert heat is very uncomfortable but my parents who are in their eighties can survive the climate over here without shriveling up," said Jobe.

While the alien leader waited on the right side of the Conestoga the prairie man entered through the rear. His children were waiting, sitting on the bundles of hay. His wife Sarah was sitting on the opposite side of the children. "Now, Sarah, James, and Jesse, you all are to remain over here because we are all going to make room for a new member of the family. This guy's name is Will Von Alien. He will be with us for some time," the prairie man said. "What does he look like?" asked Sarah.

"What do you care? You should accept him for who he is," replied Jobe. "Well, I care what he looks like. He might be a better spouse than you. Besides, I like the good looking ones better than you," the prairie man's wife said. Jobe walked off of the Conestoga, and he approached the alien leader. "Now, Will I want you to meet my family. Come with me," he said.

The alien leader hesitated. "Well, okay. I guess your kids are very nice," replied Will. "Why did you show some hesitation on that?" asked Jobe. "Forget about it," the alien leader answered. "No, tell me the reason why you don't want to meet my family," the prairie man said. "Because I suspect that they're a bunch of bigots and social Darwinists," replied Will.

"How can they be like that?" asked Jobe. "Because I came across a bunch of bigots today," the alien leader answered. "Well, I can assure you that the folks in my

family are far from bigots. They're liberals," replied Jobe.
"Okay," said Will. "Now, before I head on board, I would
appreciate it if you'd be willing to toss the barrels on
board," the prairie man replied. "I don't know about that,"
the alien leader said. "Why?" asked Jobe.

"Because I was struck by lightning more than three
times today, and I was basically punished by God the whole
day. Then, I was hit by a tornado," answered Will. "Well, I
had to pull the wagon because the oxen were tired. I am
tired. Therefore, I'd strongly appreciate it if you tossed
these barrels on board," the prairie man said. "Well, give
me another reason as to why you want to do it," the alien
leader replied.

"Because I am doing the Christian thing, and I am
more than willing to help you because you ended up in a
couple of situations. So, just do the simple task without
giving me aggravation. Besides, you have much more
muscle than I do. You're extremely strong," replied Jobe.
"Okay, thank you brought up two pretty good points. I'll do
it," said Will. The prairie man walked on board the
Conestoga wagon, while the alien leader placed the barrels
on board. Even though each barrel weighed fifty pounds,
Will treated them like they were as light as a feather. "Kids,
watch out," Jobe shouted.

"Why?" asked James."Because the barrels will be
tossed on board. I don't want any problems to take place,"
the prairie man answered. "I think I am stronger than Nat
Turner," replied the older son James. "Don't use that man's
name in vain," said Jobe. "I'm not using his name in vain.
Besides, he's not God. Also, he's a slave. He's not a spirit or
person. He's nothing but a piece of property," the bigoted
older son replied.

"You shut the hell up. If we enter the Civil War according to President Pierce, we will take the Good side, and not the side of malice!" the prairie man said. He walked out of the front of the wagon and took the circuitous route to the rear. "Will, you better be careful heading on board because I don't want you to slip over those barrels," he said. "Okay," the alien leader replied. The prairie man jumped back on board the Covered Wagon. Will followed. The prairie man was able to walk across the bales of hay on the sides of the barrels. The alien leader remained standing behind the barrels in the rear of the wagon. "Why are you just standing there?" asked Jobe. "Because I can't fit on the sides of the wagon, and I don't want to destroy the animal's food with my heavy weight," answered Will. "You won't destroy the animal's diet. Just come across," the prairie man replied. "Are you sure about that?" the alien leader asked.

"Yes, just be very careful when you're crossing over the barrels," answered Jobe. "Okay, this is not going to be easy but I'll try," replied Will. He hesitated. "Are you waiting for the barrels to move?" Jobe asked. "No, but I am thinking about how I should go across this," the alien leader answered. "It's easy. Granted, I never crossed over a bunch of barrels but I think you can do it. Will, if you're the leader of a large city in some crazy dimension away from here and you can lead the place, I am sure you're able to cross over a group of barrels," replied Jobe. The alien leader stared at the barrels.

He gradually raised his right leg and placed his right foot on top of the first barrel. For him, crossing over a group of disorganized barrels is like crossing Niagara Falls. He tip-toed very slowly across the barrels. He moved as slow as a turtle and watched his every move like a tightrope walker. The last barrel was lying on its side on the floor of the Conestoga. The alien leader is now standing on top of the fifth barrel. "What are you doing?" asked Jobe. "I am thinking about what I am going to do and what moves I have to make in order to cross this particular barrel," Will answered.

"Well, you better make your move quickly. My sons are waiting for their snacks," replied the prairie man. To a man, crossing over a bunch of barrels is very easy because most men have flat feet. crossing over the last barrel seemed like a life or death leap for him. He stared at the toppled barrel for ten more seconds. Finally, he made the three foot long daring leap. And his result was he landed face flat on the floor. The kids started laughing hard. "This is much more comical than a Vaudeville Show," said James. "You are very entertaining," Jesse said sarcastically. "Is everything okay?" asked Jobe. "Yeah, this fall might've taken my pain away from the tornado," answered Will.

"I am surprised that you were able to survive that traumatic twister. It is rare for one to survive that funnel cloud, and you come out of there with a simple limp. If I ended up in a tornado, I would be blessed by God to survive. You are very blessed and fortunate," the prairie man replied. "I guess I am very lucky to survive such a brutal storm like that but, then again, I am an alien and you're a human. I have multiple lives. You humans don't. So, you won't probably be able to survive such a thing," said Will.

"Now, before anything, I want you to introduce yourself to my sons, and my sons shall voluntarily introduce themselves to you," replied Jobe. The alien leader approached the prairie man's sons. "You better not stain my hands," said James. "Why would I do such a thing?" asked

Will. "You know that you're very insolent in your behavior. You are probably one of those freed slaves who decided to paint yourself because you thought that you'd be able to afford the trip back to Africa," answered the prairie man's older son James.

"You know that you're a snide, arrogant soul. You should really be ashamed of yourself. For God sakes, you believe in the idea of Social Darwinism, which is totally sick and wrong. You should be ashamed of yourself, and you deserve to spend the rest of your life in jail," replied Will. "Excuse me, but you're not a human. You're nothing but a piece of property that deserves to be working the cotton gin. A piece of property like you cannot talk to anyone," said James. "Where did you learn to be so condescending and bias?" the alien leader asked. "I learned it from my proud Mormon dad," the older prairie son answered. "James, is this a real creature?" asked young Jesse. "No, he came from my overalls. Of course, he's a real creature. I don't know what *kind* of creature he is. he is most likely a piece of property that decided to act crazy," answered the older brother.

"Boys, stop ridiculing our new family member. Learn how to introduce yourselves to him, and do the Christian thing. Be a good Mormon, and don't be a bigot. Just simply be nice to him, or at least pretend to be nice and compassionate to him," the prairie man answered. "What happens if he is nasty to us?" asked James. "Well, this is what I have to say: *Do unto others as they would do unto you*," answered Jobe. "Fine then, I'll do it. But, what if he's a nonbeliever?" the older sibling asked. "Still, you respect folks of all races, all kinds, and all religions," the prairie man answered. James rolled his eyes in disgust.

"Fine. Then, I'll do it to make you happy," he brusquely replied. "Yup, that's my oldest son," Jobe said in a sarcastic manner. The older sibling turned around and gave an arrogant facial appearance to the alien leader. "Who are you?" he asked. "I am Will Von Alien, the leader of Starmos City," answered Will.

"Well, what you said sounded crazy, but okay. My name is James. I am fifteen years old. I am a Mormon and I came from Jefferson, Missouri," the older son replied. "Where's that?" the alien leader asked. "I don't know how to describe it. It's a small city. It is your generic place. Its citizens live in simple farms. There are only a few sites like the Mississippi Paddler. You might see some form of entertainment in the town like street performers or simple, stupid Vaudeville Shows. I don't know how else to describe it," answered James. "Okay, well, I come from a retro futuristic city that has flying cars, and it's surrounded by sandy hills, and most of the buildings are over one thousand feet tall," replied Will.

"That sounds totally absurd. You might just probably be seeing things in your head or, you may be delusional. Maybe, it's true. Maybe, where we're living life doesn't seem to be advancing or progressing quickly. I am pretty sure that you're quite crazy and batty," the older sibling said. "Well, maybe what you're saying is totally ridiculous and absurd. You're thinking that I am crazy when you're more crazy and insane than any other soul. Now, I am wondering what is the present year that we are in?" replied Will. "What are you talking about?" asked James. "I am wondering what year we are presently in," the alien leader answered.

"We are in the year 1856," the older sibling replied. "Well, I came from the year 2047. I came from the future," said Will. "Yeah, that sounds nice; but you're in the current year of 1856. This gives me another good reason to put you in an insane asylum," replied James. "We don't have insane asylums in 2047. In fact, we don't even have the words "insane asylum" inside our dictionary," the alien leader said.

"Well, we have the largest dictionary out there, and we have the words of insane and asylum in our dictionary. Maybe, you should learn how to look them up." replied James.

"Maybe, you should learn how to not be so condescending," the alien leader said. "Well, you ought not say crazy things and dye your skin blue because I won't mistake you as a batty and mentally incompetent soul," the older sibling argued. "Excuse me, young man I never dyed my skin. I am an alien from another planet. I'll prove to you that I don't come from Planet Earth," the alien leader said. "And how would you be able to prove that?" asked James. The alien leader looked at the palms of his hands. He noticed that there weren't any fingerprints.

"You know how every human is identifiable and known by their fingerprint?" he asked. "I didn't think that I was identifiable by that," the older sibling answered. "Well, turn over the palms of your hands, and you'll notice the swirly lines in your hands. Those lines are your fingerprints," replied Will. The older sibling flipped over to the palms of his hands. He noticed his hand print. "Do you get what I'm saying?" the alien leader asked. "I sort of see what you're saying," answered James. "Now, I don't have fingerprints like you do," replied Will. "Prove to me that you're not a human or a slave. Prove to me that you're an alien from another planet," the older sibling yelled.

"Well, look at the palms of my hands," the alien leader replied. He showed the prairie man's older son the palms of his blue hands. "Now, do you have enough proof?" asked Will. "Absolutely not! For God sakes, you can have a bunch of parchment that's painted blue wrapped around your hands. So, give me some other proof," answered James. "Well, what other proof do you want?" the alien leader asked. "Show me if you bleed the same way we humans bleed," answered the older sibling.

"Well, we do have blood vessels that run throughout our body. I never got a cut and I've never seen anyone ever bleed. So, show me what blood looks like," replied Will. "Let me get my razor blade," said James. The older sibling walked over to the rear of the Conestoga wagon. He walked up to his father. "Which barrel can I find the razors?" he asked. "Why would you need those things?" asked Jobe. "Because I want to show my friend Will the razors," answered James. "Is he violent?" the prairie man asked. "Oh, he is absolutely violent. He threatened me and he even tried to kill me. He threatened to beat the hell out of me if I didn't find the razor blades," the older sibling answered. "Jesse, is your older brother lying?" asked Jobe.

"Oh, he is totally violent. He threatened me also," the younger sibling answered. "I must have been so bothered by this cold-hearted, Son of Satan," said James. The siblings clearly lied through their teeth. Jobe walked up to the alien leader who was sitting on the bale of hay adjacent to Sarah. "What are you doing sitting next to my wife?" the prairie man asked brusquely.

"Nothing. She didn't say a word to me," the alien leader answered. "I don't believe that," replied Jobe. "And where's your proof?" asked Will. "Excuse me, but my kids both accused you of threatening them with razor blades. If that is true, get the hell off of here," the prairie man answered. "I never would say such a thing to your kids. Maybe, they would say such a thing to me but I would never say anything like that to your kids," the alien leader replied. "Are you stating that my kids are lying?" asked Jobe.

"Yes, your kids proclaimed to be Christian but God is totally not in their spirit. By the way, they didn't threaten me. I didn't threaten them either but your kids are very disrespectable and evil," answered Will. "How is that possible? They've never sinned a single day in their lives," the prairie man replied. "I don't know about that," the alien leader said. "Why would you say that?" asked Jobe. "Because nobody is perfect. Mankind is born with original sin, and man can't go one full day without sinning or without abstinence," answered Will. "What are you talking about?" asked Jobe.

"Well, a couple of hours ago, God talked to me, and he told me that I am born with original sin," the alien leader answered. "Maybe my kids are right. Maybe, you are completely batty," the prairie man replied. "I don't know about that," said Will. "How can I prove that you are sane?" asked Jobe. "Well, where I come from we have mental competency tests to see if an individual is competent to be functional for society – you know to see if they are mentally incompetent or, deemed dysfunctional and cannot be with society," the alien leader answered. "Can I make a judgment?" asked Jobe.

Will answered first. "I believe that one of your Christian principles states that you shall never judge one another, and *do unto others as they would do unto you*." "Good point. I am sorry for treating you like garbage," the prairie man replied. "Thank *you* for being nice and accepting towards my kind," the alien leader said. "Now I can trust you more than my kids. Will, this is a 'yes' or 'no' answer. Did you threaten my kids?" asked Jobe. The alien leader looked directly into the prairie man's eyes. He never blinked. "No, I didn't," he answered. "I could believe you. I am so sorry on behalf of my malicious sons. Don't you worry, they shall get theirs when they meet their Creator," the prairie man replied. "Thank you for believing me and being extremely kind to me," said Will. "You're very welcome," replied Jobe.

He walked back to the front of the Conestoga wagon. The oxen are just standing there, waiting for the prairie man to strike the whip. "Will, can you get the ox whip for me?" he asked. "Yeah, sure," the alien leader answered. He walked to the rear of the covered wagon. "Which barrel contains the whip?" he asked. "Walk to the rear of the wagon, and when you see the label 'Miscellaneous.' Once you see that, you will slam your hand as hard as you can on the top of that barrel. In there you shall be able to find the ox whip. It looks like a ten feet long leather strap. It'll be easy to find," answered the prairie man.

The alien leader walked across the bales of hay to the last barrel in the very rear of the covered wagon. As Jobe instructed he slammed his fist on the top of the barrel. "There's no way this thing is opening up," he said. "What do you mean?" the prairie man asked. "Because the thing won't budge. I keep on slamming my fist against the barrel, and it still won't open or crack. What's wrong with this thing?" the alien leader asked.

"Let me come back there and see what's wrong," answered Jobe. He turned around to his son. "James watch the oxen," he said. He walked across the bales of hay to the rear of the Conestoga wagon, where the alien leader was waiting. "What's wrong?" he asked. "This thing is not opening up, and it's really annoying me," answered Will. "Well, what have you done to open the thing up?" the prairie man asked.

"I just banged my fist against the top of the barrel as you said, and the thing didn't even open up," the alien leader answered. "How hard did you bang it?" asked Jobe. He re- enacted the bangs of the barrel. "This wasn't much banging at all. This bang was as strong as a simple knock on the door. Boy, you need to learn how to bang harder," the prairie man said. "Well, how hard do you expect me to bang on these barrels?" the alien leader asked. "Hit these barrels like you're hitting something with a sledgehammer. Hit them like you're hitting your worst enemy. Hit them as hard as you can!" answered Jobe.

"Are you sure you want me to do that to them?" asked Will. "Well, I want to see you demonstrate your strength. If you could survive a heavy tornado, I am sure you would be able to knock open a barrel," the prairie man answered. "Here goes nothing," said Will. Jobe moved two steps behind the alien leader. Will formed his hand into a fist, and moved his arm all the way back. With all of his strength he hit the barrel and in two-seconds it was opened.

This alien leader has the strength of a Lion. The prairie man clapped. "Thank you very much for opening that," he said. "You're welcome. Now, do you want me to do the honors of retrieving the whip?" asked Will. "Yes, you were the one who managed to open the barrel. I think that you shall do the honors of taking out the whip," answered Jobe. "Are you serious?" the alien leader asked. "Of course, I am serious. I am a Christian. I don't think that I would be telling you any fallacies," the prairie man answered. "Okay, if you say so," the alien leader replied. He slowly reached his arm inside of the three feet tall barrel and slowly placed his right hand inside of the barrel. He placed his hand on top of the handle of the whip, and strongly gripped it. He then slowly pulled out the ten feet long whip. This whip was as brown as a cowboy belt, and it has the strength of an Anaconda. He was very careful with it. He walked to the front of the Conestoga wagon and presented this whip to Jobe. "Was that so bad?" he asked. "No, it was probably one of the most simple tasks I've ever completed." the alien leader answered.

"When you're with me, not a single chore that I'll assign you will be hard or tedious," replied the prairie man. "What happens if I don't want to do any chore?" asked Will. "Well, do you not want to be part of the family?" asked Jobe. "I would love to be part of the family," the alien leader answered in a sarcastic manner. "Are you serious about that thought?" the prairie man asked. "Of course, I am," Will again answered sarcastically. "Frankly, I don't see that you're telling the total truth." the prairie man said. "Why? Why would you be insinuating such a thing?" the alien leader asked. "Because I feel that your attitude may be leaning against us Mormons," answered Jobe. "Why would you say such a thing?" asked Will.

"You acted quirky around my family," the prairie man answered. "And what makes you say that?" the alien leader asked. "Because you were unusually talkative and when I have house guests or new comers joining me, they're generally very quiet," answered Jobe. "Well, the only thing that I would have to say about your comment is that's what we aliens do," replied Will. "Did you realize what you just said was the stupidest thing that I've ever heard?" the prairie man asked. Will looked at him as if to say why? "Because I think that your opinion, that statement, is the stupidest opinion and comment I've ever heard!" answered Jobe. "Excuse me but I don't plan on having any confrontation today," replied Will.

"Why would you want to be confrontational?" the prairie man asked. "It seems to me that *you* want a confrontation when I want to be benevolent with you," answered the alien leader. "How dare you disrespect my father like that," the older sibling exclaimed. "Well, your dad was being nasty with me first. I guess you've inherited the trait of arrogance from him," the alien leader said. The older sibling's pale skin turned red, filled with a ton of anger. He has the face of fury. His eyebrows are slanted vertically.

"You have ten-seconds to jump off of this wagon," he said. The alien leader snickered. "Just what would you do if I didn't jump off from this wagon?" he asked. "You don't want to know what I'd want to do to you," the older sibling answered. "Please! tell me what you would do," the alien leader said. "Well, if you don't jump off of this wagon in ten seconds, I shall come at you with razor blades, lemon juice, and a Cat O' Nine Tails and I won't be done yet!" replied James.

"And just what do you mean by that?" asked Will. "In addition to doing that I will tie you to a piece of plywood, and bring you to the tallest point of the Grand Canyon. Once there, I shall push you off of a cliff, and you'll have the painful plummet to your fate," answered the older sibling. "What else would you do?" the alien leader asked now becoming angry. "Well, I will take you to the Penitentiary and have you put on trial for crimes against the Mormons and you will be convicted; that's a total guarantee. Besides, the jurors would probably believe a human over an alien.

After being convicted, the judge would sentence you to force labor and death," answered James. "Ooh, I am so scared. Maybe, the court will find out the evil intents that you have, and the vendetta that you have against me. The court shall see that, and you will definitely be convicted of a serious crime, and the same punishment should happen to you," replied Will. The older sibling, being the typical con-artist that he is, told his father that the alien leader threatened death against him. "Will, do I have to leave you out in the middle of the desert?" asked Jobe. "No," the alien leader answered. James approached his father. "By the way, your favorite guest, offended Mormons," he said. "He did not say anything disrespectful towards us Latter Day Saints," the prairie man replied in anger. "He did too. He said that the practice of Mormonism should be banned in the nation. It is the most evil religion, and it doesn't even practice the beliefs in Christ, and he also said that it doesn't practice any form of the Christian Philosophy," said the older sibling. Jobe turned around towards the alien leader. "Did you say those evil things?" he asked.

"No, I didn't. Your son is nothing but a pathological, disgusting liar. All around you, you see some form of talent. Talent is often perceived as good or entertaining, but there's also another form of talent, the one that your son possesses. This talent is the art of evil and deception. Your son makes up lies upon lies upon lies about me – who knows what else- and his younger brother is just as bad. His younger brother shows some disrespect but he predominantly keeps his mouth shut. So, why don't you learn how to be a good father and tell your sons off! Yell at them for being so arrogant toward me. I am sorry for talking to you like this, and telling you about your both of your sons' disrespectful attitudes," answered Will. "You know that you seem to be more believable than my sons are. Frankly, you're probably even more trustworthy than they are. Granted, I've never seen or heard my kids lie but they might be constant liars. I probably never know what tricks they have up their sleeves. I am quite surprised that they are being disrespectful toward you because my sons were never disrespectful towards Sarah and I. I don't even think that you would even say anything offensive about Mormons., and I know that you are extremely accepting towards all races and all kinds. My kids are very bias, and arrogant," replied Jobe embarrassed and apologetic.

Chapter IX: The Conestoga Wagon

After talking to the alien leader, the prairie man cracked the whip on the oxen. "Mush!" he shouted. The oxen started to move. They moved extremely slowly. "What's this kind of garbage?" asked Jobe. The oxen remained in a state of laziness. "I think you have to jump off of the wagon," said Will. "What are you talking about?" the prairie man asked. "I am saying that you should learn how to lay down the law with those lazy bums," the alien leader answered. "Hey, don't call any of God's creatures bums. They are just as important as you are, and they play a crucial role in our society," replied the Jobe. "I don't know about that," said Will.

"Why not?" the prairie man asked. "Because, these creatures are totally nonproductive. They move so slowly. They weren't the ones that invented the wheel. A human was the one responsible for that. Humans also revolutionized the wheel. The Starmos Aliens brought the idea of the wheel to the next step by building flying saucers and LSC's (Light Speed Cycles.) These animals never would even think of such a thing. All they do all day is eat, sleep, and take a dump," the alien leader answered. "That's totally not true," Jobe argued. "Why would you argue my point?" asked Will.

"Because animals are very productive members of society. In fact, what you said was totally untrue! The animals are brilliant creatures, and they're very modest and selfless creatures. Every day on the average American farm, an animal is being sacrificed for food. I don't think a human would be willing to sacrifice his or her body for food. In addition to that, the animals are far from lazy. If you notice that most farm animals have muscles. That's because the animals are pulling the plows on a daily basis, and the humans don't have to do that because they have the animals to slave away in the hot sun. If we humans ever had to work in those animals' conditions, we would probably not even be able to survive one full day. Animals work from sunrise to every day We humans are extremely lazy as compared to the animals," the prairie man answered.

"Well, why are the oxen acting so obstinate and lazy with you?" the alien leader asked. "Look at the weather outside, today," answered the prairie man. "So, what?" asked Will. "The weather outside was terrible. The extreme heat tremendously caused damage to the animals," answered Jobe. "The weather was beautiful. What on Earth are you talking about?" asked Will. "Well, maybe you didn't happen to notice what climate zone of our current location," the prairie man answered.

"What are you talking about?" the alien leader asked. "I am basically stating that before we saw the rainstorm, the ground was as dry as a bone. In fact, the heat increased to the point that the dirt started cracking, and some parts of the dirt turned into dust. Today was the first time that we saw rain in a couple of decades," answered Jobe. "What do you mean by that?" asked Will.

"This is the first time that I saw a droplet of rain in this area in 20 years," the prairie man answered. Will stared at him in disbelief. His mouth opened wide as a crater. "I can't believe that this is so. I can't even go one week without water, and all of you can live for 20 years in a drought!?" he said. "Will, it's not me being affected by the lengthy droughts. It's my parents. I moved to safer ground.

I moved to the plains in the country, where there's not too much water, and nor is there a scarcity of water. The plains have the perfect amount of water. It is a place where you won't have to worry about flooding nor will you have to worry about constant drought," replied Jobe.

"Now, do you want me to tell you about where I live?" the alien leader asked. "Not just yet. I have to get oxen moving. So, I will be right back on board," the prairie man answered. He gave the whip to the alien leader. He walked over to the last bale of hay to retrieve, the stepping stool, which is adjacent to the hay. He reached his hand towards the wooden stool. "No," shouted Will. The prairie man was alarmed by the alien leader's shout. He fell backwards. "What are you doing?" he asked. "I want to know what you want me to do with this whip," the alien leader said.

"Are you kidding me?" the prairie man angrily asked. "No, I'm not. I am dead serious. I want you to tell me what you want me to do with your whip," answered Will. "You made me fall over the most frivolous thing in the whole entire world. The Lord would never be too happy with you based on what you just did to me, making me fall like that on my back. I'll probably have back problems later in my life because of your big mouth. You're nothing but a stupid idiot. If anyone should be ashamed, it would be you. Will, you wonder why my kids don't like you. Besides them being bigots, they also think that you're a stupid idiot," replied Jobe. "How can you say such a thing?!" the alien leader asked.

"Because of your superior attitude. You think who you are constantly. Besides, it sounds so condescending when you start your questions with the word 'and.' It sounds so arrogant and snide. Now, I hope you apologize for your disrespect towards me," the prairie man answered. "Okay, I'm sorry," Will replied in a sarcastic manner. "I can tell that was totally fake. That was so disingenuous, it's not even funny. Now learn how to give a loving, genuine, sincere, and remorseful apology towards me," said Jobe. "I am sorry for being so disrespectful toward you and your livestock. I will never do such a thing again. I would never mean to be like that, and I don't have any intents of malice behind the words that I said. I am very bothered with how I behaved towards you. I am sorry, Jobe," replied Will.

"Now, do you see how genuine you sound?" asked the prairie man. "Believe it or not, yes. I do sound very sincere. Thank you for saying that," the alien leader answered.

"Yeah, that's how you're supposed to be. I can't believe that I am treating you like a grade school kid but, you must learn like one. I don't mean to sound condescending towards you but all I am saying is the whole truth and nothing but the truth, so help me, God. Now you might be the leader of a retro futuristic alien city way ahead of our time; but you are not all perfect like you think you are. Not a single soul is perfect, whether you're a human, an animal, or some mythical deity from another world. Nobody is perfect. You must learn that. You are so bombastic with your attitude and you act like you're the best leader in all of the Universes and Dimensions combined but the only perfect and true leader that exists is God. You have the ego the size of an elephant but the brain the size of a pea," Jobe replied.

"Yeah, you keep rambling on whatever you're saying. Every word that comes out of your mouth is a bunch of misleading comments. Then, when you're truthfully wrong on your comment, you try and make somebody else look bad," said Will. "I hate to be rude but what you said is definitely not true. You are actually the type to act like that. Personally, I would like to end this argument before it becomes confrontational. Just help me up, and let me get the stepping stool so I can continue with my duties," replied Jobe.

"You are totally right in what you just said. I am genuinely apologetic about what I did a couple of minutes ago. Let me just tell you that I am not a malicious alien. I am here to help you but I am also here to learn about the world. So, I feel that it would be necessary to continue on with our trip through time," the alien leader said. He reached grabbed the prairie man's hand and helped him up. "Thank you," said Jobe. "You're very welcome, no problem," replied Will. "No, I am seriously grateful and proud of your maturity," the prairie man said. "Is everything okay?" the alien leader asked. "Yes, everything is perfectly fine," answered Jobe.

The prairie man walked right off of the Conestoga wagon. He walked up to the oxen. The oxen that he possesses have the same exact look. Both oxen have short, saddle brown hair. Their eyes are six inches in diameter. The only thing that distinguishes the two oxen is that the right one wears a silver bullring and the left one wears a gold bullring. The prairie man walked behind the oxen and tapped on each hoof. Finally, they started moving. Jobe jumped back on the Conestoga wagon. He immediately retrieved the stool and placed it in its proper spot. He moved to the front of the wagon. The oxen are pulling the wagon as fast as a horse pulling a Chariot.

"Slow down!" he shouted. The oxen continued moving at great speeds. He retrieved the rope to control the oxen. He yanked on the rope to stop the animals from pulling the wagon. The oxen dug their hooves into the ground. The oxen's nervousness grew within the matter of seconds. They jumped on board the Conestoga wagon. "Honey, what's going on?" asked Sarah. "Oh nothing, the family pets just decided to become closer to the family," answered Jobe. "Well, toss those dirty mud bags off of this wagon this instant!" replied the prairie man's wife.

"Excuse me! These animals are just as important as dogs. They are not here to help *me*. They're not here to benefit *you*. They're here to benefit the family. You're not the whole family. You're a small part of the family, who has a lot of say in this family, unfortunately," the prairie man said. "Dad, mom is totally correct. Get those dirty, slimy things off this wagon immediately. It's already bad enough that we don't have proper plumbing on the road, and I don't want to smell. Those wretched swine should get the hell off of this wagon, now," exclaimed James. "First of all, they're not wretched swine. They are regular animals. More importantly, they're God's creatures. These creatures might be huge in their size, but they are very loving and gentle creatures. Second of all, you should show respect towards your family members. They may not be human but they are considered part of your family. The selfless man, who is in love with God's creatures, shall prosper. He, who is self-centered, and hates all of God's creatures shall be a part of Satan's Lair," replied the prairie man. The older child looked at Jobe with disdain – not respect.

"I am tired of this garbage that you constantly spew out. You're always preaching love one another when we live in a society that is filled with nothing but disgust and hatred. Our society considers cruelty of humans, that don't look alike acceptable. You shouldn't be preaching to love God's creatures we hate our own kind. In fact, we treat our own kind like property. We don't even consider some of our own species to be considered human. We consider them as things that can be transported, bought, and sold. I absolutely agree with this, because property should never be valued as much as a human!" Jobe was taken aback.

"Your behavior is totally evil and inappropriate. You are just like the evil southerners, who support slavery. I guarantee you that we will be entering a Civil War because of this. According to Franklin Pierce's record, there will be a huge Civil War taking place between the North and the South. For God sakes, John C. Calhoun is pro-slavery. This is sickening. I hope that he goes to hell! For God sakes, he had a vendetta against the victims of the *Amistad Court Case*. I think somebody sick like that who supports the cruel commission of slaves to harsh environments should be ashamed of themselves and they deserve a short stop and sudden drop!" Jobe was obviously upset. "I am going to tell the authorities that you support liberation of property, which is totally against the law. You make me sick with your attitude of showing love towards people that are of color," said James. "I don't want you to run for any political office because people like you have ruined this beautiful place or will ruin this beautiful place and make it ugly and evil. Democrats like you have a vendetta for the innocent and condone the guilty.

Son, I want your attitude towards innocent people to change because I am sure they would want to be naturalized as citizens and have the same privileges and freedoms as you do. I am sure they would want to know 'good' folks like you," the prairie man replied. James remained insolent. "Excuse me, how dare you talk to me like that. I am going to be moving out of the house in a couple of years to go away to college, so that way I become a politician. I will be loose with the southern governments and legalize slavery across the nation instead of keeping this place divided," the older sibling said. "Let me just tell you this, if there is a Civil War, you will be drafted into the Union Army and if you ever betray them before, during, or after the war, you shall perish. Your good brethren shall destroy the evil side like you. So, join or die," replied Jobe.

"That is the most outdated phrase I've ever heard. That phrase was from the Revolutionary War, nearly eighty years ago. If we enter the Civil War, I am joining the Confederate Side because they are the good side for people like me. I also heard that the southerners are more technologically advanced than the northerners. Besides, they guarantee me food if I join their army because they have year round farming, which shall therefore provide me with food year round. Half of you Union soldiers will be deceased before the war even starts because you won't have enough food and whereas, you will die because death shall do its part naturally. The south will come and strike you northerners before you're even able to mobilize your military. So, you northerners should start mobilizing your military because we southerners have a lot of strength that we can use against you," the older sibling said. Now the younger son jumps into the discussion.

"He just owned you there. Come on dad, come up with a good rebuttal," said Jesse. "Listen, your fifteen year old confederate brother thinks who he is. I hope that his twelve year old younger brother doesn't act like that," replied Jobe. "Don't worry, dad. I would never join the south," Jesse said in a sarcastic manner. "Well, that's a good thing," the prairie man replied.

"Did you know that I was just being sarcastic to you?" the younger sibling asked. "No, I didn't know that, and it's not nice the way you treat me. Then again, the apple doesn't fall far from the tree because your older brother is extremely arrogant and condescending towards me, also. So, I am not surprised about your attitude," answered Jobe.

"You know that the south shall win the Civil War because we southerners will beat the hell out of you northerners. You northerners are the most evil groups of people because you want to change the tradition of our founding fathers. Ever since you folks opted to close down the Triangular Trade, the money in this place went down the tubes tremendously. This was totally unfair that the government ended the Triangular Trade. Now, the Republicans want to end slavery, which is totally unfair. Slavery is what keeps this place running; slavery keeps balance in our society and finally, slavery keeps the fairness of gubernatorial and national elections in our government. The Republicans are screwing this place up by opting against slavery, which I am strongly for," replied Jesse.

"I believe that you are an extreme genius for such a young adolescent. But, you don't use that intelligence to do good. You use it to do evil and the one who you were influenced by was your brother. Usually brothers fight over controversial subjects like Slavery but you and your older brother should be ashamed of your evil attitudes because you agree on a subject that should never be debated. This is my final statement about slavery. I think that it is the most evil thing that man can ever do or have the capacity of doing. Unfortunately, man has the capacity to do good or do evil. It's easier to do the evil. We live in a world where the easy way of doing evil is often considered acceptable and the hard way of doing good is considered taboo or bizarre." Jobe was saddened and continued.

"I can't believe that my own sons are making choices to conform with the malevolence and wickedness of the real world. This is sickening. I hope that you, James and you, Jesse, realize what you're doing wrong and learn how to show respect towards all of mankind beginning with me." the prairie man said.

"Let me just tell you this. You'll never convince me into taking another side because my political stand points will always stay with me until the day I die. I will suffer for justice, and fight for slavery. People who are ignorant like you and the Republicans are for injustice and anarchy. I despise that. I will try and make sure that we Confederates win," replied James. "Now, this is my final plea, hopefully for today but I am asking that you see the injustice and unfairness of the idea of an ethnicity of people being treated in an inhumane manner.

The South treats them worse than animals. They see them as property instead of human beings with emotions and minds. People like you who honor and support this idea should be ashamed of themselves. The idea of slavery is considered a clear violation of our founding fathers beliefs. You see nearly eighty years ago, the United States of America was formed. Yet, there was division and still, to this day, there is division. The reason why is because of the idea of taking away man's natural rights. In other words - slavery. What makes it even more sickening is that our government supports the idea of slavery. Even though we live on the prairie, I know about a lot of things that take place in the government, particularly the Supreme Court. Next year, a huge case I heard about is going to take place and it originates from my beautiful state of Kansas. Unfortunately, it became a slave state, and that's why we've bought a house in the other part of the prairie in Missouri.

That's safer than Kansas," said Jobe. "Well, what's wrong with Kansas and where's Kansas?" asked Will.

"It's in the heartland of the country. The reason Missouri is safer than Kansas is there is a lot less fighting and violence taking place. Granted, Missouri is a slave state but the fighting didn't start in Missouri. It started in Kansas is still taking place in Kansas. That's why they call it *Bleeding Kansas.* The people who support slavery are against the violence in Kansas but the people who are for slavery are for the fighting in Kansas. They can fight all they want. The evil has taken over Kansas. I remember when my native state was once a free state, but now it's a slave state. I was born there and it would've been considered as part of the North or 'the union' if it was to remain free but because a lot of Southerners moved there, it is now becoming a slave state. Because the government of Kansas states that slavery is not illegal, the wickedness of turning innocent people into property is allowed, and now it is being considered acceptable. Some are even honoring this philosophy of being Social Darwinists and racists. I despise that. The slaves are people. More important, they're Americans just like I am and my children. Will, I am worried for your sake because they might mistake you as a slave. Since you're not a Caucasian, you will be treated differently. It is not only the African Americans that are mistreated. It's also the Native Americans. When Brigham Young was leading the way into Salt Lake City, Utah, I refused to join him. I was converted to the Church of the Latter Day Saints by him but I became a Son of Perdition. This basically means that I am considered a heresy to the Mormon Church. The reason I didn't travel with Brigham was because I noticed how they were trying to force the idea of Mormonism upon the Native Americans. I consider that to be an act against John Locke, because people are entitled to Life, Liberty, and Property. The Mormons were trying to take away the Native Americans' Freedom of Worship. In addition to that, I definitely despise the way our country treats immigrants. They are treated in the cruelest and harshest manner over here. Ten years ago, an event took place in Ireland called the Potato Famine. This was a horrible event where people were starving and much poverty took place in Ireland. People were dying of starvation. Many of the Irish people escaped to the United States in the late 1840s and early 1850s. Now, the Nativists, who are against immigration over here, believed that the Irish adulterated this country by applying to jobs in factory that the natural citizens would be able to receive. The Nativists had huge problems with the Irish immigrants having an occupation. They started committing huge hate crimes. They would deceive them all the time. Violence would take place between the evil, hate-filled Nativists and innocent Irish immigrants. The Irish people would move to lower Manhattan because there was, and still is, an abundance of tenements, which are small, communal apartments. In a square, where the factories were located, violence had taken place. Blood was seen all over this particular square. The Nativists caused this whole event and brought evil towards the innocent Irish men, women, and children. The Nativists supported bigotry and evil. Nativism is just another form of Social Darwinism or Racial Superiority. Sometimes, people have souls of malice, and some folks consider this to be acceptable. To me committing hate crimes against people who want to make a better life for themselves and enslaving people that are not Caucasian is totally wicked and cruel. The wicked and heartless shall be punished when they meet their Creator," the prairie man answered.

At 6 p.m. dusk is taking place, and the argument between the Mormon father and the two sons concluded. "When are those oxen going to jump off?" the alien leader asked. "I don't know, we're still not down the hill. We only have a couple of more feet," answered Jobe. "Well, I notice that the wagon stopped moving as fast," the alien leader replied. "We have to stop this thing. That's when we'll put the oxen back in the position that they belong." the prairie man said.

"How would you expect us to do that?" asked Will. "I will have my sons put their splinter free gloves on and try and grab onto the wagon wheels. Sarah and I will push our weight to the rear of the wagon. You should jump off the wagon and retrieve a couple of boulders, which will stop the wagon," answered Jobe. "Okay," the alien leader replied. "When will this get started?" asked James. "In a couple of minutes," answered Jobe. "I don't know about that," replied the older sibling. "Why?" the prairie man asked. "Look up ahead," answered James. Death Valley could be seen in the distance. The Colorado River flows within Death Valley. "Where are we going?" asked Jesse. "Death Valley," answered Sarah. "How do you know about that place?" asked Jobe.

"Because I went there on vacation. Unfortunately, it was far from a vacation. It was a troublesome trip and a melancholy visit. This was the place where my parents died. I was a drifter for decades until I noticed a civilization by the Salt Lake. That was where I was converted to the Church of the Latter Day Saints. There I was adopted by a loving family. I am the youngest of five brothers and two sisters. I learned how to have a lot of faith in God and love for God. that moment by Death Valley is engraved in my head, and it will be a permanent, unfortunate , and sad moment," the prairie man's wife answered. As she told the story about her experience by Death Valley she became very emotional. When she was done she sobbed. The alien leader walked up to her and started to comfort her. He hugged her.

"You have ten seconds to get your hands off my mom," said James. "Who are you to say such a thing?" asked Will. "I am her son and you shouldn't be so arrogant to me. I thought the two of us resolved our dispute because of your attitud? I am disgusted that a blue skinned creature like you would cause trouble towards us Caucasians. You are just as evil as Nate Turner, who was as rebellious as can be. I think that somebody who has the intent of malice like you ought to be shanked," answered James.

"If I met any human that gave me an impression of evil and hatred, it would be *you.* You believe in the idea of racial superiority, which is totally sick and wrong. You have an egotistical attitude. Anyone like you belongs in Satan's Lair. Nevertheless, you don't care to console your own mom. You should be up quicker than I am yet I made a choice to get up to console your mom. A son like you deserves to be tossed out of the house because your attitude is disgusting," the alien leader angrily replied. "Who are *you* to tell me that I am to be thrown out of the house? Who are *you* to call me arrogant? More importantly, who are *you* to ridicule me?" the older sibling argued.

"I am somebody who lost both of his parents. I am somebody who has a similar story as your mom, and yet, I feel that heartless people like you think that it is okay to not help somebody who is crying. If you were taught that by anybody, you should get back at them, and stop them from being evil," replied Will. "I was never taught such a thing by anybody. If I was in any small way, shape, or form, it would probably be our government. The government is a major influence on my life. They were the ones that kept the tradition of slavery from the Europeans. It's considered acceptable. I am a strong supporter of it, and want to tell those Republicans like Lincoln to cut it the hell out! Tell William Lloyd Garrison to shut the hell up because he has it in for the white man. I am a strong supporter of popular sovereignty and slavery. I also support John C. Calhoun. He supported the prosecutor in the case of the *Amistad*. I wasn't alive during that case but this Supreme Court Case shall never be forgotten. I also can't stand Frederick Douglass. He is going to probably get us into the Civil War," the older sibling said.

"How dare you say such a thing! Enslaving innocent people is the ultimate heinous act that man can do. You are just as guilty as an ordinary slave owner because if I was mistaken for an African American, I would be living on the grueling plantations. Unfortunately, we live in a society completely based on bigotry and evil. I may come from another dimension but I am an American Citizen. I was named an American Citizen by Mayor Bill Stone of California County in Upstate New York," the alien leader. "What is California County? Who is Bill Stone?" asked James.

"He is the mayor of California County, a county in Northern New York," answered Will. "In school I had to remember all of the counties of the country, and California County, New York is not one of them. You must be crazy or you tell a bunch of folktales," the older sibling replied. "This is totally true. Go up 95, and travel on Scotchtown Road," the alien leader said. "What in the world are you talking about? What is 95 and Scotchtown Road?" asked James. "95 is the highway that runs up and down the Eastern Coast and Scotchtown Road is the gateway to California County," answered Will.

"I never even heard of a highway or a road. I don't know what time you come from but we are in the mid-1800s," replied the older sibling. "I come from the future. I come from the early to mid-2000s. I was born in 2022; but the year that I come from is 2047. I am only 25 years old. I come from an alien city, and I am now the ruler of that alien city," the alien leader said.

"What you're saying is bogus and unbelievable. I don't believe in a single word that you're saying. I think that you don't belong here because you're not just of color, but I also think that you belong in an Insane Asylum. Nevertheless, you're for the Antislavery movement, which is rebellious. Rather than visiting an Insane Asylum, I'd think that you'd be the perfect candidate for the gallows. When I join the Confederates, I will ask my colonel if I can hunt you down, and bring you to trial for the gallows. That is the perfect place for you. Even though I am unwilling to settle this dispute and truce over Slavery, and I think you're crazy, I want to get some information out of you, and I wonder why you're a strong supporter of the Republicans. So, I shall ask you a bunch of questions. Be prepared for the questions that I am going to throw at you. You are forbidden to hesitate on your answers. If you hesitate on any of your answers, I will think that you're lying. You'll probably lie on your answers, and I'll not be surprised if you do lie. So, you might as well lie to all of your answers," replied James.

"How dare you even talk to me like that! First of all, I am not a liar. The only time I've lied was to myself and to

God. I never lied to anybody else. I've only lied to God to save myself from peril and death. In fact, I almost died due to my sinning. In addition to that, I am not crazy. You're good at making up slander," said Will. "But you didn't give me a chance to ask my question. I shall ask you my first question now. Do you believe in God?" the older sibling asked. "I do believe that God created all heavens and Earth. I believe that he created me. I don't believe in the theory of Evolution. I believe in the idea of Creation," the alien leader answered. "Now, do you worship God? Are you a Christian?" asked James.

"No, I am far from a Christian. I am actually the complete opposite of the Christian. I am not a Pagan. I am an Atheist. I don't worship God, especially after the ordeal that I had with him a couple of hours ago," answered Will. "What ordeal would that be?" the older sibling asked. "I have a long story to tell but I shall keep it short. I fell into a long coma and I met God. I discovered that my location was inside of woodland. I was given a sermon by God that I have sinned so much in my life that I was hooked up to a chain and a ball. I managed to escape the chain and ball, and I started to slowly ease on down a trail. Then I started to run down the trail. Suddenly, I ended up in the worst snare possible. God told me that I would be heading to the Celestial City. Instead, I was on my way to Hell. I hit hard asphalt. I probably blacked out for a couple of seconds; but I discovered that I was by the Grand Canyon. I was struck by lightning for the third time. After that, I limped off of the road. That was when I was taken back into the year of 1856, and that was because your dad helped me. But, I had an encounter with God," the alien leader answered. "Now, tell me where you were born?" asked James.

"I am a native of Starmos City," answered Will. "Where's that?" the older sibling asked. "My birthplace is multiple dimensions away from here. Because it is the year of 1856, you would not only need a Light Speed Cycle to get there, but you would also need a time machine to get there. It is physically impossible to get there by any form of transportation that you have right now," the alien leader answered. "It would be impossible to get from New York to California in less than a year by this form of transportation. Now, what year were you born?" asked James. "2022. I was born in the future," the alien leader answered. "That is in the future way ahead of this time. Now, what is the current year in your birthplace or your current residence?" the older sibling asked. "Which residence are you talking about?" asked Will. "What do you mean by that?" asked James. "Are you talking about the residence that I have in Starmos City or the one in California County?" the alien leader asked.

"The one in Starmos City. Tell me what year it is in Starmos City," the older sibling answered. "It's 2047 in Starmos City; exactly 191 years from the year that we're in now," said Will. James started scratching his hair. He thought the question that should be asked next. "Now, do you have any girlfriends?" he asked. "Yes, I do. In fact, she comes from Planet Earth, but she converted to an alien. She comes from Russia. She is almost exactly my age. She came over to Starmos City when she was really young. Like myself, her parents are deceased. She is very nice. She is very compassionate, benevolent, hardworking, and caring. She is the perfect lady," the alien leader answered.

Chapter X: The Old Town of South Salt Lake

The Mormon Family and the alien leader are supposed to be heading to the prairie man's house in Missouri, but instead they're heading in the wrong direction towards Salt Lake City, Utah. Seen in the distance is a small civilization that is made up of eight buildings. The Great Salt Lake had the appearance of a dark body of water. The dusk disappeared and the beginning of the evening had taken place. It is now 7:00 p.m. The older son just finished his commentary on the support of injustice and cruelty towards the innocence. About thirty seconds ago, he finished asking the alien leader questions. Sarah remained quiet. Jesse stared into space. He showed a drowsy facial expression. His eyes were as dark as the eyes of a Raccoon. He started to lie on top of one of the haystacks. "Shall we continue the debate?" asked James. "No," the alien leader answered. The older sibling is way more energetic than the younger sibling.

The oxen finally jumped off the front of the Conestoga wagon. "What a relief," said Jobe. "Why are you saying such a thing?" asked Will. " Didn't you see what just happened?" the prairie man asked. "No, I didn't. I was talking to your older son. Don't worry, we weren't in any debate," the alien leader answered.

"I'm not angry at you for debating my son's sick, twisted ways. He has intents of malice towards the innocent and condones the guilty. He supports the government's perspective on keeping slavery," replied Jobe. "Now, please tell me what just happened," said Will. "Do you remember when the oxen jumped on the top of the wagon?" asked Jobe. "Yes," the alien leader answered. "Well, I am sure that you remembered my wife and I were scared and James was extremely angry over this. Fortunately, the oxen returned back to their proper positions. They pulled the covered wagon into the town, which is adjacent to the Great Salt Lake.

"What lake is this?" asked Will. "This is the best lake in the country and the purest one too. It is not as big as the Great Lakes. it is bigger than the Dead Sea. Some folks call this the 'Dead Sea of the United States.' Even though it's classified by that name, it does have a lot of wildlife, particularly herons and fish. Now, this is the lake where we Mormons have baptisms. Right now, we're building a huge church. This church is supposed to be three hundred feet tall. It is going to be one of the tallest religious buildings in the World. It's going to be taller than the Giza Pyramids and the Djoser Pyramids. This building is going to be the most extravagant Mormon Church present in the country. I heard that there'll be a pathway of Diamonds leading up to this Church. Now, I've been to this town not only to help on the construction of the building, but just for a couple of visits. I will never head over to the town next door to this particular town of South Salt Lake because the town next door considers me as a Son of Perdition. If I ever even crossed into this town in an unauthorized manner, my family and I will be arrested and killed," answered Jobe.

"I know you were just rambling about the Church that is supposed to be built over here, but did you just say that you were going to get arrested if you entered the area of the Mormons?" the alien leader asked. "Yes, it's not just myself that would get arrested; it would be my children too. The Mormons believe that if a family member of the first generation violates a law in the religion, the second and third generation after that other generation will suffer because of the family member's mistake or violation. This belief is called Generational Punishment. This is unfortunate because it's not only exclusive to the Mormon religion. It is also found in different countries around the World, unfortunately," the prairie man answered.

"Well, that's what we went through in Starmos City. Fortunately, my family had never fallen into that kind of trap because we were friends with Cornelius Von Alien. I noticed a lot of citizens and my fellow aliens were ending up in the third generational camps outside of the alien city. I guess that's what happens when you're ruled by a Stalinist Dictator," the alien leader replied. "Please tell me the story about your life," said Jobe. "Why would you want to know my life story?" asked Will.

"Because as an alien leader, your life seems to be quite interesting," the prairie man answered. Well, what makes you say that?" the alien leader asked. "Because you lived through a communist dictatorship and you grew up during a time of strife and trouble. I am happy that you remained fortuitous during this time of trouble," answered Jobe. "When do you want me to tell my life story?" the alien leader asked. "I am interested to hear your story when we head into town and get settled at a Saloon," the prairie man answered. "And when will that be?" asked Will. "Do you remember to never use the word 'and' at the beginning of your question?" asked Jobe. "Oh yes. I forgot what you said. answered Will "I am here to teach you such a thing because I want you to prosper well as a good Christian," the prairie man replied.

"Okay, I don't mean to sound like I possess an attitude of superiority or sound like I am having the attitude of megalomaniac. I would never want to be dominant over others because that's what the old leader Cornelius Von

Alien was like. Like we agreed to earlier, I wasn't going to tell you my life story until we reached the Saloon in the town or as some like to call it 'civilization.' This sounds fair and square," said Will.

"What in the world are you talking about?" asked Jobe. "Earlier, I might've thought it was acceptable to be superior towards a particular person or creature, but I discovered that my behavior was completely wrong. I am totally sorry. In a couple of minutes, I would like to tell my life story," the alien leader answered. "Where are we?" asked James.

"We are near the dreaded town of Brigham Young Land. Don't worry, we're not going to get arrested as long as we don't cross into his territory, but if we Sons of Perdition enter that preacher's territory, we will be done. We will be sent to the gallows by this soul of malice. He thinks he's seen God, but he makes untrue statements all the time," answered Jobe. A beautiful moon started to emerge from the dark evening. Seen in the distance is a yellow creature. This creature is a golden creature that has the wings of an angel and the face of the Lord. This angel is not a typical angel. It wore Belgian Clogs and it is only six inches tall. This Creature of God has the soft spoken voice of a male. He has facial hair and he wears the coat of responsibility with great zeal. "Will, is that a Firefly that landed on the top of your shoulder?" the older sibling asked.

"No, this creature is quite huge for a Firefly. I think that he might be some sort of supernatural creature," the alien leader answered. This creature of God landed up on top of his right shoulder as soon as Will said that statement. "You are good at saying false things," the creature said. The Mormon family and the alien leader are completely unaware the creature that is talking. The creature reiterated what he just said.

"What's that?" asked James. "I don't know. I hear some sort of talking noise, but it may just be coming from your little brother," answered Will. "Jesse, did you say anything?" the older sibling asked. "No," the younger sibling answered in a brusque manner. "Why are you answering me like that?" asked James.

"Because people accuse me of doing the wrong thing all the time because I am the young, immature brother. I am not the spoiled one like you. Instead of receiving new clothing, I get hand-me-downs. Basically, I inherit all of your old property that is considered useless to you, James. You have a lot more rights than I have. For instance, you have the right to drive a Stagecoach or a Conestoga wagon. I am definitely forbidden to even lay my hands on the whip for the oxen. In addition to that, you are able to speak your mind and speak about your opinion without getting opposition or being ostracized. Thirdly, my parents like you better because you are the oldest, but yet, you don't have a job. Unlike myself, who is mandated to plow the fields at the end of every farming season, every day after school, you don't have to do anything. You can just go home, do your homework, and enjoy your dinner comfortably without having to worry about school. Fourthly, you have such strong and powerful words. For instance, you are very influential on my political views especially on slavery. Now, I am going to be frank with you. I didn't show this in front of our new family member, Will, but now, I am going to tell you my political view on slavery. I think that slavery is the most evil thing that man can ever do. Separation and Partition of families for no reason whatsoever is wrong and inhumane. It is quite arbitrary and unjust. Our founding fathers are turning over in their graves because of people like you, who want to do evil for this beautiful place. Not only do you want to be a slave owner, but, you also want to fight against the innocent victims of an unjust system of government. The government supports people that are cold like you are. A couple of hundred years ago, I am sure you've heard of the man who was known as John Locke, he believed that man is entitled to life, liberty, and property. In the Constitution of the United States, our founding fathers state that mankind is entitled to many Civil Liberties and those liberties are Life, Liberty, and the Pursuit of Happiness. Unfortunately, we want the same rights for ourselves, but I don't think we all mean the same thing. Bigots like you have the belief that only the Caucasian man is entitled to certain Civil Liberties. People like me who are good Republicans believe that equality and justice should take place throughout the nation amongst all races. The Republicans are here to help everyone in this beautiful place. Southern Democrats like you and Beckinridge believe that evil is okay, when it is totally not. Now, I never told anybody from the family this, but I am going to prove to you that I am Abraham Lincoln," said Jesse.

He started to stretch through the costume that had the appearance of the younger sibling. The "skin" started to break apart and a huge man started to stand up. He wore a black suit and red tie and is a small town Illinois lawyer. One thing that most people don't know about him is that he is a strong supporter of justice and equality. He has brown hair with a bald spot in the back of the head. "Sarah, did we really have a second child?" asked Jobe. "No, it was really a miscarriage. I adopted a son for nine years and I made him look like James. Then he left us. So, I hired Abraham

Lincoln to stuff himself into a costume," the prairie man's wife answered.

"How do you know Mr. Lincoln?" the prairie man asked. "Well, he is a distant cousin of ours. He is a cousin from Illinois. While I was in Illinois with him, I start to talk to him about politics and one thing that he told me was that he was antislavery. He was and still is, an abolitionist, who is against the malice of slavery. He supports freedom for all slaves," answered Sarah. Jobe and James were quiet and shocked that their son and brother was Abraham Lincoln.

The family finally arrived in South Salt Lake in Utah by the Great Salt Lake. This town had a rustic appearance. An aroma of burning wood is making the town have a delicious smell. The buildings are all made out of wood. The sign to the town showed the words of *South Salt Lake, Town of Beauty and Wonder.* "We're here," said the creature from heaven. "I hear that noise again. What's that?" the alien leader asked. "You must be hearing things. You asked the same question earlier. I don't know what you're talking about. This noise sounds so soft, but yet it sounds so supernatural. This must be a creature of God. Maybe, it's not even a creature.The noise is coming from somewhere. I don't know exactly where," answered Jobe. "You know I am wondering what's on top of my arm," the alien leader replied. "Fool, I'm on your shoulder," this creature of God said. "What shoulder?" asked Will. "Your right shoulder. All of God's creatures are always on the right side of the path. We're never on the left. We always take the good road, the right, respectful road. We're not like you Satanic Earthlings," said God's Heavenly creature said. "Excuse me. Who are you to talk to me like that?" asked Jobe. "I am totally immaculate. I have every right to decide that you've committed a serious act of sinning. It is my prerogative to say that you are a sinner," this Heavenly creature answered. "Tell me your name, you occult voice," the prairie man said. "I don't really care to disclose my name," replied God's creature.

"Well, if you claim you're immaculate, you wouldn't have to cover your name. There must be something for you to hide," said Jobe. "How dare you say such a thing to me," God's creature objected. "Can you just tell me your name?" the prairie man asked. "Fine. My name is Enkel," the Lord's creature answered. "Now, what brings you over here?" asked Jobe. "Because I am the Angel of God. I am God's messenger and I am Jesus's messenger. I bring all of the good news and bad news. I bring the Gospel to all men, who do not have the opportunity to grasp it. I free the missionaries, who are good men who end up being imprisoned for preaching the Word of God. It is a must that Christianity should reach the whole world and this philosophy shall be spread throughout the World. The Bible shall be the most, well-known book throughout the World," God's messenger answered. "What brings you here?" asked James.

"Because your friend Will Von Alien was taken by God because he is the biggest sinner in history and you took him in like the benevolent Christians that you are," answered Enkel. "You didn't answer my question. Why did you come here?" the prairie man's son (James) asked. "Because I wanted to present the alien leader with an award. This award shall never remain in his hands. This award shall increase his chances of heading to the Celestial City. Earlier today, he had zero chances of going up to heaven and being in front of the Father, but now, there is some chance that he might head up to heaven," answered the Messenger of God.

"Where's the chart?" the prairie man's son asked.
All of a sudden a chart started to appear. The X-Axis is
used to show the amount of deeds and beliefs and good
behavior to deserve the award. The Y-Axis is used to show
the increased or decreased chances of Will going up to
heaven. He has a fifteen percent chance of heading up to
the Celestial City. Enkel explained the chart. He pointed to
Will. "This man has a fifteen percent chance of heading up
to Heaven, which is a very high chance, for a starter in the
Christian faith. Throughout this trip, I will give you
messages to state the chance of him going up to God's
Palace, but like I said earlier, there is a fifteen percent
chance that he is going up to Heaven."

"Angel, what's the chance of me going up to God's
Palace?" asked Jobe. "110 % chance," God's messenger
answered. "What about mine?" asked James. "57%
chance," answered Enkel. "Are you dead serious?" the
prairie man's son asked. "Of course I am. I don't think that
somebody who works for God would be lying," answered
the Messenger of God. "Well, that's not true. Missionaries
lie all the time," replied James. "Well, I wouldn't be an
angel if I was a liar. I am an angel because I am the true
messenger for God. I help God spread his word for
missionaries who can't, unfortunately, spread the Word of
God," said Enkel.

"Now, what if you are a liar?" the prairie man's son
asked. "What if you're a sinner?" asked God's Messenger.
"He just owned you on that one," said Will. "Shut up,"
replied James. "Excuse me, but I have to tell you something
that is applicable to your life. You must believe in God and
support him," said Enkel. "Since when do you suspect that
I don't believe in God, or even respect him?" asked the
prairie man's son. "It is totally true. When your parents

aren't listening, you curse like a sailor. You abominate all creatures and it is starting to show with your belief in the support of slavery. This makes your ideas totally wrong, arbitrary, and unjust. Evil has adulterated your mind. Satan has taken over your life. There is an opportunity for you to change, but the choice is yours," answered God's Messenger.

"You are nothing but a Faerie, who tells fallacious statements. You are totally good at twisting the truth. I don't know what religion you're coming from, but I know that whatever you're rambling about is bogus. We as Christians believe that slavery is acceptable. For instance, 'Mr. Smart Guy', God has enslaved the people of Israel to the Babylonians because the people were disobeying him. Also, another incident that God supported the enslavement of people was when he allowed the Israelites to be enslaved to the Egyptians. You are not a genius like you think you are. Everything you say are considered fallacious statements. You think that condemning me is acceptable when I didn't do a single thing wrong. Why don't you learn how to look at the log in your eye before looking at the splinter in your brethren's eye! I bet you've heard of that kind of a phrase before. Also, do unto others as you would do unto yourself. I bet you heard of that phrase before, also," replied James.

"Half of the words you've just said in that statement were erroneous. First of all, I am smarter than you. I have a much more intelligent mind than you do. The reason why is because I am a true part of God. I resided in Heaven since the beginning of the Creation of Heaven and Earth. While, you were living in the World of Evolution, I resided in the Heaven of Creation. I would be able to see what's going on. Like I said earlier, sometimes if a missionary was imprisoned or was forbidden to preach the Word of God to an area in the World, I would step in and spread the Bible to the World. Thirdly, what you said about slavery was totally bogus. There was only one incident where God supported the enslavement of mankind and that was when he made the Israelites become captives of the Babylonians and that was because the Israelites were practicing idol worship, which was and still is totally wrong and it absolutely goes against God. What you said about God enslaving the Israelites to the Egyptians was completely false. In fact, God freed the Israelites from the Egyptians. I am sure you've heard of the Exodus. The Exodus meant that the Israelites were fleeing Egypt and Moses led them out of Egypt and he parted the Red Sea under God's orders. In addition to that, God, for the most part, has been against slavery. He caused the Twelve Plagues to take place against the Egyptians because of what they did to the Israelites. There is no excuse to consider the idea of Slavery to be acceptable because it's not. You took the innocent rights of a whole race and you shall be punished when you meet your Creator. It is sickening that you support the curtailing of rights towards a race of a different color. You then want to enslave Will Von Alien because he's an alien from Starmos City and he has a different skin pigment than you. You kowtow to the government and John C. Calhoun because he supports what support. You spit at the Republicans because they want to save this nation and you bow down to the Democrats, particularly the Southern Democrats. This is sickening. If you don't realize what you're doing is wrong, then I don't know what to say to you. Slavery is evil. Learn how to get that through your head," said Enkel.

"Who are you to even talk to me like that? I ought to banish you from this vehicle," replied James. "Well, who are you to banish me from this vehicle? All I came here to do was to simply tell Will about his chances of going to Heaven. Then, your dad asked the chances of him going to the Celestial City or Heaven. Then, you asked and I told you and your dad the complete truth and nothing but the truth. I want to tell you this, though. Evil has taken your spirit. Satan has turned you into a malevolent soul. You were born to a loving Christian family, but you were predestined for evil. You showed the facade of perfection in front of your parents, but when Will came into the picture, you became a total bigot. If you believe in the idea of Social Darwinism in its form of malice, then you're evil. I feel that man should learn how to show respect to each other and animals. You are the epitome of evil. When you get older, I heard that you were planning on joining the Confederate Army when the Civil War happens. That is sick and wrong. When God witnesses the wrongdoings that you have committed, there will be no chance that you would end up in the Celestial City. So, instead, you will be going to your favorite place and that is known as the Pit of Evil, Hell. In fact, God will even tell Satan that you are a perfect demon to go to Hell. I would suggest changing your view on Slavery before Death will do its part. Remember, one thing that is clear is that Sin is the equivalent to Death," said God's Messenger.

"Why don't you just leave this wagon or go preach your crazy sermon somewhere else," James replied in an angry manner. "Why would you say such a thing?" asked Will. "Because this guy was only here to tell us about our chances of us going to Heaven. He wasn't here to preach the Word of God. I already know the Bible left and right.

Tell this thing to get the hell out of here because he is extremely annoying," the prairie man's son answered.

"Your behavior is extremely humiliating. You should be ashamed of yourself, the way you treat that Spirit of God. It is the most disrespectful thing one can do. This is more disrespectful and evil than condoning slavery. I am sorry for your behavior, but if you keep acting like this when you get older, you'll be going to Satan's fierce, fiery furnace. I think you want to go up to Heaven. God believes our new family member more than he believes you. This new family member is a very nice alien. He is truly one of God's creatures. He is like a Child of God. You think that you're one of God's children, but yet you haven't proven to me that you acted like any of God's children. Your attitude is the epitome of evil and you should rethink what you're doing," replied Jobe. "You're telling me that my attitude is evil, but yet, you show the intent of malice. You say that I am a slave driver, when I don't even know any slaves. You're telling me to like this guy, who is probably some sort of a slave. I pretended to like him by giving him an interview," said James.

"You lie," replied the Messenger of God. "Who's that?" asked Will. "That's probably that annoying messenger," the prairie man's son answered. The noise of a reed flute is now being heard. Random chords that sound very gloomy are being heard. "What's that?" asked Sarah. Enkel started to illuminate in a gold color in the darkness. "Turn around. I see the Angel of God turning a beautiful gold color," the prairie man answered. God's Messenger turned around without saying farewell and he flew back up to the Celestial City. When he flew up to Heaven, he looked like a shooting star. "Thank God, that thing is gone," said James.

The Angel was gone and Will turned to more earthly matters. "I'm starving. I did all this dimension traveling and yet I never had anything to eat. I don't know about all of you, but I am very hungry," the alien leader replied. "What you said was completely irrelevant to what I just said, but you brought up a pretty good point," the prairie man's son said. "Really, you're hungry? If you think you're hungry, the slaves are much hungrier than you are. Their sick owners give them food scraps and it is disgusting. They don't even feed them substantial meals. Generations of men, women, and children have to suffer through this traumatic pain," replied Jobe. "This idea of slavery is worse than the communist leadership of Starmos City. We must do something about this! It is arbitrary and cruel how man can treat their brothers in such a cruel and harsh manner," said Will. They officially arrived in the Western town.

The Stage Coaches, Conestoga's, and horses are parked in front of the different buildings. Some of the Stage Coaches had their windows opened, while the other windows were sealed shut. Very few Stage Coaches had blinds that obscured the insides. The Conestoga Wagons remained uncovered for the horses to retrieve the hay. The horses were lying flat on the cold, hard, desert ground. The lights are turned on at the Santa Maria Tavern. This Tavern featured wooden arches. The interior of the tavern is blocked by curtains. One can see that this particular place is in functional operation because the lights are on. Two shutter-type doors are the gateway into this tavern. The outside of the tavern features a deck with two crooked steps. Featured on the top of the deck are twelve rocking chairs viewing the Great Salt Lake.

The Mormon family and the alien leader arrived at the front of this tavern. James walked out of the Conestoga first; Jobe followed; and then Sarah. Will remained inside of the Covered Wagon. James walked into the tavern while Sarah sat down in one of the rocking chairs in front of the tavern. While James walked past the two shutter doors into the tavern, the prairie man returned back to the Covered Wagon. Will is sitting on top of the haystack. "What are you doing sitting over here?" Jobe asked. "I am thinking about why I shouldn't be heading into this place. The folks in here might think that I am some sort of slave when, I am not," the alien leader answered. "How about I get a bandana to put over your face," the prairie man replied.

"How will I be able to see, then?" asked Will. "Good point. Before I give you the mask, I'll cut four holes," answered Jobe. He walked over into the rear of the Conestoga wagon. A hat and a bandana are lying on the floor right next to each other. He retrieves a red bandana that has stripes of white and blue. These colors are the representation of the Mormon Flag. He retrieved a dusty pocket knife and started cutting four holes in them. One long hole for the mouth; two for the eyes; and one hole for the nose. He walked over to the front of the wagon and gave the alien leader the bandana. "How do you expect me to get this thing on?" asked Will.

"You don't know how to get a bandana on?" asked Jobe. "No, I never even heard of such a thing," the alien leader answered. "I'll be more than willing to put this on you. Just lean your head forward," the prairie man replied. Will leaned his head forward. Jobe placed the bandana around his neck. His face became obscured by the large bandana. The prairie man guided him down the small step off the covered wagon. They walked past the rocking chairs.

The alien leader stopped. "Why are you stopping?" the prairie man asked. "Because I could see that your wife is sitting on the rocking chair all by herself. She is almost like some sort of an introvert," answered Will. "My wife is far from an introvert. If you noticed the whole time that we were on the covered wagon, my wife was never talking. If she talked, she never commented about the controversial arguments that had taken place. Granted, I am a strong abolitionist, who is against slavery. My wife is considered a second class citizen. She is forbidden to speak at the dinner table. She is also forbidden from entering bars, pubs, or taverns. She is also not allowed to vote for the President, a governor, mayor, judge, or representative. Besides the fact that it is against our religion to divorce, she is not allowed to divorce without the consent of myself. In this society, women have very few rights. It seems like they have no rights from their eyes, but they have the right to move from place to place and abandon the family. Their rights cause legal consequences. For instance, if they abandon the family and trek on their own wild adventure, they'll be sentenced to death on the gallows," replied Jobe.

"Well, wouldn't you do something to stop this kind of repression towards women?" the alien leader asked. "No way, why would I? They're not men. Why should I care about them?" the prairie man answered. "I don't understand you. You're such a freedom fighter when it comes to slavery, but yet you're a chauvinist pig," replied Will. "How can you say such a thing about me when I'm helping you? Do you want me to sell you to some sort of slave owner? I am more than willing to do that and I mean it," said Jobe.

"Fine then, we won't get into any controversial subjects any more. Let's get into this restaurant or tavern and we'll disregard this subject," the alien leader replied. "Thank you," said Jobe. After that short conversation, they entered the tavern. There are twelve tables inside of this tavern. These tables are made of Redwood bark and Cherry Wood – very polished. Each table features four to six chairs. This depends on which table one would be sitting at.

The chairs that are present at every table are rocking chairs. In the back of this tavern is a stage. This stage features Vaudeville Shows every night. This is to entertain all of the aspiring gold miners on the road to California. Inside the tavern are alcoves that have cushioned seats. These cushioned seats are for guests feature small tables that pop out from the wall, quite similar to Murphy Tables. This is very futuristic for the archaic time period. Featured in the heart of the restaurant is a huge dance floor.

Sometimes, there would be a group of traveling southern belles from Florida that would come and visit the pubs of the West. A far cry from the beautiful southern belles is a bar featured on the far left of the pub. This bar featured multiple liquors including some beer. Shelves of Whiskey are also, featured behind the bar. The real and best entertainment had taken place in a small part of the restaurant. Twice, every night, the patrons of this pub would sit by a Ragtime Piano.

This Piano is made of Cherry Wood and the Ragtime Piano has the best quality of Sounds. Also, this Piano accommodated multiple Piano Rolls and sheets of music; particularly national classics like Dixie, the Star Spangled Banner, and Yellow Rose of Texas. This piano is supported by a small, six inch tall stage. Sometimes, the same songs were played over and over again. Often, man becomes tired of hearing, seeing, feeling, smelling, or tasting the same thing again. Man needs enveloping environments. So, whenever the Ragtime Piano Player would notice a small audience, he would move to another pub until the patrons wanted him back. The music that replaced the Ragtime Piano player was a huge marching band. When the patrons grew tired of that, they called for the Ragtime Piano Player.

In general, man misses the nostalgic past especially, a nostalgic past time like visiting the pub and watching the Ragtime Piano Player play his music. Basically, the entertainment in this place would change from time to time. Featured in the rear of this pub is a kitchen. This kitchen featured a wood burning oven and the aroma of fire would warm up the town in the cold winters of Utah. Also, featured in this kitchen is a Soda Fountain, which dispenses Carbonated Cola Syrup.

"How do you like this place?" asked Jobe. "I think it is quite impressive, but I'd prefer to go outside. I would like to keep your wife company. She needs help," answered Will. "Whatever, I'll order some food and drink for you," the prairie man replied. "Okay, you do that," the alien leader said brusquely. "Why are you talking to my father like that?" asked James. Will disregarded that arrogant son's belligerent question and he continued walking. He past the two, green shudder doors and approached Sarah, who is sitting down on the Rocking Chair. He walked right in front of her; she looked up. "What are you here for?" she asked. "I am here to keep you company. I heard that you were lonely and it tremendously bothers me when I see people that are lonely and uncomfortable. How would you like it if I sat next to you and talked to you?" he asked. "Okay, that sounds fine with me," she answered.

Chapter XI: It is discovered that Women are treated as Creatures instead of Humans

It is now 9 in the evening. While Jobe and James were inside of the pub, Will and Sarah were sitting outside. The alien leader is now ready to make a conversation with Sarah. She sat down and looked at him. She almost stared at him. He looked back at her. "Why are you staring at me?" he asked. "Because I am amazed that an alien from another dimension had the ability to come over to America, especially in the mid to late 1800s. It is impressive how you were able to pull that one off, but let's have a little conversation," answered Sarah. Will started rocking back and forth in his chair.

"What kind of chair is this?" he asked. "It's a rocking chair," the prairie man's wife answered. "This is probably one of the most interesting, if not *the* most interesting, chair I ever sat down in. I want you to share your life story with me. Please feel free to do that," asked Will. "Oh my God, that is amazing. Oh, wait! I'm not supposed to be using God's name in vain. Sorry, God. Now it is I that is amazed that you want me to do such a thing. Usually, a man never asks a female about anything. The female usually keeps her mouth shut, unfortunately. I am super thrilled that you are willing to hear my life story. I don't know what to say," Sarah said in awe. "Well, do you want to tell the story like an orator, or do you want to tell the story in a normal manner? How do you want to tell the story?" he asked. "Because I rarely ever speak unless I am spoken to and I am only used to that. I want you to ask me questions and then I'll tell you about each factor in my life, how I was treated, the places I've visited, and the happy and melancholy days of my life. Like I said earlier, I am so thankful that I am able to tell my life story," the prairie man's wife answered.

"You never have to be thankful. I should be thankful towards you because you're more than willing to tell me a story about your personal life. I usually ask folks that question about their life story because I want to get information out of them. Some hesitate while others decline. There are some that say that I might be a stalker because I want to know about his or her life, but I thank you very much for being more than willing to tell your story," the alien leader answered.

"Well, please ask me some questions and it would be my pleasure to answer each one of those questions in the form of a story. Face it, mankind barely speaks because their minds are immersed in stories and the children will never be able to talk because their fathers constantly silence them," replied Sarah. "Based on what I've seen so far, I notice that your children are quite talkative. In fact, I think that they're very outspoken and bias. They're also extremely bigoted and support the Southern Democrats. What makes your kids even more sickening is that they cause trouble and have a love for controversy, especially over the idea of slavery, which I never knew existed. I did know about the true dictionary definition of the word, but yet I would never imagine myself entering a place that supports that horrific and controversial idea. Furthermore, I can't believe your sons act like that. People that are pro-slavery should be ashamed of themselves because they are evil," said Will.

"You'd be surprised to hear my comment. Most parents are supporters of their children, or my child, but in this case, I will definitely not support James. This young adult is the epitome of evil, and I can't believe that he is a racist, which is even more sickening and evil. He wants to cause trouble towards innocent slaves and brutalize them. You're right. My son is very outspoken and I partially blame my husband for his evil behavior. He allows him to behave like that. My husband is two faced. He debates with my son over the subject of slavery, but yet, he allows my son to talk like that. I would love to throw my son outside of the house for his behavior. I loved him when he was younger, but when I discovered that he would be the future Confederate, I have grown to despise him. Up in heaven, I know God loathes slavery. Unfortunately, we all will have different demises and our individual demises will take place at different years in time. When I die, I will never see my son, and I might not even see my husband in the next life. I believe that I will end up in Heaven," Sarah replied. "Why would you assume that your husband is going to hell?" the alien leader asked.

"Enkel, the faerie that just came down from the Celestial City, told everyone that they would either be going to Heaven or Hell from a religious perspective. He only made his statement about their destination in the afterlife based on how many times they formally attended Church. My husband goes to church the most. He visited the church twice a week, if not more. Sometimes, he would visit Church, once every day during a specific week at his choice. James would rarely go to Church. That was the reason why he would have a 57% chance of going to Heaven. Enkel never considered the other factors about the chances of my son or my husband's destination after life on Earth. Based on the behavior that I've witnessed, I'd say that Jobe and James will have a zero chance of going to Heaven, if not a subzero chance of even seeing Heaven in their dreams. The men in my household have a high chance of ending up on the bottom of Hell. They will be with Satan's brethren.

In fact, all they do is claim that they believe in God, when they're totally against God's principles. You just don't see that in them, but it is totally true that they're against God's ideas and philosophies," the prairie man's wife answered.

"Well, maybe in the son, I was able to see that, but I would never even expect that Jobe would be like that. If he is really like that he has the intent of evil, it is quite shocking and mind-boggling that he'd do such a thing. He would be more than willing to help me, but yet he is here to cause trouble. I am not surprised that your son is like that. I can't believe you'd even marry that man. If he's not here to help me, he is really out to get me? That's totally not nice and he deserves to be cooked, tarred, and pickled for his actions of malice and evil. I don't think he did anything wrong in his life, but if he's pulling an act by debating with his son over slavery, then I ought to hurt him and beat the hell out of this low life. If he is truthfully like that, then he is nothing but a piece of garbage. James is also garbage. I believe that your son is more evil than your husband" the alien leader replied. Sarah nodded.

"Now, you will also be surprised to hear this from me but I think that my husband and my son didn't condone slavery on their own. You see, during the generations before their generation, slavery was considered acceptable because five generations ago, their ancestors brought slaves over to North America on ships from Africa. It has been outlawed for nearly a half of a century, but again, slavery is the most evil wrong doing that man can ever commit. But that wasn't my point. Since the Triangular Trade, slavery was considered acceptable in North America, particularly in three quarters of the United States. Slavery is the most evil and wicked philosophy that has ever been around and many accept it. As Americans, we should never accept slavery because it is totally wrong and sick. Nobody knows that I am going to do this, but I am going to take action against slavery. I am going to come out of the shadows and I will stop the evils of Slavery. I am going to die for these people that are considered and treated as property. I will make a choice to fight for these people under God. Unfortunately, we live in a World that is filled with sinful hatred and evil. *For God so loved the World that he gave up his only son for man's sin.* That is the Psalm. Unfortunately, I don't see man making a sacrifice. As regular human beings, we don't have to sacrifice a man or woman to God. We should sacrifice the idea of slavery so that way we show that we love God's principles and honor him," said Sarah.

"I think you are the bravest woman of all. Women from where I come from were never as brave or as bold as you. You are as courageous as a tiger and you will fight to the end. That's the kind of woman I like. I like a woman who's a fighter. I like a woman who is here to help people," replied Will. "Well, we got into enough politics, for now. It is more important that we deal with the issue that is at hand and that is about my life. Now I probably know what you're thinking. You're probably thinking that I have an ego. That is totally not true. I will tell you why as you ask me questions about my life. Like I said earlier, I'd prefer being asked questions because as a woman I speak when I am spoken to or asked questions. Even though that theory is useless when it comes to slavery, but I have concerns about my husband listening to our conversation and he doesn't like it when I talk out of turn," the prairie man's wife said.

"Okay. Where were you born and what year were you born in?" the alien leader asked. "As I said earlier, I came from a different place, but there is a huge difference between your where you came from and your origin. I was born in Boston, Massachusetts on March 5th, 1820. During the Westward Expansion of the Country, my parents moved to Utah because our family converted to the Church of the Latter Day Saints" answered Sarah. "When did your parents die?" asked Will. "Why would you be asking such a sad thing?" she asked in a melancholy manner. She started tearing up when he asked that question. "What's wrong?" the alien leader asked. "I really don't like talking about my parents' death because it is traumatic. It ruined my life and I could assure you that it changed my life, but if you want me to tell it, I'll do it," the prairie man's wife answered. As she started mentioning the factor of her parents' death, she started sobbing. Tears started to leave the alien leader's eyes, also.

"I know it's unfortunate and terrible losing a loved one, especially a parent. Even though it hurts my feelings, talking about my parents' death is kind of a relief for me. It teaches me how to move on in life. To this day, I still cry about this. In fact, this ruined me for a number of years, but I was left with no other choice. I had to stand up and fight the misery," he replied. "Well, what happened to your parents?" asked Sarah.

"Growing up in Starmos City, life was very jolly and joyful. Every day was a happy day. This is at least the way I noticed it growing up as a kid. I didn't know that the Communist reign of Cornelius Von Alien was ruling the city. My parents worked as government workers. My dad controlled the water system in the city, and my mom controlled the finances of Starmos City. When I was four years old, the Alien Aqueduct closed down. This Aqueduct was a reservoir that held a lifetime supply of water. The reason why was because Cornelius wanted the water for himself, but I didn't think about those things when I was 4 years old. I just thought about lollipops, candy canes, and toys. I never thought about my parents' jobs. The day the reservoir shut down, one thousand folks were either laid off from their job or got lucky and were relocated. My dad was one of the lucky ones and he was relocated to a solar field that powered the city. He worked there for ten years. Then Cornelius decided to go against the primary, energy efficient source and he laid off all of the employees that worked at the solar field. One of these employees was my dad, Cornelius's fourth cousin. He thought that Cornelius was overstepping his boundary. That tyrant dismissed my mom from her job because he felt that she would give my dad money because she was a compassionate person. At the time, I was fifteen years old. One day I came home from Secondary School and I discovered that my parents weren't home, but yet their belongings were still at the apartment where I lived. I walked into my room. All of a sudden two guards grabbed me and dragged me over to the Alien Estate, the place where Cornelius resided. There was a line of prisoners being executed one by one. I was held back by the guards. My parents were in the line of the firing squad and that tyrant zealously retrieved his gun and shot them in cold blood. Not a single facial expression of remorse was shown on his face. He then approached me and his two guards dragged me into the estate for dinner. That whole week, I was crying. The rest of that year, I felt miserable. I returned back to the apartment and I moved in for a temporary amount of time. I heard a loud knock on my door. It was two huge Starmos Officers. They discovered that I was living at home alone. That very day I was brought before the Court of Cornelius and I was sentenced to living at the Alien Estate for life and was forced to work as a slave chef. I was forced to make the most delectable meals without even having an opportunity to taste them. Some of the meals that I found delectable were tossed into the desert because that brute didn't like the meals that I liked. The memories at the estate were the most painful memories of my life. I don't think anything can get worse, even if I asked God to send me worse," the alien leader answered.

After telling the story Will stopped crying. The prairie man's wife also stopped crying. "This is probably the worst ordeal one can ever go through. One thing that I must advise you is that life brings goodness, but with that goodness comes adversity. Now that I am composed I'll tell my story about the trauma of losing my parents at a young age. My family and I were in Southern Utah by the Grand Canyon on vacation. This is the day that I would never expect to take place, but it was the worst day of my life. My parents and I were riding in our Stage Coach, but the horses made a mistake in its movement. All of us including the horses died – physically or mentally - in Death Valley in the Grand Canyon in Utah. The Stage Coach crashed into the Colorado River. I managed to make it to shore. My parents ended up flowing Southbound. We were separated and I never saw them again. I learned to avoid rivers and canyons. My life tremendously changed since then. I lived on the move like a vagabond roaming from one place to another until I was adopted by a Mormon Family from Salt Lake City. Despite this tragic loss in my life, I learned how to survive. When facing a tragic loss like this, I learned an important lesson from this. It is said that when man is facing adversity, they must not go through life being miserable and weak. They must face the facts headstrong and be resilient when facing misery and hell. It took a lot of endurance, but I managed to fight sadness like a bull during this loss," replied Sarah.

"You know, we both have a lot of things in common, but yet we're different. You're a human, but yet I am an alien. We shared similar stories that were both unfortunate. We watched our parents die before our eyes and the two of us came out strong. I am much more interested in your life, but I just had to throw in this one little comment," the alien leader said. "You're right. What year were you born?" asked Sarah. "I was born in the future. This may sound crazy, but I was born in 2022. I am 25 years old, but it is amazing how I was able to travel back into your time," answered Will. "Earlier, when I talked to you, I was told by you that you were ruled by a Communist Dictatorship under the rule of Cornelius Von Alien. I want to know who this guy was and if he's still around," the prairie man's wife said.

"Well, it was Hell. I didn't know that it was Hell. Nearly half of my life, I lived at the Alien Estate. Even though my city was ruled under a Stalinist Dictatorship, I never realized that I was being ruled by somebody who was influenced by the former Soviet Union. The time that I discovered he based his political views off of Stalinism was when he let two guests come visit his estate. One of the guests was a shapeshifting robot, who was a friend of his and the other one was a fool who was being victimized by the deception of the evil of Cornelius. I learned about the belief and philosophy of Stalinism when I saw deception and tyranny from this cruel, cold brute. I knew he was evil all along, ever since he closed the Alien Aqueduct, but I really discovered his wicked, barbaric behavior when he tried and killed the two guests. He told me to poison them with arsenic in their Caesar Salad and Creme Brulee. Instead, I poured kerosene on the dishes and toss them into the oven. I did that on purpose so I could destroy Cornelius's property to teach him a lesson. This tyrant was a cold, cruel beast. Death must do its part against him because he is evil. So, I made two dishes that were pure and those dishes were for the honorable guests, who later become my friends. I made the best and worst decision of my life. I tried to make the brute's plan backfire against him. I gave him a Creme Brulee, but this Creme Brulee is not your ordinary Creme Brulee. I decided to add an additional ingredient to the dish. This ingredient is a detrimental ingredient. It's called Arsenic. I served him the dish and he immediately fainted into a state of unconsciousness," answered Will.

Sarah listened intently. "That's very interesting. I have a couple of questions that are quite important. They may sound frivolous and even irrelevant to this conversation. But, I would appreciate you answer them. Would you let me ask them?" the prairie man's wife asked. "And what would you have to ask me?" the alien leader asked.

"Well, I want to know a couple of things. First, I want to know about the most exciting time of your life and the most perilous time of your life. Tell me the biggest adventure you ever had," said Sarah.

Will had no problem. "Before I get into anything, I want to tell you that the answer to your question is related to the story about the poisoning from earlier. Now, when I poisoned Cornelius Von Alien for the first time, his two guests and I made a daring attempt to flee the Alien Estate.

The three of us walked up to the side door of the Alien Estate. As soon as my hand touched the knob of the door, a swarm of 25 guards came down from the ceiling of the hall. These guards came swooping down like a group of secret agents.

They carried huge M16 assault rifles and surrounded and handcuffed us. This was the most nerve wracking moment of my life. I felt so nervous that my muscles tightened and I literally froze into the position of my hands being up. The guards arrested the two guests and myself. We were taken to a Sensory Deprivation Cell awaiting sentencing. We were kept in this dark cell for twenty minutes. Cornelius woke up and the Alien guards brought us over to him to be sentenced. All three of us were sentenced to life in the hole without parole. That was when I resisted sentencing. As we were being taken to the hole, I managed to slip my shackles. My heart started racing. It was a matter of seconds before I would be caught, fettered to the fence, and shot. The guard in the tower tried to shut the gate. Fortunately, I managed to slip through the fence by the skin of the teeth. I would say this was the most perilous adventure of my life. It doesn't seem like a full adventure, but every second felt like one minute and every minute felt like an hour. The whole ordeal was only ten minutes long, but it was the scariest ordeal of my life," replied Will.

"That's amazing. Do you want to know the most perilous moment of my life?" the prairie man's wife asked. "Sure, please tell me that in its entirety," the alien leader answered. "Okay, if you insist. When I was ten years old, I was living in Boston. It was a hot summer day in August. This weekend was a surprise weekend for my brother's birthday. My family was supposed to be going up to

Braintree and then down to Cape Cod. The Adams's House became a Historic Site and this house looked beautiful, but it was not the most exciting thing of my life. My family and I headed down South to Cape Cod. Often, my family would never go to the beach, but yet we would see the ocean every day. We lived right in front of the ocean, but we've never seen a real beach without rocks. We headed to the relaxing, white sand beach of Cape Cod. One Saturday morning at the crack of dawn, my parents, brother, and I headed down to the beach. We walked down the shoreline and came across a large canoe. I didn't know this, but this canoe was a trap. It was the most beautiful boat I've ever seen, but hidden behind the beautiful facade was danger. I was the first one to step inside the canoe. It seemed fine to me. My dad entered, and then my brother. My brother was in the front of the canoe. All of a sudden, some British Officer's hat was seen. My brother lifted the hat that concealed a hole. We nonchalantly took the hat walked out of the canoe to continue going down the beach. While going down the beach, a shadow was following us. This shadow was actually the ghost of a British officer from the War of 1812. The shadow stalked us. We turned around. All of a sudden, a British officer emerged from the ground. He retrieved his musket and tried firing it at my family. We darted over to the Stagecoach and the horses and dashed over to the Inn that we were staying at. We retrieved our cases of luggage and immediately returned home to Boston. This was the most perilous adventure of my life," answered Sarah. "But I was to ask you some questions. I guess it's okay that you asked me questions. Can I ask about how your husband treats you?" the alien leader asked.

"Sure, don't tell anybody this. If you think my husband is an angel who came down from Heaven, that's

not true. He may have the face of kindness and
benevolence, but that is just a facade. You don't know the
'real' Jobe. He is the most evil man that one can ever meet.
He claims that he is this perfect Mormon when he is far
from perfect. Like I said earlier, that faerie that came down
from the Celestial City only stated his chances of spending
his eternal life in Heaven based on going to Church. The
only reason why he goes to Church is to ask the Lord for
constant forgiveness. Granted, mankind sins every day, but
he is a huge sinner. He gets drunk every time he is at the
Saloon. The only time he didn't get drunk was visiting his
parents and my parents and he didn't want them to see that
he was a cruel savage. When he's drunk, he acts very
disrespectful and arrogant. He pretends to be Christian. He
pretends to be a worshipper of God, when he condones the
beliefs of the Devil. He tells his son to respect God's
principles, but yet, he doesn't show any respect towards the
principles of the Lord. He is nothing but a walking facade.
Every Sunday, he works at our local Church; he's a Sunday
school teacher. The ideals he teaches do not apply to him.
Perhaps, I ought to tell the preacher what he does and show
his evilness. He claims he loves African Americans in front
of folks that he first meets. You see, my husband is
extremely deceitful and deceptive. What hc said about his
love for the African American community is totally
misleading. I've heard him agree with my son on the view
on slavery. My husband is a strong supporter of slavery. I
feel that when he meets his Creator, he will not know what
to say. When he meets the Lord, he will have to admit that
he's condoned, curtailed, and kowtowed down to evilness
and wickedness. It is upsetting that I have to deal with such
a man. In addition to that, he doesn't treat me like a normal,
American citizen. He treats me like a creature or a Second

Class Citizen. I bust my back in that prairie house for him, but yet, he treats me like garbage. I work hard every hour of every day to keep the house clean. I try and keep the house pest-free. I keep that house pure. Sometimes, he tracks mud into the house from the field on purpose. He is so disgusting and despicable with his behavior. A lot of the things he does toward me are out of spite. He wants to do damage towards me and I don't like it one bit. My son James thinks he is also 'high' class like him. When my son was younger he was totally influenced by him. If you don't believe a single word that I am saying, it is quite unfortunate. My husband is the most deceitful, heartless, and deceptive man that ever walked the universe. What makes my husband even more evil is that he's not only a chauvinist, but he thinks it is okay to enslave innocent people. It is unfortunate that he thinks like that. It is unfortunate and sickening that any man or woman thinks like that. I guess that's the kind of world we live in and this must be the real world," the prairie man's wife answered.

Will was shocked. "Not to sound rude to you but I don't believe you. How could your husband who seems like he is so nice, be so evil and disgusting? It is just cannot be true. Now I am not saying that you're a liar. If he really supports treating people like property, he should be ashamed of himself," replied Will.

"Well, he does support that. Like I said earlier, my husband's benevolent attitude is a facade. He would be an evil slave driver. For God sakes, he is just as evil as those slave drivers. I feel like a slave living with him. He forces me to go through a never ending cycle of work. He never says thank you and he condones the evils of our arbitrary and autocratic government. Don't believe me? Ask him yourself, if you dare cross that boundary with him. He will bring you Hell and possibly death. I'd strongly recommend not talking to him about controversial subjects like slavery and women, but my final words are that he is nothing but a chauvinist pig and he supports and honors evil. It is unfortunate that we live in a world of injustice; bur, he is not contributing to fairness and equality amongst the races and genders. We live in a bias world. Folks like you must stop this evil," said Sarah.

"Now, what is it like living in a world of chauvinism and bigotry?" the alien leader asked.

"From the outside, it seems like a Utopian society to the white man or the Caucasian man. From the inside, we live in a world of hell. We live in a world filled with division and hatred. We live in a world where Christianity is the primary religion in most countries and the philosophy that is followed by many people. The Christians believe that all men shall be created equal, but they don't all mean the same thing. The true Christians believe that all men and women are created equal. You see, some Christians believe in the idea of Social Darwinism and I am not talking about Survival of the Fittest. I am talking about the other definition. Some folks that are Christians believe in Racial Superiority, which is sick and wrong. When this Civil War takes place in the 1860s as predicted, I hope that slavery ends because it is an unfortunate fact of life that must be abolished and destroyed," said Sarah. "Now I still have some other questions for you aside from the question about slavery and chauvinism. What would you do to stop this?" asked Will. "Well, in this world, there have been men and women that have been jailed for crusading for justice. Some of them were persecuted. Look at Nathaniel Turner. He fought for justice for slaves. Yet, he was taken down by our authoritarian government. Fortunately, the women

fighters were never jailed yet. My biggest inspirations for
female freedom fighters are Susan B. Anthony and
Sojourner Truth. Susan B. Anthony fought for women's
suffrage and women's rights. Sojourner Truth fought for
justice for the African American females and males. She
fought for African American Justice and because of her a
law against slavery was passed in New York in 1799. As
women, we must fight against the cruel men! As women,
we must fight against the evil government! As women, we
must crusade for justice and fight injustice! As Republicans
and Independents, we must end slavery! We must stop John
Beckinridge from becoming President! We must have a
good President in 1861! We must have somebody who will
treat the women with respect and love! We must have
somebody who will advocate for women! We must have
somebody who will end slavery once and for all! We shall
create a society that is non-bigoted and create a true
Utopian society based on equality and freedom," the prairie
man's wife answered with great zeal and eloquence.

"Who is Abraham Lincoln?" the alien leader asked.
"Now, before I get into his biography, I will tell you that I
only paid him to be my son for a couple of days. Jobe
doesn't know about this. A couple of days ago, in the midst
of the evening Mr. Lincoln came over to my parents' house.
He snuck through the bedroom window and I gave him a
costume that looked like son. He dressed up as Jesse. When
you saw him earlier tonight, he was really dressed in the
costume. If you're wondering where he's going, he's
heading into Illinois. He has an interesting story to tell. I've
been friends – I tell Jobe a fib that we are "cousins" - with
him for an extremely long time. He grew up in Kentucky in
the life of poverty. He wasn't raised in your ordinary Dutch
Colonial or Victorian House. In fact, he wasn't even raised

in a house. He grew up in a small Log Cabin. He freed himself from the life of poverty and became a lawyer. As a lawyer, he would represent the under dogs. He also had many opinions on multiple court cases. He denounced the Supreme Court for many rulings in many court cases. The most recent ruling he denounced was *Scott versus Sanford* ruling. He despised the judge who presided over the case. Not only was he bothered by the rulings on slavery. He also showed anger towards the expansion of slavery. Recently, slavery has expanded to the West and he feels that this movement violated the Missouri Compromise, which clearly limits the expansion of slavery. What really made him feel extremely bothered was when the *Kansas-Nebraska Act* was passed. This act basically supported the expansion of slavery to Western States. Very few people know that my friend wants to abolish slavery. I was told that he wanted slavery gone. He worked as a member for the Illinois House of Representatives. In a couple of years from now he will be running for president. This is going to be an excellent marking on his life, on my life, and on millions of other lives. I know that Abe will fight for justice! I know that he will fight for equality among all races and all kinds! He will help us women fight! Even though he says to the public that he wants to contain slavery, I know in his mind and in his heart, he wants to put an end to the idea and practice of slavery. I also know that he wants to fight for the justice of women because women are often victims of chauvinism and generational household tradition of women being bound to the house. It is a good thing that Mr. Lincoln will be the president because he will fight against injustice. He is the true epitome of a 'true' American! He is the man that honors God and fears him. He believes in this idea of letting nobody looking down at one's youthfulness, but rather in their faith, their spirituality, their conduct, and their purity. He wants every American who is true to Christianity to fight for justice. He wants every American that is good to contain and prevent the spread of slavery! He wants the good Americans to show great pride in their crusade for justice! Now, I said all good things about Abraham Lincoln, but because I don't know him that well, I am not sure if I can trust him. Look at my husband. I've been with him for nearly twenty five years and I knew that he was a slave driver, but yet, he would show a facade of trust, kindness, and benevolence. I thought that my husband was the man to fight for justice when I first got married to him, but he is really here to cause trouble and evil. He is just as evil as my son, unfortunately. I don't think Abraham Lincoln will be like that because he openly demonstrated his 'true' political views. My husband is nothing but a disgusting liar," answered Sarah.

Chapter XII: The Conversation continues with Sarah, and Will and Jobe's first feud

The alien leader and Sarah finished their conversation. The real Jobe is as evil as Satan. He is as deceptive as Serpianto. "It was nice talking to you," said Will. "Oh, thank you. I needed somebody to talk to. It is rare for a woman to have any rights, especially talking rights. You came to this Earth to fight and not to support evil," the prairie man's wife replied. "Do you have any more questions to ask me?" the alien leader asked. "Yes, this is probably going to be a very controversial question, but I request that you listen to me on this one and you answer it. I don't really care about your answer because I like you for who you are as a kind alien. Do you participate in any religion?" asked Sarah.

"No, I don't. I am an Atheist. I don't believe in any deity or any god," answered Will. "Why are you a nonbeliever?" the prairie man's wife asked. "Because I come from a place that was ruled by a Stalinist Dictatorship. If any of us practiced a religion, we would be executed. Granted, I am now the leader of this city, and I will give the citizens freedom of religion and philosophical beliefs as long as it doesn't violate an individual's civil liberties. My fellow aliens don't believe in any religion because for many years they were so used to a spiritless society that it's just the norm," the alien leader answered. "Well, doesn't it seem quite boring being in a nonbeliever society?" asked Sarah.

"No, it's not. It's actually fun. We make our own rules for everything. We have roads that folks go speeding down at five hundred miles per hour. In fact, our city is quite colorful. Every building has a different color. We do not have anything that's generic. Our parks are also beautiful. We may not have any amusement parks, but we do have a city park. It's called Starmos Park. It is more unique than any park on Earth. Now, from where you come from, the tree barks are brown and rugged. We don't have brown tree barks; we have green barks that are made of ivy plants. Now, you guys have green leafy treetops, but we aliens have brown rugged tree tops. Also our ponds are orange colored because of the sand on the bottom; you guys have brown and green water because you have different rocks on the bottom. Now, the thing that we don't have that you guys possess is water. You folks on Earth have an abundance of water, but we Starmos aliens do not have any water. You see we're surrounded by a desert and a huge mountain and range of hills. The citizens in your area have different terrains. You have the East Coast, Plains, Rockies, the West Coast, and the Bayou. You also have different climates. We just have a hot climate year round. My place is more westernized than your place on Planet Earth because all of our buildings are extremely tall. The only building that has a low height is the Alien Estate. I probably know what you're wondering. You're probably thinking,

"Why is the Alien Estate so short when all of the other buildings in the Metropolitan Area of Starmos City so tall and I'll tell you the answer to that question. The Alien Estate is short because of the threats that we've received from this Magic Castle in the place of Debelinaire. To completely answer your question, our World is not boring because we don't believe in Christianity or religion. After all, religion is not the number one thing that is important in life. What is really important in life is your personality and your love to all of mankind? Also, humility is important and modest behavior should be expressed. You don't necessarily have to be frugal and stingy with your money and spending, but you shouldn't' flout it at others and be condescending and nor should you be power-crazy," the alien leader answered.

"You know you bring up pretty good points. I am a Mormon. I've been a Mormon for the past 25 years of my life because I was adopted by a family of that religion. The reason why I asked if your place was boring was because Atheists that I've came across were boring and arrogant. You don't seem like that to me," replied Sarah. "Do you want to know how I met your family?" asked Will. "Sure," the prairie man's wife answered.

"You see, my friend ended up being kidnapped and we had to go to New York City. I met the police commissioner and we ended up going to a place named Flushing Meadows Corona Park. We came across this homeless man who was really a serial killer, who killed over 600 people. He is the biggest Serial Killer in history. I was told that Staten Island was the Gateway to safety. I lunged at the homeless man because he tried to kill my girlfriend, the commissioner, and myself. I found this talking Rock Creature and a waterfall inside of the homeless man's cave that turned into a tunnel to Staten Island. We all headed into the tunnel. There was a bright light. I stared into this luminous Emerald and met God. Instead of seeing the gateway to Staten Island, I saw trouble coming at me. I ended up in this mysterious woodland. This place had quite a bizarre appearance. There was a loud, audible voice. It was the voice of God. He hooked me up to a chain and a ball representing my sin. After that, he tried to send a chain saw blade down to chop me in half and kill me. Fortunately, it cut the chain in half. At that point the chain disappeared and I thought I was free.

I thought it would be good for me to take the path to the Celestial City. Unknowingly I stepped on a patch of leaves and fell through a hole and landed hard on asphalt. I stood up and noticed a huge desert and part of the Grand Canyon. The ground looked parched. So God wanted precipitation to do its part. Severe rain started to fall down and a bunch of hillbillies started to come down. While this rain was taking place, I was being hit by a tornado and struck by lightning. Your husband came along and joined the hillbillies. He seemed quite benevolent to me. I moved off of the asphalt road and that's when I was taken back to the year of 1856. I thought your husband was friendly and helpful. Now he it appears that he is quite unkind because he treats women like they're creatures or second class citizens, and that's not right," the alien leader answered.

"How did you like my husband?" asked Sarah. "He seemed like the nicest man that you would ever meet. He seemed like the holiest of holy. He seemed like a true worshipper of God. He seemed like the perfect man who supported the liberation of slaves," answered Will. Will shook his head. "Do you have any more questions for me?" the prairie man's wife asked. "Yes. What is it like dealing with a husband who acts like a drunken sailor?" the alien leader asked.

"You see my husband is nothing but a two face. One person he will be nice to and the other person he will be malicious and cruel to. I am the one who he's cruel to. My kids support his nasty and arrogant behavior. Every night, he comes home drunk and acts extremely disrespectful. I can't say anything because he's the one that's always bringing in the money. He is basically the bread winner and thinks that it's his prerogative to be an arrogant person. It's not. He thinks that women should often be silenced, but he is wrong. Women should never be silenced. Women are just as important to the American society, or any society, as men. Women deserve the same rights that men have. Women are mistreated in our society. I want to lead a movement that stands up against the drunken animals in this world. I want to lead a movement that fights for equal rights for all men and women. I don't want to live in a world that tolerates hatred towards anybody. I want to live in a world of kindness and benevolence, not malevolence. We must ban alcohol from our society," answered Sarah.

"That's unfortunate that your husband and a lot of the men are cruel and disgusting in their behavior. What a world are you all living in!" asked Will. "I have the answer to that. A world of cold heartedness a world of hatred and a world of malice, but yet we live in a world of hope a fighting world and a world that shows love. The more love we show to God, he will liberate us. The more we accept, the better our world becomes. I didn't tell too many people this, but my husband is nothing but a fundamentalist Mormon. He is also a fake and he's a phony," the prairie man's wife answered. "What other questions do you have for me?" asked Will.

"What time period did you grow up in? What is Stalinism? Who even created the idea and philosophy of Stalinism?" asked Sarah. "Well, like I said earlier, I come from the distant, distant future. I come from the year 2047, even though I was born in 2022. In answer to your question about Stalinism, it is a communist movement that came from the Union of Soviet Socialist Republics (U.S.S.R. for short.) This idea is basically that there's no such thing as freedom of speech, freedom of religion, the right to assembly, or the right to any liberty. We lived in a place where there wasn't such a thing as laissez faire. We were ruled by a government that took away all of our rights. We didn't have any freedom of movement. We were never allowed to leave our city or our dimension. The Starmos Station was only for government officials. If we showed any political dissent towards the government, we would have been shot and throughout the years of there have been many citizens being executed by that evil Cornelius Von Alien. If you want to know about somebody that had an ego, it would have been him. Even though he was related to me, he had nothing but an ego. He was just like your husband. He tricked new comers into thinking that he was a nice gentleman, but he was really a tyrannical dictator. If anybody suspected him of being a dictator, he would send them to a hole that was worse than a gulag. He claimed that he was the emperor of Starmos City and he claimed that he was a fair leader. He was the most arbitrary and unjust authoritarian. He was not an emperor. He was really a tyrant and he tried to ruin the lives of innocent aliens and even humans. He was really influenced by Josef Stalin, who was the dictator of the Soviet Union. He had pictures of Karl Marx in his bedroom. He worshipped that man. If you want to know the biggest tyrant in all of the dimensions of the universe, it would be Cornelius Von Alien, a brute and an unjust, cold blooded alien," answered Will. "What was the Soviet Union?" the prairie man's wife asked.

"Have you ever heard of Russia?" the alien leader asked. "Yes, it's that huge country that spans from the Baltic to the Bering," answered Sarah. "You're a very smart woman. Now, the former Soviet Union was basically Russia," answered Will. "You didn't answer my question. I wanted an explicit explanation," the prairie man's wife replied.

"Well, the Soviet Union is also in your future. It's in your near future. The Soviet Union was a country that was in existence from 1920-1991. This place was founded by a revolutionary, Vladimir Lenin. He fought against the Czarist Government, which was basically a monarchy that was ruled by Czar Nicolas II. Vladimir Lenin destroyed the Czarist government and wanted to cause a bunch of trouble. He was a two face just like your husband. He told the people and citizens of Russia that there would be goodness and equality, and he also stated that there wouldn't be any such thing as poverty. He changed the place into a horrible status. He forced every Russian farmer to give up his or her tools which he kept the tools for himself. He then decided to move the capital from Moscow to Leningrad. He made life in the Soviet Union Hell. In 1930, he died and Josef Stalin took over the Soviet Union. He made Lenin look like an angel. Stalin committed vile and wicked acts. He killed over twenty four million political dissenters. He committed horrible acts of genocide. Unfortunately, he was never put to trial. He was also extremely deceptive. For instance, he would align with the Allied Powers trying to fight against genocide. Meanwhile, he committed those vile acts himself. He took the lives of men, women, and children who hated Stalin's way," the alien leader answered.

"You're saying all this as if it happened, but it didn't happen yet. It is the year 1856. You're talking about the 1920s and 1930s. Will, get with this century. I can see exactly where you're coming from. In our country now, we do some acts that are similar and I feel that these vile acts must be stopped. The acts that we've committed are not done by the government; they're done by cruel slave drivers and white supremacists. There were still some politicians in the government that support slavery like that sick, low life,

Southern Senator John C. Calhoun. Fortunately, he's dead, but his sick ideas still are around. For instance, that evil *Fugitive Slave Act* of 1848. We must stop people like them. We must stop his descendants, who have malicious intentions towards an innocent group of people. The Soviet Union must be the past for you, but it is the future for me. We must destroy the evils of racism and bigotry so that way nations like the U.S.S.R. doesn't exist. As citizens, we must fight for justice! We must fight against the evils of slavery and racism! We must discourage racial superiority! And we must fight for justice for men and women! We must battle the government," replied Sarah.

"I strongly agree with you. Maybe there won't be such a thing as the Soviet Union because of people like you. It is unfortunate that you all live in a world like that. It is unfortunate that you live in a world of injustice, fear, and cruelty. Sarah, it was very nice talking to you," said Will. "You're more than welcome. It is my honor to talk to somebody like you. You're extremely brilliant. But I wonder how you know and use these big words and know all that history. Please tell me," replied Sarah. "You might not be able to understand this, but some call this a learning disability. I call this a learning advancement. I have a disorder called Asperger's Syndrome. Don't tell anybody this because people might think I am crazy," the alien leader said. "Why would you say such a thing?" asked Sarah.

"Remember, we're in a society of bigotry and hatred. Even though, Dorothea Dix fixed the mental institutions, equality is never in existence, they would institutionalize me. If somebody suspects that I have an above average IQ, they would not even think twice about making an investigation. After investigating, they would put me in a mental institution. That is the kind of world that you live in and this is my current location. Along with a society of evil and politics, we also live in a society filled with kindness, action, and fun. For instance, you guys are not bound to roads. You guys can drive your Conestoga where ever you want to go. You live in a world of free movement. You can go any place that is on your mind that particular day. You don't have to do any planning. You're not bound to a single road. The only problem that you have with transportation is that your wagons can't go up any terrain and our Light Speed Cycles are like ATVs. We can fly above the ocean, travel through the Grand Canyon. We live in a world on the move. Also, we don't have this because our dimension is different than your world. For instance, we don't have a whole delta, nevertheless, a river almost as wide as the delta. We only have a small pond as our body of water. You guys could do whatever you want on the delta. You can go up and down the river on a Steam Boat, enjoying Vaudeville Entertainment, Ragtime Entertainment, and gourmet food. You all live the best lives. Some of the things you do, we aliens will never be able to enjoy," answered Will. Sarah reminded him, "Maybe the men. We women are forced to be accompanied by our husbands onto the delta ships. We would be denied entry and service because we're females. For God sakes, we are treated like creatures. We are constantly alienated because we're females. Tell our government to fight against these chauvinist entrepreneurs, who hate females. I bet females can do a lot better than males in this world. Face it, one thing that is clear is that men came from women and women came from men. We can't live in a world without women. Women are needed to build up American society. Who created George Washington? A female. This World wouldn't be existing without God, who created all of mankind," the prairie man's wife replied.

"I totally understand the miseries of the world that you have to encounter, but you can't look at the negativity in life. You have to look at the positivity in life. And as a positive person, you are going to put a positive and a loving vibe out there. Instead of being vengeful towards the folks who hated you and the innocent people, be forgiving. Doesn't your religion or denomination preach forgiveness?" asked Will. "Absolutely, I was taught how to forgive, but one thing that is clear is that I will never forget, I will love all of mankind and God's creatures. I will treat all of God's creatures with love and respect. I regret talking the way I talked earlier. I was a little too extreme. One thing that I will do is fight for justice for women by being kind. If I am kind to government officials and a little outspoken, then people will listen. If I show the path to light instead of darkness, this world might be a perfect society. Will, I strongly appreciate you for teaching me that there is good in the world because, ever since my parents died, I've felt miserable internally," answered Sarah. "You are welcome. You will be fine if you listen," replied Will. He started to push himself up from the rocking chair. He walked slowly on the wooden porch outside of the Saloon. He reached the mat. "Wait," the prairie man's wife exclaimed. "What's wrong?" the alien leader asked. "I have to tell you that you've taught me a lot," answered Sarah. "Thank You."

He pushed the two shutter doors and walked inside of the Saloon. As he walked through the doors, he noticed twelve oil lamps gleaming and making the darkness disappear. As he walked past the doors, the piano player started playing *Yellow Rose of Texas*. James was sitting by the bar drinking a cold mug of Ale and Jobe walked up to

Will from the bar. "Hi, Will. I heard you were talking with my wife. What were you all talking about?" he asked. "What are you implying?" the alien leader asked.

"I mean that you were talking with my wife. Don't you treat women as second class citizens like I do? Women are not worthy of our time. We men have better things to worry about than women," the prairie man answered. "Oh yeah, women are second class citizens," Will said in a sarcastic manner. "Yup, I totally agree with you," replied Jobe. "You're right," the alien leader sarcastically said. "Say, what's your view on slavery?" the prairie man asked. "I think that slaves are victims of a cruel society. The slaves should never be victimized by the evil Southerners and the evil senators and president in our government should never kowtow and curtail to the malevolent slave drivers," the alien leader answered. "Oh, you must be sarcastic with what you're saying. Right?" asked Jobe. "No, I am dead serious. People shouldn't be mistreated in the harshest manner and no one should be treated like property," answered Will. The prairie man's face started turning red and filling up with extreme anger and fury.

"What are you talking about?" he asked in a furious, ferocious manner. "Yeah, I believe that slavery is the most evil and vile act that man can do to one another," the alien leader answered. "How dare you talk to me like that? I am here to help you and you are here to bring me trouble. It's a good thing that I am a supporter for slave drivers. How do I know that you are not one of those slaves who escaped from one of those plantations down South?" the prairie man asked.

"I told your son the same thing. I thought you were here to help me and slaves? I thought that you were against slavery? I thought you supported people like Nathaniel

Turner and Dred Scott. People like you make me sick and you are extremely evil. You ought to be ashamed of yourself for your attitude. I am not a slave because I am not a human and what if I was? What would you do about it? You can't do anything about it because Utah is not even a slave state. For God sakes, it's territory. People like you are as evil as can be! Now, you're probably drunk. It is despicable how drunk people like you support the bullies instead of the victims. Shame on you! You can be zealous in two ways. You can be zealous in the good way in fighting for justice and you can crusade for man kind's rights; or you can be zealous in the evil way. Basically, you can curtail and bow down and support the evils of this world. As productive American citizens, we should be here to stop evil, not condone it. Slavery is sick and wicked. Right now, I would like to shoot you. I wish that somebody can give me a double barrel shotgun because I'd like to shoot people like you. You should go to hell, you little monster! I thought you were kind!" the alien leader answered in an angry manner. Will was furious. Jobe's fists tightened, his lips curled up and his pale face became red with rage. Fury ran through his body. He's about to act as mean as a snake. "Who told you this?" he asked. "Your wife," answered Will.

"When we get into the hotel, I am going to murder her," the prairie man replied. He grunted like an angry boar. "Do you want death to do its part against you?" the alien leader asked. "Oh sure, you can go right ahead and kill me. There'll be serious consequences that will be going against you. When somebody hears the shots of a man from out of town that is not a white man, you will die and it will not be with a bullet to the head. You will get arrested, put to a fair trial, and a jury of white men will convict you in a heartbeat; and there will not be a judge that will think twice about giving you a short stop and a sudden drop and I think you know exactly what I mean," answered Jobe.

"Oh yeah, I know exactly what you mean. You're basically saying, I'll be hung from the gallows, but you all will have to catch me first," replied Will. "Oh, we'll catch you. Some way, somehow, somewhere. You'll eventually catch up to us. Besides, you will eventually die. Death shall do its part against all men, women, and animals," the prairie man said. "I don't know about that," the alien leader replied. "What the hell are you talking about?" asked Jobe.

"You often use the H-word very easily. And you know what I mean by that. You claim to be so holy. You claim to be this excellent, religious Mormon, but all you do is go to Church. Being present in front of God, does not get you into heaven. I may be an Atheist, but I know a lot about theology. I know that God and Jesus are omnipotent and omnipresent. I know the ways to get to Heaven. I would have been more Godly to all men and women whether he or she is white, black, green, yellow, red, or pink. I am accepting to all races and all kinds. You are not! Your attitude is disgusting and atrocious. You are nothing but a walking facade. And the reason why I am so angry is because you treat minorities in the most evil way. You probably love John Beckinridge. I hate people like Beckinridge! He is the most evil man that has ever walked the face of this Earth. He has a vendetta against all minorities. He probably treats women like crap! Jobe, I am surprised by your attitude. And you! You lie like an idiot. Remember, earlier tonight when that faerie from the Celestial City came down? Well, guess what? You didn't care to see him. You just acted like a quirky introvert.

Shame on you! You are just as evil as my cousin Cornelius Von Alien!" answered Will.

"You know something. I'm not afraid of you. We Mormons will come to destroy you, Atheists. You think who the hell you are. You think that you're some sort of hot shot when you're not. You think that I have a Superiority complex when I do not. I am not above the law. I have to obey the laws of the land that was created by me! You are the most belligerent man I've ever met! For God sakes, you think who the hell you are and you are here to cause trouble. Like I said earlier, you think that you're so holy when you are not. You are nothing but a fraud that has fallacious beliefs. You are sick! You deserve to eat excrement," replied Jobe. Will shrugged his shoulders and started snickering in a sarcastic manner.

"Oh, you think I deserve to eat excrement. You are denying that you have a superiority complex. No, not to you. You are nothing but a piece of garbage that should go to hell. You are as stupid as can be because I do not intend to be holy. You didn't talk to that faerie from Heaven for long. You just asked him a self- centered question. 'Oh, what are my chances of going up to heaven', you asked. Well, I have the perfect answer for you; negative one billion. That faerie was here to talk to me because he needed to tell me something quite important. He basically told me about my chances of going to Heaven in a true way. He only told you that you had a 110% chance of going to Heaven so he can butter you up. He only based that answer because you go to Church a lot. That is probably to confess to the preacher about your sins. You claim that you're in love with Sarah and that you give up your life for her. Meanwhile, you are a self-centered bastard, who just gets himself drunk all the time. I bet that you don't even go to Church. You probably tell your wife that so that way you can shut her up. You probably go to the Saloon with your friends to get even more drunk! That is ridiculous! They ought to ban alcohol from this society because that's what is ruining all of your brains. You come home drunk and you commit violent behavior. How dare you! If you claim you have all the guts in the world, why don't you go to the gallows post and hang yourself in town! You are a low life, and you are nothing but a Social Darwinist," he said in anger.

"Really? I am a Social Darwinist? Shame on you because you're a piece of dung. You should be ashamed of your attitude. You are an Atheist and I should've known because I'd refuse to associate myself with Atheists like you. You hate people like me who are here to cause trouble. For God sakes, you have a vendetta towards the white men. Right now, I have many choices. I could take you, fetter you, flog and pickle you, and sell you as a slave. I could also bring you to the local constable because I could report you as a slave and I would have to do that by law because of the *Fugitive Slave Act.* I could send you to the prison and that place is not pretty. It is quite ugly in there. I could do whatever I want to you. If I want to murder you, I can murder you. So, I have many choices. I'd prefer not to go through with any of these choices because I don't want to hurt you because you are a bizarre looking creature, who looks like a monster from another planet. If you are going to act insolent with me, I shall go through with my plan of taking your life. I liked you when I first met you, but I think your attitude is maniacal. You basically act like an egomaniac and you think who the hell you are. You think you can come to this planet and adulterate us with the garbage from Starmos City," the prairie man argued.

Will stopped him. "You know something? I just want to end this. This is terrible. Even though you're wrong and I'm right, your attitude is sickening. I don't feel like fighting. Unlike, you I am benevolent. This battle is over because it doesn't make any sense fighting this. Fighting is for folks with malice intent and fighting is for world class idiots. In any place, world, universe, or even dimension, fighting will keep you stationery or move you backwards. Peace will move you forward and it will make you travel many leagues in one second," the alien leader replied.

"Yeah, you keep saying that," Jobe said sarcastically. Will walked away. He went up to the piano man, who is dressed in a dapper suit. He's wearing a yellow striped buttoned-down shirt and teal pants. He has a handle bar mustache as facial hair. He has brown hair and as he played, he would always entertain people with a smile. He had a black, ragtime, upright piano with a mirror. He wears circular specs so he can see the keys. His name is Carter, the good ol' ragtime player. The alien leader walked up to him. "What's your name?" he asked. "You can call me Carter. I've played for this saloon for many years," the ragtime piano player answered. "What song are you playing?" asked Will. "The *Yellow Rose of Texas*," answered Carter. Will like it. "Play some more."

Chapter XIII: Say "no" to Violence

The ragtime piano player continued serenading his guests with good old American tunes. He started playing the *Armed Forces Medley*. The surrounding environment has a cheery vibe. Everyone is now dancing and singing to his ragtime tunes. Some were even going as far as clanging their bottles and mugs of ale. Everyone enjoyed the music except for Jobe and James. After the piano player finished his serenade for that Great American tune, he asked, "Does anyone want to hear any more tunes?"

"Well, we don't know too many tunes for ragtime. Ask this guy over in the corner," one of the men answered. "Will, what song do you want me to play for you?" asked Carter. "Can you play me the *Maple Leaf Rag*?" the alien leader asked. "Who wrote that?" the ragtime piano player asked. "Scott Joplin. Here I'll play it for you on my a-Phone," answered Will. He started playing it. While he played the song, everyone in the saloon mingled. The song concluded. "Oh, I've heard that song. That is a timeless classic. I've heard this in 1982. Oh damn, I just incriminated myself that I came from the future," replied Carter. "You know, I'm also from the future," the alien leader said. "What are you talking about? I thought you were a runaway slave," the ragtime piano player asked. "No way. Why would you insinuate that I'm a runaway slave?" asked Will. "Because you have blue skin. You're not Caucasian," answered Carter. "Well, do you support slavery?" the alien leader asked.

"Absolutely not! Why would I support an act that is absolutely cold and barbaric? Now, I know that there are some that claim that they don't support it, but they really curtail and honor it. I am dead serious when I'm saying this.

I hate slavery! It is the most evil thing man can do," answered Carter. "It is evil that we live in a world that allows and offers support to it," the alien leader replied. "Now, let's get off of the slavery subject because that's a very controversial subject. Maybe, we don't have different views, but most of the men in this saloon are supporters of slavery. What brought you over to this period in time?" the ragtime piano player asked. "Well, to make a long story short, God brought me over here. It is a quite funny story," answered Will. "What year did you come from?" asked Carter. "2047. I was born in 2022," the alien leader answered.

"I came from 2012, but I was born in 1954," replied Carter. He started to play the song on the ragtime piano. Everyone stood up from the barstools and jumped up from their tables. Most of the guests at the saloon wondered what he was playing, but it seemed to be their favorite song. Most of the men were dancing. The waiters ran down the hard wooden floors and started spinning their serving trays. Despite half of the crowd being drunk, they were able to dance. The ragtime piano player concluded the song; everyone applauded. The darkness of saloon illuminated. Seen in the distance was the angel that came down from heaven. It was the size of faerie. This angel flew in front of the alien leader. Everyone didn't know this angel was present except for Will. "Hey, Will! How are you?" the angel asked. "Who are you?" the alien leader asked. "I'm Enkel. Remember me, I saw you earlier. How's everything going?" the angel from heaven asked. "Good," answered Will.

"Now, I am sure you know the reason why I am here. I am here to tell you your chances of going up to Heaven. They just increased because you chose not to fight with Jobe. You have a thirty five percent chance of seeing God's Celestial City and you're right now on the road to that place," said Enkel. "Say, what are the chances of the others going to Heaven?" the alien leader asked. "Well, it depends on what you're talking about. Now, there are three ways that you can have some chance of going to Heaven- through church, fighting for justice, or being benevolent. Now, Church will give you a 10% chance of going to that place. Fighting will justice will give you a 60% chance and being benevolent will give you 30% chance. Church is a minor thing. In order to reach the Celestial City, you must have a 90% chance and then the Board of the Lord will look at how you behaved on Earth and they might give you a passport to Heaven," the angel answered. "Now, just wondering, I do want Jobe to go to Heaven, but what are his chances?" asked Will.

"That is confidential, but I am allowed to tell you. It's my prerogative to tell you what other man's chances are to going up to Heaven. He has a 5% chance of going to be honest. His son has -1,000,000,000 (negative one billion) percent chance of even seeing that place. Basically, the father will remain on Earth and the son will be on the road to Hell unless he changes his view on slavery. I don't think he'll do that though," answered Enkel. "Say, did you hear any of the ragtime songs this piano man was playing?" the alien leader asked.

"Oh, absolutely. God gives me the powers to do whatever I want whenever I want as long it doesn't violate the Ten Commandments. I hear everything and see everything that goes on and takes place in the World. I can even read a pupils' mind. I can even tell what you're thinking right now," the angel answered. "What do you think I am thinking?" asked Will. "You're thinking when is that piano player going to play my song. You're also thinking about your chances of going up to Heaven," answered Enkel.

"You are totally right. Now, can you tell me what Jobe and James are thinking?" the alien leader asked. "Sure, they're so drunk that they could barely even think. They must've drunk about six mugs of ale. I can tell that the father is going to beat up his wife and the son is going to sit there and watch," the angel answered. "How do you know that?" asked Will.

"Because think of it; God knows everything that goes on. Do you know how he knows it? Because he sends folks like me who have the skills of a prophet to come down and predict what happens. The prophets are always right because they're sent down from God in the form of human beings. I live with God. They live over here with you Earthlings. They predict everything that happens according to scripture. Now, I must continue on with my journey. It was nice talking to you and I hope to see you soon, but before I say *'Bon Voyage'*, we must make one thing clear. Now Jobe and his son are drunk. I warn you. Do not interact with them because they have it in for you; and also, protect Sarah because I am afraid for her," answered Enkel. "Well, aren't you here to protect vulnerable people like her?" the alien leader asked.

"Yes and No. I am here to make sure that there isn't any violence, but I can't control a man or woman's actions. Remember, *Man has free Will*. They can do whatever they want whenever they want, but one thing that is clear is that everything you do has a consequence. So, basically, if you do something wrong, you are held accountable and responsible for that action. If you do something right, you are also held accountable and responsible. It won't be in the form of a painful consequence. Doing things right shall bring you good results. Also, remember something else. There is such thing as the Fruit of the Spirit that very few men or women have. I think you have the potential to have this. There are a couple of components that you lack," the angel answered. "What is the Fruit of the Spirit? What are the components that I lack?" asked Will. "Well, the Fruit of the Spirit clearly states that mankind must have love, joy, peace, patience, kindness, gentleness, and self-control. The components that you lack are peace, kindness, and self-control," answered Enkel.

"Well, what kindness do I lack? What makes you say I don't have much self-control? And what makes you say I am not peaceful?" the alien leader asked. "Well, first of all, you are trying to tell Jobe off because of his attitude and you are not supposed to be doing that. You are basically being a hypocrite because you claim that he has a superiority complex, when all of mankind has a superiority complex. I know you're an alien because you come from another planet, but you do have a gender. Second of all, you don't have any form of self-control. You know what Sarah goes through. She is a battered woman! Her husband is cruel to her and when she explicitly tells you not to tell anyone, you open your big mouth and you do the exact opposite as she tells you. That is terrible because you clearly knew that she was a battered woman. Thirdly, you're not peaceful. You are like a little war-monger or hawk. I am not talking about the hawk in terms of the animal. I am basically stating that you like to cause trouble and ruckus. You lack those three components. Maybe if you change your behavior I'll tell you differently. That is the clear truth. The truth might cause you to wind up in Satan's lair or, it can set you free. It's basically your choice," the angel answered.

"Not to sound like I am questioning the angel or the extension of God, but I am basically telling you this. Not to sound violent or belligerent. You are saying things that are incorrect. I never intended to start a war with Jobe. He was actually trying to be belligerent towards me. I am very peaceful with individuals. Second of all, I do have self-control because if I didn't have any self-control, I would have probably lunged at that sick ragamuffin and kill him. Thirdly, he is the most malicious man. How do you expect me to be nice to such a man with evil intent or malice? He is here to do evil in this World. For God sakes, he supports evil slave drivers like his son. Isn't there something wrong with that? Then, he claims that he's so holy when he's really not. He is nothing but a walking facade," Will replied in an angry manner. "Excuse me, but you shouldn't talk to me like that. I am the one who will be determining your fate in the afterlife. I am sorry that you had to go through all that, but according to God, those are the three components that you lack. You have a huge window to improve yourself. Now, if you don't improve yourself, your chances of reaching Heaven will stay the same. That won't be good. If you do improve, you shall make it to the Celestial City of God. I want to tell you this, Jobe is the worst husband in all of the world and dimensions, but the point that I am trying to make with you that you're apparently not getting, is that you shouldn't lower yourself down to his level. Remember, who's the one that has the higher chance of reaching Heaven? I think I know the answer to that one. It must be you, Will. You'll be the one going up to Heaven. So, don't lower yourself down or stoop down to his level. Thank you for talking with me. I rest my case," answered Enkel.

"Wait! Don't go! I have to tell you something else," replied Will. "What would that be?" the angel asked. "I am sure you remember about what happened today between me and God, right?" the alien leader asked. "Yes, what do you need to tell me?" asked Enkel. "I must say that I am apologetic for my behavior. I should've never thought that I was above God. My ego must've kicked in. That's probably why I am going through this situation. I am not complaining about the situation. I am accepting of it, but I am sorry if I caused any trouble," the alien leader answered.

The angel's gold color became brighter. It changed from gold to platinum. Fortunately, he didn't blind the alien leader or anybody at the saloon. Besides, all of the patrons at the saloon are drunk and in a state of oblivion. How do you expect them to understand what the heck they're doing?" asked Will. "Well, I don't think they know what they're doing because you're absolutely right. More importantly, I will tell God that you're apologetic. I am extremely happy that you're sorry and that you finally held yourself accountable for your actions. This fills me up with elation and ecstasy. Thank you for telling me that, but just remember one thing, and this will be clear, if you are not true to your word, I might as well not tell God this. So, now, there's one question that I must ask and are you true to your word? You can take your time to answer this question," the angel said.

"Sure, give me some time and I'll have an answer," the alien leader replied. "Okay, you can take your time. I'll wait," said Enkel. His brightness became darker. "Why are you turning dark?" asked Will. "Because I was so excited that you held yourself accountable," the angel answered. "Are you a prosecutor or angel?" the alien leader asked.

"Well, I am an angel who believes that individuals should be held accountable for their actions and that individual should himself or herself accountable for their actions," answered Enkel.

"That sounds totally absurd. First of all, you didn't answer my question. I shall reiterate what I just asked. *Are you an angel or are you a prosecutor?* I don't think that's hard to answer. Remember, it's either one or the other," the alien leader replied. "Yup, that will get you into Heaven quickly," the angel said sarcastically. "You didn't answer my question," replied Will. "What was that question?" asked Enkel.

"I just asked you the question and you don't remember the question already. You must be trying to question my authority. How dare you take that kind of attitude with me! You ought to be ashamed of yourself," the alien leader answered. "You know something. You brought up some pretty good points. We should've never had this fight in the first place. Now, to keep you quiet the answer that you want to hear is that I am a prosecutor, but the truth of the matter is that I am not. I am a normal angel like all of the angels up in Heaven. And the words that I spew out are not my words. Those words are God's words. I am God's messenger," replied Enkel.

"You know something, you're right. I should've never tried to make a fight with you. It doesn't make any sense starting fights because fights don't get anyone anywhere. He who fights moves one hundred steps backward and he who is peaceful and benevolent moves one thousand steps forward. I know that I sound like a hypocrite for saying that, but whatever I am saying is true. Forget about the question that I've asked you because that question doesn't make any sense whether or not you're a prosecutor or an angel. You are clearly an angel. You may not sound like one, but then again the one that butters you up and acts extremely nice to you is your worst enemy. He who tells you the truth and beats you when you're wrong is your best friend because, that individual is here to help you. That man or woman is not out to get you. So, I am sorry for acting belligerent towards you and from now on, I will be peaceful," said Will.

"Thank you. Now, I just received a text message from God to my brain. This basically stated that your chances of going up to Heaven have increased by ten percent. Now, you are at a 45% chance of seeing God. Now, keep going on the right road and don't slip off track. Be peaceful, but don't be a softy. The reason why is because big, husky men or women will come after you. Continue on the road fighting for justice and you shall be blessed. Fight for evil, you shall be cursed and ruined for life and eternity," replied Enkel.

The angel levitated from the ground. He started to glow brighter and levitate higher. Eventually, he reached the ceiling. He disintegrated and disappeared. "Who were you talking to?" the ragtime piano player asked. "I was talking to an angel that came down from Heaven," the alien leader answered. "That sounds crazy. What are you talking about?" asked Carter.

"Well, do you want me to tell you the story how I ended up here?" asked Will. "Absolutely, tell me everything that happened," the ragtime piano player answered. "Okay, you see. I come from an alien city and I just so happen to be the leader of that city. I was not affiliated with any religion or theology. So, I fell into a deep sleep and then I met God. I was in disbelief of meeting him because I was asleep. I knew that it was my reality. I was hooked up to a chain and a ball because I sinned so many times. Fortunately, he cut the chain and the ball. Then, I started running down the wrong trail and I ended up over here on Planet Earth in 1856. There's much more to my story, but you get the point though," the alien leader replied.

"Yes, basically, you met God and he told you that you were going to go to Hell, and so you wanted to redeem yourself and he took you back over into this time period," the ragtime piano player said. "You're exactly correct. You're right on the money! You are a genius! You must be very intuitive or you must know my every move," replied Will. "I'm just a musical genius. I didn't know you're every move, nor did I follow it, nor do I care to follow it. Just based on what you said, I can easily tell what you're doing or what you've done," said Carter. "Well, that's amazing. Do you have some sort of telepathic powers?" the alien leader asked.

"Now, why would you think a normal human being would have telepathic powers? Maybe the prophets in Bible times did, but I sure don't. I am just an ordinary ragtime piano player. I am not a fortune teller or a prophet. Now, I don't have any special gifts in that field, but one thing that is certain is that I am good on the piano and that has nothing to do with this. Any man can have the capability for intuition. It is true that we live in a world that is filled with questions and eventually, there shall be answers to those questions. Mankind has to be instinctive and think outside of the box all the time to find the answers to those questions," the ragtime piano player answered. "Good point. Thanks for the tip. Now, can you do me a quick favor and play the original rags," replied Will. "Absolutely. Anything for you, buddy," said Carter.

The ragtime piano player started to play *Original Rags by Scott Joplin*. Everyone in the saloon disregarded the fact this song except for Will. 3/4 of the patrons of the bar are drunk or their minds must be fogged up with cigars. As the song concluded, the prairie man and his son grabbed the alien leader. Will started kicking the two. He kicked those two mean prairie folks in the stomach. "Carter, help me," he said. The ragtime piano player continued playing his song. He was so immersed that he didn't even hear the surrounding environment. James and Jobe grabbed Will by his legs and started pulling him. The song concluded.

Everyone in the bar started vomiting and acting crazy. Some were loopy. The place looked like a nut house. The alien leader was eventually dragged out of the saloon past the shutter doors. "Jobe, what are you doing? Have you lost your mind?" he asked. "Absolutely not, I am doing what I am supposed to do. We drunks don't stand by morons like you. You think that you can talk to my wife, especially about me!? That's despicable and what you did was a complete atrocity. I am dragging you out of this bar because I didn't want you monopolizing this guy's time.

Also, you were acting like a fool. You probably got drunk," the prairie man answered angrily. "Who are you to drag me? When was I ever acting like a fool? When did I get drunk? When did I drink anything?" the alien leader asked. Jobe stopped dragging him because he fell to the ground and started to vomit. Will pushed himself back up from the ground and Jobe did the same thing shortly after him. "You don't seem quite drunk to me; you appear to be sober," said Will.

"Well, I am not sober, I am extremely drunk. For God sakes, I drank six to eight large mugs of ale. The reason why we dragged you was because you were talking to my wife and when you're at the saloon, men are forbidden to talk to women. Secondly, you were acting like a fool with that piano player. You're not worthy to be in the presence of an excellent piano player, especially a ragtime one. Thirdly, you had four mugs of beer. Fourthly, you are nothing but a pathological liar," the prairie man replied.

"Excuse me, you seem quite sober to me to even talk like that, but then again, you talk like the Biblical folk when you are sober, but when you're drunk you actually talk intelligent. Let me just tell you this! I didn't have a single drink. Why would I have a drink when there are people around me acting like idiots and vomiting? I don't think I want to drink with stupid people and I would never even have an alcohol beverage because I don't believe in drinking alcohol and getting drunk. You should be ashamed of yourself because you also said that I was acting like a fool because you were the one that was clearly drunk. In addition to that, you thought that I was acting like a fool in front of that ragtime piano player. We both had common interests. I am very good at the piano and he's also very good at the piano. We also love ragtime and Western piano music. Now, don't say any erroneous statements about me. You look at the splinter in the other man's eye when you have a huge log in your eye. You're so drunk that you probably don't know what's going on," the alien leader said.

"What are you talking about with the log in my eye and the splinter in your eye? That's a stupid phrase and you didn't even use it in the right context. For God sakes, the phrase means that you shouldn't look at the bad act that the other man committed when you have committed the worst act. You think that I've done evil when you've done more evil. So, you should be ashamed of your attitude because your attitude is malicious. So, shut the hell up. I know the place where you belong. That would be Satan's Lair. You think that you're such hot shot when you're really not. I know the reason why you want to talk to my wife. You want to take her away from me. So, you were basically flirting with her! That's sick and I can talk to the Town Government about putting you in jail. Shame on you! Right now, I have every right to kill you," Jobe was furious in his drunkenness. Will was angry but cautious.

He remembered what Enkel told him. "First of all, I didn't do anything to your wife. I was never even thinking about anything in the flirtatious way. Besides, why would I want your old wife? I would want somebody that's 25. How can you accuse me of doing such a crime? Do you think I am as evil as Young? I don't think so. You try and turn me into an evil monster when I never did anything with any intent of harm. You are the harmful one! Also, you have the guts to say that I have the log in my eye and you have the splinter in your eye. No, no - it's the other way around. You are the one with the log in your eye and I have the splinter in my eye. Do you understand smart one? I own up to my wrong doings and what makes it even more wrong is that you don't own up to your own terrible actions. You always like to feel sorry for yourself.

Then, at home, you beat your wife in a senseless and cruel manner. That is bad enough alone. AND you do that almost every night. You come home from work and you decide to get yourself drunk. Smart move." Will was on a roll. "That's despicable! Your attitude is horrifying and evil. Somebody ought to shank you because you deserve that! I am not evil like anybody. I already have a girlfriend and if you think I am a polygamist, I am not. Polygamy is evil and folks who do that also deserve the short stop and sudden drop! That has nothing to do with this conversation, but I knew what you were thinking in your head. You were trying to compare me to a polygamist. To me, your attitude leaves me with no other choice, but it is necessary to call you this name! You're nothing; but a World Class Idiot, who doesn't belong in this society. You are the epitome of evil and instead of your mind being made up of brain cells it is made up of cells from alcohol. Alcohol poisons your mind. Before you know it, you will get older and become worse if you keep drinking. That's even if you make it to your later years in life. Alcohol is probably destroying your liver," said Will. The prairie man vomited again.

"How dare you even talk to me like that? Who are you to talk to me like that? I was staying with my family enjoying the perfect conclusion to a vacation with my family, enjoying the rain that they haven't seen in quite a long time. Then, I notice you flying in a tornado. I do the benevolent and Christian thing and I come and help you. I take you on board the covered wagon and bring you to South Salt Lake with my family, but then you talk with my wife, who is nothing but a pathetic wash woman. She is a consistent gossiper. She plants thoughts in your head and you try to flirt with her and make her your wife! You are such an arrogant thing. You're not even a human being. All you do is gossip, gossip, and gossip," he argued.

The alien leader clenched his fists in anger. "How dare you even accuse me of doing such a thing? Your attitude is the most evil attitude! You're telling me that I am flirtatious when I really have a girlfriend. The only reason why I talked with your wife was because you chauvinists think who you are. You deny women rights because you can. Well, guess what? In my society, we don't do that. We used to do that. We used to even enslave women. I couldn't stand seeing that. When I killed Cornelius Von Alien, the former tyrant, I made a vow to improve our society and I fought against the evils of slavery. When the former regime of Cornelius was challenged by the other dimensions over this controversial subject, the government would deny that they enslaved women and made them work. The old government claimed that they paid the alien women to work when they didn't pay them a single dime. That is sickening! I vowed to end slavery and when I became the leader, I liberated all prisoners and all women. Starmos City was nothing but a city under a Stalinist Dictatorship except it was ruled by Cornelius. To me, Stalinism and Communism were evil practices in running the government. Women are victims of government and chauvinist pigs like you. So, shut the hell up and treat your wife with respect!" he replied.

Jobe looked at his wife and then Will. He loosened his fists and a sarcastic smug appeared on his face. "You were - oh so right. I guess I should be apologetic for what I did to you and my wife. I guess my actions were so wrong. I shouldn't have treated my wife like that. I guess my actions were totally inappropriate," he said. He snickered after he said that. Will glared at him. "Do you think I am stupid? Those words are not even genuine. You are good at being sarcastic. I can't stand the ones that are sarcastic. Your behavior was and still is abominable. Even though I am an Atheist, who practices some form of the Christian philosophy, I do have every right in the world to hate you. I will forgive you if you ask for forgiveness. It doesn't seem to me that you're owning up to your actions. If you think that you're wrongdoings of mistreating your wife is acceptable, it's totally not. In fact, it is completely unacceptable. Your attitude is wrong. You deserve death to do its part against you. You have an attitude of superiority.

In addition to mistreating your wife, you think slavery is okay; it's not. Again, slavery is the most evil thing that man can do and slave drivers deserve to be shot. I wish Nathaniel Turner was alive today to see your evil. He would probably spill your guts. I may sound evil when I am talking like that, but I came into all of the dimensions and the world so I can stop evil. God brought me over here to fight against injustice! You are a fake; a fraud; a phony. If anybody should be ashamed of themselves, it would be you! You're the most evil human I've ever met," the alien leader replied. Jobe was listening and trying to think of a good reply. "How dare you have the audacity to talk to me like that? This gives me another reason to bring you to Court or, even kill you. To all men, death shall do its part, but to some, death will come early; and I think you're the one who will be the victim of an early death. Now, I want you to hold yourself accountable," said Jobe. "Well, unlike you, I do hold myself accountable for my wrongdoings. I do not have the intents of malice. What I must say is this; I am sorry for threatening you. I am sorry for threatening to spill your guts. That sounds gross in my eyes. I know that I would not like to die like that. I am sorry for sounding so disrespectful to you because I do not have the intent to do such a thing," the alien leader replied.

"I don't believe that for one second. I don't believe that apology. It's just another one of your misleading statements. You love twisting the truth. That's one thing that I know. Let me just tell you this. And if you think I have to hold myself accountable for my actions, think twice. I think that you deserve to be punished. I'm not going to punish you. Instead, I am going to do the more Christian thing and bring you to the hotel. And I know what you're also thinking. You're probably thinking why I am so mean to

Sarah. Well, I am not mean to her. I am perceived as mean man, but there's one phrase that is universally accepted around the World. *Women and Children should be seen and not heard,"* the prairie man said.

The alien leader's blue skin started turning red. His hands clenched into fists. An emotion of fury ran through his body. The prairie man snickered. "What are you going to do? Are you going to beat me up?" he asked. All of a sudden, Enkel came down from Heaven. Will turned around. "Do I have the permission to beat him up?" he asked.

"Well, based on the terms of the situation because he's trying to intimidate you, I would beat him. If he's threatening you, you have the right to beat him and even kill him. Despite, the commandment of *Thou shalt not commit murder*; there are exceptions to that rule. If somebody is threatening you or intimidating you, you have every right to defend yourself even if that means to kill him. You may be penalized in a court of law, but you won't be penalized by God," the angel answered.

"Well, you didn't answer my question. Let me reiterate what I just asked. *Do I have the permission to beat him up*?" the alien leader asked. "Yes, it's justifiable under those conditions. If hc threatens you or intimidates you, lethal force or violence is applicable. Say 'no' to violence, when he is not doing any violence towards you or somebody that is vulnerable. You should never have it in you to be violent," answered Enkel. "Okay, thank you," replied Will. "You're more than welcome. And by the way, your chances of going to Heaven increased from 45% to 50%. You made a very wise decision for consulting me before acting violent. Thank you very much for doing that," the angel said. "See you later," the alien leader replied.

"No, actually, I'll see you later," said Enkel. The angel disappeared. "Who were you talking to?" asked Jobe. "Oh, I was talking to an angel of God. A messenger that speaks the Word of God better than you, as he's a genuine messenger and you're not," answered Will. He turned around. All of a sudden, the prairie man lunged at him. Fighting this prairie man is going to be as hard as David fighting Goliath. The alien leader fell to the ground.

"What are you doing?" he asked. "Oh nothing, death shall do its part on you. I am tired of you having the access and ability to talk to God; and I will never be able to talk to God unless I make it up to Heaven. That's even if I'm able to go up to Heaven. I'll probably never be able to see God because of my alcoholism and my lies," answered Jobe. He started to choke Will. Will kicked him in the face and he fell back. The alien leader ran from the scene of the fight in the saloon. He ran up to the bar tender.

"Do you guys have any 22 calipers over here?" he asked. "No, but we do have a couple of double barrel shotguns," the bartender answered. "Hurry up! Somebody's threatening me and trying to kill me. I just escaped him," replied Will. "Okay, I'll do that," the bar tender said. He ran to the back of the kitchen and asked the head chef, the owner of the saloon, for the location of the double barrel. While, he is retrieving the double barrel, the alien leader is in a nervous state of mind. His heart is racing and he is sweating bullets. Finally, he was given the gun and he ran out of the saloon and pointed the gun at Jobe.

"Go ahead shoot me. You'll see where you end up. On the gallows, on your road down to hell," Jobe said. The alien leader shot him twice in the head and twice in the stomachs. These were the shots heard around the world. This will change the town forever.

Chapter XIV: Sarah and Will are arrested and interrogated by Sheriff Joe for the Crime of Capital murder

It is now the crack of dawn and the alien leader shot Jobe in cold blood. Was it defense or murder? That will be the question that will be answered throughout this chapter. The four shots caused all of the seventy five townspeople to come out of their homes. The folks from the outskirts of town heard the noises of the four loud shots of the double barrel. The females before the males noticed the bloody crime scene. Some of the females fainted. While others returned back to their home to get their black gowns and pretend to weep. Some of the faces remained stone cold while the other females broke down into tears.

The husbands comforted their wives by holding them. Some of the other husbands were horrified by the gruesome scene. The only male that wasn't crying was Will Von Alien. He started breathing heavily. Sarah disregarded her husband's death and made like nothing ever happened. Some of the men at the bar ran out while others were so drunk and in a state of oblivion and they didn't even know the bloody scene that had just taken place outside of the saloon. To add insult to injury, James, the son of the deceased man, didn't even know what took place because he was too drunk.

The universally accepted fact is that the man is dead and it is quite sad that the man had such an abrupt and sudden end to his life. Questions are being raised in the minds of the individuals who actually care. Some are wondering whether or not this death was an intentional homicide, a suicide, a homicide because of self-defense, or even a justifiable homicide.

Others have been overtaken with emotion that they can't even think straight. Sarah just continued rocking on the chair on the porch of the saloon. She didn't show any emotion. She just continued staring into space, not even giving a care about the dead man's body. There are lines of citizens waiting to see the dead body and pay their respects. Everyone joined to see the dead body except for the alien leader, James, the bar tender, and the drunken male patrons of the saloon. After five minutes, the townspeople finished paying their respects to the dead body.

Everyone formed a semicircle around the deceased prairie man and started singing *Amazing Grace*. As the emotional song was playing, the women dressed in black wept and they showed true emotion. After the song concluded, the preacher from the town placed frankincense on the body.

"I hereby bless this body. May he go up to Heaven and rest in peace. It is sad seeing such a Great Mormon die like this. I am not a coroner or the mortician. I am going to recommend that this body is reviewed by the mortician, but I believe this was a homicide and it doesn't seem like a justifiable homicide to me," he said.

The alien leader walked up to the body and carried it. The blood from the prairie man's deceased corpse started to drip on his hands. "Yes, it is sad that this man died. I believe this homicide is justifiable. Unfortunately, I noticed a fight that was caused by this belligerent soul and he caused trouble and he sadly caused his own demise. Not to sound like I am defaming the dead man or disrespecting any member of the deceased. Some people have an inclination to cause their own death. This man fell victim to that inclination. To those who think he's a victim of an unjustifiable homicide, they are completely mistaken. To those who think that he's this innocent man, who died from violence, they have a false impression. I knew this man very well. He lived by violence because every night, he would come home drunk and he would beat the hell out of his wife. This man's primary cause of death were two bullets to the head and two to the stomach. His evil caused that. This man was a supporter of slavery and chauvinism and his malicious behavior caused his own death. So, death should've done its part against him. Not to say that he deserved it, but his vile attitude caused him to die," he said.

The preacher was listening to this than replied "How dare you say such a thing! It is extremely wrong and evil. You should be ashamed of yourself!" "Why would you say such a thing?" the alien leader asked. "Because your attitude is arrogant! You should definitely be ashamed of yourself because you think that the death of this man is not a big deal. You think that people dying in the streets is okay when it's really not. You think that a man dying from four huge bullets is acceptable and justifiable when it is clearly not! I wish I was God because if I was God, I would send you to Hell. When you meet him, he'll see how you're behaving and you shall be sent to Satan's lair. I have the authority to do this. I'll make you a Son of Perdition in my church, even though you're not part of my church. I'll deny you access to the church of the Latter Day Saints. We Mormons have better individuals than you. You know what I can also do, I'll return you to your slave master, or even better yet, I'll send you to Sheriff Joe. That Sheriff will have you hung before you even go to trial and I hope that you *do* get hung because once he kicks that wooden stool, death shall do its part against evil bastards like you," the preacher answered.

Sheriff Joe started to walk in the distance. He wore brown, leather boots, size 42 blue jeans, a brown vest with a white button down shirt. His silver grey hair shined in the South Salt Lake sun. His 9 millimeter is concealed in his left pocket. He had a spherical body shape. He drew his gun and pointed it at Will. He finally arrived at the gruesome scene. "Whoever has the double barrel, I demand you drop it and you place your hands in the air because you're under arrest," he said. The alien leader dropped the double barrel. The preacher walked up to the county sheriff.

"What seems to be wrong?" the sheriff asked. "One of the followers of my faith was brutally murdered and I believe this slave and this woman sitting on the rocking chair killed him. I don't know why. The slave is stating that his homicide was justifiable because the dead man would always come home drunk and beat his wife senselessly. I believe that's his wife sitting on the rocking chair over there," the preacher answered. "You two are coming with me for questioning," said Sheriff Joe. He pointed at Will and Sarah. The prairie man's wife placed her hands against the wall and the sheriff handcuffed her. Meanwhile, the alien leader approached the sheriff. "Why should I be arrested, sir?" he asked. "Because, I feel that you were the man behind the gun. You, therefore caused this man's death," the sheriff answered. "I didn't cause this man's death. He caused his own death," argued Will.

"Silence! Because you're a slave you should be charged with the crime of capital murder, and you will therefore face the death penalty. You will be detained at the jail until arraignment this afternoon," said Sheriff Joe. "What is arraignment?" the alien leader asked. "No need to know about that now. You're under arrest," the sheriff answered. He handcuffed Will. "Sheriff, am I under arrest?"

asked Sarah. "Well, I have a question for you. Were you involved in this?" asked Sheriff Joe.

"Well, I guess I must say yes. I wasn't the one that pulled the trigger. He did that. I just talked to him, but not about that," the widow answered. "Well, you're under arrest under the charge of the accessory for Capital murder. You could also be facing the death penalty," the sheriff replied. He pulled her from the chair and restrained her. The preacher carried the dead man's body to the lake. Will started to resist as he was being taken to the county jail. He started to run like a penguin being handcuffed. "Come back here," Sheriff Joe shouted.

The townsmen grabbed him and brought him back to the sheriff. They walked three hundred feet to the county jail. The building has a similar appearance to the saloon. Yet it's much different. The building is painted brown and redwood makes up the building. A gallows post stood proudly adjacent to the building. In front of the gallows post are benches. The townspeople see executions as a part of their daily entertainment. A small, covered porch features two rocking chairs, one for the sheriff and another for his wife. The sheriff lives on the top level of the building. The only way to get into the building is by entering the door that has three bars on its window. The alien leader and Sarah are now being escorted into the building. "I hope you all enjoy your home over here because, this is going to be the place that you're staying at for a while," said Sheriff Joe.

The first level is made up of one huge room. There are two jail cells. Each cell is made up of stone walls and metal bars. The two cells are separated by a wooden wall. In front of the two cells is the sheriff's desk. The desk is made of cherry wood. His desk has many features. He has secret drawers in this desk that contain grand jury transcripts.

The drawers are so secret that one would have to open one drawer and three would have to pop out. The individual would have to guess which drawer to open next. Another unique feature on this desk is that instead of the lamp being powered by oil and fire, the lamp is powered by kerosene and fire and it would be functional for eternity. The jail cells had two small cots and a wooden floor. One item the sheriff always kept on him was a chain of keys. Each cell has a different lock so the sheriff would have to remember which key has to be used for what cell. That would be hard to remember especially for an old sheriff. This old bugger can work like an intelligent, agile horse. The alien leader didn't resist being placed into the cell and nor did Sarah. "What's happening?" he asked.

"You're being taken for questioning," the sheriff answered. "Fine, if I am being taken for questioning, that'll be acceptable," replied Will. "Well, that won't be it. Your charges will be read fully to you and you'll be arraigned and brought to bail. That's even if you make bail. If you don't make bail, then you'll get brought before a grand jury proceeding. If you get indicted, then you're screwed and you'll have to be brought to trial. If you get convicted, you will be hung, unfortunately," said Sheriff Joe.

"Well, I'm scared that I'm going to get convicted. I am worried for myself. I'm worried for Sarah. She's definitely not my girlfriend. We live in a world that's filled with injustice, and I am worried for her because she is a true victim," the alien leader replied. "Enough with the chit chat! Let's get serious. Before I get into interrogation, do y'all realize why you're here?" the sheriff asked. Neither the alien leader or the widow answered the sheriff's question.

"Let me rephrase that. Do you realize that you're here for interrogation and do you also realize that you're going to be awaiting arraignment and indictment?" asked Sheriff Joe. Both detainees answered Yes.

"Good. Now, we're going to get into the real interrogation. First, I'll interrogate the slave, the blue guy. Come out of your cell," said Sheriff Joe. He walked up to the cell door and opened it. It is now interrogation time for the alien leader. He closed the door to ensure that Sarah wouldn't be able to escape. Then, he started interrogating Will. "What's your name?" he asked. "Will Von Alien," the alien leader answered.

"Now, are you a slave or are you an alien?" the sheriff asked. "I'm an alien," answered Will. "How can you exactly prove to me that you're an alien?" asked Sheriff Joe. "Look at the palm of my hand. Then you'll be able to tell that I'm not a slave and that I'm an alien," the alien leader answered.

"What's so special about the palm of your hand?" the sheriff asked. "I don't have any fingerprints or palm prints," answered Will. He placed his hand on the desk and showed the sheriff the palm of his hand. "Oh, I see. That's quite interesting. How did you get here? Did you come here on some sort of a Space ship?" asked Sheriff Joe. "No, I didn't. God sent me here. You can ask him yourself," the alien leader answered. "That's physically impossible. How would he be able to do such a thing?" the sheriff asked.

"Because God works in mysterious ways. Ask him yourself and he'll give you the answer," answered Will. The sheriff smacked his male detainee. "What's wrong with you? Are you out of your mind? Do you need to be placed in an insane asylum?" he asked. "No, I am perfectly sane," the alien leader answered. "Not according to your charges.

You've been charged with Capital Murder. I don't think anybody in their right mind would commit such a heinous crime - killing a good Mormon in cold blood. I don't think you have an ounce of sanity. You may just be plain evil," replied Sheriff Joe.

"No, I'm not insane; nor am I evil. And why are you presuming me guilty when we live in a society when all men and women are innocent until proven guilty?" asked Will. "Oh, are you trying to interrogate me, now? That's not going to work around here. I am here to interrogate you and enforce the law of Utah. I take an oath to preserve the laws of the Constitution of the United States, the Constitution of the Territory of Utah, and the Charter of South Salt Lake. I take an oath to protect your rights. I was not told in this oath that men like you are allowed to interrogate the sheriffs. Maybe that's a new law they just added last week. I go to the county conventions and town hall meetings every two weeks. Now, let's get into the questions that I'll ask you about this recent alleged incident that had taken place about a half hour ago," the sheriff answered.

"Okay, well can I interrogate you before you interrogate me?" the alien leader asked. "No! I don't want to do this, but I may have to fetter you to this chair. You don't want me to do that and that's the last thing that I want to do, but one more mishap, you are going to get in so much trouble and I mean it! Don't test my patience because if you do such a thing, the scene is not going to be nice. You'll be encountering Hell quite early. Let me just interrogate you without a problem," answered Sheriff Joe. "Okay, that sounds quite acceptable to me," replied Will.

The Sheriff was exasperated. "No, you're not supposed to like an interrogation; you're supposed to be willing to accept one. Now, let me ask you the first 'real' question. What made you want to commit the crime of capital murder?" the sheriff asked. "I didn't *want* to commit that crime. I was left with no other choice but to kill him," the alien leader answered. "This is a 'Yes' or 'No' question. Well, did you feel killing this man was justifiable?" asked Sheriff Joe. "Yes," answered Will. "Why did you feel that way? What did he do to you?" the sheriff asked. "You see, I heard that this man was very aggressive to his wife and he was cruel to her. He would come home at night, drunk and vomit on her and do all cruel things," the alien leader answered.

"Well, do you realize that's what a vigilante does?" asked Sheriff Joe. "Yes, I did. I was protecting somebody from being a victim of domestic violence," answered Will. "What other reasons do you feel that this homicide was justifiable?" the sheriff asked. "Well, think of it. If you were in Sarah's shoes and your husband came home drunk with an aggressive and violent attitude, I think you would go after him," the alien leader answered. "That still doesn't justify homicide. I think that she can fight the battles herself against her husband. What other ways do you feel that this justifies homicide?" asked Sheriff Joe.

"This is the only way and leave me the hell alone," Will answered angrily. "Hey, don't be testy with me young man. I have many years behind me with the law enforcement. I have the right to shoot you if I want to, and I can tell the judge that I shot you in self-defense because you were trying to get my gun," the sheriff argued. "Okay, I'll tell you the other way that his homicide was justifiable. You see, I was talking to Sarah, his widow in the cell, and she told me that her husband was aggressive and cruel to her. He was in the bar and I met him and asked him in a kind way why he would do such a thing. Him and his son were drunk and in a state of oblivion. So, he threatened to kill me. I him and I ended up in an argument outside of the saloon.He lunged at me and tried killing me. I kicked him and ran for my life back into the place. I ran up to the bar and the bar tender retrieved the double barrel and I shot Jobe, the aggressor," the alien leader said. "How long did you know this man?" asked Sheriff Jobe. "About six hours," answered Will.

"Tell me how he was like during this six hour time span?" the sheriff asked. "Before anything, can I tell you the whole story?" the alien leader asked "Sure," answered Sheriff Joe. "Now, I was struck by lightning 2 times and then I fell into a tornado and I landed on asphalt. I fell off of the asphalt and I was taken back to the year of 1856. I met Jobe. He seemed nice and claimed he was actually a supporter for the abolitionists, which I really liked. His son was an arrogant and zealous supporter of slavery and I couldn't stand that. We arrived in the City of South Salt Lake and we headed over to the saloon. His wife was forced to sit outside of the place because they're a bunch of chauvinists. I sat next to her and talked with her. She told me that her husband is a walking facade and he is a strong supporter of slavery and chauvinism. When I confronted him about that, he started to show his true color of evil. That was when I knew the real Jobe; the evil man," the alien leader said. "Now, what made you want to get a gun and shoot him?" asked Sheriff Joe.

"Because I wanted to ensure that he wouldn't kill his wife or act violent towards his wife," answered Will. "This is the last question that I have to ask you. This interrogation is over for now. Go back to the Cell. I'll open the door and you'll come back in. If you think that I presumed your guilt, that was not true. Remember, all criminals are innocent until proven guilty," the sheriff replied. He escorted the male alien detainee back to the cell. He then pointed to Sarah "Come out of the cell, lady," he said.

The widow immediately walked out of the cell on his command. She sat down in the chair. "Now, do you realize that you're here for interrogation and you will be detained during your trial and possibly sentencing?" he asked. "Yeah," she answered. "No, you are to have respect for me. You must say 'yes, sir'," the sheriff replied. "Fine. I'll say it, but I want you to repeat the question you asked me," said Sarah. "Do you realize the reasons why you're here?" asked Sheriff Joe. "Yes, sir," the widow answered. "Now, you were supposedly married to this man. Is that correct?" the sheriff asked. "Yes," answered Sarah. "How long? Give me specific details?" asked Sheriff Joe. "17 Years. I was married 17 years," she answered. "That's a good answer. Now, what is your maiden name?" the sheriff asked. "Sarah Rosenthal," the widow answered.

"What was your husband like? Please give me a few words to describe him," asked Sheriff Joe. "A rude, two-faced monster," answered Sarah. "That sounds like some harsh words. Can you tell me how he had a two-faced personality?" the sheriff asked. "Well, when he met new people, he would act extremely nice and benevolent. When he was in the house or drunk, he would act extremely nasty and evil," the widow answered. "How did he act evil? What would he do?" asked Sheriff Joe.

"He would try and beat the hell out of me for little issues or for no reasons whatsoever. He would come home from work drunk. He would sometimes even threaten to kill me if I tried to stop him from being arrogant and cruel," answered Sarah. "Do you have any children?" the sheriff asked. "Yes, I have one son," the widow answered. "How old is he?" asked Sheriff Joe. "15 years old," answered Sarah. "Does your husband have any will in the house?" the sheriff asked. "Yes, the house will automatically be given to my son," the widow answered.

"Where is this house?" asked Sheriff Joe. "It's in Kansas City, Missouri. It's over in the plains in Missouri," answered Sarah. "Now, is your son mentally competent to live on his own and maintain that house?" the sheriff asked. "Yes, absolutely. Half of his life was dedicated to school and farming. I think he'd be able to live on his own. I would think he'd know how to farm his own property," the widow answered. "Okay, I'll arrange transport to bring him back to Missouri," replied Sheriff Joe.

"That'll be fine with me," replied Sarah. "I didn't ask you if it would be fine. I must ask you this question. Does your son have any emotional problems or separation anxiety?" the sheriff asked. "Absolutely not. I don't think so," answered Sarah. "I don't know if you know the true definition of a sheriff. We are supposed to do many jobs and one of these jobs is to interrogate people. The person that is to be interrogated must give me a straight, eloquent, and full answer. If that person doesn't give me the full answer, I can charge them with providing false or misleading information to a law enforcement officer. Now the question that I asked you is *if your son had emotional problems or separation anxiety?* This is a 'yes or no' question," said Sheriff Joe.

"No," Sarah answered abruptly. "Young lady, that's no way to answer the sheriff's questions. You are to answer his questions with respect and I don't think being blunt is stated in the definition of respect. Now, how does your son behave in the house?" asked the sheriff. "Fortunately, my son is not a two-face. He is genuine. But, is he genuine in a good or bad way? I know the answer to that; he is genuine in the bad way. He is also the epitome of evil. My son is a strong supporter of slavery and chauvinism also. Quite recently, he started becoming an alcoholic with my husband. After working on the fields, he also gets boozed up or drunk. Fortunately, he doesn't act violent with me. I worry for my son, especially now. I am worried because I'm in jail, he won't have anybody to turn to. He'll drink until he's dead. When you hear the phrase 'the apple don't fall too far from the tree,' my son is the epitome of that. He's just like my husband. Fortunately, he's not violent like him. Now, I am also concerned that my son is going to take revenge on me because of my husband" the widow answered.

"Earlier in your statement, you said that your son wasn't violent. Later, in your statement, you said he wasn't as violent as your husband. Now, is your son violent?" asked Sheriff Joe. "Yes, he is. He is not as violent as my husband. He does have a violent attitude and a short temper," answered Sarah. "How is your son violent? What does he do that's so violent?" the sheriff asked. "When my husband punches me, my son repeats my husband's evil attitude. Evil is, unfortunately, found within the household. I am the victim of those two evil beasts. My son is not as cold and barbaric as my husband. He's bad enough that if I had the authority to, I'd throw him out of the house," the widow answered.

"Well, was he always violent?" asked Sheriff Joe. "No, he started becoming violent when he started drinking. I am sure you notice how alcohol can ruin one's mind," answered Sarah. "How long has he been violent for? Be specific," the sheriff asked. "I don't know exactly how many months. I do know that this violent behavior has been around for a year or a couple of years, ever since he started drinking," the widow answered. "How old was he when he started drinking?" asked Sheriff Joe. "I'd say about fourteen years old," answered Sarah.

"Do you have any recollection of his first alcoholic beverage?" the sheriff asked. "Ale. The only alcoholic beverage that he would drink was ale; sometimes brandy. It was usually ale," the widow answered. "Did your son have any criminal history?" asked Sheriff Joe. "I don't think he did," answered Sarah. "You weren't clear with your answer. I'll assume it's 'no.' Next question. How old were you when you were married to Jobe?" the sheriff asked. "I was about 16," the widow answered.

"That's quite a young age to get married. Now, when did you have your son?" asked Sheriff Joe. "17 years old," answered Sarah. "So, you're quite young! You must be 35. Is that correct?" the sheriff asked. "No 36," the widow answered. "That is still quite a young age. Your life will be hell if you get sentenced to life imprisonment. Hopefully, that won't happen," replied Sheriff Joe. "Hey, do you feel bad for her and not me?" shouted Will.

"Hey! You in the peanut gallery, did I ask you to talk?" the sheriff asked. "No, you have the full stage. Continue interrogating Sarah, while I just sit in that cell like a stupid jailbird," the alien leader answered. The sheriff stood up from his chair. "Put a cork in it," he said. "Okay, you can stop talking to him," replied Sarah. The sheriff sat back down in his chair and continued with the interrogation.

"Now, do you think that you have any disability?" he asked. "No," the widow answered. "Why would you say such a thing?" she asked. "Because I've dealt with this before. Women who kill their husbands have battered woman syndrome and they get sent off to an institution if the jury finds them not guilty on reason of insanity," answered Sheriff Joe. "Hopefully, I don't have that," replied Sarah. "Don't say such a thing because that might save you from the gallows. Now, what made you want to tell Will about your husband's true colors?" the sheriff asked.

"Well, you see this is what really happened. Since, the pubs and saloons in this nation are so bias and chauvinist towards women, I was denied entry. So, I was forced to sit on the rocking chair outside. That was when I met Will. You see, Will had a warm heart of compassion. He noticed that I became lonely and he chose to sit next to me and talk to me. He basically interviewed me about my life and he talked about his life. He also felt bad for the women like me and I told him about the true colors about my husband. He originally loved my husband because he seemed so genuine and kind. I wanted to show him the true colors of my husband because my husband is nothing but an evil savage and chauvinistic pig. This alien loved my husband because of his views on slavery. I told Will the real views of what my husband thinks of slavery. I basically told him that my husband is a strong supporter of slavery and treating other human beings like property. I also told him that my husband treats me and women like slaves because makes me work around the house all the time, and I am forced to do nonstop work," the widow answered. "Do you realize what you caused because you told Will about your husband?" asked Sheriff Joe.

"Well, you see, after I told him about my cruel husband, Will) confronted my household beast. He asked him why he's mean to me and my husband threatened to hurt him in the saloon. They came out and my beastly husband lunged at him and tried to choke him. He managed to kick my husband and he shot him four times," answered Sarah.

"Well, do you realize how your husband died?" the sheriff asked. "Yes, four blows to the head from a double barrel," the widow answered. "Now, did you have anything to do with the cause of his death?" asked Sheriff Joe.

"No, I didn't. I never told Will to get the gun and shoot him. I didn't say a word when this fight had taken place. I just sat on the rocking chair and watched. When he died, I didn't show any emotion. I wasn't the one who committed conspiracy and I didn't plan this murder," answered Sarah.

"Do you have any sympathy for your husband's passing?" the sheriff asked. "Absolutely not. Why should I have sympathy for a selfish man who brutalized me for nearly twenty years? I'm sure if your wife terrorized you that long, you wouldn't show any sympathy for her passing. Look at my husband. He's the cruelest man around," the widow answered. "Now this will be my last words for this interrogation. Personally, I feel that you are a battered woman. You're not mentally ill. When you meet your attorney, you'll be able to talk to him about this. For now, just remain here and you'll be safe. Place your trust in me," replied Sheriff Joe. He escorted her back to the cell and locked the door.

He left the building and walked down the block to the law office of Attorney Harold Blackmon. The office looked like a small cottage. This building had a rustic appearance. On the front of the building, there's a sign that states *Harold Blackmon, Attorney At Law. Specialty: Capital Homicide*. The office had a large awning on the outside.

The sheriff walked through the door. As he opened the door, the bell on the hinge rang. Inside was one wooden desk that stood on top of stone tiled floor. The stones came from the quarry outside of town over yonder. A fire place kept the office warm in the cold Utah winters. The fire place is not running because of the hot weather outside. The white hearth is covered with ashes from the cinders. The stairs is located perpendicular to the fireplace behind the attorney's desk. The stairs leads up to his sleeping quarters and kitchen. The attorney is sitting at his desk counting gold coins.

His desk has a lamp and a gold scale. He's counting the value of his gold, not realizing who's in the room. The sheriff sat down in the wooden stool in front of the attorney's desk. Attorney Blackmon just continued counting his gold without a regard in the world. The sheriff slammed his fist on the desk. The attorney finally realized who was in the room. He picked up his head and his long, brownish grey hair shined in the brightness. Harold Blackmon has a pleasant voice whenever he speaks. "Good day, Mr. Blackmon," the sheriff said. "Good day to you, Sheriff Joe. What brings you here?" the attorney asked. "Do you happen to know about the shots that were heard earlier today?" asked Sheriff Joe.

"Oh my, yes. What happened?" asked Mr. Blackmon. "Well, you see the defendant shot the alleged victim in self -defense, so he says. The alleged victim's wife is at the county jail waiting with the defendant and myself," the sheriff answered. "What was the reason why you came over to me?" the attorney asked.

"Because, I need you to defend these two and represent them at trial as their legal counsel. You're the only attorney in the town and I believe you specialize in homicide cases so I'd figure that you'd be willing to take this case" answered Sheriff Joe. "Well, I have to think about it as there are only two reasons why I would be the attorney," replied Mr. Blackmon. "What are those reasons?" the sheriff asked.

"Because I specialize in homicide cases and I believe that everyone is entitled to an attorney. Besides, it would be extremely hard for a defendant to represent himself or herself at trial. I think a jury would believe me better than a defendant. Those are the only reasons why I'd represent them," the attorney answered brusquely. "Why would you not want to represent a case of your specialty?" asked Sheriff Joe. "Because, I'd rather represent somebody who ran somebody over with their coach, who is not a harm to society, rather than a man who is actually armed with a double barrel and can snap at any moment. For all you know, he can snap at me," answered Mr. Blackmon.

"Now, you'd be surprised to hear this, especially coming from the sheriff. This man and this woman are clear victims and they're unfortunately charged with capital crimes. I didn't charge them with the crimes; the prosecutor immediately did that. They're very nice and cooperative for the most part," replied the sheriff. "Okay, I'll believe that when I meet them. I don't want to be defending somebody that'll go out in this world and commit crimes," said the attorney.

Chapter XV: *Utah V. Rosenthal and Von Alien*

Attorney Blackmon and the Sheriff walked out of the law office. "My clients better be nice to me because I will do a terrible job at trial on purpose because I don't want some bloody murderer getting off because nobody who commits such a heinous and vile act should get off like that," Mr. Blackmon said angrily. "You know something, I am surprised with you. You usually have a cheerful and pleasant voice and a confident attitude. You are acting very unpleasant and miserable, maybe, even arrogant. Why are you acting like that? Your behavior is totally wrong. What happened to you?" asked Sheriff Joe.

"Because I usually defend people who commit petty acts that are considered acts of violence. For instance, I'll take the case of somebody who accidentally ran somebody over with their Conestoga, who is facing the death penalty for murder; rather, than some murderer, who shot a man in cold blood who deserves the death penalty," answered the attorney. "Now, do you not specialize in homicide cases?" asked the sheriff. "Yes, I do specialize in homicide cases. I don't specialize in the cases of intentional and murderous homicides. I specialize in the cases of negligent homicides that are considered as murders by the law, even though they're not murders. I will not take the case of some sociopathic killer," answered Mr. Blackmon.

"I don't know about that. You see, this man is being accused of capital murder because of the color of is skin. You'll see him later, and this woman is being accused of conspiracy because she's the alleged victim's battered wife," replied Sheriff Joe.

"You know what? You'll see if I agree with you when I meet them. We shall make a bet on this. I don't do much betting when it comes to legal cases or even the law. I don't usually don't do things that are considered unethical, but in this case, I must do something that's unethical. Let's make a bet. Since this town is so small, I know everybody over here, especially you. Because you have a stagecoach that is your prized asset, you will be forced to give it to me. You'll have to give it to me if you don't win this competition. These folks are your detainees and you are responsible for their behavior. If they misbehave in front of me, your stagecoach is now my property and I can go out of town whenever I want to. If they're well behaved, I will do an excellent job on their case and you'll be able to keep your stagecoach. Does this sound like a fair deal? Because to me, it's an extremely fair deal," said Mr. Blackmon.

"This is hard to say, but I will agree to the bet," replied Sheriff Joe. "Really?" the attorney asked. "On second thought, no. This is my most prized possession. There are more important possessions to me than a stagecoach but betting on this sounds quite stupid and unfair to me," answered the sheriff.

"In life, we have many decisions. You have an important decision to make. Do you want to give up your stagecoach? It's your choice yes or no. You could hesitate all you want, but I suggest that you join this bet," replied Mr. Blackmon. Sheriff Joe hesitated. He started scratching the back of his head thinking. He's making like this is the most important decision of his life. He finally spoke up.

"You know that this stagecoach is a material object. Besides, the folks that I detain don't act violent or insolent when they're in front of me, especially these two. I don't think they'll act insolent in front of you because you're here to help them. I think they'll be on their best behavior." The attorney laughed hard and slapped his knee. He fell to the sandy road in laughter.

"You must be joking with me when you're saying that. I don't find what you're saying to be true. I don't mean to be disrespectful towards you, but I think you're lying and the phrase the sheriff never lies is very important. That sounds so pathetic. The sheriff is just like any other politician. If the politicians are a bunch of liars, the sheriff must be a liar because the sheriff works for the government," he said.

"Let me just tell you this. I can put you in jail for harassing me. The only reason why I came to your office was for you to help my two detainees get an acquittal. I am usually favoring the prosecution of criminals and detainees. I know how to lay down the law in this town. Before I came into the picture in South Salt Lake, this place was nothing but a lawless town. When I came into the picture, I laid down the law. Now, laying down the law doesn't mean convicting everybody before they get tried or having a vendetta for defendants. Making sure the law is enforced means that you are fair with all of the men and women. Unfortunately, we live in a world that is filled with people being extremely unfair and not being willing to accept others. I don't do the bad things that others do. I accept all men and women for who they are," argued Sheriff Joe. "Even if they're a true criminal who would've committed the most wicked crimes?" the attorney asked.

"It depends on the circumstance. You see, I don't torture my detainees in a physical, mental, or an emotional way. I know they're going through a lot, having to go on trial, and some of them facing the death penalty because they committed a capital crime. You see, some of my detainees, particularly women, are victims of cruel husbands who commit the most wicked acts. Then, there are others, who committed heinous acts themselves and they show remorse. It is a rare occasion where I come across somebody, who commits a wicked act, that doesn't show remorse. My detainees usually show remorse and there is a low recidivism rate in my jail. I think you should be more than willing to defend my prisoners in court, especially these two because I feel that these two are the bigger victims more than the alleged victim in this case," answered Sheriff Joe. They arrived in front of the county jail and walked right in.

"These inmates better behave in front of me," muttered Mr. Blackmon. "Trust me; they're excellent. I usually don't say that the criminals are innocent, but in this case, they're clearly innocent," replied Sheriff Joe. He retrieved a second chair and placed it in front of his desk. The attorney sat down in the sheriff's spot. Sheriff Joe escorted the two defendants from the cell. Both Will and Sarah are quiet and solemn proceeding out of their cell. They have some intuition of who's present, but they're not too sure. They sat down in the two chairs in front of the sheriff's desk. Sheriff Joe walked upstairs to his apartment. "Introduce yourselves, individually. I want the blue man to start," said Mr. Blackmon. The alien leader smiled. "It's an honor to see you. I'm Will Von Alien and I come from Starmos City. I'm from the future. Specifically, from the year 2047," he said. "Okay, that's good enough. You must be crazy or something. I might not be able to believe you," replied Mr. Blackmon.

"Why are you saying that I am crazy when I'm clearly sane?" asked Will. "Are you trying to be insolent with me?" the attorney asked. "No, sir. I'm not crazy, but I do come from another dimension and I do come from a different year. Ask God," the alien leader answered. "It is hard for me to believe that you're an alien because I never dealt with an alien. I've dealt with slaves that looked similar to you. So, maybe, you might be a slave trying to pull an alibi of being an alien," replied Mr. Blackmon. "And what would be the difference if he was a slave or an alien? Would you still take his case?" asked Sarah. "I guess so. I don't know if he's a slave," the attorney answered.

"Well, you should look at his handprints and then you'll be able to tell the difference," the widow replied. "Fine then, I'll be more than willing to look," said Mr. Blackmon. The alien leader placed his hands on the desk and flipped them over. "Now, do you believe me?" he asked. "Yes, I am extremely sorry for accusing you of being a slave because I would never mean to accuse you of being a slave. Even if you were a slave, I'd still take your case. Now, I'll interrogate you. I know you don't want to go through the same ordeal that you guys went through with the sheriff. In order to get some information about this case to defend you, I must ask you guys questions," answered the attorney. "Sir, I'm a female," the widow said. "Yeah, whatever. That's not that important to the case. Let's get serious now. I'm going to interrogate y'all," replied Mr. Blackmon. "Well, who are you going to start with?" asked Will. "I am going to start with you," the attorney answered. The alien leader grinned.

"Okay," he said. "Now, I am going to ask you similar questions that the sheriff asked. What are your charges?" asked Mr. Blackmon. "Capital Murder. That's my only charge," answered Will. "Well, that's not such a minimal charge. Do you realize that you're facing the death penalty if you get convicted of that charge?" the attorney asked. "Yes, sir," the alien leader answered in elation. "Why do you seem so happy? Do you realize that you might be facing the end of your life?" asked Mr. Blackmon.

"Because you're here to protect me. Besides, if I was to get convicted and sentenced to death, I would never die. An alien could only die if he or she drinks a huge bottle of poison or has poisonous syrup on their breakfast," answered Will.

"Well, I don't think you want to get poisoned because you might lose your head on the gallows. Stop smiling because this is not funny. I am here to help you and I want you to tell me the whole truth and nothing but the truth, so help you God. Let me continue on with my interview. Now, did you know this man before the alleged incident had taken place? And if so, how long?" the attorney asked.

"Yes about 6 hours," the alien leader answered. His elated face disappeared. Now, his normal face reappeared. He is going to answer the attorney's questions in a nonchalant manner. "Now, how did you meet him? I can tell this is going to be a long answer. Answer this question in its entirety," asked Mr. Blackmon.

"Well, you see, I was heading down the path of God and I fell into this abyss. All of a sudden, I hit asphalt at a hard impact. All of a sudden, I hear a jolt of thunder and a bolt of lightning. Rain started to come down in the area that surrounded me. A bunch of rednecks came down. I was struck by lightning. Before I knew it, I ended up in the middle of a large tornado that was five hundred feet tall. I ended up flying to the ground. I hobbled down off of the asphalt road. As soon as I hobbled off that road, I was brought back to the year 1856. The asphalt disappeared. A benevolent and kind prairie man came down from the Grand Canyon Mountain. He was willing to help me, but my overconfidence kicked in. So, I told him not to bother doing it. It was a struggle for me to move through a crowd of rednecks. So, I screamed for this prairie man's help. He helped me. Him and I walked up the hill in the harsh desert heat. We arrived at his Conestoga wagon. I met his family. I thought he had two sons. One of them was really Abe Lincoln dressed in a costume. The other son was nothing but an arrogant social Darwinist. He was a strong supporter of racism, which was and still is an evil philosophy. His son was a strong supporter of slavery. In fact, I heard there's a Civil War coming up and his son would join the Confederates. To answer your question, this is how I met Jobe," the alien leader answered.

"That's a good enough answer. Now, what made you want to kill him?" the attorney asked. "Let's get one thing clear. I never intended on killing him nor did I want to kill him. He wanted to kill me and act violent with me. When we arrived at the saloon, he was welcome into the saloon because it was a men's only place and his wife was forced to sit outside. Since she was lonely, I wanted to keep her company. She told me that her husband was really a walking facade. He was really a strong supporter of slavery and chauvinism, just like his son. I felt so bad for his wife. His wife told me not to confront him over this. It was my just duty to do so," answered Will. "Why didn't you listen to her?" asked Mr. Blackmon.

"First of all, I wanted to make sure that she was telling the truth and she clearly did tell the truth. Second of all, I wanted to tell that man to stop doing what he was doing and also to change his political views, particularly on slavery and chauvinism," the alien leader answered.

"Well, this is my question. Were you trying to cause a confrontation with him?" the attorney asked. "No, he was trying to be belligerent to me. You see, he started out through saying demeaning words. Since I am fascinated with ragtime piano music, he tried to say things like 'I wasn't worthy enough to listen to that kind of music' and he would ridicule me. He also mocked me because of my race of being an alien and coming from the future. Those mocks and ridiculing comments eventually became threats. He told me that he was going to put me in an insane asylum or prison because he thought that I was a slave and he threatened even to kill me. He claimed that it was his prerogative to kill me, when it was clearly not. Then, we walked outside of the saloon. Sarah was just sitting down in the rocking chair. He lunged at me and tried to kill me. He started choking me and I kicked him and he fell backwards. Then, I ran into the bar and met the bartender. I asked for the double barrel rifle. Once he gave me the gun, I ran outside and shot Jobe," answered Will.

"Did you shoot to kill or did you shoot to stop?" asked Mr. Blackmon. "Even though I wanted to kill him, I shot to stop him from beating me up and I also shot him to stop him from being evil to his wife," the alien leader answered.

"Did you get satisfaction from murdering him? Did you act as a vigilante or simply somebody who was defending himself?" the attorney asked. "Let's make one thing clear. I am not a murderer. A murderer is somebody who commits intentional homicide. I killed him so I could defend myself. This is an answer to your first question. An answer to your second question is that I acted as both. I acted as a vigilante because I wanted to stop him from being cruel to his wife because whenever he was drunk or, sometimes even sober, he would be aggressive and nasty to his wife. I acted more in self-defense than a vigilante. You see if somebody lunged at you and tried choking you, would you kill them? I think you would. That would be considered self-defense and a jury would vote in my favor because of the reason of self- defense," answered Will.

"That's a good point. My interview is done with you. I want you to stay here because I might have further questions to ask you," replied Mr. Blackmon. "What questions do you have for me?" asked Sarah. "Give me a couple of seconds and then I'll ask you them. Lady, have some patience," the attorney answered. "No, I'm the one with all the patience. Maybe, you don't have any patience. Let's get into the interviewing. Did you have a criminal history?" asked Mr. Blackmon. "Why would you think I had a criminal history or, even have one? That sounds ridiculous, but to answer your question, I don't have one at all," answered the widow. The attorney disregarded her snooty answer.

"What are your charges?" he asked. "Conspiracy to commit capital murder," answered Sarah. "Can you describe to me your husband in a short or simple phrase?" the attorney asked. "A coward, a piece of trash, an evil and wicked soul, a two-faced, a walking facade, and a drunk," the widow answered. "That sounds like some pretty harsh words. Now, did you actually premeditate this murder with Will?" asked Mr. Blackmon.

"No, I didn't. I never even have the thought of killing him. Now, you see, I know that one thing is certain. He threatened Will. When, he died, I didn't show a tear. The sheriff insinuated that I conspired to kill him. You see, the reason why I didn't cry was because I never knew anything nice about him. He was nasty to me since day one," answered Sarah. "Well, what do you remember about him?" the attorney asked.

"Like many other husbands, he was nothing but a slave driver. He not only supported slavery towards African

Americans, he supported slavery in the house towards women. He made me do an endless amount of chores, and I would be forbidden to leave the house. If I ever left the house, he would suspect that I was having an affair and he would try to kill me. My husband treated me like an animal, if not worse. He was nothing but a creature. My son would just sit and watch. My son eventually learned his ideas of Social Darwinism and now he's going to be like that to his wife. My husband is not only a supporter of Social Darwinism towards women, he also believes that people that are not Caucasian are inferior. That really gets me pissed off. In terms of gender status, I should be dead and I shouldn't have any right to get angry at my husband. I was expecting to have an excellent relationship with him," the widow answered.

"I can see you're a battered woman. Even though you didn't conspire for his murder, I feel that you should've shown some sympathy, but then again, I can understand what you went through. Hopefully, this won't go to trial and you'll be exonerated quickly. I even think the town prosecutor will even feel some sympathy for you. When the arraignment happens, I'll talk about having bail. I feel extremely sorry for you. You're clearly a battered woman and you're an unfortunate victim of a cruel man. Hopefully, I can arrange a plea deal where you plea guilty in exchange for immunity," replied Mr. Blackmon. "Why would I plea guilty even though I'm innocent?" asked Sarah.

"Because it might save you from serving time and possibly the death penalty," the attorney answered. The attorney finished his interview with Sarah and Will. Within a matter of seconds, after the interview, loud knocks are being heard on the wooden door.

"What's that?" the alien leader asked. "I don't know who's behind that door. It sounds quite loud," answered Mr. Blackmon. The knocks became louder. Sheriff Joe rushed down the stairs. "Hold on a second, you annoying thing behind the door," said Sheriff Joe. He opened the door. The county prosecutor stood behind the door. This prosecutor wore a professional suit. He is bald and he always wears a tuxedo. He's well groomed and has a handle bar mustache. He has a voice that sounds quite condescending and grim.

"Bring those two to my courtroom," he said. "You look like a new and dapper prosecutor," replied Sheriff Joe. "That's because I'm new. I've only been around for a couple of hours. I am here to prosecute Will Von Alien and Sarah Rosenthal," said the cruel prosecutor. "Give me your name, sir," said the sheriff. "Old man, you don't talk to me like that. Do you understand? You must be as evil as sin. How dare you commit such a wicked crime of talking to me like that! I'll give you my name. You are to address me by this name. I'm Mr. Douer," replied the arrogant prosecutor.

"What are you doing here?" asked Sheriff Joe. "You don't talk to me like that or I'll bring terror to your town," answered Mr. Douer. "Yeah right, I don't believe you for one second. I'll be willing to give you my detainees to bring them safely to court," the sheriff replied. "Okay, take them out of their cells. On second thought, I only want Will," the prosecutor said. "Fine then, I'll bring him over to you. Does he need to be brought in handcuffs?" asked Sheriff Joe.

"Yes, it would be much appreciated. After all, he committed such a heinous crime," answered the prosecutor. "Let me just tell you this, a*ll criminals are innocent until proven guilty*," the sheriff replied. "Well, in America we don't do that," said Mr. Douer. "Really? Well, go back to your own country because in America we have a fair justice system towards all criminals. Shut up because you're nothing but a world class idiot who should be ashamed of himself," argued Sheriff Joe. "Just bring that thing over to me," the malicious prosecutor said. The sheriff disregarded that prosecutor's nasty comment and he escorted Will in shackles to the prosecutor. "You better treat him with respect," he said.

"Oh, I'll treat some low life with respect," Mr. Douer replied sarcastically. The prosecutor escorted the alien leader from the jail. He started kicking him and beating him as they continued moving to the courthouse. Will didn't say a word as this torture had taken place.

They arrived in front of the courthouse. The courthouse had a similar shape to the Alamo Fort. It is made of wood instead of clay. There are twelve stairs going leading into the courthouse. The prosecutor and the male defendant met Attorney Blackmon, who is standing outside of the courtroom. The room outside of the courtroom features five seats. There are two body guards in this room to make sure that a ruckus does not take place. The prosecutor walked inside the courtroom. "Will, how were you treated?" the defense attorney asked.

"That prosecutor is nothing, but a cruel bastard. He started kicking me and beating me up as I was being escorted to the courthouse. I would like to strangle him, but unfortunately, I couldn't. I was placed in handcuffs and he tried to restrain me," answered Will. "How can he mistreat you in such a harsh manner?" asked Mr. Blackmon. "Well, that's how these damn prosecutors are like," the alien leader answered.

"Let me take you and Sarah for arraignment. Now, don't be nervous, but don't look cold. The judge will read you your charges and then you'll be escorted out of the courtroom. We'll also determine if there should be any bail," the defense attorney replied.

He escorted the two detainees into the courtroom. The spectators are sitting in the seats quiet as a church mouse. The courtroom has polished wooden walls and a white carpet to symbolize the peacefulness of a courtroom. The judge sat behind a desk on an eight foot high pedestal. Two witness boxes are adjacent to him. A small window is behind the judge.

This window is very significant because it is the gateway to the jury room. The jury can hear everything that takes place in the courtroom. The only time the jury leaves that room is if there's a recess or a verdict reading or if the trial is over. Typically, the jurors are present in front of the defendant, counsel, and the judge.

The jury is always present in a small 15' by 15' room. Judge John Stevenson is present on the bench. He's wearing the traditional judge clothing. His bald head shines in the sunlight. The two defendants are being escorted to the defense table. "Ladies and gentlemen, the counsel and the defendants are present. Is that correct?" he asked.

"Yes," the defense attorney and prosecutor answered. "Now, what are their names?" asked the Mr. Stevenson. "Will Von Alien and Sarah Rosenthal," answered Mr. Blackmon. "So, one's an alien and another is a human being. Is that correct?" the judge asked. "Yes," the defense attorney answered. "Now, Will Von Alien is charged with Capital Murder and Sarah Rosenthal is charged with conspiracy to commit Capital Murder. Now, this is a question for the prosecutor to answer. Are you pursuing the death penalty?" the judge asked.

"Yes, your honor," answered Mr. Douer. He snickered as he answered the judge's question. "Now, does the defense want bail for these clients?" asked Mr. Stevenson. "I don't necessarily want bail. I want my clients to be remanded to the custody of this town. Due to the lack of criminal history and the lack of a violent past, I think they're more than worthy of being kept in this town," answered Mr. Blackmon. "Well, we have to set monetary bail," replied the judge.

"Well, these two don't have any financial support or money. Can we just remand them to the custody of this town?" the defense attorney asked. "Sure, if the prosecutor approves," answered Mr. Stevenson. "Despite the fact that they don't have a violent history or any criminal history, I would deny them bail because of the crime that they committed," the arrogant prosecutor said. "Well, I hereby deny them bail. Next case," the judge replied.

"Your honor, I beseech you. My clients are more than deserving of bail," said Mr. Blackmon. "Too bad, they are not worthy of bail. You bother me again, I'll hold you in contempt and they'll be forced to represent themselves at trial," replied Mr. Stevenson. The attorney and the defendants walked out of the courtroom. As they walked through the double wooden doors, the prosecutor snickered. "Judge, we did an excellent job. What a good start to a good trial," he said. "I know, this is going to be great," the judge replied. "Because you're the judge, the defense will be so weak. I hope that you rule against all their objections. Then, we'll have a strong case against them," said Mr. Douer.

A group of random people were escorted into the jury room, escorted by a paralegal. The judge started to instruct the grand jury. "Now, you've all been called here to see whether or not this case will go to trial. The defense and the defendants are not present. The only representative from counsel is the prosecutor. He will try and persuade you to bring this case to trial. Hopefully, it'll go to trial and justice will be done." He snickered and snarled as he said that. The prosecutor started to present the case to the grand jury.

"In every case, we have troubled criminals; and in this case we definitely have troubled criminals. They may have not come from a troubled home. They do have malicious intents. One of them is charged with the crime of conspiracy to commit capital murder and the other one is charged with capital murder. Based on other cases, I'm sure you know what they're facing. But, you are not to have any bias opinion according to what Judge Stevenson said. Now, let me tell you this. An innocent man, who was a devout Mormon came home from a bar because he was enjoying himself. Since he was this devout and benevolent Mormon, he took this alien slave into his family because this alien was in a horrible situation. Meanwhile, the victim didn't realize what was coming at him. He really had taken in a malevolent monster. So, his family arrived in the City of South Salt Lake and they decided to stop at a saloon. Fortunately, women are not allowed in saloons. This alien talked to the wife, who was supposedly lonely and while they talked to each other they conspired to commit murder of Jobe, the victim. He didn't know what was really going to strike him. He came out of the place. The wife was sitting comfortably on the rocking chair not giving a care in the world and Will Von Alien, the defendant, decided to retrieve a double barrel shotgun and shoot his gentle caretaker. Now, who would do such a thing? I don't think anybody in his or her right mind would let this man walk free. I think this case would be the perfect case to go to trial. So, please, I beg you to simply bring these two to trial so they face justice like they deserve."

It is now up to the grand jury to deliberate on whether the two defendants, who are not present in the courtroom, should go to trial. The grand jury took six hours to deliberate on whether or not this case should go to trial. This is the first moment that'll make or break the prosecutor. Mr. Douer is smirking in excitement hoping that his two defendants should go to trial. As a result, his hope comes true. The grand jury indicted Will on one count of Capital Murder and Sarah on one count of Conspiracy to commit Capital Murder. The indictment finished and the members of the grand jury walked out of the room. The prosecutor thanked them and gave them hugs. "Thank you so much for fighting for justice," he said. The members of the grand jury just kept walking past the prosecutor disregarding every word he said and they walked outside the courtroom. "So, Mr. Doure, the case is going to trial. Are you happy?" asked Mr. Stevenson.

"Of course I am! It was my lifelong dream to ruin Will Von Alien. Maybe Sarah, could join his fate, too," replied the prosecutor. "If the jury wins this case, I'll get so much money and my name will be known throughout this whole town," the judge said. "This is going to be a great case. I'll be happy if we destroy Will's reputation forever," replied Mr. Doure. The arrogant judge and prosecutor smirked at each other in a sinister way. They laughed in an evil manner. It is now half past three in the afternoon. A jury of twelve men was selected. Women aren't allowed to serve on jury duty. The men were immediately escorted into the jury room. As soon as the jury was brought into the jury room, the defendants and all counsel returned back into the courtroom.

The trial began. 12 hourglasses stood on top of the judge's desk. Each hour glass would be turned over every five minutes. The opening arguments are about to take place.

"Ladies and gentlemen of the jury, it is a must that we must fight for the justice of Jobe. This is a sad death that would've never taken place if these two monstrosities weren't here and if that one monstrosity didn't come to planet Earth, but unfortunately he did. We're not here to set them free. We're here to bring them to a sentence that I'd like to quote a famous phrase that was used by the British. *'This man must face the short stop and a sudden drop'*, end quote. We're not dealing with one man who committed petty piracy. We're dealing with a man and woman who committed the wicked crime of capital murder and conspiracy. I will prove to you that these two are clearly guilty in my examination of witnesses. The first witness I'd like to bring to the stand is the bartender from the local saloon over here."

The bar tender boisterously busted through the double doors. He started dancing all his way to the witness box. The judge laughed and never even had a thought of holding this man in contempt. "What's up y'all," he said. "Now, let me ask you this. Did Will tell you that he was going to kill Jobe?" asked Mr. Douer.

"Of course, he did," the first witness answered. "And what did he say to prove that he premeditated this murder?" the arrogant prosecutor asked. "Get me that double barrel now," answered the bar tender. "Did he use those exact words?" asked Mr. Douer. "I have no recollection, but they sounded similar," the first witness answered. "Did he ask for anything else?" the arrogant prosecutor asked.

"Well, before he asked me for the double barrel. He told me that he wanted to kill him with a twenty two caliper rifle," answered the bar tender. "Very well then, you could leave," replied the Mr. Douer. About seven more witnesses were called up to the stand by the prosecutor. The first witness would either make or break this prosecutor's case. The opening statements for the prosecution's case ended. Now, the defense will be heading up for their opening statements.

"We live in a world filled with trust and deceit. Unfortunately, there is more deceit than trust. Will Von Alien was in a detrimental situation and he met Jobe. My client figured that Jobe would be such a nice gentleman. But he was an extremely violent man. He had a history of violence. Now, I'm not saying he deserves to die, but he caused his own death. First of all, he would come home drunk every night. He would be aggressive and violent towards his wife. This man was nothing but a brute. Now gentlemen, the prosecutor will say in the State's Rebuttal that I am putting Jobe on trial. My clients are really on trial when they shouldn't be. You see, I worked across the street from the saloon and I saw the unfortunate death scene take place. I was not too sure about what happened, but I have some witnesses to prove my case to you. The prime witness in this case that will help exonerate these defendants is the ragtime piano player at the saloon." Carter brought is bicycle ragtime piano from home and started playing it in the courthouse. He started to play *The Entertainer.*

"Enough is enough. Stop playing you idiot. This is not some sort of a Vaudeville Show. This is a Court Room! I could hold you in contempt," the judge yelled. The defense's first witness sat down in the witness booth. "What did Will tell you about Jobe?" asked Mr. Blackmon. "He told me that he was violent," the ragtime piano player answered.

"Did the alleged victim show any form of violence?" the defense attorney asked. "Yes, he grabbed Will and tried pulling him out of the bar," the defense's first witness answered. "Did Jobe use any words of violence?" asked Mr. Blackmon. "Yes, he threatened to beat him and even kill him," the ragtime piano player answered.

"Well, do you feel that's enough to justify homicide?" the defense attorney asked. "I would say that would be enough to use lethal force," the defense's first witness answered.

After this witness was cross-examined by the defense attorney, ten more witnesses were cross examined and questioned. After the opening statements, the closing arguments had taken place. The prosecutor basically stated that this was a crime of passion and the defense argued that the alleged crime was justifiable homicide and self-defense. It is now half past 7 in the evening; the jury is going to determine the two defendants' fate. After two hours of deliberation, the jury reached its verdict. The foreperson walked out and handed the papers to Judge Stevenson. The alien leader folded his hands in nervousness. Sarah started sobbing in nervousness. The jury foreperson is about to read the verdict.

"For the people of the Utah Territory versus Will Von Alien, as to the charge of First Degree Capital Murder, we the jury find the defendant guilty. We further find that this defendant used a deadly weapon in his crime to be true. The people of the Utah Territory versus Sarah Rosenthal, we the jury find the defendant not guilty of the crime of Conspiracy to Commit First Degree Capital Murder. We further find that this defendant didn't tell the co-defendant to kill Jobe in the fashion that he was killed." The jurors walked out of the jury deliberation room.

"Would any member from counsel like to poll the jury?" asked Judge Stevenson. Both members of counsel answered. The prosecution answered "Yes" for Sarah and the defense answered "Yes" for Will. The jury foreperson turned around and asked every individual juror whether this was his true verdict. Every juror answered unanimously against Will. The foreperson then asked if this was the jury's true verdict referring to Sarah. The jury unanimously ruled in favor of Sarah.

"Thank you, ladies and gentlemen of the jury. I love your verdicts. These were the best verdicts of my life. Come back soon, you hear," said Mr. Stevenson. "Oh yeah, they were great," replied Mr. Douer. "Sarah, you're, unfortunately, exonerated. You can go free. I hate to be you. I'd suggest you leave this country because you still won't have your rights outside of the courtroom walls. Will, you are to return back here for your sentencing. All counsel must be present for sentencing tomorrow. I am ordering that Sheriff Joe is to attend the sentencing hearing. Thank you everybody. Get out of my courtroom," the judge said. The guards dragged the convicted alien leader to the county jail for the sentencing hearing tomorrow. The defense attorney followed Will to the county jail for further discussion. Everyone was cleared from the courtroom except for the judge and the prosecutor.

"So, how did you enjoy this case?" asked Mr. Stevenson. "I think this was the best case that I ever dealt with and it didn't even take much fighting," answered Mr. Douer. "I can't wait to hang him. This is going to be the best execution of my history with sentencing people to death. Better yet, he's not even a person. He's an alien," replied the snide judge. The prosecutor and the judge snickered in an evil, conniving way. "This is going to be great," the arrogant prosecutor said.

Chapter XVI: Will Von Alien is sentenced

It is now 9:00 in the evening, the courtroom is now solemn and desolate. The prosecutor and the judge are not present. The alien leader just finished his horrible ordeal and this ordeal will not come to an end. The jury ruled against him and ruled in favor of Sarah. She checked into the Horseshoe Hotel. The alien leader is spending his night in jail. This night is not spent for enjoyment.

She walked into the hotel which is adjacent to the courthouse. The clerk at the hotel is standing behind the wooden table that has many unique features. This table was imported from Europe 60 years ago and it has many carvings inside the legs of the table. These carvings come from the Templars.

This table has Christian artwork carvings including scenes of The Last Supper and the Stations of the Cross. This table has been well kept for 60 years. A large bell stood adjacent to the ink well that stood on the right side of the table. Seen behind this table, is the check-in lady. She's an alien. She used to work at the Star Hotel over in Starmos City, years forward. She has a Russian accent because her origin was Russia.

"Who are you?" asked Sarah. "I'm Rubi. I came from Starmos City, years forward," the check-in lady answered. "Say, do you know Will Von Alien?" the widow asked. "Yes, he's my boyfriend," the alien leader's girlfriend answered. "How long have you been here?" asked Sarah. "A couple of hours," answered Rubi.

"May I speak with the manager?" the widow asked. "Sure," answered the alien leader's girlfriend. Police Commissioner Clayton walked down the stairs. "Who are you?" asked Sarah. "I am Commissioner Clayton. I also come from the year 2047. I come from New York City," he answered. "How long have you been involved with this place?" the widow asked. "A couple of hours," answered Clayton. "What brought you here in such a short amount of time?" asked Sarah.

"You see, an angel told me that Will was arrested and falsely accused of the crime of capital murder. So, Rubi and I were taken back 289 years back in time to this place. By the time, I got here, my buddy was put on trial and he was facing the death penalty. Unfortunately, he was falsely convicted by a malevolent judge and arrogant prosecutor. The stupid jury believes this prosecutor. I was told by this angel that this hotel was up for sale for $50.00. So, I decided to buy this hotel and fix it up. Now, we're here. Say, I want to know what brings you here," the police commissioner said.

"Well, you see I was put on trial for the crime of conspiracy to commit Capital Murder. Fortunately, I was acquitted because the prosecutor didn't really present his case well. One thing that is for certain is that the prosecutor has an attitude as wicked as a serpent and he definitely has a vendetta for Will. Unfortunately, in a death penalty case, his appellate rights have been taken away. So, there's no way he can escape the gallows. If he has any chance of getting off the gallows, he'll have to escape jail and he'll be a fugitive and I don't want that to happen. He'll be left with no other choice," the widow replied.

"Did you just say he'll be left with no other choice? No, it's *we'll* be left with no other choice. The reason why is because we're his best friends and Rubi is his girlfriend. We're here to fight for justice. We are a team. If one man goes down, the whole team will go down. If one man triumphs, the team shall therefore triumph. Don't say he'll because we'll be hung as a group if we have to do. We'll escape as a group. I know I'm a cop and I know I'm supposed to be protecting the society from escapees. I know what happened to Will and this is a horrible scene. He was falsely accused by that wicked prosecutor, who I think deserves to be hung by his hands. I'd like to beat the hell out of that malicious soul," said Clayton.

"You're right. I totally agree with you. If Will goes down, we'll go down. We will help in the fight to escape and justice will be done," replied Sarah. "Very well then. I shall take you to your sleeping quarters," the police commissioner said. "Good, thank you," the widow replied.

The police commissioner and the widow walked up a wooden spiral staircase and down down the narrow hallway. This hallway featured three small chandeliers. Each one is made of pure gold. The hallway is adorned with drapes from old curtains and the walls are covered with crimson colored wall paper. There are five rooms in this hallway. Each room is closed off by a wooden door. The rooms are color coded because only one gender is allowed in one bedroom.

There are three bedrooms for men and two for women. The male bedrooms face the Great Salt Lake. Meanwhile, the female bedrooms face town. She was escorted in the first bedroom to the left. This bedroom looked like any other ordinary hotel room of the time period. Fortunately, it didn't have a dilapidated or decrepit appearance. She sat down on the bed in the room. Standing adjacent to the nightstand is a small desk. This desk featured parchment paper and an inkwell. She started writing a telegram to Judge Stevenson.

"Your honor, on behalf of my friend, I request that you don't sentence him to death. As a witness, I request that you toss out the conviction because I know what happened. You see my husband intimidated him in the bar and he

threatened him. My husband, the alleged victim, was all boozed up (drunk at the time.) I never said a word to Will when this had taken place. Unfortunately, the jury noticed the malicious words of an evil prosecutor. Nwo the only punishment that my friend is facing is death. He doesn't deserve to die because he didn't commit any crime. He was just simply defending himself. I know that you think he's guilty because you're an arrogant and cruel judge. But don't sentence him because he doesn't deserve it. I request that you don't convict him of any crime because I'll tell you what really happened. My husband dragged him outside of the saloon. Will started talking to an angel, who was and still is here to help him. After that, my husband lunged at him and started choking him.

He kicked him (my evil husband) in the face and he fell to the ground. Will ran back into the saloon to seek refuge and retrieve a gun to shoot him to stop him. You see, the one who you want to execute did not shoot to kill; he shot my husband in self-defense. I felt that the homicide was justifiable. Normally, a widow would be crying but you don't understand what I went through with my evil husband. My husband would come home drunk and he would beat me up. So, I'm glad that he's dead. Sincerely, Sarah Rosenthal," she stated this in the telegram. As she was writing this letter, she read the letter. She folded it up. A pigeon flew up to the window. "Bring this letter to, Judge Stevenson," she said. The bird flew to the courthouse and slid the telegram underneath the double doors. Sarah fell asleep.

The next morning, half of the town walked up to the courthouse either to watch or speak at the sentencing. The other half of the town went to the 9 a.m. service at the Church of the Latter Day Saints. Sarah walked up to the

Courthouse. The police commissioner posted a FOR SALE sign on the front window of the hotel. He and Rubi walked up to the courthouse for sentencing as well. This is the day that shall determine Will Von Alien's fate.

This will determine whether he gets sent to the gallows or gets Life in Prison. Everybody is present in the courtroom including all of Will's confidants and Jobe's son, who is now sober. The judge walked up to the top of the bench, where he would deliver the sentence. The impact statements will take place now for the victim. There are two victims in this case; the fake victim, Jobe or the real victim Will.

Sentencing is about to take place. The members from counsel and the defendant are present in the courtroom.

"Ladies and gentlemen, today is an exciting day for all. We will have a monster being kept out of this society. It's time for the start of the sentencing hearing. Before we start, I want to say that the defendant and counsel are present. The members from the victim's family are present and so are the defendant's confidants. One important thing that we must bring up at the sentencing hearing is that I received a letter that sounded quite threatening. Fortunately, this woman had a right mind and she didn't write anything that was considered illegal. She just asked me to give the defendant clemency. This letter is not important so, I shall therefore toss it. I think we'll start off with the prosecution for the victim's impact statements," said Mr. Stevenson.

Sarah was saddened. The dishonorable judge sat down in his seat and leaned backwards. Instead of treating the courtroom with respect, he treated the hallowed courtroom like it's his living room. James walked up to the stand. The prosecutor covered his nose and snickered in an evil manner. The son of Jobe stared at the alien leader directly in the face.

"Will, I had some respect for you when I first met you. I thought you were this great leader of a great city. Later I discovered that you are a conniving man filled with evil and hatred. To me, you are now considered a monstrosity. I hope somebody kills you. You won't be dying at my hands. You'll be dying at the hands of the Justice System of the United States. Fortunately, evil masterminds like you will disappear from this World. To add insult to injury, you tried to lasso my mom into committing this crime. Now that she's free, you're not going to cause any evil to this world. In your short life of 25 years, you have caused great harm for so many. I hope you die," he said.

"Do you have any further words?" the judge asked. "No more, your honor. I don't have anything else to say. I shall give the other victims a chance," answered James. "Do you have any victims to come up to the stand?" asked Mr. Stevenson. "No, your honor. This was the only other unfortunate victim," answered Mr. Douer. "Now, do we have any impact statements for the defense?" the judge asked.

"Yes, your honor," answered Mr. Blackmon. "Who do you want to start with?" asked Mr. Stevenson. "Sarah Rosenthal," the defense attorney answered. She walked up to the stand.

"Your honor, my only request is that you throw out the defendant's conviction. The real victim in this case is not my former husband. It's the alien, who's facing the death penalty. He doesn't deserve to be going through this ordeal. That prosecutor I believe clearly has a vendetta for him. Besides, Mr. Douer intended to do evil to him. What is even sadder is that the stupid jury believed this world class idiot of a prosecutor. It is wrong how a jury of one's peers can convict an innocent man because of the prosecutor's malicious attitude. Your honor, I would rather be the one hanging than this man, Will. Spare him his life for I shall be more than willing to take the punishment. It is not right how we live in a country with such a great justice system that we have a bad apple like this prosecutor, who is here to cause nothing but, trouble and evil. That is unfortunate. We shouldn't tolerate injustice. I feel this homicide was justifiable. First of all, you would want to hang my husband because what he did to me was totally wrong and evil. Every night, he would come home drunk and beat me senselessly in the worst manner possible. My husband had anger management problems, especially when he was drunk. My husband was a strong supporter of slavery and chauvinism. I don't think anybody with a right mind would believe in doing such a thing. My husband did not deserve to die. He caused his own death instead. The reason why was because he dragged Will outside of the saloon and then threatened him, and I'm not talking about petty threats I am talking about real cold hearted threats. He would threaten to kill him multiple times. I saw a struggle take place outside of the saloon. You see, my evil husband lunged at Will and then he started choking him. Will kicked my husband in the face like he deserved. Then, to make sure that my violent spouse would not kill him, my friend, the defendant sitting over there, shot my husband. It seemed like such a sad moment. Everybody knew him as this great, benevolent Mormon. My husband was not the great Mormon. He was nothing but a walking facade and an evil man. He had intents of malice and my husband was the true epitome of sickness and horrible behavior. You see, we live in a world, where there is a Court of Public Opinion and the 'real' Courtroom of Justice. In this world, even in this nation, there are courtrooms that are supposed to be used to support justice, but unfortunately, a lot of courtrooms support injustice. The courtroom that you're presently sitting in supports evil and injustice; because, if this was a just courtroom, a different jury would've been selected and we would not be here for sentencing. Will Von Alien is clearly an innocent victim of an overzealous prosecutor and a malevolent judge, who supports that evil prosecutor," she finished her statement. She walked over to the defense table.

"Now, let me just tell you this, I am an extremely fair judge because if I was unfair, I would hold you in Criminal Contempt of Court especially during Capital Murder hearing and that can carry out a 10 year sentence. You were lucky that you got acquitted yesterday because I feel that you were a conspirator for the death of Jobe and if I was on that jury, there'd be a mistrial. I think you are the most evil woman that God has ever put on the face of this Earth. How can a woman like you be so cold and have the heart of evil? I don't know any woman like you. There's this one phrase that goes, If you commit a crime on Earth and you don't get punished on Earth, you will be punished when judgement day takes place and that's when you meet your Creator. Sit down now! You should be ashamed of yourself," the arrogant judge said.

"Now, who's next?" he asked. "This lady right here," answered Mr. Blackmon. "Oh, what is she another alien?" asked Mr. Stevenson. "Yes, your honor," the defense attorney answered. Rubi walked up to the stand to testify on Will's behalf.

"Your honor, this gentleman and I are soon to get married in December and you want to hang him before he even sees his wedding cake. That's totally evil. You see, I know what it's like to be a battered person because in my past life in Russia, my mom was a battered woman. The only exception is that he's a battered man from an alien city. Unfortunately, we live in a society that is based on the idea of Social Darwinism and I'm not talking about the idea of Survival of the Fittest. I'm talking about the idea of Racial Superiority. You see, my boyfriend Will, has been the victim of that. I know the details of what happened that caused him to end up in this situation. Now, your honor, I don't base my beliefs off of relationships or that individual's talent. I base my opinions off of the evidence, and based on the evidence from this alleged incident, this man is clearly innocent. If he wasn't an alien, you would probably treat him differently. We'd probably not be here right now. He's just as important as a man. We unfortunately live in a world filled with injustice and hatred. The one who should be on trial right now is that evil prosecutor. He's the one that is here to cause trouble. He's the one with the vendetta against my boyfriend. Your honor, the reason why I came up here was to save my boyfriend's life. I simply don't want anything to happen to him. If you send him to the gallows, you are doing the most evil action that man can do. I think you know why, but I'll tell you anyway. You see, Will would never even thinking about committing an intentional homicide. He would never even hurt a fly. He will bring somebody out of this world that has evil intent. Sarah brought up a pretty good point. She said that her husband caused his own death. This particular phrase sounds cold. It is not cold and nor, is it arrogant. When one says that somebody deserves to die, that sounds arrogant and cold.

When one says that somebody caused their own death, it sounds more intelligent than arrogant. Based on what I've seen, Jobe's violent behavior caused his demise. If he never came home all boozed up, he would be living today and maybe, this whole thing would've not taken place. One thing that I must say is that my boyfriend is clearly innocent. If I was on that jury, I'd vote not guilty on reason of self-defense. Another, reason why this homicide should've been considered as a justifiable homicide was because Will took the life of a man who was nothing but a beast. Like Sarah said earlier, Jobe would act in an animalistic manner. Jobe was nothing but a malicious monstrosity and he was a walking facade, but one thing that is for certain is that he's dead. To some, his demise is sad. To others, his demise would have caused a celebration. Will is being used as a scapegoat and being turned into the monster because he simply defended himself. Unfortunately, I might not be able to see my boyfriend because he is going to be hung because of dirty judges like you," she said. As she walked off of the stand, she started sobbing. She sat down at the defense table. "Lady, stand up, now! You should be ashamed of yourself. Who are you to talk to a judge like that? Do you think I am a monster? Because if you think that, you can get the hell out of my courtroom! You think what your boyfriend did was acceptable? Well, guess what? It's not acceptable. It's totally sick and wrong. I can't believe that callous creatures like you even exist. I'd like to hang you like your boyfriend. Unfortunately, the stupid justice system in this country doesn't allow that," replied Mr. Stevenson.

"Let me just tell you this. You're a piece of garbage. How can people call you the 'honorable' or 'your honor'? You are very dishonorable because you're nothing but a tyrant. I've dealt with tyrants like you. You are as evil as that bloody prosecutor. Then, you have the guts to call me a callous creature, when you're the cold-hearted soul. If I was the judge, I would give you ten years behind bars. You want to hang me? That's ridiculous and absurd. When you meet your Creator, he will see how you have been. If you think it's your prerogative to be the way you are, then you ought to be ashamed of yourself. As a judge, you take an important oath not to be bias and you're the exact opposite of that oath. When somebody is testifying, you have the craving to hold them in contempt for no reason whatsoever! That is sick and wrong. How dare you act in such a way! You need to reassert your soul because you are harmful. You are as evil as a serpent; and you have the heart made of stone. Your blood is frozen in time and you are locked in stone. You think you're this great and almighty judge. You're not! Somebody should speak up to you and have the guts to fight against you. You're not even a human being. You are nothing but, a racist. That is sick! May God send an Eagle to swoop down and grab you from this Earth and drop you in Hell! That's where you belong. Hell is your little nest," the alien leader's girlfriend argued.

"Oh, you're so right," the dishonorable judge said in a sarcastic manner.

Rubi continued "I know I am. I am here to fight for justice. You are the epitome of injustice. Why don't they just brand the letters of 'SOI' for Supporter of Injustice or 'EOI' for Epitome of Injustice because you are clearly the Epitome of Injustice. May Satan curse you," replied Rubi.

"You're right. I'm more right. And to show you that I'm more right, it'll be my honor that I shall hold you in contempt of court on two counts. One count for threatening me and another count for calling me a dishonorable judge.

The guards shall take you out of this courtroom. I hereby charge you to be guilty of the crime of criminal contempt of court. You'll serve 60 hours in jail without food.

That'll be your punishment. If you have a problem, you have your appellate rights so you can file for appeal, but because I'm the only judge in this town, I could deny your appeal. So, goodbye to you. and by the way, you're evil," said Mr. Stevenson. "This evil behavior should be destroyed. You are a true supporter of evil and may the Lord see what you're doing," the alien leader's girlfriend replied. The guards started to drag her out of the courtroom. The double doors shut.

The judge smirked in an arrogant manner. He laughed in an evil manner. "You knew that would happen to you, Rubi," he muttered under his breath. The double doors of the courtroom closed. "Do we have any more advocates for the defendant coming up?" he asked. Sheriff Joe walked up to the stand. "Yes, your honor," he answered. "Well, what a surprise. We have the sheriff coming up to testify on behalf of the defendant. I've never seen that. There might be some chance that I might throw out the conviction," replied Mr. Stevenson.

"Ladies and Gentlemen, I am the Sheriff for South Salt Lake. I was the one who apprehended Will and Sarah. As a sheriff, I initially believed that they were guilty before their trial, even before arraignment. I was reminded of the theory that all criminals are innocent until proven guilty. When I understood that theory, I interrogated my two detainees especially Will. Since we live in a racist and chauvinist society, the prosecutor pressed charges against him and that was totally wrong. When I interrogated him, I noticed that the victim in this case was him. Jobe wasn't really the victim. The dead man was the belligerent soul.

Unfortunately, they're portraying the defendant to be the bad man when the dead man was the bad man. I felt this case should've never even been indicted because there was a lack of evidence in this case to even go before a grand jury indictment. So, your honor, I strongly request that you overturn this alien's conviction because he is clearly innocent. And so is Sarah. Fortunately, Sarah got acquitted like she should've been. It is wrong that we live in a society that is filled with bigotry and hatred," said Sheriff Joe. "Well, let me just tell you this, you crazy sheriff. I used to like you and I thought you were the best sheriff because you have the strength of stone. You don't; you have nothing but a soft spot, especially for these monstrosities of society like Will Von Alien. I request that you leave my courtroom now. Unfortunately, I can't tell you to leave this town. If I had the authority to do that, I would toss you out of here," the judge replied.

     The sheriff walked out of the courtroom. He reached the double doors. "You keep dreaming," he said bluntly as he made his departure. After the sheriff left the courtroom, the judge asked, "Are there any other individuals coming up to defend this creature?"

     "Yes, your honor," the defense attorney answered. "and is this person the last one testifying on Will's behalf?" asked Mr. Stevenson. "Yes, your honor," answered Mr. Blackmon. Police Commissioner Clayton walked up from the seating area of the guests. "What's your name?" the dishonorable judge asked. "Commissioner William Clayton," the police commissioner answered.

     "And, are you here to give a statement on the defendant's behalf?" asked Mr. Stevenson. "Yes, sir," answered Clayton. "Good. At least some mortal like you shows some respect for a judge," replied the arrogant judge.

"Your honor, we live in a world of accusatory men and women. I am a cop and I believe that all criminals are guilty unless they're cops. The reason why is because we cops and police commissioners see what takes place in the court systems. I know Will Von Alien because he came to Planet Earth when the train derailed from Starmos City. He was supposed to be heading to California County. He headed into New York City for that reason. You see, I believe Will is a victim of a cruel injustice system. As an American, I believe that all criminals are innocent until they're proven guilty and that should go within the Justice System of the United States. Your honor, I know this defendant very well. And I figured that he would be discriminated in this time period because there's such a thing as what is called 'Social Darwinism.' This is a belief of what is well known as racial superiority and in the year that we're in now, 1856, racism is acceptable. It's not acceptable. In fact, it's totally wrong. I bet if Will wasn't an alien, we would not be here during sentencing because he would be a free man. Because he's an alien, we had to take him to trial. If you had some sort of random John Wilkes on the street, you'd probably think what he did is acceptable. Unfortunately, your court system believed that Jobe's arrogant behavior was justifiable. As a police commissioner, I deal with many women who come into my office being accused of Capital Murder, who kill their husbands because their husbands were so nasty to them; they acquired the disability of Battered Woman's Syndrome. That's unfortunate because no women or man should have to suffer what some women suffered. Look at Sarah Rosenthal. She had to suffer the cruelty of her evil husband. That is evil and we shouldn't have to live in a world like this. Then, your court system that is supposedly fighting for justice does not fight for justice. Instead, your court system curtails and kowtows to injustice and you all think injustice is acceptable. You see, justice covers a lot of territory. Books have been written about justice. We see justice every day. Justice is a relative subject. One person might think that somebody else being prosecuted is considered justice. Others will think that this is injustice. Then there are those that think acquittals are just and the others think that acquittals are wrong. That's because they're simply stupid and ignorant, and yes, there's the phrase that ignorance is bliss. It's not. Ignorance is the epitome of evil. Ignorance is what tears down a society. Mankind should have an open mind and be willing to listen. Now, my preaching does not have much to do with this case. Besides, I'm not a preacher. I am just a police commissioner. Ignorance is sort of related to this case and so is the idea of racial superiority. The reason why is because this prosecutor is an arrogant man. I am able to read every prosecutor's mind and I know their motive to charging a defendant with a crime. Based on what I see, this prosecutor believed that Will was a slave even though he was clearly an male alien. The reason is your world believes that men, who are not Caucasian are inferior. That is totally wrong and evil. I can't believe that you think that's acceptable because it's not. This prosecutor is sick in his head. He is a sociopath; he supports injustice. If you look forward in history, you'll be able to look at Italian prosecutors, who had vendettas against innocent defendants. The worst prosecutor in the world is a prosecutor in Perugia, Italy, who had a vendetta for many innocent defendants, but we shouldn't be getting into the future and talking about foreign prosecutors. We should talk about this prosecutor right here. He has it in for Will because he, Will that is, is a strong man. He is benevolent and intelligent. This prosecutor was (and still is) a jealous freak. He had something against Will and he had it in for one of my good friends. Your honor, I hereby request that you reverse the conviction of my good friend because anybody in his or her right mind knows he is innocent. If you sentence him to the gallows, then you might as well sentence Rubi, Sheriff Joe, and myself to the gallows. We'll be more than willing to go for our very loyal and benevolent friend, Will Von Alien. So, your honor, I beg for your mercy on behalf of one of my best friends," said Clayton.

"Yes, you know something. It is very nice that you want to be benevolent for your friend. He must unfortunately suffer the consequence for his actions. A jury of his peers found him guilty and now he will have to receive the consequence. You are basically stating that he's above the law because he's an alien. He's not. If he does something that's illegal, he has to face every consequence like everybody else. I appreciate the fact that you want to fight for your friend, but it's too late. He must suffer the consequence," replied Mr. Stevenson.

"I just beg you for mercy on his behalf," the police commissioner said. "Well, that's nice, but it's not going to happen. Now, I need to give a chance for the defendant to say his words before I impose the sentence," the arrogant judge replied. Will Von Alien stood in the middle of the Courtroom.

"Your honor, I do not want to say that I don't hold myself accountable for a crime. I didn't do anything wrong. I never had the intent to kill Jobe Rosenthal. He had the intent to kill me. I know I'm innocent of these malicious allegations and this case should've never gone to trial, but to the victim's family, I wish them a better life and happiness because I know they had a tremendous loss. It is extremely upsetting for what happened to Jobe. I am not here to say that I'm innocent or preach my innocence, but your honor, I am innocent. I killed Jobe was in self-defense and I hereby felt that this homicide was justifiable. When I first met the alleged victim, Jobe, he was extremely nice. He was willing to take me in with his family after my ordeal with God. When we came to the saloon in this town, I discovered that the men mistreated women. For instance, they banned them from going into these places. I discovered that Sarah was all lonely and she needed somebody to talk to. Hence, I found out about how she was being mistreated by her husband. So, I decided to confront him, but not in a violent way. Since, he was drunk, he started acting extremely belligerent and animalistic to me. So, that was when I felt that my homicide was justifiable. Your honor, I hereby beg for mercy because I feel that I definitely deserve it. I am innocent," he said.

"Is that enough?" asked Mr. Stevenson. "Yes, your honor," the alien leader answered. He sat back down at the defense table and started crossing his fingers in nervousness about the sentence. "Very well then. Before, I impose this sentence. I will say that I announce you to be guilty of the crime of First Degree Capital Murder. Look at yourself, you're an arrogant monster. When God was thinking about creating his creatures for all of the dimensions, he shouldn't have created you because you are the true summary of evil. And evil creatures like you don't belong here. So, I shall therefore impose the sentence of death by hanging. In other words, you'll go to the gallows.

You are not entitled to file for an appeal because you're an alien and you're not Caucasian. You're an animal; you're a beast," the arrogant judge said.

"Oh your honor, I beseech you," replied Mr. Blackmon. "Don't give me that bull crap. I don't have time for that garbage that you're spewing out. I want the guards to take him to the county jail. I hereby order Sheriff Joe to sentence Mr. Von Alien to death. The defendant shall die at the hands of the government," said Mr. Stevenson.

The guards swiftly dragged Will across the street to the County jail. He should be brought to the gallows and executed. It is a horrible moment. Half of the courtroom started crying. The judge ordered every individual to leave the courtroom except for the prosecutor. After everybody departed from the courtroom, the judge and the prosecutor laughed in a diabolical way. As the prosecutor laughed, his fangs started coming out of his mouth. So, did the judge's fangs.

"You did such an excellent job, your honor," said Mr. Douer. "Of course, I gave that creature what he deserves, but then again we're creatures that are humans," the judge replied. "We're all God's creatures," the evil prosecutor said. "I know," Mr. Stevenson replied sarcastically.

Chapter XVII: The Escape from South Salt Lake

It is now 4:00 the next afternoon. Everybody is lining up to see the execution of Will Von Alien. he's in his jail cell waiting for execution. Sheriff Joe is sitting at his desk preparing the paper. "Sheriff, what are you doing?" the alien leader asked. "Preparing your papers for execution. You must answer my questions when I ask you the questions that are stated in the papers," the sheriff answered.

"Well, would you mind not organizing these papers? Judge Stevenson is going to deny me from going forward from being executed if they're disorganized," asked Will.

"Unfortunately, I can't disorganize those papers because that arrogant, nasty judge would go after me. I wanted to burn those papers. Unfortunately, I couldn't. That judge is clearly out to get all of us. You know that. He's as evil as a serpent and he is not a human. He looks like a human but really in his heart, he's a creature. That judge should go to Hell because that's where he belongs. It's too late to fight for justice because that sick judge denied you from filing an appeal against your conviction. Another reason why I can't disorganize those papers is because I can be sent to jail, possibly the gallows because that judge could say that I violated the *Fugitive Slave Act*, which shouldn't have been put into place but that garbage senator John C. Calhoun put that law into place. Let's get back to this case. Will, I know you are a victim. I knew that Jobe was a drunk and I knew he had a violent attitude. Unfortunately, we live in a world filled with evil and injustice. It is said that our own justice system is flawless. That's not true, our justice system has its flaws," answered Sheriff Joe.

"Well, is there any hope out of this case?" the alien leader asked. "I don't think so. The only possibility of that happening is if you escape this place. You'll be able to run into the woodlands of Utah," the sheriff answered. "Can we come up with an escape plan?" asked Will. "Sure," answered Sheriff Joe. "Would you let us out of the cell and then we can talk?" the alien leader asked. The sheriff opened the cell door and he brought Will and Rubi out of the cell. "Can I join the escape plan?" the alien leader's girlfriend asked.

"Sure, why not." answered Will. They both walked up to the sheriff's desk. Sheriff Joe told them about an escape plan. "So, I'll join you in this plan. But before I get into this I want to tell you all something. You must be very discreet about this because I don't want that damn prosecutor finding out; nor do I want that sick judge finding out either. This is how you *must* escape. You are allowed to bring four friends with you to the gallows post, but before you get up there, I'll cut the rope a little loose. In order to keep that hidden, I'll tell everybody that I'm adjusting the rope to fit your neck. I'll cut this rope so loose that you'll fall out of there. So, be prepared to fall six feet to the ground. Then, run as fast as you can into the wilderness. I'll come and join you abandon this town once and for all," he answered.

"What would Rubi do?" the alien leader asked. "I'm sorry, but I initially thought that she would be standing behind you. She'll stand in front of you waiting to catch you when you fall. I think she's physically strong. She'll break your fall and there won't be any possibility that either you or she will have a broken bone. Then, we'll all do the same thing," answered Sheriff Joe.

"What would you do?" the alien leader asked. "Well, you see I would do the exact same thing everybody else is doing. I would make sure that there wouldn't be any individuals trying to go after you during the escape. In addition I'd make sure that the judge or that prosecutor would come after you. If they even tried to lay a finger on you, I'd murder them myself. We shouldn't let their evilness get to us. That would be lowering ourselves down to their level," answered the sheriff.

"That sounds like an excellent escape plan. I understand that there's no way we can be surreptitious. One thing that is certain in this plan is that we must have quick reaction speed. It is a life or death situation," replied Will. "Excellent analysis," said Sheriff Joe. "Thank you," the alien leader replied. "Now, can I ask you some questions before you supposedly hang?" the sheriff asked.

"Sure, you know I'm not going to hang, right?" asked Will. "Yes, I said 'supposedly'. Let's get into the 'interrogation.'" Sherriff Joe went through the motions. "Okay," the alien leader replied. "Now, do you realize that you're going to be executed by the gallows?" the sheriff asked. "Yes, I know I'm not going to get hung," answered Will. "Very good. Now, where did you come from?" asked Sheriff Joe. "Starmos City," the alien leader answered. "Very good. When did you come over to Planet Earth?" the sheriff asked. "36 hours ago," answered Will.

"Good. How old are you today?" asked Sheriff Joe. "25 years old and counting," the alien leader answered. "What is your birth year?" the sheriff asked. "2022," answered Will. "Is that in the past or future?" he continued. "The future," the alien leader answered. "Have you ever been to this town before?"

"No, I haven't. Quite frankly, I never knew this town existed," answered Will. "What states have you been to or through?" asked Sheriff Joe. "I've been through the Carolinas, Virginia, Delaware, Maryland, New Jersey, and New York. I have been to California County, New York and New York City," the alien leader answered. "What year have you been to New York?" the sheriff asked. "2047," answered Will.

"Now, do you like the judge that you're dealing with?" asked Sheriff Joe. "No, I can't stand him. He's the most unfair judge. He knew exactly what happened. The only witnesses that perjured themselves onto the stand were the prosecution's witnesses. This judge was extremely unfair. Whenever the prosecution made an objection against the defense attorney, the judge would rule in favor of the prosecution's objection. When the defense made an objection against the prosecution, the judge would tell the defense attorney to shut the hell up. Then, when somebody who supported me curses in the court room, he would tell his guards to actually drag that individual out of the courtroom. That's quite arbitrary and unjust. So, simply, the answer to your question is 'no.' I am sure you're going to ask me if that judge was fair. He was totally unfair and he should be thrown off the bench. If that judge was here right now, I'd grab him by his neck and strangle him until his head exploded. Then, I'd decapitate him. That judge thinks he has the right to call me a monster. He knows that he's the real monster. He takes the oath to preserve, protect, and defend the Constitution of the United States and the Charter of Utah, when he's violated this oath numerous times. The Constitution clearly states that an individual is entitled to a fair trial. My trial was unfair because the prosecution had more of a chance to prove its case than the defense," the alien leader angrily answered.

"That sounds quite vile. I can understand how angry you are at the judge. You shouldn't say that you want to decapitate him. That's just plain terrible. I'll take the answer to your last question as 'no.' I would probably write the same answer even if I am the one that enforces the laws," replied Sheriff Joe.

"Good thing, you agree with me. I like you," said Will. "Let's continue with this interrogation. I have one more question. Would you like to have a last meal?" the sheriff asked. "Yes, sir," the alien leader answered. "You could look from this menu in front of you. Select what you want because the delivery guy is waiting outside," replied Sheriff Joe.

Will selected a Southern Cobb Salad. The sheriff presented him with the dish in a formal manner on an ornately decorated dish. The alien leader started eating. He finished the meal in ten minutes. "Sheriff, tell me about your life," he said.

"Sure. I've surpassed my expected age by twenty years. I am about 79 years old but am still as strong as a cannon. I was born in 1777, the year after the Declaration of Independence was signed by our founding fathers. It is important that I must say that we were still involved in the ordeal with Great Britain, The American Revolution. It is unfortunate that the British didn't give us independence and regrettably I was too young to fight. I would have been a strong fighter. Fortunately, we won the revolution in Virginia and became a free country. Unfortunately, we weren't fully free. You see we didn't have an established government, nor did we have a Constitution. We did have the Articles of Confederation. Did that work? Absolutely not. The reason it didn't work was because it created division between all of the states. The Constitution wouldn't be much better. As you see, we lived in a society where we had to worry about an unfair government because the Constitution was set into place. We Americans insisted that the Bill of Rights would be included in the Constitution because our rights weren't initially guaranteed. So, the first ten amendments were added to the Constitution to preserve our rights. Our government didn't guarantee rights for all of mankind. These rights were only given to Caucasian men. Women and African Americans were denied those rights. Instead, the women and African Americans were treated like slaves. African Americans would be forced to work on Plantations and women would be forced to work within the homes. And we both agree that was wrong! People perceived the Constitution as a document that would protect man kind's rights, and if you ask a government official why they didn't guarantee all men and women rights, that official will tell you to shut up, get lost, or they're property. One thing that is for certain is that women and people that are not Caucasian are not property. They're human beings like everybody else. Now, the reason why I am talking about Slavery is because it relates to this case with you. The government thinks you're a slave because you're not Caucasian. They think you're property because you don't come from America. That prosecutor is nothing but a nativist and a cruel creature. I remember that we used to have an excellent and fair prosecutor. This thing took over the courthouse and you were unfortunately put to trial. That was wrong because I know that you were innocent. Slavery unfortunately ties into this case because that prosecutor and that judge are two Social Darwinists. Those two are bigots, who are here to cause trouble. Then the jury that was selected was an unfair and partial jury because they thought that you wouldn't understand the true definition of an impartial jury and they figured that you didn't have any rights because you're not Caucasian. They didn't want to show their true opinions because they knew they'd be ostracized and held accountable," explained Sheriff Joe.

"I totally agree with you. Now before I supposedly get hung. I just want to know if there are any spectators waiting for the public execution," said Will. The sheriff walked out of his seat over to the door. He peaked out the window. Not a single individual is standing outside waiting to see the execution. "No spectators over here," he said.

"Please check the side window," the alien leader replied. "Okay," said Sheriff Joe. He checked out the side window adjacent to the door. Not a single individual is standing in front of the gallows post. "Nobody over here," he said.

"Very good. Not to sound like I'm being bossy, but I would appreciate it if Rubi would come outside," replied Will. "Why would you make such a stupid request?" asked the sheriff. "Do you remember the escape plan?" the alien leader asked. "Oh yes, it clearly states that Rubi is to stand in front of the gallows post," answered Sheriff Joe. "Good, so why don't you escort her outside," said Will. "Okay, I think we can have that arranged," the sheriff replied. He walked up to the alien leader's girlfriend and removed her cuffs. "Am I free?" she asked.

"Yes, you are. All that judge wanted to do was throw you out of the courtroom. He figured that I would keep you in a cell because he had a vendetta against you, but at the end of the day, I freed you. Just go outside and stand in front of the gallows post. Just pretend you're crying or praying," answered Sheriff Joe. He escorted her out the door up to the gallows post. Will remained safe inside. After the sheriff did that, he dashed back into the county jail.

"Mr. Von Alien, it's a good thing that I can trust you to stay here. Remember, we don't want to foil the escape plan. We want everything to go as it should go. I want you to be safe here. I don't want anything to happen to you," he said. "Sheriff, you don't have to call me Mr. Von Alien. Besides, Mr. Von Alien was my father. Call me Will; that's what my name is and that's what it'll always be." the alien leader replied. "Okay, 'Will', you're going to go up to the gallows post. I'll tell you what to do next. Be very cooperative like you have been because I'm not here to imprison you. I'm here to help you escape safely," said Sheriff Joe.

He escorted the alien leader up to the first four steps of the side door which was the gateway to Hell. "Stay there," he said. While the alien leader waited by the gallows post, the sheriff returned to his desk, to retrieve the scissors in the third drawer to the right. He opened the drawer and chose the 18" long scissors that are as sharp as shark teeth.

He walked back up to the gallows post and started cutting the rope that chokes the individual who is being lynched. The judge and the prosecutor noticed the sheriff cutting the rope. They dashed down the courthouse steps and ran across the street. They are surprised by the scene of the sheriff cutting the rope. Within a matter of seconds the prosecutor arrived at the jail. The sheriff continued cutting the rope.

"What the hell are you doing!?" asked Mr. Douer. Sheriff Joe turned around. His eyes and nostrils widened, his pupils dilated, and his heart started pounding. "What's wrong? Why aren't you answering me?" the arrogant prosecutor asked. The sheriff dropped the scissor. "Do you want me to charge you with attempted murder?" Mr. Douer asked.

"No," answered the sheriff. "Well, tell me what you were doing with the scissor," the prosecutor shouted. "I was adjusting the rope so that way the defendant can die slower," Sheriff Joe sarcastically replied. "That's my man. Torture the monster and then kill him," said Mr. Douer. "Yup, you're right. Torturing the beast is the right way to go. That is surely the nicest deed one can do," the sheriff replied so convincingly. "Yup. I'll turn around while you do that," the prosecutor said. The sheriff continued cutting the string loose so that way when Will steps up to the gallows post, he falls into Rubi's hands.

While he's doing this, the prosecutor turned around. He noticed Rubi. He placed his hand on his heart and almost fell backwards. "Rubi, you're supposed to be in jail. What are you doing here?" he asked. "Oh, Sheriff Joe freed me," she answered. "and since when does he have the right to free you?" asked Mr. Douer. "Well, you see the judge stated that I would be sentenced from 1-60 days in jail and I was very well behaved in the county jail. I was freed because of my good behavior," the alien leader's girlfriend answered.

"Well, don't you need my approval to be freed?" the arrogant prosecutor asked. "What makes you think I need your approval you low life, piece of shit?" asked Rubi. She punched him after he said that. He bounced back up. His nose swelled up to the size of a clown's nose. "Ha, ha, ha. Instead of you looking like a prosecutor, you look like a clown from the circus. Looks like you won't be signing any autographs anytime soon," she said.

The prosecutor dashed back to the courtroom. Meanwhile, Will is standing on top of the gallows post waiting for all of the town's people to be coming out. He looked at the sheriff. "Are you finished?" he asked. "Yes, sir, you'll be ready to hang there all you want," Sheriff Joe answered in sarcastically. "Okay," the alien leader replied. "Do you feel that you're ready to be hung?" asked Sheriff Joe.

"Yes," answered Will. "You DO know I'm being sarcastic when I asked that question?" the sheriff asked. "Of course, we're pulling an act in front of the prosecutor," the alien leader answered."Hush! Don't say anything! That creature is here. He's going to tell Judge Stevenson and then you'll be in serious trouble," replied Sheriff Joe.

"I don't care; they can do anything they want. I'll fight them. If Rubi was able to punch that prosecutor in the nose, I can kill him. I'm stronger than that prosecutor. I wish some horse can kick dirt in his face. If I had a horse, that's what I would make him do. You know something, I know a much worse punishment that I can inflict on that prosecutor. I'd go to the Quarry and make an acidic formula and dump acid on this crazy prosecutor," said Will. The sheriff laughed.

"You know that you're going to the extremes with what you're saying? I have a much simpler thing that I'd do. Have you ever been to Spain or Mexico?" he asked. "No, but I've heard of those countries," the alien leader answered.

"I'm sure you very well may know about the bull riders and bullfighters. You see, I would put the prosecutor in a rink with a bull and he'd have the crap beat out of him.

The prosecutor would be dead in seconds. He doesn't have the strength to fight off the bulls," replied Sheriff Joe. "I know that. Unfortunately, he had the strength to persuade the jury," said Will.

"The only strength that this prosecutor has is verbal strength. His only talent that was given by the devil was to tell lies and twist the truth. He might have the capability of going up there, twisting the truth, and trying to put you on the gallows. He doesn't have any strength against God. When he meets God, he'll be destroyed. This prosecutor will be going to Hell when he meets God and I hope he spends a lengthy amount of time in Hell," the sheriff replied.

"When is everyone going to watch the execution take place?" the alien leader asked sarcastically. "In just 5 minutes," answered Sheriff Joe. Suddenly, women dressed in black came down from the Church of the Latter Day Saints. They wore black gowns and hats. Two of them were paid two mourn; while the other three started singing *Amazing Grace* for 10 minutes. The preacher also came down. He wore a white cloak and shoes. He tossed Holy Water on top of the Will. The rest of the town followed the Mormons.

Many town officials are present at the execution and so are the employees of the saloon and the dance hall. The mourners from the Mormon Church stopped singing the song. The preacher walked up to the gallows post. "We are here as a town and a community of Christians. We are not here to celebrate a holiday. We are here to mourn the execution of an individual from another Planet, Will Von Alien.

Unfortunately, he was falsely convicted of the crime of First Degree Capital Murder. This man being hung did an excellent action. He took the life of a Son of Perdition, who is now going to go to Hell. He didn't intend to take the life of Jobe because he was a Son of Perdition. The reason he took that man's life was in self-defense. The prosecution accused him of committing a heinous crime. I don't think it's a crime to defend yourself. God will see the action Will did and on judgment day Jobe shall go to Hell and Will shall visit the Celestial City," he said.

"Is that it?" asked Mr. Stevenson. "Yes," the preacher answered. Commissioner Bill Clayton came up to the gallows post. "You know that you're part of the escape plan," whispered Sheriff Joe. "No, I didn't know that., but I'm more than willing to join this great escape," replied the police commissioner. "Good, go up and speak your heart out," the sheriff said. Clayton walked up to the gallows post. "Now, ladies and gentlemen, we live in a world that is filled with the guilty and the innocent; harshness and lenience; fair and bias behavior stupidity and intelligence; unfairness and fairness; and finally, justice and injustice. Will Von Alien had to suffer through injustice of a system that is bias and filled with individuals whose minds are filled with stupidity.

Furthermore, he was innocent and endured the harshness of a cruel, stone-hearted, unfair judge. I researched this judge's history through a "Judge" encyclopedia and this judge would always give defendants that were not Caucasian the harshest sentences possible. This judge is clearly a bigot and he knows he's a bigot. He just doesn't want to open up about that because, he's afraid he'll be held accountable. You should not like this judge. In fact, deface his house! Throw mud at his house! Sneak a bucket of frogs in his house and make him feel like he's not welcome in this town. Better yet, make him feel like he's not welcome in this country! This judge has an ignorant mind and he's nothing but a Southern racist," he exclaimed. Rubi walked up to the gallows post.

"Will Von Alien, it is sad that you're going to be dying. In fact, it is miserable. One thing that is for certain is that you'll be going up to Heaven. And you know that judge shall be going to Hell and so should that prosecutor. You were unjustly tried and you know that the whole town is here to support you. Yes, it is a form of public humiliation being executed in public but it won't be humiliating to you, and you know why. That prosecutor can get up there and lie all he wants. He can dance around the truth; he can even twist the truth. But one thing that is for certain is the prosecutor won't twist the truth against God! He knows and you know that when you meet the Creator, he'll say that you're completely innocent because he *knows* you are innocent. Remember, God has an omnipresent power. He knows who you are and he knows who that prosecutor is. He knows that you never shot Jobe to kill him. He knows that you shot him in self-defense. Maybe, that stupid jury didn't believe you. That jury was not an impartial jury, it was a jury filled with all old men. If there were women on that jury, the verdict would have been different. Unfortunately, we're in a chauvinist society. I want justice to be done for you because you are clearly a victim of injustice. You are the victim of an unjust government and a cold- hearted prosecutor. When this prosecutor perishes, may he perish in vain! When you perish, your heart shall be cherished! Mr. Douer had a vendetta towards you because you were an alien from Starmos City, and you had special abilities that he did not have. You knew how to get along with Earthlings. Some Caucasian men had a problem with you. Sadly, we are in a society where slavery is mundane.

Unfortunately, some Caucasian men misconstrue you to be a slave when you are not. Some Caucasian men are strong supporters of slavery and that's also wrong. Now, Will, I've finished addressing my speech to you and I shall address this speech to the people in front of us. Ladies and Gentlemen, what Commissioner Bill Clayton said was quite important and significant. Unfortunately, we live in a world filled with injustice and we must destroy this injustice. We are living with it. Mankind says that there's nothing you can do about it. But there is something you can do about it. You can destroy this unjust government! You see one factor in this world that causes injustice is lying. Lying spreads like wildfire. It is easier for a man or woman to lie than tell the truth. It may be hard for that individual to do it because he or she might have to come up with a good story. It doesn't take long to tell that story or a fib. It is very easy to tell a lie, but is it easier to tell the truth? Is it easier to face the truth? You see, one thing that this prosecutor did that should never have been done was that he lied the whole time. This prosecutor is nothing but a pathological liar. He has the heart of an evil serpent. As a matter of fact, he doesn't even have a heart. His mind is the personification of evil and he is sinister. And Judge Stevenson is also a creature of the same ilk. This judge thinks he is as nice as Hercules. But he has the mind of Hades. This judge could have easily thrown out the conviction or choose to not even sentence Will. He did the complete opposite. This judge is as evil as sin. A Jolly Roger symbol is engraved in his head. It's not visible for all to see. The reason is that judge is really a serpent. If any of you were in the courtroom, I'm sure you might have stared at the judge's and the prosecutor's eyes. If you looked at them, you noticed their eyes looked like triangles pointed downwards. These triangles had the appearance of scalene triangles. Therefore they have scales hidden in their clothing. So they're not really human. That judge is not really a judge. He's really a beastly serpent and so is that prosecutor. I don't think any human would have the heart to prosecute my boyfriend because he was simply defending himself, but didn't you notice that this judge and prosecutor had shady appearances. I know I noticed. I just didn't want to announce this in open court and possibly humiliate them. They know who they really are. If they really had guts to stand up and fight, they'd show their true identities to the world; not some stupid disguise that they're trying to put on. If they had the guts to prosecute Will and send him to the gallows, why don't they have the guts to show their 'real' selves. They should identify who they really are," she said.

The judge and the prosecutor started turning red in anger. They didn't want to reveal themselves. The alien leader's girlfriend walked down from the gallows post and returned back to her spot. The prosecutor and the judge approached her in a warlike manner. "So, do you think being arrogant is okay?" asked Mr. Douer.

"No, I'm not the arrogant one. You're the arrogant one. You're the evil soul. You're the evil creature and you know who you are," answered Rubi. "No, I'm not the evil creature. The one who is the evil creature is you. For Godsakes, you're an alien. You're not even a human. You're not Caucasian; you wouldn't be a functional member of this society. You deserve to go on the plantations like everybody that is not of Caucasian color," the arrogant prosecutor replied. Rubi looked at them defiantly.

"You know that you're really a serpent," the alien leader's girlfriend said. "Yes, I know that. I'll show it after everybody finishes their speeches. I will show everyone that I'm a Serpent and it won't be in a nice way. So, let everybody finish their speeches," replied Mr. Douer.

"Yeah, I'm also a serpent. I don't want to admit that I'm a serpent, but if I have to shut you up, I shall admit that I'm a serpent. Once I admit that, this ordeal will be over and it won't be over in the pretty way. It'll be over in the ugly way. Death shall do its part against you, my dear. You think you're a nice lady when you're really not. You have an ego and you are here to cause trouble. You may have the strong voice, but do you have the strength to fight against me. Nobody can kill me unless they are born of a man, moved from another planet, or if they were related to a tyrannical dictator. I am stronger than you when I am in the form of a serpent. When the speeches are over and Will dies, I will poison you with my venomous fangs," said Judge Stevenson. The last individual came up to the gallows post to say her final wishes to the alien leader.

"Will, you have always been on my side when I first met you. When we met on the Covered Wagon heading to South Salt Lake, you sort of knew that my husband was being nasty to me because he would forbid me to say a word to you. He felt that women had no rights and that they should be seen and not heard. He felt that women were inferior to men. That is not a surprise. We, unfortunately, live in a bigoted and chauvinistic society. The majority of men in this society are nothing but walking phonies. The men in this supposedly 'free' society are not fair toward women, and what makes this even worse is that our government tolerates this unfairness. We as women won't tolerate this. We will rebel against our cruel, drunken husbands. We will revolt against the government who tolerates this and we will not curtail and bow to an unfair justice system. We as women should fight for justice. I am kind of going astray from this case, but one thing that we must say about Will Von Alien is that he is here to help the women of this society and he does not deserve to die like this. If anybody has a right mind or a mind filled with sanity, we would kill that judge and that prosecutor. Like Rubi said earlier, a human being wouldn't treat another human being like that. We must fight for Will because he is the true victim in this case. The partial jury might perceive him as a cold-blooded killer. He is a victim of injustice. Before he dies, I'll tell you what really happened. I told him that my husband was drunk and so he confronted my husband but not in the violent way. My husband was drunk and nasty. So Jobe, my husband started demeaning him and saying nasty comments about him right to his face. Eventually, those nasty comments became threats. My husband threatened this man who is unfortunately going to be hung. Then Jobe decided to make a fight with Will by lunging at him and choking him. Will was left with no other choice, but to simply stop him. He shot him to stop my beastly husband. He didn't shoot to kill. One reason why this case went to trial was because of this bigoted society that we live in. You see Will is not of Caucasian skin color so this evil prosecutor decided to pursue this case to make an example out of Will and turn him from a nice man into a wicked killer. He is not a killer. Then a jury that is supposed to be made up of his peers convicted him. This jury, however, was not made up of his peers. This prosecutor picked a jury of old men, who probably wanted to get out of that room. So, the old men just voted guilty because of that prosecutor's gut feeling. Now, I have withdrawn from speaking to all of you. I shall say my last words to the real victim the one who is standing next to me waiting to be hung. Will Von Alien, for you have been an excellent and loving figure in my life. You have cared about women and many victims of injustice and you are here to fight. You won't stand up to a cruel justice system. And I know when you perish, you'll perish in harmony, not in vain. Know that when Mr. Douer and Judge Stevenson shall perish they'll go right to Hell where they belong," she said.

She hugged the alien leader. She stepped down from the gallows post and Sheriff Joe escorted him to the Stool of Death.

"Mr. Von Alien, do you have any last words to say before you meet your death?" he asked.

"Yes, Sheriff. To all of those who wanted to help me, they've done their job and I am extremely grateful. To all of those who wanted to prosecute me, may they ask for forgiveness when they meet their Creator. And to those who have been there for me during this whole ordeal, I owe a lot of gratitude. Maybe as a productive member of American society, I was never able to fight for justice. It is up to all of you to fight for justice and stand up against injustice. You know how evil our government is and you all must fight. Remember, he who helps the weaker man shall be strong. I don't want to say that I am the weaker man because I am not. Instead, I am the stronger man; I'll fight for justice. And I do love God," he said. The alien leader placed the loop around his neck. He kicked the stool and the loop broke apart. He fell into Rubi's arms. Judge Stevenson and Mr. Douer ran up to the gallows post.

"Ladies and gentlemen, we are not a judge or prosecutor. We are really Serpents of the Under World. We are really Serpianto and Korbian," said "Mr. Douer." Everyone in the crowd started laughing. The judge and the prosecutor shapeshifted from humans to Cobra Snakes. The crowd started running out of the Western Town. The sheriff jumped down from the gallows post. Everyone ran into the woodlands including the escapees. The Boom Town of South Salt Lake became a Ghost Town within a matter of 30 seconds. The town is now desolate.

Chapter XVIII: Four Years Later: March of 1860: Abraham Lincoln (Republican) versus Stephen Douglas (Northern Democrat)

Will Von Alien, Commissioner Clayton, Rubi, and Sheriff Joe survive in the wilderness for many years. Their clothes are all rugged and their hair has an unkempt appearance. They are dependent on fires, stolen tents, and animals. Sometimes, one of them would come out of the woodlands to steal some crops from a farmland. However, they would only be able to survive for a month off the crops they've retrieved.

Eventually, they reached Illinois. They've just emerged from the woodlands. Right now, they're hearing political opinions in a debate going back and forth. "It sounds like Abraham Lincoln," the alien leader said.

"How do you know what Abe Lincoln sounds like? What are you inside his mind?" asked Sheriff Joe. "No, but I met him on the way to South Salt Lake. He was paid to be in the disguise of Sarah's younger son so that way Jobe didn't think that there was a miscarriage," answered Will. "Well, what is he doing?" the sheriff asked. "Let's go and check," the alien leader answered. They walked up to a seating area with about one hundred and fifty chairs. Most of the chairs were occupied except for the ones adjacent to the Northeast tree. Three quarters of the attendees showed signs that were for the support of Abraham Lincoln. While, the other quarter had signs that supported Stephen Douglas.

"Ladies and gentlemen, we just finished the debate over the Mexican American War. I need somebody to raise their hand and ask a question about a debatable subject," said Stephen Douglas. One of the attendees raised his hand. "I'm going to direct my question to both of the candidates. What's your view on slavery?" he asked. Abraham Lincoln answered the question first.

"Personally, I am against slavery because I feel it's unfair. For national interests, I can't just abolish slavery because it'll create national division and we don't want to be more divided than we are politically. Our country might not be divided by an actual border but we are divided by a border on political views. You see, the South supports slavery and they think it's acceptable. The North is against slavery and they think it's unacceptable. You see, we must draw a line between the two because one phrase that I must bring up, that is quite important, is *A divided House cannot stand*. If you get a giant saw and cut the house from ground, it will still be standing, but for how long? Not too long because a strong wind is going destroy it because the house is cut off from its foundation. In order to keep tensions low and keep the balance between the North and the South, we must not abolish slavery. As your president, I will keep slavery, but stop its expansion. Eventually, it'll die out. If you keep a firefly in a jar that doesn't have small holes, the firefly will die out because of lack of oxygen. If we stop the expansion of slavery, then it shall eventually end. I rest my case. It's time for you to answer this gentleman's question Mr. Douglas," he said.

Stephen Douglas walked up to the podium and started speaking. "I am not for the expansion of slavery nor am I for the abolition of slavery. Mr. Lincoln is for the abolition of slavery because he wants it to die out by containing it and not letting it expand. You see, I don't believe that we should force states to become a slave or free state based on its location. I do believe that people are entitled to choose if they want to make their individual state a slave state or free state. Like I said earlier, I am not here to expand slavery nor am I here to kill slavery, I just believe people have their choice. Now, I know some may ask what if there is no unanimous agreement. Then I will make the state's legislation choose their individual vote. Then, if they vote against the people's favor, then the people have the right to go up to Capitol Hill and discuss with Congress and The Supreme Court about what happened. The Supreme Court shall be able to make a decision about this idea of Slavery. If the people in that state are still not satisfied with the decision, they could fight it two ways. They can fight in the illegal way by rebelling and causing ruckus, or they can fight the legal way. People are entitled to file an appeal against the Supreme Court. That doesn't mean that the Supreme Court will rule in their favor. That's my view on slavery," he said.

Another attendee raised his hand. "I am directing this question to Mr. Douglas. Do you support national division?" he asked. "I do not support national division because it ruins this country. I don't think you would want this country divided because that will eventually lead to a Civil War and I feel that having a Civil War will destroy this country as well. We don't want that to happen. If you are insinuating that my support of popular sovereignty is wrong, then you're totally wrong. One right that man has that can never be taken away is that man is entitled to his opinion and you're entitled to your opinion. But, it's wrong," answered the Northern Democrat. The same attendee stood back up.

"You didn't answer my question. What I asked you was that 'did you know that slavery creates national division and so does popular sovereignty.' I live in a state that is filled with popular sovereignty. I read the press and I see the reports about violence with regards to popular sovereignty," he said.

"You've just brought up a good point. What Mr. Lincoln said was true. The reason why is because it does create division. I am apologetic that I questioned your opinion and said it was wrong because it is not. Nobody's opinion is wrong. Man is entitled to his opinion. He should have facts. You see there are some good parts and bad parts about Popular Sovereignty. The good part is that the people are entitled to choose whether they become a free state or slave state. As an example of a bad part, for instance, I am sure you all have heard of *Bleeding Kansas,* was a bloody battle that had taken place between the people who supported slavery and the people who were against slavery. Mr. Lincoln brought up a pretty good point when he said drawing a line between the two. My line between slavery is different than Abraham Lincoln's. I do not support slavery but nor am I here to abolish it. I am here to basically say that I am a supporter of popular sovereignty because people are entitled to their individual choice," replied Stephen Douglas.

Rubi stood up because she had a question to ask. Everybody in the audience stared at her. "What are you? An alien?" asked Mr. Douglas. "Yes, I am. I am a normal American like all of you," she answered. "Well, what question do you have to ask me?" the Northern Democrat asked. "I am going to direct my questions to both candidates. What are your views on women and what are your views on women's rights?" she asked. Mr. Lincoln walked up to the podium.

"I feel that women are being mistreated in the society that we live in. Women shouldn't be outspoken, but there are some women that are being victimized by their cruel husbands. And as your president, I will fight for the women's rights. I will pass a federal law against domestic violence because no spouse should be cruel to the other. Anybody who violates a woman's rights will go to federal prison. I will pass a law stating that females are entitled to file for a divorce if they have to because their husbands act like beasts. In addition to that, this law will also state that women don't have to explain to their husbands where they're going, and women don't have to be accompanied by their husbands when they're going out of the house. You know what, I will bring all of you to my home and I will show you the respect that I show my wife Mary Todd, and maybe, you all will show your wives the same respect. Sadly, we live in a world where women are treated unfairly. For many centuries, the world as a whole viewed women as second class citizens; some of them viewed women as creatures, not even humans and we have to stop this. Sometimes, women are treated as slaves and that is just as evil and sickening as the idea of slavery. We will not give in to this idea. We must fight for justice! We must support our women! We must fight for our wives! We must stop the deadbeat husbands! As a nation, we are here to fight for justice and justice shall prevail for ALL men and women whether you are white, black, red, yellow, or green," he exclaimed.

Stephen Douglas then walked up to the podium. "You see, I strongly oppose Abraham Lincoln's idea of equality for women. I feel that women *are* nothing but second class citizens. He claims that it's unacceptable to mistreat women. Women are not even human. Look at who were the true pioneers of this country - the men. Look at who discovered gold - men did. Look at who conquered the world- men did. And look at who showed the strength to fight- men did. Women didn't do anything. You see, God, put people on this Earth for different reasons. Men were put on this Earth to do all of the work and women were put on this Earth to sit at home and produce. Redskins were placed on this Earth to move off of their land and people that are not white were selected to work on plantations. So, different people were selected on this Earth to do different things. These ideas are not from my mind. They're from the mind of Charles Darwin. I am just spreading his word. I feel that it is okay to do that because the idea of Social Darwinism is acceptable," he said.

Rubi stood up again. "I am directing this to you Mr. Douglas. Have you ever thought of putting a twenty-two caliber against your forehead?" she asked. "No; And why would you say such a vile thing?" asked Stephen Douglas. "Because you deserve it. *You* are not a human. You are an animal. Wait a second! I made a mistake. You are as evil as the Son of Satan. May God have mercy on you because you are an accident. Instead of coming up from Heaven, you came down from Hell! You think women are non - productive members of society?! Well you're totally wrong," the alien leader's girlfriend exclaimed.

"Now, ma'am, was the other question you asked about slavery on women?" asked Mr. Lincoln. "Yes, sir," answered Rubi. The 1860 Republican candidate Lincoln walked up to the podium. "Mr. Douglas, I'll be the first to answer this question," he said. "Okay, that sounds fine with me," replied Stephen Douglas. He is still flustered over Rubi's comment. Mr. Lincoln faced the crowd.

"You see, we live in a world that is filled with many factors of life. Some of these factors are debatable and controversial subjects. Slavery is the most controversial subject and widely discussed in this nation. There are two kinds of slavery: racial slavery and gender slavery. Racial Slavery is when the white man enslaves somebody who is not of their skin color and that's where the evil idea of Social Darwinism comes into play. Slavery because of gender is also wrong. That's a subject of slavery that is rarely ever talked about. This is one of the primary ways husbands are cruel to their wives. Now, the idea of natural selection comes into play regarding this subject. Mr. Douglas said that people have different callings in life because of gender or race. That is true. It is the negative truth. You see, my opponent tried to say that natural selection is okay and acceptable; it's really not. Nobody should be forced into anything because of the idea of natural selection. That's like saying if your parents are killers, you have to be killers or because you're a British man, you are a tory. That's not true. There are British men that are Patriotic. I am sure you all know about Thomas Paine. He was from Great Britain. He was a Patriot. He supported the 'true' American people. That's not related to this subject. You see, the white man thinks that if you are not their skin color, you are inferior to them and you must be a slave. Also, if you're not a man, you must be a slave. That's what the white man believes. We, unfortunately, live in a world that is based off of the idea of tradition, which poisons the individual's mind. Tradition can and should be changed. Women should be able to have all of the rights in the world. They shouldn't be forced to be confined to the house. I think it's totally wrong, and the men say that women are outspoken when they are not. They are here to help you and be loving toward you. To all of the men out there, you must be loving to your wife. I am loving to Mary Todd. As your president, I will pass into legislature a new law that clearly states that husbands are not to confine their wives to the house. So, to those who want to violate my proposed law, I will have you investigated, hunted, captured, arrested, tried, and convicted. And you'll have the choice to have a jury or judge preside over your case. This jury will not be made up of a jury of your peers, it shall be made up of judges from the Supreme Court and therefore, you will hopefully get convicted. The mandatory sentence that I will give you evil husbands would be 10 years per count. So, if you enslave your wives, we will charge you with every criminal count concurrently and you will be sentenced per count. So, if you have 10 criminal counts, you can face up to one hundred years. Nobody should have to be enslaved, especially our wives, and slavery must be contained. Our founding fathers had principles that clearly stated that all men are created equal. They don't mean men as the gender of men and they're not pointing to the Caucasian men. They're stating that all of mankind that was created by God shall be treated equally and the same. Currently, the only group that has rights are Caucasian men and they think that they're superior to all other races. We should not tolerate any form of racism because racism is evil," he said.

The Northern Democrat walked up to the podium. "Mr. Lincoln, you gave a pretty important speech. I am totally against it. The reason is that speech clearly states that you want equality for women. To me, that sounds like an idea of chauvinism. Women don't deserve any rights. God basically states that women are not entitled to the same rights as men. Like I said, earlier, women didn't have the same accomplishments as men. I know some idiot in this audience will say that women never had the opportunity to fight for their rights and fulfill an achievement because they didn't have any rights. Well, guess what? Women were never meant to achieve anything. Women were meant to be confined to the house and that's acceptable to me. I make my wife do constant work at the house. She does everything for me at my beck and call. She even does extra for me. Do you know why? I have the answer to that question. She knows that it's her calling in life to do the work and she knows that she'll have the heck beat out of her if she acts rebellious. Women are not supposed to act rebellious. Just like sons and daughters should be seen and not heard, so should women. Women should not have any say or any rights. In fact, I am going to pass a law that totally contradicts Mr. Lincoln's law. This law will state that women will have to do at least 16 hours of work in the house every day. And if they do less than one minute of that work, they shall go to jail and rot there for 20 years. If they try to leave the house without their husbands being present or if they leave the house without permission, they are to get a life sentence. If they yell at the husbands or try to cause an argument with their husbands they'll get the death penalty. Also, if they voice any political opinion anywhere they'll get the death penalty. Essentially, what I am saying is that women will have to suffer through Capital Punishment. Then, if they try and stop their husbands from going out of the houses, they shall be sent to the stockades where the townspeople should throw stones at them. We, unfortunately, live in a world where women are tolerated. We live in a world where women are becoming more free. And these women demand more freedom than they have. Don't they have enough freedom as is? What more freedom can you give them? And Mr. Lincoln, you Republicans think liberalism is okay. Well, guess what? We Northern Democrats will kill you crazy Republicans. Yeah, people? We will destroy Candidate Lincoln," exclaimed the Northern Democrat.

He expected all of the attendees to start shouting in joy and support for him. None of the attendees applauded. The only candidate the attendees applauded was Mr. Lincoln. Rubi stood up from her seat. "Stephen Douglass, you shouldn't even be running for president. You know that you belong in the most secluded part of the Grand Canyon. You should be shackled to the heaviest rock in the Grand Canyon because you are evil. Your views are sick. You are totally wrong and you should admit that you're wrong. Slavery is wrong and nobody is superior to another. Learn to get that through your head you evil bastard. May God smack the living Hell out of you. I hope that he smacks you so hard that you spit out a couple of teeth. I hope that somebody kicks so much dirt in your eye that you go blind because you are an evil man. I didn't mean to say man. I meant creature; you are nothing but a creature," she declared.

"Well, your opinion is not important to me because it is unfair and stupid. Now, you're the epitome of a world class idiot," replied Douglas. Everyone in the audience started laughing at Stephen Douglas for his stupidity. Will stood up from the audience.

"Now, I am going to direct my question to both candidates. What would you do to fix our justice system in cases involving individuals that are not of Caucasian skin color like myself?" he asked. Mr. Lincoln walked up to the podium.

"Well, Mr. Von Alien, I see that there are many people that are not Caucasian that get falsely accused of crimes. I don't know if you were one of them. These non-Caucasians are usually tried by a partial jury and that is clearly a violation of the Constitution because every individual should be tried by an impartial jury. To those in the audience, this basically means a jury shouldn't be bias. Because an individual is of a different skin color, his or her rights are taken away. The case can come before a judge or an unfair jury. Sometimes, they get falsely accused because of skin color and that's not right either. Throughout this speech, I would often say 'as your president, I would pass an important law', and that's totally true. I am going to go through with all of the laws that I've proposed. This new law that I will propose will be a federal law. Though it won't be a law that results in punitive consequences; the case just doesn't get tried and it gets dismissed if this proposed law is violated. The law that I shall pass is called *IJAFTA*. This is known as the *Impartial Jury and Fair Trial Act.* This Law will basically state that everyone is entitled to a fair trial and all juries must be impartially selected. In addition to that, the judge that's presiding over the case must be fair to both the prosecution and defense. I have defended many criminal cases and some of these cases were people that were not of Caucasian skin color. The jurors were selected by the prosecutor only in cases like this. That's just totally unfair. It's not only unfair to the defendant, it's unfair to the defense attorney. What is even more unbelievable is that the judges allow this to take place. Our founding fathers had many great intentions for this country in the early years, but did they mean these rights for all people. This is clearly stated in the Constitution. Specifically, in the Bill of Rights and it is one of the first Ten Amendments. Every individual must be tried by an impartial jury that is selected by the prosecution and the defense. In cases that don't involve Caucasian people, the jurors are selected by a prosecutor. We must stop this because our society is being based off evil and malice. We as Americans should not be subject as witness to this kind of despicable behavior. As your President, I will fight for justice for all! I will make sure that every man and woman, whether you are white, black, green, yellow, or any color, will be entitled to a fair trial. Sadly, our founding fathers who fought for equality didn't believe in equality for all men or even women. Like I said earlier, our Declaration of Independence states that '*all men are created equal.'* It meant for all of mankind. Yet, Caucasian men were only given the freedom. Women and individuals that were not Caucasian were treated as property and that is evil and wrong. All of God's male and female creations should be treated as equals and nobody should be treated differently than another. Now, my final words to all of the judges out there, every individual of any race or color should be treated as an equal, hence, they should be tried fairly. To all of the prosecutors: you are to be fair to the individual that you're trying because that individual's rights are clearly protected in the Constitution of the United States. And finally, to all of the defense attorneys, you are to ensure that your clients receive a fair trial and, you must object if the prosecutor is choosing a partial jury. You must show them how the 'real' Constitution works-not their Constitution. We will end up with a nation that is filled with injustice, a breeding ground of evil and authoritarian leadership shall take place. A nation that supports fairness and is filled with justice, a seed of goodness shall be planted and thus, the plant of fairness shall blossom," the Republican Candidate answered.

The Northern Democrat walked up to the podium. He had a disgruntled appearance on his face. His hands were tight in fists and as soon as he approached the podium, he appeared angry to the attendees. His eyebrows are slanted; his left ear is red and he is smirking. "Now, to all of you in the audience, there must be something wrong with you for listening to this idiot of a candidate, Abraham Lincoln. Would you all vote for a candidate who is a hideous Republican from a crappy log cabin? That is ridiculous. If I was a voter, I wouldn't vote for some redneck from some log cabin in the sticks!. That sounds ridiculous to me that you'd consider a vote for him. You all think he's going to be this excellent president. Right? Well, guess what? He's not. Do you realize what he's trying to do? He's trying to twist the idea of our founding fathers that *All Men are created equal.* Our founding fathers only meant Caucasian males are to be created equal not women and people who are not white. Mr. Lincoln says we live in a world that is filled with bigotry. Well, he's wrong. He's probably so stupid, he doesn't know what bigotry means. I don't see our world being filled with bigotry. I did not run for president down South because I wanted to persuade the North that slavery was okay. Women and people that are not Caucasian are meant to be enslaved. Women are meant to be enslaved around the house and non-Caucasians are meant to be enslaved in the fields and plantations. So now I shall willingly answer that stupid alien's question. So, basically, I feel that it is the prosecutor's and the judge's prerogative to decide whether or not the jury is impartial. I know what you all are thinking. You all are probably thinking that if the prosecutor is the only one to select the jury, then, you're basically stating that I think that all criminals are guilty before they are proven innocent. That is not true. You see, the defense doesn't have to show the burden of proof. The prosecution has to show that at trial. So, I think we should cut the prosecutor a break and besides, I do think all criminals are guilty until they are proven innocent; whether they commit something as petty as stealing a loaf of bread or as heinous as First Degree Capital Murder. I feel that every criminal is guilty before they are innocent. The world famous phrase is that if you do the crime, you do the time. That's what I think. Nobody should be accused of committing a crime but anybody who is guilty of committing a crime is guilty. Our justice system is too lenient and we must be a little more stringent and accept my idea of all criminals being guilty before they are proven innocent. The more our government works against the defendant the lesser amount of crimes are committed. That's how I see it. So, basically, Mr. Lincoln's idea is erroneous, stupid, and ignorant. Ladies and gentlemen, behind me, my opponent who is lobbying for the same political position as I, is an ignorant idiot. I hereby rest my case and I will give Mr. Lincoln to present an objection. If you want crime off of your streets, you can vote for me. If you want a lot of violence on your streets, vote for Abraham Lincoln. I am done," he said. Mr. Lincoln walked back up to the podium to object to despicable Douglas's idea.

"Mr. Douglas, you are a despicable bilge rat. Ladies and gentlemen in the audience, I am sorry that I just ridiculed Stephen Douglas. He has the most evil intents for this country. He is going to turn the colors of this flag from red, white, and blue to grey, orange, and evil. Mr. Douglas is here to cause trouble and I will tell you the reasons why.

When I said, our jury system was unfair, I meant it. It is too stringent on the defendant and is usually working against them. What kind of defendant? For the Caucasian male defendant, the jury system is extremely fair because the jurors are selected in a fair way. When it comes to a female defendant, the jurors are selected in an impartial way. Also, when it comes to a defendant who is not white, they jurors are selected in an impartial way. I just received a telegram from a woman named Sarah Rosenthal. She experienced a battering situation because her husband would come home drunk every night. While he was in one of those drunken stupors, she was placed in another situation when she talked to a man he took in named Will Von Alien, who came from the future in Starmos City. I think he's one of the attendees. I am not going to show his identity. Anyway, Jobe, the alleged victim, started demeaning him because he said that this alien was not worthy of listening to ragtime music. Those insults became threats. Sarah's husband Jobe eventually threatened him. He started acting violently toward Mr. Von Alien. He lunged at him and then started choking him. Will kicked him in the face and shot him four times. Will and Sarah were brought to trial because of their gender and skin color and that is not fair. Sadly, Will was convicted. He managed to escape death. Fortunately, Sarah was acquitted because the prosecutor didn't do a good job proving the case against her. Those two should have never been arrested. They were the real victims. Jobe was not the victim; he was the aggressor. There were many flaws in this case according to Ms. Rosenthal. First of all, the jury was made up of 12 old men. How can that be? You can't choose all old men as part of the jury. Besides the fact they want to get out of the jury room immediately, so that is not an impartial jury. This case that should have never gone to trial was picked by a partial jury. I am not here to ridicule Mr. Douglas. I am not here to object to him. Another part of this case that was important was that the judge and the prosecutor were fakes. They were not even human. They were both evil, shapeshifting, serpents. That sounds crazy but it's the truth. They don't call me *Honest Abe* for nothing. I have never lied a day in my life. Maybe, I shouldn't have said that because it sounds like I have an ego, but I don't have an ego. Don't let this man cajole you all into voting for him for president. Mr. Douglas will not be a good president because he will ruin this country. He will state that tradition must stay the same. In spite of tradition sounding great, it is not great in all cases. Tradition is evil in some cultures. For instance, mistreatment towards women and individuals that are not right is wrong and this was passed on from generation to generation to generation. This is an evil tradition. Chauvinism, bigotry, and slavery are the evils of American tradition and we must destroy that," Mr. Lincoln declared.

"Aye," declared everyone. The major debate concluded.

Both candidates walked off the stage. The Northern Democrat had a scowl on his face. Meanwhile, the Republican candidate, Abraham Lincoln, proudly walked off of the stage. Every attendee started to act informal. One of the individuals carried him and he was passed throughout the audience. Everybody started chanting,

"Lincoln for President!" Faces of elation are seen throughout the crowd. Everybody showed approval for Abraham Lincoln to be president. Everybody passed him to the back right near Sheriff Joe. "So you're the man who is going to be the excellent president?" the sheriff asked.

"Yes, I am going to be the president. My goals are quite simple. God placed me on this planet to stop bigotry and mistreatment towards people who are not white males. I will fight for the women and the non-Caucasians. You should join me in my crusade," the Republican candidate answered. "I totally agree with you," replied Will.

"I want to make sure that you are who you are. Are you Will Von Alien?" asked Mr. Lincoln. "Yes, I am. Are you the one who I saw when we were on the Conestoga wagon?" the alien leader asked. "Why, yes. I dressed up as Jesse for two days because Sarah wanted me to. I am Sarah's distant cousin," the Republican candidate answered. "Why did you dress up as Jesse?" asked Will. "Jobe didn't know Sarah had a miscarriage. So, she had to pay people to dress up as her younger son so her cruel husband didn't find out. If he found out that she had a miscarriage, there would be fury taking place. Her conniving husband would commit the most evil act to a woman possible and vulnerable women shouldn't be treated in such a malicious manner," answered Mr. Lincoln.

"I am sure you know exactly what happened to Sarah and Will. That is a clear example of injustice," replied Commissioner Clayton. "Yes, I know. You brought up an excellent point. I must ask you this question. I know of Will but what is your name and what year do you come from?" the Republican candidate asked. The police commissioner reached his right hand out to the best candidate, Abraham Lincoln. "It is an honor to meet you Mr. Lincoln. I think you are going to be the best president our country had in history so far. Let me introduce myself to you. My name is Commissioner Bill Clayton and I come from New York City. I am also from the year 2047," the police commissioner answered. "Well, you are a nice gentleman. You come from a place that I loved the most. I know you're from the future so it must look like a place that I have dreamed in my wildest imaginations. It is an honor to meet you Mr. Clayton. What kind of commissioner are you?" asked Mr. Lincoln. "Police Commissioner," answered Clayton.

"So, you protect the people from the evils of society?" the Republican candidate asked. "Yes," answered the police commissioner. "Good, perhaps, you can join me in my crusade to help improve the society that we live in," said Mr. Lincoln. Will approached him. "Say, can we stay at your house? We've been homeless for four years," he asked. "Sure," the Republican presidential candidate answered. "Thank you very much. Those wilderness conditions can't get harsher," the alien leader's girlfriend replied. "I know," said Mr. Lincoln.

Chapter XIX: Inauguration Day. The arrival on the train to Washington D.C: March 4, 1861: Nearly One Year Later

Abraham Lincoln won the election for president against Stephen Douglas by a large number. All of the Northern states voted for Mr. Lincoln because he was and still is an excellent speaker. He spoke eloquently in his speeches and he spoke in a bipartisan and fair manner. Another reason why he won the election of 1860 was because he spoke in a non-bigoted manner and the Northern states looked for somebody who was a non-bigot and that would be the now and new 16th president who would strongly improve the country.

The Northerners felt that this new president would be rid of the ideas of slavery and chauvinism. The Northern Democrats would be destroyed and the great Republican would fight for justice that the Northern Democrats oppose. The monstrous opinions of Stephen Douglas will unfortunately go down in history. he will never run again for president after he received zero approval. Yesterday was the campaigning for the fight for justice. Today, is the day where the fight for justice shall take place. and tomorrow is when justice shall be involved in our beautiful society. The weather may be beautiful. The political climate is stormy.

Today is the day where Mr. Lincoln gets sworn in as

president and the evils of James Buchanan's presidency disappears. This is the day where a new president who is here for all will fight against evil. This is the day where the best president will fight for justice. This is the day where the United States of America will listen to the powerful words of a new president. Today is the day, where the World will listen to the words of this great incoming president.

Today is the day, where the beginning of the end of slavery takes place. This is the day where the beginning of the end of chauvinism takes place. And this is the day where spouses will go to jail if they mistreat their partners in the harshest way possible. This is the day where the beginning of the limits on the containment of slavery takes place.

Ladies and Gentlemen, behold your great new president! The idea of evil shall be ceased! And this is also the day that will be the opening of the Horizon where all men and women are created equal. Most of all today is the day where the evils of the Buchanan administration disappear and the excellence of the Lincoln administration shall appear.

Within the next four years, the Pledge of Allegiance will show its true meaning, and this is the beginning of where all men and women shall be created equal in terms of freedom. This is the definite future under Mr. Lincoln. Let's get to the present day. It is March 4, 1861 and Abraham Lincoln, Mary Todd Lincoln, Tad Lincoln, Willie Lincoln, Will Von Alien, Sheriff Joe, Commissioner Bill Clayton, and Rubi Woschinskiwitz are sitting on the honorable Presidential train to the majestic Washington D.C. The train is made of strong wood and steel.

The train is colored red and blue to represent the colors of the Chessington-Baltimore Railroad. The railroad traveled from Ohio to Virginia. Right before Washington is the temperate woodlands of the Northeast region. This steam train is passing through Baltimore. Mr. Lincoln is the first president to ride this train. He and his family and guests are sitting in the caboose of the train. The blue caboose has the most coveted interior.

There are extremely comfortable chairs that feel like one is relaxing on cloud nine. Every chair is decorated in the same way telling the same story of American History. The carvings in the legs on all the chairs are the same. The carvings take the individual through American history. On a typical chair, the carving on the rear right leg shows a portrayal of George Washington crossing the Delaware during the American Revolution. This is to show that the foundation of the United States required a lot of strength and endurance.

The rear left leg carving shows a portrayal of the signing of the Constitution and the presidents who signed it. Then the front right left shows a portrayal of the War of 1812 and the day when Francis Scott Key wrote the lyrics to the patriotic song of the *Star Spangled Banner.* The last leg showed a portrayal of miners in California panning for Gold and this is to represent the expansion from East Coast to West. Today, there will be a fifth leg added to all of the ten chairs in this room to show the strength and greatness of the new President Abraham Lincoln. The train car features cherry wood floors that are polished and well kept. The windows were dressed with curtains that are adorned with paint made of pure gold. Everybody in the train cars are well dressed including the four honorable guests who lived in the woodlands for four years. The guests are dressed in dignified suits and they are wearing top hats to fit the suits.

Every tie is the color of red and blue to show some patriotism for the jubilation of the inauguration to take place later today. Abraham Lincoln is dressed in the most honorable suit for the President of the United States. He is wearing a perfectly clean white shirt that doesn't have a crease or wrinkle. He is wearing two rings on his hand - one wedding ring on his fourth finger and one for the honor of President of the United States.

His suit jacket is neatly pressed. He is wearing a long overcoat above the suit. He is wearing black, cotton pants that are neatly pressed. Mary Todd sat in the seat adjacent to him. Her brown hair is curled up for this honorable day. She is wearing a kerchief on the top of her head. She is wearing a svelte, green gown to show the colors of March. The two younger Lincoln sons are sitting in the back of the Caboose. They are both playing chess. Willie and Tad Lincoln are dressed in tuxedos for their father's day of honor.

Commissioner Bill Clayton grew a mustache within the past year. He retrieved his mustache comb from his shirt pocket and he made some last minute changes. He wanted to make it look stylish. The alien leader walked up to the right door of the train car. Adjacent to the right rear door of the car, is a mirror that is hanging on the wall. He fixed his hair in the mirror and retrieved the cologne in his right pocket. He tossed the cologne on top of his head. A cough left his mouth. After coughing, he stared in the mirror. A flashback started to play in his head. He traveled forward into actual time. He started reminiscing when he was a lad. In this daydream, he was at the Star Hotel and his father was the host of a 2032 convention about the status of the water in Starmos City. He is remembering walking proudly alongside his father. He showed great pride at this convention.

"Dad, how did you get to where you are?" the young alien asked. "Well, it is a complicated answer to explain to you son, but in simpler terms, I must say that if you work hard, you will be extremely successful. Hence, you shall go on and move on the right road in life. And also through aggression, but nonviolent aggression. Be aggressive in your spirit for your career. Take everything with pride and excellence. Show great zeal when it comes to justice and excellence, but most of all, follow your calling," the alien leader's father said.

The short flashback is now over. The alien leader stopped staring in the mirror. He sat back down on the chair. Mr. Lincoln finished his glass of wine. "Will, what were you staring at?" he asked. "Nothing," the alien leader answered. "I don't think anybody stares into the mirror for no reason whatsoever," replied the 16th President. Will hesitated.

"I was staring at a blemish I just noticed and tried popping it," he said. "Now, don't lie about that. You were thinking about something," replied Mr. Lincoln. The alien leader started to grow emotionally melancholy. He started tearing. "You see. I didn't tell many people this. My parents died. I was just thinking about a great moment with my dad," he answered. Those tears became a sobs. "Before you get into your full story about this flashback, tell me how your parents died," the 16th president said. "Do you remember when I told you about the tyrant Cornelius Von Alien?" asked Will. "Yes, I remember vividly," answered Mr. Lincoln. "Well, this brute shot my parents in cold blood because they wouldn't stand up to the raising of tariffs and the closure of the reservoir," the alien leader replied. He sniffled. "That's sad. Continue on with what you were telling me about the flashback," the 16th President said.

"Now, what I saw in this flashback was when my dad and I were at a water convention and we walked alongside each other. He said to me a very important phrase. The words I remember he told me were that I should push to be successful, do everything with excellence, be zealous for goodness, and fight for justice. I felt I made him proud and I am going to continue to make him proud in life. Those words are literally engraved in my head. It is important that I remember those words for the rest of my life," the alien leader replied.

"I can definitely relate to you. I am sure that you remember me telling you that I lived in a log cabin when I was a lad. So, now I shall tell you something quite important in my life that I haven't told anybody because my parents would have gotten lynched. Sadly, they didn't die in such an inhumane fashion. Now, my dad used to be a logger and a farmer. In fact, he was the one that made the cabin that my family lived in. So, more importantly, my parents and I grew up in a slave state, Kentucky. My parents were against slavery because they felt it was wrong. Near them were plantation owners and that was evil. We lived in area that was ruled by a stringent government. I had to live my boyhood under the radar because if anybody found out that my family was against slavery, we would be killed and that would be horrible if such an event would take place. If my parents would die in such a brutal way possible, then I would be depressed for many years and that would ruin my life. I wouldn't be in the position that I am today. Let's get off of our parents' death. It may be important, but we shouldn't let that ruin our day," said Mr. Lincoln.

A luminous light started to show on the top right hand corner of the train. Enkel, the messenger of God came down from Heaven. He flew down to Abraham Lincoln and flew into the palm of his large hand. "Mr. Lincoln, for all the years you have feared God, he has taken you on an excellent journey in life. And here you are today going to be the 16th President of the United States and that's a respectable honor. I am ecstatic for you. I have a strong request from you. Keep on fearing God while you're in office the way you've feared him outside of office. Keep fighting for justice and equality and your chances of going up to Heaven. Don't have any ego and show constant humility. The more humility you show the better the person you shall become and I would be extraordinarily proud of you because of that. Keep on showing your respect for the true American Justice System and your chances of going up to the Celestial City and being on the right hand of God shall increase to 150%. Mr. President, I will stay with you the whole time today. And if you're wondering why, some mystical effects will take place, it is because of me. I am going to create good, magical effects," said Enkel.

"Thank you very much," the 16th president replied. "Stand up," God commanded. Mr. Lincoln stood up faster than the drop of a dime. All of a sudden, the presidents on the wall started talking. There are five presidents featured in paintings on walls. The paintings of the first five presidents started talking. "Enough is enough. One must speak at a time and the first commander-in-chief is ordered to start talking," God's messenger declared.

"Thank you Enkel. Now, I want to make this address to Mr. Lincoln standing on board the train. I want him to face me and look me in the eyes," said George Washington. The 16th president turned around. "Mr. Washington it's an honor to talk to you," he said. "Thank you. That's very nice. I have a message to give you and it's quite an important message. Do you realize that you are taking the most honorable and respectable office of the United States?" the 1st president asked.

"I do," the 16th president answered." and do you realize that you will have to be taking an oath to protect this country and fight for individuals civil liberties stated in the Constitution?" asked George Washington. "Yes," answered Mr. Lincoln.

"I will tell you what it was like on the day of my inauguration. I can tell you that trains were non-existent. They were just a thought in Great Britain at the time of my inauguration in 1789. Granted, I didn't want to become president because I felt my job was done fighting for independence. The American people insisted that I became president. Now, let's get to the date of inauguration. I remember it was a warm October Day on the island of Manhattan. In fact, it was on October 3, 1789, that was the day of my inauguration. It was called the Thanksgiving Inauguration. I have a clear recollection of standing outside of the Federal Building in New York City shaking people's hands. After I shook their hands, I took the honorable oath of President of the United States. One of my very first initiatives as president was to create a three house legislature and create the national bank so I can prevent Britain from committing an act of evil by trying to regain our country and taking away our freedoms. Aside from doing that, I decided to start the construction of a new capital. And that capital wouldn't be located in Philadelphia. That capital would be located on the Potomac in Washington. I built many buildings. The most important job that I didn't complete unfortunately was the creation of the Executive Mansion. Instead, I died and here I ended up on the top of this wall; whereas this is my story as being the president, the one thing that you should know Mr. Lincoln, is that you are going to be an excellent president. Even though I was a slave owner; while I was up in Heaven, I realized the true evils of slavery and I agree with your politics. Mr. Lincoln, I wish you great luck being president. I think you're going to do an excellent job," George Washington replied. The painting of the first president stopped talking. The portrait on the opposite side of George Washington started talking. Thomas Jefferson started speaking. "What is your name?" he asked. "Well, which one are you talking about?" the 16th president asked. "You know who I am talking about. I want to know what your name is in its entirety," answered the 3rd president. "I'm Abraham Lincoln. You can just call me Abe," Mr. Lincoln replied.

"Well, I want to sound respectful because I hear you're taking office of President of the United States today. Is that correct?" asked Mr. Jefferson.

"Yes. And how did you know that?" the 16th president asked. "My intuition told me that. Nobody goes in this car on the train down here unless they are a president on their first inauguration day. Every time the president gets inaugurated, we presidential portraits know," answered the 3rd president.

"Say, you are the president with the most intelligence? Is that correct?" asked Mr. Lincoln. "Yes, I am. I have a lot of intelligence. I have Aspergers," answered Mr. Jefferson. "Say, that's what I have also," replied Will. "That's nice. Who are you?" the 3rd president asked. "Will Von Alien of Starmos City," the alien leader answered. "Well, I would request that I talk to Mr. Lincoln because his day is more important than yours. He is going to be the sixteenth president. Or, I should say he is the 16th president," replied Mr. Jefferson.

"Okay," Will said rather embarrassed. He sat back down in the seat and requested wine. "Mr. Lincoln, I would request that you listen to me because I have a couple of pointers to bring up with you before you take the oath of the most respectable position in office. When I took presidency, I don't want you to repeat the flaws that I had during my term in office. Granted, at the time I pushed for these decisions. But I realized there were flaws. I don't want you to put a halt to trade unless it's really necessary. When I was President, the British committed such vile and horrible acts, but don't focus on the past because Great Britain will probably become our allies. Besides, they are one of the biggest traders with the United States. Mr. Lincoln, as president you should be willing to listen to your cabinet and review your cabinet because if you act ignorant in office and you cover your ears, you're not going to last in that position for long. The third thing that I must say that is also quite important is that you have to tell the people that all men and women are created equal. Unfortunately, I did not include that in the Declaration of Independence. As president, you must include women and people that are not Caucasian. Mr. Washington brought up a pretty good point about regretting slavery. Sadly we were not able to realize that it was wrong back then. Even though we were the founding fathers of this country, we had some flaws too. But, one thing that is for certain Mr. Lincoln that we say all the time for our future presidents. Do not make the same mistakes that we did when we were in office. No president is flawless. Bad and harmful history cannot and shall not repeat itself. Unfortunately, it has, but as president insure that the history will not repeat in a bad way. And now these are my last words Mr. President. I wish you safe travels and good luck running for president. Thank you for taking the honorable office of President of the United States," the 3rd president said.

The first five presidential portraits returned back to its inanimate state. The life in the cabin became normal. Mary Todd looked at Will.

"So, what is it like to be an alien leader?" she asked. "Oh, I don't think I am fully the alien leader because I haven't been there for four years, but at the time it was an honor to be the leader. Think of it. If you were leader, you would receive a bunch a luxuries. You're not. Hey, you never know though. If I die, you might be the successor to my leadership. I want you to insure freedom for the citizens whether they are aliens or humans. And you would have to change the clothing that you wear to ultramodern clothing. It would be quite homely and unpopular if you wore prairie clothing. In addition to that, with great power comes great responsibility. If you don't show any responsibility, you will be impeached. More importantly, the chance of you being leader of Starmos City is slim to none. I won't give up my city or my citizens to anybody," the alien leader answered.

"That's what I like to call a strong leader. If I was the leader of a place, it would be Heaven. Unfortunately, in this society, I can't be leader. Everybody is quick to lynch women and that is quite arbitrary and unjust how I along with many other women are mistreated in such a cruel and malicious way. The society is unfortunately dysfunctional without women. And, justice cannot be done without women. The world we live in is evil. People like my husband Abe, will be here to fight for justice. My husband will not curtail and give in to evil. Fighting will take place. This fighting might cause many lives to be lost. My husband will fight for women like a tiger fighting to protect its live young. We as Americans will overthrow those Southern tyrants and we shall destroy bigotry and racism forever. I won't tolerate a country that allows this kind of evil to take place. I won't allow a government to enslave innocent people. I will make sure that my husband sticks up to his word. For he who tells the truth shall prosper; and he who tells lie will live a miserable live. My husband is going to be the best president in our very young American history. He will be the exemplary president for other presidents," she replied. The conductor opened the door. He wore a crimson cap and crimson suit. A gold pin is featured on the upper right hand corner of his shirt.

"Mr. Lincoln, Mary Todd, Tad, Willie, and Mr. Lincoln's VIP guests, get your trunks because we are approaching Union Station. There's no time to dilly dally. We must hustle now. Mary Todd, get your dress ready because it is crucial that you look beautiful. You don't want to look to homely or too comely. You want to look perfect like the most perfect first lady. Mr. Lincoln get your family's trunks and place them on the luggage wagon when the train gets to the station. For now, you must get your hat ready and make yourself look dapper. And sons of Mr. Lincoln stop playing chess. It is time to get ready. We can't afford to be late. You must get ready to head over to the Saint John's Church for the 9:00 service. Going to Church will be a great start for your inauguration day. You can't afford to be late. March to the doors now everybody and exit out the right. Thank you and don't be late. If you're going to be late, you all are playing with fire," he exclaimed.

The president laughed. "You know that I can call my bodyguards to come here and arrest you for being bossy. You'll be eventually released from prison, but by the time that happens, you won't be able afford anything. So, you'll be poor, but you know something? I should have some sympathy for you because I was poor at one time and that was during my boyhood and maybe I shouldn't be so superior to you. Besides, I fear God," he said. He walked up to the conductor and patted him on the back as a gesture of endearment. They walked up to the rear of the train. The president's kids stood on the top of the back of the caboose. Followed by that, Mr. Lincoln and Mary Todd stood in front of them. The guests knelt down. The photo is about to be taken. The March sun was interrupted by a blue flash. The sons of the 16th president walked off of the train and they started walking into Union Station. He, his family, and his guests walked over to the right door and departed from the train.

Lines of spectators are standing on the platforms. The spectators aren't cheering. They are applauding the honorable and respectable president and his confidants. The platform is adorned with gold coins and the tossing of patriotic confetti had taken place.

They walked past two glass doors caged in ornately designed silver. They opened the doors. They walked inside the main area of Union Station. It had the appearance of a big empty room. Wooden desks are featured on the right. Each wooden desk contains a small bell which signals the train company that somebody has purchased a ticket. There are nine desks. Hence, there are nine bells. There are wooden benches in front of these desks where the families can wait for their loved ones to depart.

Across from these seats, there's a huge mural that depicts the history of transportation around the world. The left of the mural shows cavemen creating a wheel. This wheel would be a revolutionary item for the future according to this mural. A portrayal of the Roman and Greek Chariots is shown adjacent to the simple, but yet so complex wheel. The stage coach and Conestoga followed the portrayal of the Greek and Roman Chariots. The last portrayal of transportation depicted in this mural is the train. The best form of motion to ever be created in society. The stone floors reflected in the strong sunlight.

"This station looks exactly like Starmos Station," said Will. "Where's Starmos Station?" asked Mr. Lincoln. "Well, obviously in Starmos City. I don't think any other station can be found in any other city," the alien leader answered. "I believe you come from the future as you have told me numerous times. Granted, I have been told to believe none of what I hear and half of what I see, but you have brought up a good point," the 16th president said. "I know I've brought up a good point. Often, good leaders bring up good points. One thing that is certain that you have taught me was honesty and modesty. You are in such a highly regarded political position and yet, you don't act showy or egotistical. That is what I call an exemplar who demonstrates fair behavior. Now, let me just tell you this about the place of my origin. Starmos City is a place that is filled with irony. One minute, you'll think my place is the most ultramodern, retro-futuristic city of all. And the next minute you'll think my place is the most anachronistic, obsolete place," replied Will.

"That's quite interesting. I would never even think that the place you came from had such out-of-date buildings. Over in this country, we have out-of-date buildings. Some of them are 200+ years of age. These buildings are in Jamestown, Virginia, not too far from here. Perhaps, we'll see them at some point soon. That's if they don't get destroyed by the idiotic Southerners," the 16th president said.

"Why would you think they'd be destroyed?" the alien leader asked. "Because the Southerners show a great deal of animosity and hatred against the people who were antislavery. If they learn to open their minds up, maybe the country will be better. Their hearts are as evil as fierce, fiery furnaces. I don't think I told you. The South is planning on withdrawing from the nation. The reason is because they didn't have me on their ballots and tickets. They are going to start the American Civil War and there will be tremendous horror. Families will be separated due to political views and geography and the nation will be divided into two. There has always been political division between the North and the South and this political division was on the idea of slavery. *A divided house cannot stand.* As Americans, we can't live in a world of injustice and cruelty. And unfortunately, the evils have turned this beautiful red, white, and blue nation into an ugly nation," said Mr. Lincoln.

"Move faster," the conductor shouted. The president, his guests, and family moved much quicker. They opened the glass door that is contained in an iron cage. The conductor walked back toward the train. Waiting at the station is a Black Stagecoach. The Stagecoach was drawn by two gallant horses on the front. These horses stood at thirteen feet tall; and each weight one-half of a ton.

The alien leader showed a facial expression of amazement. His eyes are wide open. His mouth is agape. "What's on your mind?" asked Rubi.

Her yellow skin turned into a pallid color. "I love it here. It's the most unique place I've ever seen. The roads are quite amazing and unique here. Some of them are even irregular. I looked at the circle of Union Station and one part is paved with Cobblestones and another part is not even paved; it is still with dirt. It is also amazing that this place features such beautiful buildings," answered Will. He turned his head around and he showed a great deal of honor for the capitol. The Stagecoach driver walked out of the vehicle. He is wearing a grey toupee that looks similar to a powdered wig. He opened the door. The 16th president and the first lady walked into the Stage Coach. The sons followed and then the guests entered last. This is an amazing moment for the Lincolns and their guests. The interior of the Stagecoach has a quite unique appearance. There are two long, cushioned seats one behind the driver and another, facing the opposite seat. Traditionally, at most inaugurations, the president would sit facing the front. He decided to face the opposite side of the driver. There are four windows that are tinted to block the president from being seen in the public's eye. Everybody sat down in the vehicle.

"Where are you all heading to?" the driver asked. "Saint John's Church in Lafayette Square," the 16th president answered. "Very well, then," said the Stagecoach driver. He cracked the loud whip and they departed from Union Station. They are heading on their way to Saint John's Church for the 9:00 a.m. service. They have officially departed from the Union Station, leaving Columbus Circle and heading down Pennsylvania Avenue.

Chapter XX: The Official Inauguration

The stagecoach departed from the train station and started heading down Pennsylvania Avenue. A crowd of 500,000 people lined the street. "I have to stand up and greet the crowd," the 16th president said. He stood up on top of the seat and started greeting the crowd of citizens. Every citizen had a facial expression of joy. The president waved to crowd. Some of the individuals in the crowd are dignified. Others are screaming in happiness; others are whistling.

Then, there are those who salute the president. The marching band started to follow the stagecoach. The president had a smile on his face as the crowd admired him. The honorable 16th president sat back down in the stagecoach. "I want all of you to stand up on the rooftop," he said. "No thanks, I don't want to get my dress ruined," replied Mary Todd. "Me neither," said Will. The president laughed. "Since when do you wear a dress?" he asked. "I was just saying me neither because I don't want to stand up and show myself to the crowd," the alien leader answered. "Well, guess what. I don't usually force people to do things. I want you to show the world who you really are and I want you to represent the place of your origin. People would think that you are a unique individual. I think they'd show a great amount of respect for you and they might even show some possible form of adulation," replied Mr. Lincoln.

"Really?" asked Will. "Of course. I'm not here to lie to you. I would be honest and quite frank with you. I am going to tell you the truth," the 16th president answered. "Okay, here it goes," the alien leader replied. He opened the sun roof of the stage coach and climbed up on the hood. Instead of the crowd praising him because he is an excellent leader of Starmos City, the crowd stared in a skeptical and questioning manner.

This is a far cry from the praises that were given to Mr. Lincoln. Within a matter of seconds, the crowd started throwing jeers at him. Some of them called him a *bloody slave.* Some of the members in the crowd started throwing small stones at him. Fortunately, they missed. He jumped back into the stagecoach. It is mind-boggling how the crowd shows respect towards somebody else; singing praises and honoring that individual. On the other hand when another individual comes out who is not of Caucasian descent, the crowd shows disrespect and hatred towards that individual.

"Why did you come in here so abruptly?" the 16th president asked. "Do you realize what kind of society we live in? We are living in the most evil society of all! This is disgusting. I know I sound jealous. I am not. I am clearly the victim of a racist and bias group of individuals. You shouldn't have told me to come out on the rooftop of this vehicle because I know you have racist intents. You are just like all of the other politicians. You are nothing but a bigoted president. In fact, I don't want to live with you because you're not here to free the slaves. The world we live in mistakes me for being a slave. They treat anybody who is not of Caucasian color like garbage. That is disgusting, and so, Mr. President, I believe that you knew that I was going to be treated differently than you, and you were just trying to test my agility and emotional strength. That's not right. That is totally wrong. You should be ashamed of your attitude," Will answered in an angry manner.

"Why are you talking to me like this?" asked Mr. Lincoln. "Because you are very snide and nasty. You are nothing but a deceptive, surreptitious snake," the alien leader answered.

"Whoa. Those comments are quite strong," the 16th president replied. "Yes, it's not fair how the crowd would honor you, but they don't honor me. Granted, I didn't do much to contribute to American society. I did enough," said Will.

"That's not true; you are a huge contributor to American society. For God sakes, you saved us from a massive alien attack in the future. You saved Rubi from being turned into a slave and you saved Commissioner Clayton from ending up in a mental institution," replied Mr. Lincoln.

"Why would you believe that he would end up in a mental institution?" the alien leader asked. "Because, look at him. He's wearing a police uniform that is so futuristic. They can't sew any yellow colored clothing and they can't even sew a good hat. That's at least in our time. They'd think he comes from the future, which is true but our current society would, unfortunately, try to institutionalize him. But that's the ignorance of the South," the 16th president answered.

"You are totally right. I might've just been overreacting. It is sad that we live in such an evil society," replied Will. "Do you know what I am going to genuinely do as your president?" asked Mr. Lincoln. "No," the alien leader answered. "Well, I am going to bring those slave drivers to justice. I will destroy the men who come home drunk and mistreat their wives. And I will destroy the deadbeat spouses. We will live in a nation where there is truly freedom and justice for all and our pledge of allegiance will be true to this country," the 16th president answered. "Don't be like all these other politicians. Are you sticking to your word?" asked Will. "Yes, when I say I am genuine, I mean to be genuine. That's why my name is called 'Honest Abe'," answered Mr. Lincoln.

"Lately, you haven't seemed quite honest to me about the way I look for this event. Are you really the 'Honest Abe' that everybody says you are?" asked Mary Todd. "Of Course, I am. I don't think people would give me that title if I was dishonest or not genuine," the 16th president answered.

"Good point, I guess I should keep my mouth shut. There is some form of skepticism in my head about you. Well, what do I care? I am only your wife," replied Mrs. Lincoln.

"Hey, don't say such a thing. You're my wife. You're the only one who I have. We had many losses in our lives. Two of our kids have gone to college and the other two kids are like quiet introverts. You're the only one who I have to talk to. And besides, you are going to be here to represent me and the Executive Mansion. Do you realize that you are going to be one of the very few women who take a political position?" the 16th president asked.

"No, I thought women in this nation were forbidden from taking any influence in the government. I don't even think women are allowed to have any Civil Service Jobs either," answered Mary Todd.

"Well, that's true, but that won't apply to my wife because while you're in office, you're not going to be sitting around being any ordinary first lady figurehead. Oh no! You will have a lot of say in the government and I might even try to make you the Secretary of State. You would have to get elected by the people to be considered Secretary of State; and there's a 1 out of 1,000,000 chance of you getting that position because women are not allowed to vote and most of the men in this society hate women. I love you Mary Todd. And I will always love you and our sons forever," replied Mr. Lincoln.

"Oh, Abe, you are the best husband. You are here to help me. I can understand why I can't get a political position. And I can tell that you relate to me. You didn't have to say such a thing, but one thing that I must say that is for certain is that we can do something together. I may just be a political figurehead, but with my name known to the public, we can fight together and we will be a strong team, who will fight for justice. Together, we will fight against the evils of slavery. We will destroy the malevolent plantation owners and make them face justice for turning innocent people into property. If anybody had the right mind, they'd stop these plantation owners. We will free as many slaves from these harsh plantations as possible. We will set up the Freedmen's Bureau and that is when justice will be served. We will not give in and curtail to evil. And you know where evil comes from. Evil doesn't come from above; evil comes from below. All men and women have good sides to their souls. All men and women have evil sides. We won't be the ones who have evil sides. We will fight for goodness. We will fight for righteousness! And as 'true' and loving American citizens, we will destroy the evil actions of the Southern plantation owners. After we stop the plantation owners, we will fight for justice for women because women cannot be victims of their evil husbands, but Abe, while you take all these actions, make sure you are not violating the Constitution because; if you violate the Constitution, you could potentially be thrown out of office and some sick Southern Democrat can take office and slavery will be legal in this country. So, make sure that you consider the fact that you must *preserve, protect, and defend the Constitution of the United States. And* being that you fear God and this oath is under God, you must defend the Constitution under God, and not to sound arrogant. The only one who gave you the special ability to hold the honorable position of President of the United States was God. So, while you're in office, cherish God and do not lose your faith. You are here not only to please your nation, but you're here to please God and you must trust him, and *without faith, you will not be able to please God,"* said Mrs. Lincoln.

The stagecoach was approaching Lafayette Park. The park looks picture perfect. The pathways are extremely clean and pure of litter because there was snow. The fountain in the center shined in the March sunlight. The kids are climbing the trees enjoying the beautiful weather. The pollen on the trees fell and the fresh, green leaves permeated the park with a spring scent.

The benches are occupied with visitors waiting to see the inauguration of the honorable President Mr. Lincoln. Some folks are even looking at the statue of Marquis De Lafayette. Meanwhile, in the stagecoach Will stared at the park in fascination. He is more intrigued at this park than Flushing Meadows Park.

"What's this place?" he asked. "Oh, it's Lafayette Park. It's not just any ordinary park. Nothing is ordinary in

Washington D.C. Washington is the most unique place in the nation, if not in the world. This is Lafayette Park. I am sure you know who this park is dedicated to just based on the name of the park, but it would be my honor anyway to tell you about who this park is dedicated to. It is dedicated to a French General who fought during the American Revolutionary War in the 1770s and the 1780s. Now, Will, I know what you're probably wondering. why would a French general be fighting in the American Revolutionary War? Well, we wouldn't be winning the war without France on our side. We might've still been ruled by the British. The French primarily joined the Revolution was because they wanted to help us. There was another reason. The French were at war with Britain in the Seven Years War and they managed to have some partial victory through one of the treaties of Paris. Now, the French wanted to keep the British weak. And that was a good thing because the more the British were weak, the more we had a chance of winning the revolution and we did. Sadly, for the French, during the monarchy of Marie Antoinette and Louis the Sixteenth, a revolution had taken place because France wasn't able to pay off their debts to the British. The first French Revolution had taken place, but I think we should get back to the point of your question. You were asking about the nomenclature of this park; so, I shall answer your question. The overall reason why this park was named after Marquis De Lafayette was because he was a major help in the American Revolution," answered Mr. Lincoln.

"I didn't know that such a small park would be named after such a significant person on American History," replied Will.

"Let me just tell you this. You can underestimate parks and streets in other cities and places. Do not underestimate anything in Washington because everything in Washington is significant. Washington is the foundation for American history. This place is the most patriotic place in the nation. It is the most important place in the World. It is the most interesting place in all of the universes. And it is the most respectable place of all dimensions. It is the place that is prominent in all of the Heavens," the 16th president said.

"You are totally right. After reviewing the attention to detail in this place, it is more important than Starmos City. I don't even know how to describe this place. It is very modest how there are some buildings that look like mundane houses; but yet, it's sort of retro-futuristic because Union Station and Starmos Station look exactly the same. There's something exotic about this place. The exotic thing about this place is that there is an Obelisk going under construction and that is just impressive. Well that's just impressive enough to me. To me, this place is the most indescribable place that one can ever visit. I have never even been to a place where everything is so significant. I am going to fix Starmos City and make it as nice as this beautiful city," the alien leader replied.

Elation started showing in the 16th president's face. A wide grin started to appear. His grin is so wide that some of the beard strands started falling off. His face turned flush with color. He is in an overjoyed state of mind. He sighed in joy.

"Do you know what you said made me very happy. In fact, this is one of the happiest days of my life. You are here to do an excellent job to improve this beautiful place; and you will spread the cheer of this beautiful city to the other places. The citizens in your city would think that this place has an anachronistic look. I've never been to your city, but based on the stories you have told me, your place is quite interesting. In fact, I may want to come with you to the future," he said.

The alien leader reached into his shirt pocket to find the Intergallactic and Inter Dimensional Regulation Handbook. He put on his specs. "It is surprising that I need glasses at the age of 25. It is a must that some need reading glasses. Besides, the print is extremely small. Anybody who is born before 1950 will not be allowed to travel from Dimension to Dimension as clearly stated in this rulebook. I am sorry to say this Mr. Lincoln, but you will never be allowed to dimension travel," he said.

"Please, don't call me Mr. Lincoln. Just call me Abe. I want to know if you can find any possible loophole that you can bring my family and I into your dimension," the 16th president replied.

"Well, you see, I'm in some sort of a dilemma. There's no way I can dimension travel because God revoked my rights to do that. Right now, I'm supposed to be in the year 2047. I am stuck in 1861. Until I learn how to reconcile with God and until I qualify to go up to Heaven, there's no way that I am leaving this dimension," the alien leader said.

"Why would you brag about the rules in front of me?" asked Mr. Lincoln. "I never intended on bragging or being a show off about the rules," answered Will. "I think you were trying to show the rules into my face to gibe at me and show that I don't know too much of anything. One thing that is for certain is that I had to know a lot of things to be president. I had to know a lot to become a lawyer and congressman," the 16th president replied.

"I object to your wrong statement. You see, the reason why I told you about the rules was because I didn't exactly know them. I am not trying to rub anything into your face! I am not trying to torture you or tease you. And I don't have any intentions to insult or gibe at you. So, don't try and be arrogant or snide to me," the alien leader argued.

"Did you just realize that I was just kidding with you? I would never be nasty with you. Just learn how to take a joke," said Mr. Lincoln. "You know you're right. I shouldn't take too many things so serious. What you just said scared the living heck out of me," replied Will. "I am truthfully apologetic because what I did was quite nasty. From now on, I won't joke with you. I know that Mary Todd can take a joke that I make and so can the kids. I didn't know if you were able to take a joke though," the 16th president said.

"You see, I don't remember if I've told you this, but I have Asperger's Syndrome. You're probably asking yourself. What is he talking about? Well, you see, Asperger's Syndrome was diagnosed in 1944 by Austrian doctor Hans Asperger. This is a Learning Disability that basically states that you are extremely intelligent, but socially challenged. Even though, I might seem sociable, I am not able to take sarcasm or jokes very well. So, you would have to respect that," the alien leader replied.

"You know something, this may sound crazy, but throughout the years that I have known you, I have learned a lot about the near future and the distant future, but it is a great thing to know about the future because, the future is quite important. Futures can be bright. Futures can be a failure. You are the one who determines your future. And not to sound like I have an ego, but as president, the future of the nation is in my hands. Thus, I shall make sure that the future is in the county's best interest. Even though I have said this dozens of times, I believe the ending of slavery, chauvinism, and bigotry will be in the best interest of this country. When man learns to accept each other for who they are, our World will be better. This nation and this world needs a big bandage and stitches and it will take eternity to fill the gash in the World because there will always be problems in the World for eternity, but before we try and heal the World as a whole, we must heal the problems in our nation," the 16th president said.

The Stagecoach finally pulled up in front of Saint John's Church. Everyone stepped out except for the driver. "What is this place?" the alien leader asked. "Saint John's Church. It's a non-denominational Christian Church. This small church is what I like to call the 'national church.' It is extremely significant in this country because every president would come here to have his term blessed. Basically, he would ask the preacher to bless him during his term as a president. It is a significant place in Washington," answered Mr. Lincoln.

This church is surrounded by shrubbery and vegetation as well as grass. Featured on the property are circles of floral patterns. There are two steeples on this church. Each steeple is made of wood and metal. The front steeple is significant because the United States flag waves on the top of the steeple.

The back steeple features the Cross of Jesus Christ. The church has a year-round Easter appearance. It is painted green and yellow. Two wooden doors lead the believer into the church. These two wooden doors have engraved Christian symbols. The 16th president is the first one to walk up the first four marble stairs into the church; the rest of his family proudly entered right behind him; then his guests.

The rest of the attendees entered the church. The Baptist preacher is wearing a tuxedo; he is standing on a small stage that has a similar appearance to the altar. Featured in the rear of the stage is a large pipe organ with eighty eight brass pipes. The seats in the church are made of polished cherry wood. The choir stood in the back of the church. The choir is made up of African American women and Caucasian young men.

This is the only interracial choir during this time period. The president, his family, and his four guests walked up to the front of the church and sat in the first row in front of the preacher. Everybody else entered the church in a dignified manner.

Within minutes all 48 rows of polished wooden seats were filled up with people. The preacher stood in front of the altar. He adjusted his patriotic tie and his glasses. He retrieved his comb in his right pocket and fixed his black hair. He also combed his mustache. "Ladies and gentlemen, today is just a Sunday. That's what some of you must be thinking, but this is not your ordinary Sunday. This is a national holiday.

This is a holiday under God. This day is the day where an old president departs from office and a young president enters the honorable office of the President of the United States. And as Americans, we must respect that. Today is the day where Abraham Lincoln sits in the front row and today, is his day of honor. Today, is the national holiday that should be dedicated to him. This day is considered a day where the spirit of jubilation runs through our body.

On March 4, 1861, Mr. Buchanan departs from the honorable presidential position and Mr. Lincoln enters this honorable office. Today, is not only a day filled with happiness and jubilation, this day is also a serious day. This day is the day of where the new incoming president will have to handle huge problems. He will take on the responsibilities that are going to be handed down to him. I will tell you all a true story, but before I tell you all this story, I want the new president to stand up before all of you," he said. The 16th president listened to the preacher and stood up proudly in front of all of the attendees.

"Thank you, very much, pastor," he said. "This goes to show that we have a man that possesses a great feature. Now, it's not his height or the fact that he was able to take the office of President of the United States; it's actually because he is a person that possesses great humility. Not too many people can do that. I don't even think that I can do that. This man is the epitome of a God-fearing individual. Will he continue to be a God-fearing individual when he takes the office? Will he still have faith in God when he faces the problems of national division? Abraham Lincoln may be over six feet tall, but he will be facing Goliath sized problems. Let me tell you all about the story of David and Goliath. David had to fight off a gigantic human named Goliath who was a monstrous sized individual. At the time, David was a teenager when he had to fight off Goliath and nobody even thought that he could. People thought that he was going to end up being killed. But, he disregarded everybody's comments. At the end of the day, he disproved everybody and defied their expectations. Just one simple stone killed Goliath and Jerusalem received a new leader. This true story is similar because Mr. Lincoln is entering the honorable office of President of the United States and he is going to be facing many problems. Not to make this day sound like a negative day; I must tell the truthful problems that are coming his way. Well, one problem that has engulfed this nation is slavery and bigotry. For all of the years since the first president, not a single president cared to put an effort to fight the evils of Slavery. They just either supported it or ignored. Some even honored the idea and that was just plain evil. Slavery is an unfortunate national problem that must be ended. And another problem that must be ended that we have in this country is bigotry and racism, especially the idea of Social Darwinism or racial superiority. The racism is spreading like wildfire in this country. It has been in this World for many years. In fact, it has been in the World since the beginning of Bible times when the evil Ancient Egyptians enslaved the Israelites because they were not polytheistic. Racial superiority will still exist, but it should not exist in this country because all men and women whether they are white, black, green, yellow, or blue, they should all be created equal. Sadly, that's not the case because the white men are enslaving and mistreating people that are not of their color. So, Mr. Lincoln, I want you as president to listen to God and fear him and never lose faith because the loss of faith is the worst sin possible in the Bible. *And without, faith you may not be able to endure.* You will not be able to hold the true office of President of the United States. You must be strong. Be strong like a warrior and be an example to your people. As president, show your people how the country should really be governed. Fight for justice. Stand up against fundamentalism and Social Darwinism. Stand up against the evils of society and stand your ground and crusade for equality. Make sure that all men and women are created equal. Follow the principles of the Constitution. and don't forget to preserve, protect, and defend the Constitution of the United States. Support the Bill of Rights and be an honorable humanitarian. Respect every American in this country and every individual. All of God's creatures must be treated in the best way possible. I know you want to please God. So, as president, do everything to please God. Faith is necessary because *without faith you will not be able to please God,"* he said.

The president returned back into his seat. The preacher pointed at the alien leader. "Come up here, sir," he declared. Will hesitated. "Really?" he asked. "Do you think I would be asking you to come up here if I didn't want you to come up here?" asked the preacher. "I guess not," the alien leader nervously answered. He walked up to the altar.

"Now, please tell the ladies and gentlemen in the audience your name," the preacher said. "Will Von Alien," the alien leader muttered. "I don't think I was able to hear you. Can you declare your name to this great audience?" asked the preacher. Every attendee showed a wide grin. The alien leader's face showed some form of embarrassment. His blue skin started turning red. He started sweating. "Are you nervous?" the preacher asked. "Yes," shouted Will.

"Whoa," the attendees exclaimed. "Fine then, I'll tell you my name. It's Will Von Alien, okay?" the alien leader declared. He started crying. "Why didn't you want to say your name to the audience?" the preacher asked. "Because I was nervous," answered Will. "Why were you so nervous?" he (the preacher) asked.

"Well, I don't want to sound like a bigot, but the majority of this audience is comprised of Caucasian people and most of the Caucasians that I came across so far were bigots or snide to me. Some misperceived me as a slave because of our racist society and we must stop these societal problems. Now, I am going to direct this to the audience. I am sure you know the true significance of the red stripes on our flag. The reason why there are red stripes on our flag is because it shows the bloodshed of the individuals who died or who ended up being up injured in the wars. Most white men think that the red applies to their own color and gender, but that's not the case. If you really think about it, there aren't too many anatomical differences between the white men and the non-Caucasians. At the end of the day, we all of the same organ systems, we breathe the same air, drink water, have emotions, care about society, and we bleed the same color of blood. The only difference between the people who are white versus the people who are not white is that we all have different skin colors. That doesn't really matter. If man can really be born blind, we wouldn't be able to tell who has the same skin color and maybe, there wouldn't be bigotry and slavery. We all shouldn't have to be blind to see a man who truly fears God and shows a great deal of respect towards God. If you see, we are all God's children and we are all God's creatures. He brought us to this Earth to love one another and unfortunately, man doesn't do that. We all must learn how to treat one another with respect. People should not act superior to others because superiority, particularly racial superiority is wrong. So, ladies and gentlemen, at the end of the day, people who possess malice will go to Hell and they shall meet Satan. If we all learn how to treat everyone as equals, we would live in an almost Utopian Society, but sometimes, there is such a thing as what I like to call too much equality. Marxism is too much equality which basically means that everybody is to be in the same monetary class and you don't have to work in order to get into that monetary class. That's not true. Man has to work his or her way up. My final words in this particular statement are that *Slavery must be abolished, for once and for eternity. Racism and Bigotry should be destroyed,"* the alien leader declared. He sat down after he made that statement.

"Ladies and gentlemen, for our exiting song, the church and the choir should play *O Happy* Day."

As the song is being played, everybody is walking outside of the church in a respectable and dignified manner. The men and women are walking out in a synchronous motion, standing side by side, and holding hands. The president, his family, and his guests are the last ones to walk out of the church. Waiting outside the church is the Stagecoach. The horses started kicking their heels into the ground.

The Stagecoach driver cracked the whip to discipline them. Mr. Lincoln opened the door and escorted his wife into the Stagecoach; he and his sons followed; and then the four guests. Every individual sat in the same spots as they were sitting in a while ago. It is now 10 in the morning and the stagecoach returned back to Pennsylvania Avenue from the Church.

They drove down Pennsylvania Avenue past the National Mall to the Capitol Building. The Capitol Building is a building that is the color of an angel. The building is pure white all over the place. There are two wings in the building. One for the senate and one for the House of Representatives. This building is also the place where trials are held and this is the justice building of the nation. There are many citizens and spectators standing cheering.

The Stagecoach pulled up in front of the monumental building. The president is the first to walk out of the Stagecoach; Mary Todd and the two Lincoln sons followed; and then the guests. The cheering stopped at the drop of a dime when the president emerged from the vehicle. Not a single sound is heard from the spectators and the setting is now formal. One can even hear a single pin drop, that's the silence of the environment.

The president walked up to the podium. The marching band started playing *Washington Post* and *Hail to the Chief.* The 16th president met James Buchanan at the podium. They started talking to each other. "I'll wish you luck," Mr. Buchanan said. "Thank you," replied Mr. Lincoln. "I heard from Mr. Douglas that you're against slavery. What kind of an American are you?" the 15th president asked.

"I am more American than you," the 16th president answered. He walked up to the podium.

"Good day, ladies and gentlemen. We are here as a nation, united against evil and to fight for justice. Typically, most presidents refuse to break tradition. I am going to break tradition. This tradition is not a good tradition. It is the worst tradition of all bad traditions. This tradition is known as bigotry, slavery, and chauvinism. At the end of the day, these ideas come down to the tradition or the idea, rather, of Social Darwinism. As your president, all men and women shall be created equal. Currently, in our society, that's not the case. The only ones who have rights are Caucasian men; or simply known as 'the white man.' As your president all men and women, whether he or she is white, black, green, yellow, or blue; will have equal rights, not necessarily economic rights, but they will have the rights of Life, Liberty, and the Pursuit of Happiness. In addition to that, by the end of my first term, I am going to pass a law that ends Slavery and Chauvinism. People that are not of Caucasian color will have the rights to pursue work, marriage, or independence. Women will have those rights also. And I will also pass a law that individuals are only limited to two mugs of ale because anybody who is drunk has the tendency to act violent towards their spouse and that's not right. Nobody should have to suffer because of some arrogant, drunken sailor. I am not against alcohol, but I am not for people's overconsumption of such a dangerous drink. I will also pass a law against slavery and I will stop slavery from spreading. Those are my primary goals as president and if you have a heart, you will help me in my pursuit for fairness and justice for all races and all kinds. Remember, we are all God's creatures," he said.

These words do not have any meaning to the evil Southern Plantation Owners. South Carolina seceded before Mr. Lincoln became president. After the inauguration of President Lincoln, the rest of the South seceded. This started the American Civil War. Mr. Lincoln's presidency is going to be a tumultuous roller coaster.

Chapter XXI: 2 Years later: Gettysburg, Pennsylvania

Two years later, the Civil War has just begun. In Gettysburg, the people in the Union army are mobilizing in case a battle shall take place. While Rubi stays with the Lincolns, the alien leader, Bill Clayton, and Sheriff Joe joined the army in the fight for justice in the Civil War. A number of Caucasian Northerners and former slaves make up this army.

The Union is here to fight for justice and the Confederates are here to fight for evil. Life is very hard for these troops, but they are willing to fight. The temperature outside is bitterly cold; almost to the point of freezing and all these soldiers have to wear are their blue button down shirts, their hats, and saddle-brown worn out boots. The only cover that these soldiers have from the bitter conditions outside are their shelters, which are only made up of soft cloth and two pieces of 12 feet rope.

Over 1,000 tents are used for lodging and house the individuals fighting in the war. Four individuals are held in every tent. Then there are about 20 other tents that are used to house mobile weaponry. Finally, there is a large tent for the general of the Union Army. These tents are guarded by a large rampart. This rampart is made up of four layers of thick walls. These walls feature small arches that are used during battle. Some of the larger arches house cannons and semi-automatic firearms. The most honorable part of this fort is the United States flag that stands proudly on the top. Also, the flags of the Union States stand on the top of the fort. The top of the fort features sod, which prevents rain from seeping through the top and making the conditions musty for the soldiers.

It is now 5:00 in the evening. Most of the people in the fort occupied with their own jobs. Some are loading their guns for battle; others are waiting in line to ask the general questions about their assignment. Then, there are those who are organizing their tents with their artillery and arms.

Other folks are getting their horses ready for battle. Lastly, the rest of the soldiers present at the fort are doing menial jobs that are not crucial and are considered as 'nonessential' for the war but necessary for the soldiers. Some of the soldiers are repainting the numbers on their tents. Each tent is identified with a number it shows who they belong to, but repainting the number will not affect their performance in battle because the tent is also color coded.

This also shows the identification for their association. The tents that are painted navy blue belong to the Union Army and the tents that are painted grey belong to the Confederate Army. In the rear of the fort is a bunker. Typically, the bunker is used to house weaponry, but in this case it is used to house prisoners of war. The prisoners on both sides are treated in the harshest way possible. Some of the prisoners even have a gaunt appearance when they are released because that particular army who is housing them malnourishes them.

All of the Union prisoners of war have a gaunt appearance when they are released because the Confederate army has a barbaric and demonic soul. If a high ranking Union official is apprehended and taken as a prisoner of war by the Confederate army, he will be shot before even having a chance to serve his time. Granted, both sides treated their POWs (Prisoners of War) in a similar way. The Union side at least treated their prisoners with some respect and in a semi-humane form.

The Confederates were and still are completely inhumane, cold-hearted, and despicable. War is the most evil part of life; sometimes it is necessary. The battlefield is extremely quiet and clean. Not a single spatter of blood is on the brown soil.

Yet, the Union soldiers are getting ready for war. The grass on the field is slowly dying because of the weather. Later tonight the temperature outside is supposed to increase to 65 degrees. That will be the day when the Union army sees Mother Nature's beauty.

That will be the day where there'll be Heaven for the army. Will, Commissioner Clayton, and the sheriff are staying in tent 997, which is in the fiftieth row from the actual ramparts. It is right near the General. The interior of their tent has the exact appearance of all the other tents in the fort. There are two crooked, wooden steps that bring the individual into this tent. The tent is colored blue and 9-9-7 is clearly painted in white on the right side. When one walks inside this tent, 19 wooden boards make up the floor of this tent. In the rear of the tent is a small bunk bed.

This is not a typical bunk bed though. For instance, there aren't any bunks. Instead three small hammocks connected to two wooden poles house the soldiers when they are at rest. In addition to that, there aren't any mattresses or even cots. The soldiers have to sleep on small pieces of cloth.

Adjacent to the bunk bed, is a small table. The table is the only fancy item that is in the possession of a typical soldier. The reason why there is a fancy cherry wood table for the soldiers in tent 997 is because the individuals in that particular tent resided with President Lincoln for nearly four years. The table features a checkerboard as well as a Backgammon set.

Along with that, there is a small drawer located inside of this table for spare clothing. In the rear of the tent are three muskets. Each musket is engraved with the initials of U and A. The initials show the identification of the property owner of the gun. All of the guns have been unloaded and will have to be reloaded later in the evening. Will, Clayton, and Sheriff Joe are present in the tent. They are all honorably dressed in their uniforms.

The alien leader is lying on the bed dressed in his uniform. Fortunately, the uniform does not camouflage with his teal, oceanic colored skin. He is twiddling his thumbs staring into space. Like every other soldier, he is constantly thinking about the outcome of the war. He is trying to think of ways that the Union will have the ability to win. A couple of seconds later, he started scratching his bristly mustache that he had grown over the course of the past couple of years in the war. Sheriff Joe and Commissioner Clayton are trying to divert their minds from the traumatic thoughts of war.

So, they are playing chess. The sheriff is wearing his large specs. His left lens is broken; hence, he can't see out of his left eye. Clayton's hair is already grey from years earlier because of the stress of war. He is only sixty years of age.

"What move are you going to make?" he asked. "I am going to make a move that you will be hit so hard that you won't even know. I am the best at chess. When I worked in Boston, I used to play chess all the time. I even played checkers; 'bet you can't play that," answered Sheriff Joe.

"You know that I am good at all of the board games on the face of this universe, including some of the harder ones like Backgammon and Dominoes. When I worked in New York at One Police Plaza, we used to play Backgammon and Dominoes all the time. In fact, we ordered pizza that looked like dominoes. That's how sophisticated we police men are," the police commissioner replied.

"What the hell is pizza?" the sheriff asked. "What? You don't know what pizza is?" asked Clayton. "No, what is pizza?" asked Sheriff Joe. "Oh, God, it would take a lot for me to describe it. I might be able to describe it in simpler terms. Pizza is an Italian dish that is a triangular piece of baked bread and the toppings are at your request," the police commissioner answered.

"Now, why do you think we've been driven in a Conestoga this whole time when we have such furniture that is for the opulent?" the sheriff asked.

"Well, let me just tell you something quite important that I'd think would be necessary for minds like yours. In life, some things come handed to you; while, there are others that you have to work for. If you work for those things, you will most likely receive them. Now, a lot of the things we received in life were handed to us. Basically, we were almost sort of spoiled when we lived with the Lincolns. As compared to some of the other soldiers, we are being treated the best; so, don't complain.

For instance, we are able to sleep at night comfortably without having General Grant come into our tent and holler at us to go into the ramparts. We should just be grateful for that alone. In addition to that, we are able to cook our own meals. Most of the soldiers at this fort don't even have any cooked meals. Some of them don't even have substantial meals. Some of them have to live off of hardtack. That's another thing that you should be thankful for. You should show some thanks to the president that we have a fancy table filled with board games that are extremely entertaining. These games take us off of the horrible and melancholy thoughts of the horrors and sorrows of war. So, we are basically entertained in our own little tent. Very few soldiers are lucky that they are even able to get their hands on a board game. Granted, with the perks come some negative parts. Like all of the soldiers on both the Union and Confederate sides, we hear the sounds of gunfire. In addition to that, we might have to be on constant guard. Our minds cannot think straight because we have to be aware all the time of the bullets flying. Fortunately, we are guarded by a huge rampart. It is sad having to worry about that. Sadly, another part of war is that we are not able to comfortably lay on our beds or cots. We have to lay on cloth-like fabric because cots cause fires. Then, lastly, we are not able to see our families. If I am not home for 24 hours, my wife will have a panic attack. Imagine being gone for nearly 7 years. My funeral probably had taken place. Then, we have to show some form of sympathy for the slaves because they have to be on a higher watch than us. Rather than worrying about being captured the evil Southern plantation owners will return them down South to be tortured and face Hell. Now, let me just tell you this, don't try and think that you don't have enough because you have more than a lot of other soldiers. In fact, you have been spoiled. When man is given a lot of luxuries, he or she will have the tendency to act in a spoiled and stupid manner. They will take advantage of that individual who spoiled them. When given gifts, he or she should be grateful and appreciative. If that individual is grateful for his or her gifts, then he or she will be prosperous and live a happy life. Not only will there be happiness in that individual's life, there will be some joy. Now, joy and happiness seem to sound the same, but they have two different meanings. Happiness has to do with your external personality and your internal personality. Joyfulness is when you remain true to God and joy is seen in your heart. You can be as happy as you can. But you don't have to be joyful. Joyfulness and happiness are synonyms, but they both have different meanings. We are living in a World that has a lack of joyfulness and happiness, particularly in this war. People are losing their faith in Jesus because of the situations that they face of losing a loved one in the war, being imprisoned by an enemy army, getting permanently wounded, and losing limbs. When people lose joy, they lose their happiness. Now, I know that I said that joyfulness and happiness are two different definitions. They are related because if you are not happy; in some scenarios, you might not be joyful. You might not have both. Now, let's get back to the idea of gratefulness. Now, you should be extremely grateful to Mr. Lincoln because he has given you a lot. You and I and Will are the only ones that have a lot of material items in this Civil War because we are the president's closest friends. Remember, this a lot of the other soldiers don't have a lot,"answered the police commissioner.

"Now, I must admit that those words that you said are quite prophetic and important. They really did sink into my head. Now, I realize that I should be grateful for the good things and life. I not only should be grateful. I should be joyful," replied Sheriff Joe. "Are you serious?" asked Clayton.

"Of course, I am. A sheriff must always be serious," the sheriff answered. The police commissioner chuckled. "Well, for all of the years that I have known you, I have always witnessed that you were a jolly gentleman. You would always laugh constantly. Besides, you were a complete fool sometimes, but one thing that I know is that you were never a fool with politics and that you would never act like a jackass in public. You would always present yourself as an intelligent man. In addition to that, you would be serious when it came down to the legal matters. For instance, you would be insane when it came to somebody who would try to violate the law. And I'm not talking about insane in a good way. You would be very upset if somebody tried to violate the law. At the same time, you wouldn't be a tyrant when it came to laying down the law. You would try to be fair with the victim's family and the defendant. And that's what I like about somebody like you. You weren't too stringent. You weren't too lenient. You would be an extremely fair sheriff and that's somebody that I like. You are extremely fair because you go by the Constitution of the United States. That's somebody who I like. You are somebody that'll fight for justice. You won't bow down and honor a government that's unfair. Nor will you honor a government that's too loose. You are somebody who is what I'd like to call the 'square sheriff.' Now, you would be a perfect deputy commissioner for New York City. We all need a commissioner like you," he replied. "Sheriff Joe, What is your view on women's rights?" the alien leader asked.

"First of all, don't call me Sheriff Joe. Just call me Joe. I am just plain ol' Joe. Now, when I was younger, I was initially against women's rights. I was brought up in a time when chauvinism was acceptable. When I started getting older, I noticed how chauvinism violated women's rights. Then, I started to review the Constitution. When I read the words, *All Men are created equal*, I interpreted those words as all humans are created equal. Just to make sure that my interpretation of the Constitution was the correct interpretation, I went up to visit a historian. He said that I was totally right and these historians are extremely Conservative. He told me that my interpretation was fair and correct and the government totally misinterpreted the Constitution of the United States. I didn't advocate for women. I do believe that they are treated in a very unfair way and we must stop this unfairness because it is evil and unjust. In the early 1840s, I noticed a lot of women killing or hiring people to kill their husbands. And a lot of these women were battered women. Their husbands would come home at night, get drunk, and commit acts of domestic violence. Fortunately, Mr. Lincoln took office and he is fighting for women's rights. I treat my wife with a great deal of respect. Still, a lot of men, particularly the ones who work on the farms, treat their wives in the most arrogant ways possible. To add some insult to injury, our evil government considers women as second class citizens. The government denies women their rights because they think that the females are below the status of males. That's not the case. Hopefully, evilness towards women will end during Mr. Lincoln's presidency," the sheriff answered.

"What is your view on Judge Stevenson and Prosecutor Douer?" asked Will. "Oh my God, don't get me started with those pieces of garbage. Let's just get one thing clear. They are fakes and before they shapeshifted into beastly serpents, I knew they were fakes because they had eyes that looked like upside down scalene triangles, but if they were in real political positions, I would like to drag them up to the gallows post myself and hang them upside down. They are the most evil individuals I have ever come across. For God sakes, they are worse than the worst criminals I have ever dealt with. They're both monsters. First of all, they wanted to deny bail to two innocent individuals: you and Sarah, even though you just defended yourself and Sarah was in the wrong place at the wrong time. That's why that prosecutor wanted to charge her with Conspiracy to commit Capital Murder. That is despicable and evil. That prosecutor should have never charged you with a crime because you were just simply defending yourself against a drunken hound. And that judge, I have something against him. Judge Stevenson is a bigot. He only supports the wan and Caucasian ones. That's extremely bigoted and arbitrary. I never knew that this judge and prosecutor worked for the courthouse. That leads me to another thing. In our town, we elect our judges and prosecutors. There was no way that they were able to work at the courthouse unless they either paid their way up or slithered their way through the doors; and threatened the judge. This clearly shows that they were serpents and we found out that they were beastly and of the devil. One thing that is for certain is that demons will never dominate the World and evil will never win. We will all come face to face with God. So, when 'Judge Stevenson', really Korbian, and 'Mr. Douer', really Serpianto, come face to face with their Creator, he will realize that they have done evil and never rebuked their wrongdoing or repented, they will go straight to where they belong and that place is spelled in these four simple letters: H-E-L-L, formally pronounced as Hell," answered Sheriff Joe. "Was it necessary to spell out Hell?" the police commissioner asked. "Yes, it was. I was just trying to add some emphasis," the sheriff answered. "Whatever, let's just continue playing Chess," replied Clayton.

The alien leader walked out of the tent all the way past all of the tents. He continued on walking over to the General's tent. Now, General Grant's tent is the biggest tent in the fort. The exterior of the tent has an American flag on the right side. The tent features seven wooden steps. The wooden steps are polished. They look like the complete opposite of the all the other steps at the other tents. The alien leader walked into the tent. The tent is also unique on the inside. There are three tables. One table is used for recreational board gaming; another table is used for eating; and the third table is used for strategic planning for war.

The third table is used more often amongst the military leaders. The third table features a large map and chess pieces. The chess pieces are used for marking out the location of the troops. Adjacent to the tables, is a large telegraph. The telegraph is used for the high ranking soldiers to communicate in Morse code to one another.

Behind the tables, is a giant, navy blue curtain. The tables blocked somebody from going behind this curtain. Will is wondering about what is hidden behind this curtain. He is thinking hard and his intellectual wheels are turning. He started studying the situation like an analytical scientist. Immediately, he discovered that the telegraph is present in the tent. He communicated to tent 997 and asked Sheriff Joe to come to the General's tent in a heartbeat. The sheriff raced down to the general's tent. The alien leader walked out of the tent onto the stairs. He noticed the sheriff running as fast as a bull. He is breathing heavily and his face is flushed; he is sweating bullets. His head is at a high temperature.

His chest is expanding and contracting and he is not able to even think totally straight. "General, what's wrong?" he asked frantically and out of breath. "Oh, I'm not the general. I am Will," the alien leader answered. The sheriff is still not thinking straight. "General, is everything okay?" he asked. "Listen, sir! I am Will. Will Von Alien," answered Will. "General, why are you calling me sir?" asked Sheriff Joe. The alien leader approached him and smacked him. "What the hell is wrong with you? Have you had whiskey? Have you drunk beer? Did Serpianto poison you? Did Korbian poison you?" he asked in an angry manner. "Oh my God. Will, it's you! Where have I been? What's happened to me?" the sheriff asked.

"You see, I was communicating to your tent on the telegraph to let you know that I was here and to come here immediately. Nothing has really happened to you. You must've gone into a fog. It must be the conditions for Neanderthals like you," answered Will.

"What did you just call me?" asked Sheriff Joe. "I called you a Neanderthal. You must have some sort of disease for Neanderthals because you're sure quite senile. At your age, you should be intelligent and you shouldn't forget too much of anything especially how to run. And being that you're the sheriff, you should be able to recover quickly from being out of breath. Remember, you need to be able to catch criminals and most criminals are quite fast. If you're not able to catch any criminals, then you are incompetent to be the sheriff," the alien leader answered. In spite of the sheriff having a bull-like attitude, he does have a soft spot and he can become emotional very easily. He started tearing. Eventually, his tears became a sob.

"Why are you telling me that I am incompetent to be the sheriff?" he asked. "Because of the fact that you are not agile. In order to be the sheriff, you must be agile and fit. You must be able to catch criminals easily. The crime rate in your town will increase if you are not able to catch the criminals," said Will.

"You should have never called me senile or Neanderthal; then, I wouldn't cry the way I did just now. You can call me anything else but Neanderthal and senile. I have grandchildren and I would not want to be called those names in front of them because they would be able to call me those names and my life would be miserable. I want to make one thing clear to you. I bet if you owned your own business you would discriminate against old people and that's not nice. That's just plain wrong," replied Sheriff Joe.

"What you're saying is totally not true! You are basically telling me that I am a callous bigot when I am totally not. Somebody that is a bigot is Cornelius Von Alien or James Rosenthal. Those people are bigots. I support old people and I am for everyone. If you were not the sheriff, you would have either been put in a mental institution because of the ignorant people or even worse. You would have been slaughtered and killed in a cold-blooded manner and the government in the town wouldn't do anything about it because they would say that the homicide is justifiable because they say that old people are among the 'undesirables.' and that is despicable that we live in a world like that. You see, I know what goes on this World based on the small parts that I see. I can tell how a government runs based on my first impression. And the government running your town is filled with bigots. Maybe, you're not the bigot.

The mayor of your town is a bigot; the district attorney is a bigot; and 90% of your town is made up of a bunch of bigots and racists," the alien leader said. The sheriff stopped crying. General Grant emerged from the curtain and crawled under the tables. The alien leader took off his military hat.

"Good day, General," he said. General Grant is standing in a tall, valiant manner. He is showing the true epitome of the strength of the Union army.

He is also dressed and groomed in a respectable and dignified manner. His beard is combed and shining in the sunlight. His uniform is perfectly buttoned and his socks are tucked into his pants. His boots are perfectly even and shining. Not a single crease or wrinkle is seen in his pants. His patriotism is also seen in his clothing. His shirt features a small patch on the upper right hand corner.

This patch is not an ordinary military patch that just states the ranking in words. Instead, this patch shows the meaning and significance of his ranking in the Union Army.

The patch shows a Lion, a Donkey, and a Horse standing side by side. The Lion is the symbol of strength and courage. And the Donkey is the symbol of loyalty and patriotism. Finally, the Horse has a lot of significance on this patch. The horse symbolizes agility and distance.

General Grant fits all of those categories. He is doing an excellent job leading the Union army against the Confederates. This shows his strength of the Lion. He is a proud fighter for his country. And he will never give up in the war. This shows his loyalty. He will go the distance for justice and freedom for all. That shows a man of true loyalty and honor.

He stood in front of Will. "What's wrong?" he asked. "Oh, I am just wondering where I should stand in the middle of battle," the alien leader said. "Well, come on into the tent and then I'll tell you," the great general replied. He escorted Will and Sheriff Joe into the tent. He showed him a map of Fort Gettysburg. He pointed out the location where the alien leader should fight. "I am going to place you right over here in the middle of the fort. Now, I believe that you are here to fight for justice and you won't honor the evils of the Confederates," he said. "No, sir," the alien leader replied. "Now, first of all, I must tell you two important things. First of all, you must know that you don't have to call me sir or General Grant. Those titles are not my name. My name is Ulysses. You are to address me by that name from now on; and this will be a secret that is to be kept between you, your friends, and me.

In addition to that, I want to promote you to the General of Cannons. Basically, you will be the one to order the troops when to fire the cannons at the Confederates. And finally, I want you and Sheriff Joe to come behind the curtain," said the Union General. The alien leader, the sheriff, and he crawled underneath the tables and walked behind the curtain. They walked in the General Grant's sleeping quarters. The sleeping quarters features a hammock and four chairs.

Each chair is cushioned. "Stay right here, I have a surprise for you," he said. He walked to the second curtain, which is in the rear of the sleeping quarters. There is somebody waiting behind the second curtain. He emerged from the curtain. He is an African American who stands at a staggering six feet plus. His parents were basketball players and he came from California County. "Tom," shouted Will. "Whoa! What a surprise to see you here," replied Tom. "I know. This is truly a surprise. I thought you wouldn't make it out when Brutis captured you a while ago," the alien leader said. Tom gulped.

"Well, you see, I made a deal with him. He just took me hostage for ransom. I gave him a lot of information about my life and he released me. I was told by some mysterious messenger of God that you were here. So, I decided to come to see you and I had no other choice but to join the army and escape those beastly, murderous, callous Southerners. So, I joined the Union Army just to be safe," he replied.

"Well, I have a couple of questions to ask you. When did you get here and what's your ranking?" asked Will. "I got here about ten minutes ago and I am a rookie, but let's just make one thing clear. All of the positions in the army count. And one position is just as important as another," said Tom.

"Good point. You are totally right. Say, has Brutis educated you while you were imprisoned?" the alien leader asked. The rookie laughed. "Of course he has. I wouldn't be aware of Starmos Station if he didn't teach me," he answered. "Really?" asked Will. "Do you think I'd be lying to you for one second?" asked Tom. "Well, you have brought up a pretty good point. In fact, let me just see that you're not Brutis," said Will. "Why do you think that I am Brutis? Besides, Brutis would have a more evil demeanor than I would," the rookie replied. "I don't believe you. You are more intelligent than Tom and you are a little huskier than him. You are nothing but a fallacious soul. You *are* Brutis. Show me who you really are. Tell me who you really are," the alien leader answered angrily.

"Fine. Do you want to see the real me?" asked "Tom". "Yeah, well, I am really Brutis," the false impersonator of Tom answered. He took off his costume of

Tom and showed that he was really Brutis. His voice changed from Tom's voice to his (Brutis's) raspy voice. "I have to go to Jacqueline Langyaw. I have to help her guard Light," he said. He ran off back to Planet Earth to return to 2047 at Swinburn Island. "What a traitor!" exclaimed General Grant.

"I know. I am at odds with that monstrosity," replied Will. "Where's your friend, Tom?" the Union General asked. "He was abducted a couple of years ago at my estate in Starmos City," the alien leader answered. "Well, we'll deal with that after this war. For now, it is necessary that this war must be fought," replied General Grant. "What do you want me to do?" asked Will.

"You, Clayton, and Sheriff Joe did enough work. You guys can enjoy the rest of your day," the Union General answered. The soldiers in tent 997 ate dinner and like all of the other soldiers, the individuals in tent 997 fell asleep at 6:00 in the evening. Six hours into everybody's sleep, an alarming noise has been heard. Everybody awakened from their short sleep. It is now 12:00 a.m. Every Union Soldier is rushing from their tents to the barracks at the fort. It is now 12:03 in the morning and the confederates are lined up ready to fire. The alien leader ordered the firing of the cannons. The bloody fight for justice is taking place. Lives are being lost. The beautiful grassland has turned from a simple field in front of the fort to a death field. Thousands of lives are being lost. Bullets are being shot all over the place. This particular scene is a sick and gruesome scene. Everywhere you look, somebody's life will be lost to a bullet. Then, in pockets of the field many lives are being lost by cannonballs. Groups of people are falling to their demise due to a callous cannonball. People are losing their limbs because of grenades and dynamites. This is a horrific scene. Families are losing loved ones. Dozens of soldiers will be suffering from mental ailments or physical ailments because of this horrible battle. The Union won the battle by the skin of the teeth. Both sides have over 23,000 casualties. A ceasefire has taken place. It is now 2:00 a.m. Every soldier returned to their base. The Confederates returned down South. Meanwhile, the Union soldiers stayed at Fort Gettysburg. Two mornings ago the field in front of Fort Gettysburg was the natural color of green, now it is painted the color of blood. It is now 9:00 in the morning. Seen in the distance is the Presidential Stagecoach. The 16th president walked out of the stagecoach and he is here to deliver an important address to the troops.

Four score and seven years ago our fathers brought forth on this continent a new nation, conceived in liberty, and dedicated to the proposition that all men are created equal. Now we are engaged in a great civil war, testing whether that nation, or any nation so conceived and so dedicated, can long endure. We are met on a great battlefield of that war. We have come to dedicate a portion of that field, as a final resting place for those who here gave their lives that that nation might live. It is altogether fitting and proper that we should do this. But, in a larger sense, we cannot dedicate, we cannot consecrate, we cannot hallow this ground. The brave men, living and dead, who struggled here, have consecrated it, far above our poor power to add or detract. The world will little note, nor long remember what we say here, but it can never forget what they did here. It is for us the living, rather, to be dedicated here to the unfinished work which they who fought here have thus far so nobly advanced. It is rather for us to be here dedicated to the great task remaining before us— that from these honored dead we take increased devotion to that cause for which they gave the last full measure of devotion—that we here highly resolve that these dead shall not have died in vain—that this nation, under God, shall have a new birth of freedom—and that government of the people, by the people, for the people, shall not perish from the earth," he declared.

After the speech, every single Union troop applauded the honorable president for his honorable speech. He spoke with General Grant about the war and returned back down to Washington to continue his presidential duties.

The Battle of Gettysburg was the bloodiest battle in the Civil War. Many lives were lost; many families were ruined; and the trauma in Gettysburg is unforgettable. Since then, there have been many other bloody and ruthless battles. On April 9, 1865; two years later, the Confederates surrendered. After this, slaves were liberated and Union POWs were freed from those brutal Confederate soldiers.

Chapter XXII: April 13, 1865: one of the worst days in History

In spite of the war being over, reconstruction is necessary. The South and the North are completely obliterated. And Amendments must be passed to end slavery, make it illegal and fight for justice for all races. Sadly, slavery is not officially illegal. In addition to that, people would have to fight for the voting rights of non-Caucasians. So, justice must be done. The president, his guests, and his family are staying at the Executive Mansion.

It is a quarter to Seven in the morning, and everybody is still sleeping. The bedrooms are on the second level. There are about nine bedrooms. The president and his wife are sleeping in the grand bedroom; the alien leader and Rubi are sleeping in the bedroom facing the front lawn; Sheriff Joe is sleeping the bedroom facing Lafayette Park; and Commissioner Bill Clayton is sleeping in the bedroom facing Pennsylvania Avenue. The guests are sleeping on the West side of the Executive Mansion and the Lincolns are sleeping on the exact opposite side. The rays of the sun beamed inside of Will's bedroom.

The rays are much brighter than a simple oil lamp. Rubi and he are sleeping in a King- size Canopy Bed. The drapes of the Canopy are the colors of red, white, and blue. The linens on the bed are just plain white. There are two closets in the bedroom; one for Will and another for Rubi. The floor is very unique. The floorboards are made of three different woods from three different trees: birch, spruce, and cherry wooden floorboards make up this floor. In the center of the floor is a huge square carpet. This carpet has ornate red and gold designs that look like Julius Caesar's Civic Crown. This carpet is custom designed, measured, and fitted for this particular room. In the center of the carpet are two designs of United States flags waving proudly.

Featured between the flags is a design of the Presidential Seal. Electricity has just been invented. So, the alien leader used a lemon to charge his aPhone. He is sleeping. Loud snores are coming out of his mouth. At 7:15 a.m, the alarm is making a loud noise that sounds like a repetitive chime. Despite the loud, mind-numbing alarm being heard, he is still in a sleepy state. Rubi moved her hand. Her pulchritudinous blonde hair is in curlers. Will is drooling because he is out cold. The alarm repeated. It started to talk.

"Wake up," it said. "What?" the alien leader asked in a fatigued manner. "Wake up, Will," the alarm said. The alien leader stood up from the bed. He walked up to the phone charging. "You're going to shut the hell up," he said. He unplugged the phone and turned it off. "That was a relief," he then said. He is wearing blue and grey striped pajamas.

He is wearing white socks and grey slippers. His hair is messed up and unkempt. He opened the curtains.

The sun's rays stopped beaming on the bedroom. He stared into the window. As he started into window, he started to have a flashback as to what happened earlier about the 'good' morning.

He is having a recollection of the loud noises that caused him to wake up a while ago. He is recalling when Jacqueline Langyaw invaded the Alien Estate and kidnapped Light. He is thinking about that morning. Within a minute, the flashback ended. "Why did I think of something painful like that?" he asked himself. He paused.

"Maybe I should go back to bed," he then said. He stepped back into the bed and tried to fall asleep. Unfortunately, for him, he is not able to fall asleep. He just remained laying down staring at the armoire. Rubi started waking up. She yawned. She slowly started walking out of the bed. She walked around the bedroom at a slow pace. She is in a state of oblivion.

After pacing for two minutes, she fainted. The alien leader jumped out of the bed. His heart jumped and he started panicking. "Rubi, is everything okay?" he nervously asked. He placed his hand up to her wrist, trying to feel her pulse. Her pulse is normal. He felt her heart. The heart rate is a little higher than usual. Then, he felt her head to make sure she didn't have a fever.

Fortunately, her temperature is normal. Skepticism is running rampant in his mind. He walked out of the bedroom and entered the hallway. The hallway features seven small chandeliers. The three tier chandeliers are made of brass and diamonds. The hallway features a burly wood floor that has a nautical appearance. He walked up past the stairs all the way to the president's door. The Presidential door is painted a patriotic red, white, and blue. He knocked very loudly on the door.

Mary Todd opened the door. President Lincoln is sleeping comfortably in the bed. "What's wrong?" she asked. "I think my girlfriend is either dead or in a huge faint. She has a normal pulse and an above normal heartrate. I am nervous as can be. I don't know why she is in such a bad bodily state. I am worried that she's dead. I will not be able to live with myself if she is dead," Will answered nervously in a panic.

"I want you to tell me what happened in a more calm manner so that way I am able to help your girlfriend," replied Mrs. Lincoln. The alien leader reiterated exactly what he said verbatim. Mrs. Lincoln and he walked back to the guest bedroom where he and Rubi slept. His girlfriend is lying on the floor unconscious. "What should we do?" he asked. "Well, I am going to try and make sure that she'd be able to survive," answered Mary Todd. " and how exactly are you going to do that?" asked Will.

"I'm going to put her on the bed for now and call a nurse up here to try and investigate what's wrong," the first lady answered. "How exactly are you going to call the nurse?" the alien leader asked. "I am just going to shout for the nurse to come up here," answered Mary Todd. "Is there an on-site nurse?" asked Will. "Quite frankly, I don't know. You know what? On second thought, I am going to ask my husband to order his secretary of state to call the nurse. Once he does that, your girlfriend will be safe," the first lady answered. She walked out of the bedroom. As she walked past the door, Will grabbed her. "What do you think you're doing?" he asked in stentorian manner. "Nothing," she answered nervously. He returned his voice back to normal. "I smell something quite fishy. Did you happen to kill my girlfriend?" he asked. "Why would you say such a thing?" asked Mary Todd. "Well, you are not able to think when you're speaking. Face it. You are saying that I said a statement when I simply asked you a question. Now, answer this question in an answer of 'yes' or 'no.' Did you murder my girlfriend?" the alien leader asked. The president's wife hesitated.

"No," she answered. "Come down the stairs," replied Will. While, he placed his unconscious girlfriend in the bed, Mrs. Lincoln waited by the door. After placing Rubi in the bed, Will escorted Mary Todd into the parlor room. The parlor room features arched windows. Inside this parlor room, are four elegant sofas. They are covered with silver and gold quilts. By the windows are two musical instruments. A Steinway Piano stood on the West part of the room and a Harpsichord stood on the East part of the room. The room is an alcove because in order to get into the room, one would have to climb down two wooden stairs. The room has a floor that is carpeted with green rug. The alien leader is sitting on the couch in the Northwest part of the room in front of the coffee table and the first lady is sitting on the other couch across from the coffee table on the opposite side of the alien leader.

"Okay, now not to sound like a police officer because I am your guest, but I am going act like one if I suspect that you've murdered my girlfriend. Now, let me ask you this question again from earlier. Did you murder my girlfriend?" he asked.

Mary Todd looked up at the white ceiling. She then stared at Will and shifted her almond eyes at the arched windows. "No, I didn't kill her," she answered. "Now, you've hesitated. You looked upward; and you shifted your eyes when you answered this question. Now, there must be more that you might be hiding. Don't worry, I won't prosecute you. Tell me exactly what has really happened," the alien leader said.

"Okay, I'll tell you. You see one night in 1863, the mansion was burglarized by this beastly alien. He identified himself as Brutis. He walked into the library; ransacked through all of the books and discovered a couple of hourglasses filled with quicksilver. He cracked them all open and retrieved a teacup. He forced her to drink the substance inside of those hourglasses. I remember one thing that he stated that will keep on replaying in my head every time I mention this. He stated that she would die on April 13, 1865 at 7 in the morning. In addition to that, he also stated that he would be coming to kill you next. So, you better leave Earth and return back to Starmos City," the first lady replied.

"Thank you, but the information that you supplied me with was inefficient. Can you give me a detailed description of the perpetrator's physical appearance?" asked Will. "Well, this might sound a little crazy, but I must give you two descriptions of the perpetrator's appearance. Well, when he came in, he had a similar skin pigmentation to your pigmentation. He had blue skin. It wasn't a teal blue like yours. This beast stood at a staggering height of over eight feet. He was much bigger than my height. You might describe him as a Goliath. He wore a bizarre uniform. The uniform looked like it was made of this aluminum. And I remembered that there were 'bout seven letters and two rules. I have a vague recollection of the uniform showing the letters of CVA rules and SSGM shall dominate. Those letters and words were featured on a badge that looked similar to a police badge. I also remember that he was very muscular when he came in and poisoned Rubi," answered Mary Todd.

"Even though I am interrogating you, I must tell you something quite important. If you don't know what CVA or SSGM stand for, I'll tell you what they stand for. CVA rules means *Cornelius Von Alien* rules and SSGM shall dominate means *the Starmos Socialist Governmental Military shall dominate.* Now, let me just get one thing clear. I killed Cornelius Von Alien, who was a tyrannical beast who ruled Starmos City; and I ended the SSGM, which was a military controlled under the Starmos government that was influenced by the former Soviet Union. The spirit of Cornelius Von Alien is still in existence; and many evil individuals are still loyal to the old SSGM and show a deceitful attitude towards the new and improved leadership," the alien leader replied.

"What is the Soviet Union?" the first lady asked. "Remember, I live in a time when I learned about the Soviet Union. For your generation, the Soviet Union is going to be a tyrannical communist country. For my generation, the Soviet Union was a former Soviet Union; it was a communist dictatorship country ruled by evil leaders. You see, your generation will not know that the Soviet leaders are evil; but they are. Unfortunately, the former Soviet Union politics influenced Cornelius Von Alien's head and ruined my city. We will not curtail and give in to injustice! We will fight against the Communist ideas and rip the Soviet Union into shreds," answered Will.

"Would you mind getting back to the interrogation?" asked Mary Todd. "Sure," the alien leader answered. "Very well, then. I'd appreciate it if you'd continue interrogating me," the first lady replied. "Okay, I must've gone a little off on a tangent. Now, I remember you told me that this perpetrator looked differently when he entered the mansion and when he departed from the mansion. Can you tell me how this perpetrator looked when he departed from the mansion?" the alien leader asked.

"Well, I can tell you one thing. This beast looked totally different when he departed the Executive Mansion versus how he entered. He looked quite unkempt when he walked out. In fact, he looked like a homeless introvert. His clothes looked totally different. His hair looked like it was unkempt when he departed. Instead of having neatly combed brown hair, he had hideous black hair that was that looked like it had lice. He didn't wear the SSGM cap. Instead, he wore a checkerboard flat hat that looked like it had been worn for over fifty years. He had a beard that was scraggly. His eyebrows looked like they were overgrown. I can tell you he didn't depart out of the mansion in strong boots; he departed from the mansion in clichéd laced shoes. Instead of wearing leather gloves, he wore gloves that were knit by a homeless shelter; and I remembered that he carried a gondola boat," answered Mary Todd.

"Did he look like he kind of shape shifted?" asked Will. "Yes, how are you able to know that this beast is a shape shifter?" the first lady asked.

"Well, first of all, I am a very intuitive alien. I know everything that goes on. You can provide me with very little information and I will be able to piece a story from that little amount of information that you have provided me with. In addition to that, I have dealt with this beast on a number of occasions before. One occasion that I will remember was back in 2047, I was at a talking fox's house because my friend's town was forced under evacuation because the tyrannical aliens were invading. So, being the good alien, I decided to help keep the humans safe. I didn't know that I was going to deal with a beast like Brutis. I met him in the woodlands. He looked like an unkempt Goliath sized human. He shapeshifted into an alien and tried to capture me. I tricked him into thinking that I was by the lake when I returned back to the fox's abode. Unfortunately, he found out, but I managed to resist him, but one thing that is for certain is that he'll never be able to win any battles and I can assure you that he will not hurt any of you because if he lays a finger on you or any Lincoln, I am going to hunt him down and hang him," replied Will.

"You know, I have always liked you. You're a very protective and loyal individual. You will go beyond all limits to protect my family, the nation, and I. That is somebody who I'd think would qualify to be the vice president or secretary of state. The only problem that you have is that you go off on tangents that sound crazy, but sometimes those tangents are relevant to the conversation. Now, I can understand the reason why," said Mary Todd. "I don't think you realize that the interrogation is over with. Now, please answer these three questions. What were you doing at the time of the poisoning? What was your current location during the time of the burglary? And did you know beforehand that my girlfriend was going to die today before she was poisoned?" asked Will.

"To answer your first question, I was finishing up cleaning the kitchen and I was helping make dessert with the chefs over here. That was when I heard the sound of glass breaking. To answer your second question, when the beast walked up the stairs, I was in the kitchen heading up to my kids' bedroom to put them to sleep. That was when we heard the loud noise of the break-in. So, while he entered Rubi's room, I sneaked upstairs and locked my bedroom door. That was when I noticed him running on the lawn escaping. To answer your third question, I had no idea that such a wicked crime was about to take place," the first lady answered.

"You claim that you snuck up to the bedroom when you saw this burglar, but how are you able to clearly read the initials, even though you were so scared?" the alien leader asked. "Well, I want to tell you that when I thought about the incident, I became very nervous because that incident was a horrible incident. Now, I'll tell you the more truthful details, but before I tell you the truthful details, I was not lying to you. I was trying to be as clear as I should be when I am being interrogated. Now, he entered through the kitchen window. I finished cleaning off the plates and he approached me. He told me what he was going to do and he claimed that he would be going after you next; and I would not be able to stand by him. I threw my knife at him but that didn't stop him. He just continued running. I was so bold, but yet so scared. And the only reason why I was bold was for my sons. I remember he wore a tin uniform and I remembered that his patches fell on the floor. When, he entered Rubi's bedroom, she was sleeping because she was ill with the common cold. I was so nervous that I started acting stupid. I brought the kids up to my bedroom with my husband and we stayed in the bedroom that whole night. Fortunately, the burglar left five minutes after he committed the crime," answered Mary Todd.

"Was the vice- president present at the time of the crime?" asked Will. "Like I said earlier, this incident was a traumatic and emotional incident that has taken place, but I don't think the vice-president was there when the incident has taken place. If the vice-president was there, I'd know he'd protect my family, the guests, and I. I know him very well. Unfortunately, he wasn't here during the time of the crime," the first lady answered.

"You have answered my questions in a cooperative manner. Quite frankly, I was surprised on how you seemed to be lying at first being that you didn't have a straight answer, but when you told me what happened in its entirety, I was able to understand it better. Thank you for giving me the details," replied Will. "Are you the constable?"

Mary Todd asked in a sarcastic manner. The alien leader chuckled. "No, I'm not," he answered. It is now half past seven in the morning and the Executive Mansion is still quiet. The only ones who are currently awake are Mary Todd and Will. The president started to walk down the stairs. He is wearing crimson striped pajamas. His hair looks unkempt and his beard looks scraggly. He walked up to his wife and Will. "What are you doing up at this time?" he asked. "Well, I didn't happen to tell you this but my girlfriend, Rubi, has been brutally murdered by this man named Brutis. Did you happen to discover a burglary that had taken place a couple of years ago?" the alien leader asked. The president paused and he started trying to recall about Brutis's burglary.

"Oh, yes. I absolutely do remember. This definitely does ring a bell. I was in my bedroom about to fall asleep at the time of the incident. I do remember Mary Todd running up the stairs with the two kids, nervously going into the bedroom," he answered. "Very well, then. Did you happen to know if this beast entered the guest bedroom where Rubi stayed?" asked Will.

"Oh yeah, I heard her door open, also. I remember she also needed some sheets on that evening too," answered Mr. Lincoln. "What else do you remember?" the alien leader asked. "I remember that the burglar brought up a cacao mug and I believe he administered some sort of a drink to her," the 16th president answered. "Okay, now what is a cacao mug?" asked Will.

"A coffee mug," answered Mr. Lincoln. "Now, that sounds like sufficient evidence for me. I must ask you this question. Did you happen to..," the alien leader replied. The 16th president interrupted.

"Whoa, whoa, whoa. Before you say anything else, why are you asking me such questions?" he asked. "Okay, my answer does kind of relate to the last question that I was 'bout to ask you. To answer your question, the reason why I am asking you and Mary Todd so many questions is because I found my girlfriend Rubi pacing and then she fell to the floor unconscious. I was told that Brutis poisoned her with some quicksilver and that she was to die today at around this time. Nobody knew that she was going to die today. She unfortunately died and I don't think this day can get any worse," answered Will.

President Lincoln became nervous. He dashed out of the parlor room and started running up the three flights of stairs to the alien leader's bedroom. There, he had discovered a horrible sight. Rubi is dead on the bed. He felt her pulse. The wrist felt cold. He felt her chest. Not a single heartbeat has been heard or felt. He felt her forehead and there wasn't a single temperature to show that she was either alive or ill with fever. She is officially dead. He crashed to the floor and started sobbing. Five minutes later, somebody knocked on the front door. He stopped crying and ran down the stairs to open the door. The knocking became louder. He sees this as the scariest moment of his life. He hesitated and then opened the door. Fortunately, it's only the secretary of state, William Seward. He has a clean grey haircut. He is wearing a professional suit with a red tie and a white shirt. His shoes are brown laced shoes that are well kept and professionally polished and shined to the point of squeakiness. He has a quite cheerful but that is a little bit raspy voice.

"Good day, Mr. Lincoln," he said. "Just call me, Abe," the 16th president replied. "Very well then, Abe. I think we shall get going to Capitol Hill to discuss about the new 13th amendment," said Mr. Seward. "Even though this is quite important, we have a crisis taking place upstairs. Somebody has died and she is an alien from Starmos City, who I made a member of my family." replied Mr. Lincoln.

"Oh my God, that's terrible. How exactly did she die?" asked the 24th secretary of state. "Well, you see, I didn't tell you this because my family and I were scared, but the Executive Mansion was burglarized a couple of years ago back in 1863 by some shapeshifting alien. The shapeshifting alien poisoned Rubi," the 16th president answered. "Oh my God, that's terrible. How exactly do you think such a thing can take place?" asked Mr. Seward. "Well, somebody managed to break into the place because the kitchen windows were brittle before I put the iron reinforcements. And that individual was a shape shifter. When he entered, he looked similar to a Goliath-sized alien. I was told that he stood at a staggering eight feet tall and he had a large head. In addition to that, he was very muscular and had a well-built body," answered Mr. Lincoln. "and where did he go when he left?" the 24th secretary of state asked. "Well, the only time when I exactly witnessed this burglar was when he departed from the front lawn. I witnessed him running through the side yard all the way up to the Lafayette lawn. I was in the bedroom the whole time this had taken place because I was about to fall asleep because I was tired from a hard day's work," the 16th president answered.

"Now, I didn't ask you this question from earlier. How did you know the perpetrator's physical appearance even though you didn't see him?" asked Mr. Seward. "Well, that's not true. I didn't see him most of the time. I was only able to see him on the front lawn and he looked like a dirty ragamuffin. I don't like describing homeless or poor individuals in such a nasty manner. If he committed a wicked crime of murder in the first degree, he deserves the death penalty," answered Mr. Lincoln.

"How did you know that he was a shape shifter? And why would you say such a thing about him being a shape shifter?" the 24th secretary of state asked.

"Well, first of all, I found out he was a shape shifter because my wife told me. In addition to that, you can't be so strong, bust through a tall window, and then look like a short, gaunt, and impecunious homeless man. Now, you're probably going to say that just because you're short and gaunt doesn't mean you're weak. If you do not have the proper nutrition, you must be quite weak and I don't think somebody who is gaunt would be able to bust through such a tall window. Granted, the window was weak at the time, but I don't think a supposedly gaunt man would be able to open a window like that. I don't think he would be able to handle a crowbar; nevertheless, climb through the window and thus, from that theory alone, he was a shapeshifting creature. I believe my wife's side of the story. Besides, she was a firsthand witness as to what happened sadly. Now, in order to rest my case, I will state this, the intruder entered through the side window in the form of a goliath sized alien, but he came out of the front door in the form of feeble and gaunt homeless man. Not to sound like a snob, but my opinion counts and I don't think your opinion will count," the 16th president answered.

"How did this intruder affect Rubi?" asked Mr. Seward.

"Well, you see, this intruder had a motive. He wanted to kill Rubi because she was and still is Will's girlfriend. Will is the alien leader of Starmos City. Before I continue, I must remind you of something. There are good aliens and bad aliens. Will Von Alien and Rubi are good aliens who are here to help American society and Starmos society. I know I sound crazy or even delusional. I am not. If you want to meet Will, you will be more than welcome to meet him. He is a very kind and genuine man. He is an excellent male alien. For now, let's get back to answering your question. My theory is that Brutis killed Rubi because he was jealous that Will became the leader of Starmos City and also, that he (Brutis) was jealous of the fact that Rubi was Will's girlfriend. That is just plain despicable and atrocious. Why do we have to live in a world like this? I am constantly asking myself the same question every day," answered Mr. Lincoln.

"Let's continue asking the questions about what happened. This my last question because I can understand that you don't have too much information. Besides, your answers are probably erroneous and theoretical," the 24th secretary of state replied.

"They're probably theoretical, but those theories are not erroneous. At least, they don't sound erroneous. Now, I believe she was murdered with the involvement of a cacao mug. She was not murdered in the way that you'd expect to be a normal way of being murdered. She wasn't struck with the mug. Instead, Brutis decided to poison her with some quicksilver, commonly known as mercury. I found this out because I noticed my hourglasses in the Presidential library were destroyed. So, I believe that he grabbed the mug, broke the hourglasses filled with quicksilver, and filled the mug with the substance. Then he decided to pour liquid in the drink to make it appear like drink coming from a cacao plant," the 16th president said. "I'll leave the body as it is and make sure that nobody can tamper with it. We must get over to the Supreme Court to head over to a proceeding about the passing of the thirteenth amendment and I have a new proposal for the annexation of a frozen land up North," the 24th secretary of state replied.

The black Stagecoach is waiting outside of the Executive Mansion. The president walked up to his wife and kissed her good bye. He entered the Stagecoach and departed from the Executive Mansion all the way down to the Capitol Building.

They finally arrived in the Conference room for the important meeting regarding the idea of passing the Thirteenth Amendment. This is going to be the start of justice. The president walked inside of the Congressional Hall. The Congressional Hall featured multiple tables. These tables are made of cherry wood and burly wood. Each table features seven ink wells.

Every table features a piece of parchment paper that is used to take notes and propose new bills. In the Center of the Congress Hall is a large chair, which is used for the seating of the president. Adjacent to this seat are two chairs that are used for the vice-president and the speaker of the house. The Congress Hall is filled to the brim with politicians from all over the nation.

The president arrived in his position. He stood up. "Ladies and Gentlemen, we have just gotten over a war a week and a half ago because Jefferson Davis and Robert E. Lee surrendered themselves to authorities, but that doesn't mean war is over. In addition to just getting over a horrible but, necessary war, we have to face the effects of war. The biggest effect of war is the Reconstruction Process. I do not like to tax people. I am left with no other choice, I am going to raise the taxes by 2% because since, the South is now part of the nation, we must treat that region as if it was the same as the North, but the biggest factor in reconstruction of the South is that we must end slavery, for once and all! For God sakes, this war occurred because of the ideas of slavery, bigotry, and chauvinism which all tie into the idea of Social Darwinism. Now, the reason why I am here is to pass probably one of the most significant amendments and that is the Thirteenth Amendment. Now, this amendment shall end slavery and chauvinism. This amendment is put into place because it will discourage bigotry and hatred. People must give up their slaves within thirty days after the law goes into effect. In addition to that, if they possess a slave illegally, they shall be remanded to the custody of their local department of corrections and sentenced to a imprisonment for the rest of their natural life. This amendment is supposed to end slavery and make the possession, distribution, importation, purchase, or sale of slaves illegal. In addition to that, this law will state that all races must be treated as equals in the work force. Now, these are the first few parts of this law that I am hereby proposing. You all would be surprised to hear this coming from a governmental figure. I must state that women should be treated equally to men. Most of you don't know how I treat my wife, but I treat her with a great deal of respect. I may not be sounding like somebody with great humility, but I want to be an exemplar to show the world how I honor my wife and how she honors me. I notice that there are a lot of women going to jail because they're battered by their husbands. No longer am I going to sit and wallow in a country where women are mistreated. I am going to fight for the justice of females. I will make a law that will set up houses for women that are battered. Also, husbands will think twice about beating a woman up in a heinous way, especially because of a miscarriage. I want to let you know that I had to dress up as somebody's younger son because her husband would beat her wife up because he would find out that she'd have a miscarriage. So, my good friend Will decided to kill this man because he was violent and aggressive. Also, I don't think you all will show some approbation for this law that I am proposing. The law that I am proposing that shall also go into effect along with this amendment is that Sarah's Law shall be passed. This law states that if you are a battered woman, you have the right to shoot your husband and you won't be arrested. Now, I know that there will be some that will misuse this law. Most women won't kill or come home drunk unless they are deranged. In addition to that, I am going to pass a law that pubs and saloons are to serve one individual two drinks that are alcoholic. And those drinks will have to be in bottles. Basically, bars will not be allowed to serve two mugs of ale any more. They will only be limited to serving one mug or two average sized bottles. If they violate this law, they will have to face fines. Now, you'll probably think what I am saying is quite Socialist, but it's not. I am not violating laissez faire. I am trying to be fair to all of the citizens. This is going to take you a while for you to deliberate on approving this amendment and Sarah's law, but it is important to society", said President Lincoln.

The congress deliberated for twelve hours. A unanimous agreement was not able to be reached. The president will have to make a new speech or he will have to continue to wait for Congressional deliberations.

Unfortunately, Abraham Lincoln was not able to make it to see the Thirteenth Amendment to be passed because he died at the Ford's Theater by a wicked and callous killer John Wilkes Booth. Later, that week John Wilkes Booth was shot. Andrew Johnson had taken office and part of thirteenth amendment was passed to end slavery. That was when justice was done. God brought Will, Rubi and Commissioner Clayton back to the year of 2047 in the cave in New York City.

Chapter XXIII: Back in the year 2047, but life is still not stable nor normal

Sheriff Joe returned back to South Salt Lake and Will, Rubi, and Commissioner Clayton arrived in New York City in 2047. They are right back in the cave. "Where are we?" the alien leader asked. "We're back in New York City and we are still in the cave," answered Clayton. "It seems like we've been gone for nearly seven years," replied Will. "Well, that sounds odd because it only says that we've been gone for ten minutes according to my digital watch," said the police commissioner.

"It seems like we've been gone for a long time. Quite frankly, I feel like sleeping right now because I feel like I'm going to puke," the alien leader replied. "Well, there's no way that you'll be able to sleep because we have a huge problem that we must face," said Clayton. ", and what problem would that be?" asked Will. "Oh my God. How can you not remember that your friend, Light, has been kidnapped? How can you not remember about Jacqueline Langyaw? Better yet, how can you not remember about Serpianto, Korbian, Mitchell, Brutis, or even Howard Carterson?," the police commissioner angrily asked. "I guess when you travel two hundred years in the past and two hundred years back into the future in ten minutes, amnesia and nausea might do its part," answered Will.

"Buddy, you can't afford to go through this. Your girlfriend is unconscious; you have to rescue two of your friends and bring six hardened criminals to justice. If you forget about those people, then they'll eventually do evil to the world and we can't live in a world where this injustice and evil. We can't even look at a world filled with evil. Besides, I don't think you want your girlfriend to die," replied Commissioner Clayton.

"You know something? You're right because we can't live in a world where there is such a thing as injustice. If we live in a horrible world, then I have failed as an alien leader and a member of the Earthly alliance. As a police commissioner, you have failed because you are here to protect the public from the menaces and rogues of society. And we might as well not be alive because God has selected us to have different jobs in life. He has selected me to be the alien leader of Starmos City and he has selected you to be the police commissioner in New York City. God gives people different jobs and man has different callings in life. Every man and woman has a different purpose on this planet, in the universe, and in all dimensions combined. We all have different meanings and callings," the alien leader said. He walked up to Rubi and placed his hand over her forehead. Her fore head is as cold as ice. She has a very low temperature. He placed his hand over her heart. He felt slow heart beats. "She's alive! She's alive," he exclaimed ecstatically. He sprung up from the cave floor. "What do you mean she's alive?" the police commissioner asked in an anxiously excited manner.

"She's alive! She's alive, I tell you," said Will. "How is she alive when she's not moving?" Clayton asked in a moody voice. "Well, if you know biology, you should know that if a heart is beating and if that individual has a pulse, then, that particular individual is alive. Therefore, that individual might survive. It's not a guarantee. There's a high chance of survival," the alien leader answered. "Well, I haven't taken a Biology class in 30+ years, so, I probably don't remember anything that has taken place in that particular class since then. Now, what are we going to do with this body?" the police commissioner asked.

"For your information, this body is not just any deceased body. First of all, you shouldn't be treating my girlfriend like she is any ordinary dead body because she is not, and I mean she is not, any ordinary dead body. She is a normal human being and you shall treat her as such. And second of all she has a name. Her name is Rubi. Learn to get that through your thick head," the alien leader angrily answered.

"Hey, young man, don't be so snooty with me because if you're snooty with me, I'm not going to help you and you will not be able to survive on your own in this cave. Besides, I have been through numerous situations that I had to survive on my own. I will respect you. She is your girlfriend and I shall respect you and her. Thank God she's not deceased. Now, let me rephrase the question. What do you want to do with Rubi?" asked Clayton.

"I strongly appreciate the fact that you have asked the question in a respectful manner. Now, I shall respectfully answer your question. To be honest with you I don't know what to do with her," answered Will. "Buddy, you used to tell me not to say I don't know and I can't believe that you're saying I don't know. Besides, aren't you the one who always comes up with the solutions to many different problems? Aren't you the one who tries to be the heroic one and fight for justice? Aren't you the one with the intelligence?" the police commissioner asked.

"I have been the one to fight for justice. I don't have the most amount of intelligence because if I was intelligent, everything would have been going nice and quite peachy. I am not even a hero because if I was a hero, Jacqueline Langyaw would have been killed. If I was a hero, I would not be rebelling against Cornelius Von Alien, who was nothing but an extreme tyrant. Instead, I would be just like any other Starmos citizen," the alien leader answered in a pessimistic voice.

"Listen up! Don't be pessimistic or weak with me. You were the one who fought for justice. You were the one who fought for the justice of all men, women, all female and male aliens. And now you're going to give up like this? What's wrong with you, Will? If your fellow aliens were standing in front of you, they wouldn't be happy. If your family members were standing in front of you, they would be extremely disappointed. Thirdly, if your father and mother were standing in front of you they'd probably start crying. So, do you want to give up so fast in life and make a lot of folks unhappy or do you want to fight till the end? It's your choice," declared Clayton.

The alien leader started sobbing. "Why are you talking to me in such a scathing and demeaning tone?" he asked. "Because I feel that you are giving up so quickly after you have devoted your life to fighting for justice. That sounds quite ridiculous to me because somebody who is a fighter does not give up. Somebody who is a good fighter is persistent, strong, reliable, heroic, courageous, honorable, charitable, chivalrous, benevolent, amicable, respectful, bold, and respectable. You fit the true epitome of a hero. You must fight. You can't curtail and give in to evil. You can't just give up so quickly, especially on your girlfriend. Besides, you should think about how you're going to rescue her. And don't say that this is physically and mentally impossible because there is a possibility of saving your girlfriend. Maybe, it'll take more than a simple resuscitation or a true love's kiss. You need to find a way to rescue your girlfriend," the police commissioner answered. "Are you insinuating that I'm not smart? Are you trying to say that I am unintelligent to think of a plan to rescue my girlfriend?" asked Will.

"Well, you were very quick to give up. I don't think that's showing intelligence. You must show some great intelligence of which you possess," answered Clayton. The alien leader started thinking to himself about what he can do to rescue his girlfriend, although there are huge limiting factors. "I think I've got it. You know that luminous emerald?" he asked.

"Yes," the police commissioner answered in an excited manner. "Well, guess what? I plan on waking my girlfriend up that way. I am going to pull the emerald out of the rocks and place it in my girlfriend's mouth and then, she will come back to life and spit out the emerald," replied Will.

"Excellent thinking," said Clayton. "Great, thank you," the alien leader replied. Commissioner Clayton stood by Rubi. Meanwhile, Will is looking for the emerald. The emerald keeps blinking in different parts of the cave. Finally, the emerald started blinking incessantly in the center of the rear of the cave. Will placed his hand over it and the emerald stopped blinking. It became brighter. He tried to remove the emerald. Unfortunately, it's jammed between the rocks.

"There's no use," he said. "Silence, Will! There is a lot of use. You're just not using the talents that I have given you," a loud audible voice said. This voice sounds exactly like God's voice. The alien leader's heart skipped a couple of beats. He froze in nervousness and his muscles locked. He ended up getting some cramps. "Why aren't you speaking to me?" asked God.

"I'm sorry. I didn't know that you were talking to me," answered Will. "What do you mean you weren't able to hear me? Who doesn't hear me? Are you trying to be a pathological liar? Do you make me out to be a fool?" the Creator asked.

"I am sorry for lying to you, God. I would strongly appreciate it if you gave me some mercy. I didn't mean to lie to you like that. It was just that your alarming voice scared the living daylights out of me," the alien leader answered. "Thank you for owning up to your wrongdoings because I like somebody who's honest. Now, the reason why I came to talk to you was to let you know about your status of going up to my kingdom. It is amazing how your chances have increased from zero percent to eighty percent. And I hope that it will be a one hundred percent chance of you getting full citizenship into my kingdom. And you will be allowed to go where ever want as long as it's a place that's filled with justice. And if you visit a place that is filled with injustice, you are to crusade for righteousness. You don't want to be somebody that sits around and vegetates all day like a nobody. You want to be an important member of society, for which you have because you've became the leader of Starmos City. The second reason why I came to talk to you was to tell you not to give up on your fight for justice and fairness. I don't want you to give up on rescuing your girlfriend; so, I am going to help you by opening up the emerald, but I must do that after I tell you what I must tell you. And thirdly, I know you're probably wondering why you were forced to travel back in time. I didn't do this with Cornelius Von Alien because I didn't feel he had the potential of enduring what you have endured. Besides, Cornelius was a Son of Satan and you are one of my sons. and I wanted to teach you not to be evil to your future wife like Jobe; I wanted to teach you not to be a bigot, but most of all, the reason why I brought you into the past was to make sure you wouldn't repeat the same evils of that former beastly dictator," replied God.

"Let's get to some real business. What are the things that you want me to do in order to have full citizenship and guaranteed citizenship for eternity in your kingdom?" the alien leader asked. "Well, first, I want you to put the emerald in Rubi's mouth so that way she comes back to life. I want you to drop the emerald on the floor. Once you do that, an earthquake will take place; and you will be on board a fishing boat. And you will be forced to drive this boat to Swinburne Island. Rescue Light and bring the beasts to justice," the Creator answered. "Okay. Is that it?" asked Will.

"Absolutely not. The only way that you'll be able to bring them to justice is if you find the secret door into the Skull Castle. You are to head to Skull Castle and you will have to go on a massive manhunt to find the villains and Light," answered God.

"Okay. Thank you," the alien leader replied. "You're very welcome. And just remember one thing. I am the omnipresent one and the omniscient one. I know everything you do. And so I say, Will, you must carry out this mission in the right way. You must be considerate of others; and you must be willing to fight for righteousness and fairness. You have been here to fight in the Civil War and I have taught you well about really fighting against injustice. I showed you the wickedness of the government during the Civil War times. It's not the government that's wicked. It's Jacqueline Langyaw and I will not penalize you for murder if you kill her because once she dies, you will be given citizenship for all dimensions. Justice will be done for everybody and let me tell you this. Evil shall never win. Man shouldn't let evil win. If man lets evil win, then there must be something wrong with the world we live in because evil shall never have the opportunity. Unfortunately, they use their free will in the wrong way. Also, keep your confidants safe while you embark on this mission because you are the leader. You are not the follower; you are the one who will be telling Clayton and Rubi what to do and how to do it, but do not be like Cornelius. If you do anything that he did; if you even contemplate evil, you will be punished; and if you try to take away an individual's rights, you will never be able to live with yourself. So, Will, I must give you blessings or how mankind says it as 'good luck.' Granted, luck comes from the devil but I just want to wish you good luck in a nice and a sort of benevolent way. You are the chosen one; you are the one who is going to conquer evil. Fight Will, Fight! Fight when it is the time to fight. Don't fight if you don't have to. Fight only when you need to and I shall give you the strength to fight when the time comes, but for now, you are to do the first few things that I have told you and I am sure you know what they are. It is nice talking to you. I will be watching your every move. You will see my face when you are inducted in the citizenship ceremony in Heaven," the Creator answered.

God stopped speaking. Granted, his voice is clearly audible. When the God directs something at a particular individual, he will speak to that individual and that particular individual only. "Who were you talking to?" asked Clayton.

"I was talking to God. Weren't you able to hear the whole conversation?" asked Will. "No, I was just wondering who you were talking to the whole time. I would think that you were crazy and that you would have to be put in an insane asylum," the police commissioner answered.

"Well, I am not crazy. I don't know why you weren't able to hear God's voice because his voice is quite audible. You can hear that voice from anywhere you go. Besides, he is omnipresent and omniscient. He can see everything you do, hear everything you say, and provide you with everything you need. Just now, he provided me with directions to help Rubi and bring her back to life from unconsciousness," the alien leader replied. "Does he know the every move that you make?" asked Commissioner Clayton.

"Of course, did I not just say that?" asked Will. "Who am I kidding? I must look like the crazy one. If I am the crazy one, then I must go into an insane asylum," the police commissioner answered.

"No, why would you say such a thing? You are the best police commissioner in the world. And I am not saying that because you are the best crime fighter in the world. I am saying this because you are the one who was willing to take Rubi, Officer Valencia, and I with you and that's an accomplishment. Otherwise, we would be ridiculed by a bigoted society and I can understand the reason why. Like I said earlier, God has many different purposes for us. My purpose in life is to fight for justice. And he has given me the spirit of optimism and I shall set that spirit free and show that spirit to the World," the alien leader replied. He walked up to the luminous emerald. He pulled the emerald out of the rocks and placed in Rubi's mouth.

"What are you crazy putting that in Rubi's mouth? Have you lost your damn mind?" asked Clayton. "Absolutely not. If I was crazy, I wouldn't be listening to God and I would not put that in my girlfriend's mouth. And then she wouldn't have to survive. I love her and I will do anything for her," answered Will.

The emerald caused the alien leader's girlfriend to illuminate and start glowing in the dark. She started floating to the ceiling. "I am in such disbelief," said the police commissioner. Her eyes started blinking. She floated back down to the surface and started walking. Her eyes widened. She started moving her arms and she looked at the palms of her hands. She started moving her digits. After that, she spat the emerald and it fell into Will's right hand. He gave the emerald to Commissioner Clayton and he kissed her.

"I love you," he said. "I love you too," she replied. After one minute of kissing, they stopped. "Let's continue the mission that we intended to work on. And say, it is quite miraculous how we were able to make it back to Earth in time," the alien leader said. "How are we going to get out of here?" the police commissioner asked.

"Well, don't we have an emerald to get us out of here?" asked Will. "I don't know where you put it last. Besides, aren't you the supposedly responsible one?" asked Clayton. "I gave you the emerald and you were supposed to put it in your pocket. What did you do with it?" the alien leader asked. "I don't know what I did with it. I recall I placed it in my right pocket. I think I should check both pockets," the police commissioner answered. He placed his hands in the two pockets.

"I am sorry. I can't find anything in those pockets. I don't know what to do," he said nervously. "Great. That's just the perfect time to have the emerald gone. And it's all your fault. Good job, Bill. Good job," Will said sarcastically. "Hey, don't you be sarcastic with me. I am the police commissioner. Do you realize that it's my prerogative to arrest you right now?" asked Clayton. "Hey smart one, you would have to have a warrant to take me down. And there's no way that you're going to do that. Besides, we're in an area with no cellular service. We are not near a court house. In addition to that, there's no probable cause to even have a search warrant. So, you can't arrest me," the alien leader said.

"Fine then. We are not here to argue because arguing and quarreling will not get us anywhere. We must find a way to get out of here. There must've been some occult effect that has taken place because I don't think the emerald would easily disappear like that. Maybe, God must've made the emerald disappear because my pockets are sewn shut. There's no way that anything would be able to fall out of my pockets. I don't think there's anybody here to pick-pocket me. There must've been a supernatural effect that has taken place and I am going to get to the bottom of it," the police commissioner replied. "I don't know about that because don't you remember that Brutis lives here?" asked Will.

"Don't you mean Buck, the homeless man?" asked Clayton. "Well, I don't know if you were paying any attention. Buck is actually Brutis. He is able to travel back and forth from one dimension to another whether it is a travel through time or a travel from literally one place to another place. Granted, for a human who was born before 1950, dimension traveling will definitely be impossible, but for anybody born after that year, dimension traveling is definitely possible," the alien leader answered. "How could Brutis be an alien and a homeless man?" the police commissioner asked.

"Well, you see, in our alien population, there are some individuals who possess certain talents aside from talents pertaining to the aesthetics. There are some aliens like Brutis who can easily shapeshift. So, basically, one minute he can look like a Goliath-sized alien or the next minute he can look like an introverted vagabond. I know it sounds like an anomaly but in Starmos City, it is quite mundane. I do not have that ability to shapeshift because I don't have it in my genetics. Fortunately, there's no way that I am able to get this kind of ability," answered Will.

"Why are you saying that it is fortunate that you are not able to get that kind of an ability?" asked Clayton. "Well, you see along with the perks of shapeshifting there are some serious consequences. First of all, there can be some crazy flaw that might take place where half of your body is a human's body and half of it is an alien's body. Basically, there might be a mistake in the middle of the shapeshifting process which can turn you into a mutant. Second of all, if you shapeshift into a tree, you might remain a tree because trees cannot move. So, you might mistakenly shapeshift into something that you were not intending on shapeshifting into. And thirdly, death will come more easily to you. Aliens cannot die with a bullet to the head or a knife to the throat. The only way an alien can die is if he or she gets poisoned by a dangerous element like Arsenic or Mercury. When you are a human, you can die from anything. Basically, it takes more to kill an alien than to kill a human and humans can die more easily than aliens," the alien leader answered. "I can see that you are wary of the idea of shapeshifting, but are you wary of your surroundings and do you believe in taking chances?" the police commissioner asked.

"There are many factors of life, particularly in humans, but also in aliens. I do take chances in life. I feel that humans are too timid and I can understand why. It's because you all have one life to live on this Earth, but I believe the humans should learn how to make the most of their lives because man doesn't have a long lifespan. Man only has a short lifespan of 200 years. That's if man is healthy and doesn't eat like a pig. We aliens have a lifespan of eternity unless our lives are cut short because of poisoning. We aliens are quite strong because we are sort of genetically superior to human beings. In spite of that factor, I don't believe in treating you humans in a condescending or bigoted manner. You see how the white men in the Civil War times treated women and non-Caucasians in the harshest ways possible and that was not right. That was just plain racist. In addition to that, women and African Americans were enslaved by their brutal white captors and that should have never taken place in a country whose Constitution states that all men are created equal and that basically means that all of God's children have equal rights. Now, I was in disbelief when this kind of evilness has taken place. So, to conclude this particular statement, we shouldn't live in a world that is filled with evilness and Social Darwinism. Besides, that idea is evil and nobody should be mistreated because they are genetically inferior to that individual," answered Will. "You didn't really answer the question that I've asked you. I clearly asked you if you believed in taking chances and you stated that you believe in taking chances. You did not have to go on a wild rant about Social Darwinism and bigotry. Yes, we all get your point. Bigotry is totally wrong," answered Will.

"Rubi, I didn't hear too much talking from you during this whole ordeal. Do you believe in taking chances?" the police commissioner asked. "Of course. Yeah, what he said," the alien leader's girlfriend. "Wow, you must be very well acclimated to the 'gangsta' culture. That's not a good thing," replied Clayton. "How dare you tell my girlfriend that she's living the 'gangsta' culture! Look at the city that you're in. New York unfortunately has people that act like they are a bunch of street urchins. You shouldn't be calling my girlfriend a street urchin because your city is filled with not only street urchins but parasites," the alien leader argued. "Yeah, leave me the hell alone. Just because you're the police commissioner doesn't mean that you have the right to call me whatever you want to call me. It is not right that we live in a world that people who are in power think that they are superior to others because they are not. Let's just end superiority and treat each other like we are all human beings," said Rubi.

"You know something; you all are right. Granted, there has to be a division between rich and poor because if there's no division between the rich and the poor, then there'll be communism and that's evil. There should be equality between races; and I might've crossed the line because when I am a politician, I am actually equal to all of you. Besides, you folks are the ones that place me in the political arena. And I should be an example to the rookie politicians. You are right and I was the one that was completely wrong. Simply, I want to just say that I am sorry and I would appreciate it if you forgave me," the police commissioner said.

Noises started being heard. The noises sounded like a small man walking. He is wearing clichéd clothing that a ragamuffin would typically wear. He has a small black beard and he has black hair. He is wearing a small checkerboard cap. He is wearing boots with holes in them. He has an evil personality but, he acts deceptive when he needs something. This man has committed over six hundred murders. He is a serial killer and he is a shape shifter. When he is in the form of an alien, he has a normal voice that sounds deceptive and conniving, but when he is in the form of a human, his voice sounds raspy and unintelligent. He started staring at Will with his eyebrows slanted in a downward position. He has evil confidantes and was a former soldier for Cornelius Von Alien. He is as evil as a former KGB soldier. He is currently five hundred feet away from the motley trio. In spite of the cave-like location, he is able to see them quite clearly.

He has excellent vision. Standing proudly next to him are the two malevolent serpents, Serpianto and Korbian.

"Brutis, who do you want me to kill?" Serpianto asked in a sneaky manner. "Why are you calling me, Brutis? You know I am supposed to be Buck when I am this cave. Will might notice that I am here and I might be killed. What is my name?" the shape shifting homeless man asked. "Buck," answered Korbian.

"Who am I?" asked Buck. "Yes, your name is Buck," answered Serpianto. "Now, I will tell you who I want you to kill. Serpianto, you must kill Will. Korbian, you must kill Rubi. And I will kill Clayton," the malevolent shape shifting alien replied. "Thank you," said Serpianto. "On second thought, don't kill them. Instead, we're going to capture and torture them. Then, we will take them to Skull City where they will be forced to work as slaves along with the humans we've captured," replied Buck. "Oh, even better idea," Korbian said. The snakes slithered their way up to their captives. Serpianto grabbed Will by the hands and he tied them together with his tail. Korbian grabbed Rubi and dragged her into the cave and Buck brutally beat Commissioner Clayton and dragged him into the cave. Sadly, the motley trio was not able to defend themselves. They didn't have a fighting chance against those sinister souls. The trio is being dragged past the waterfall. They're so nervous that they are not able to speak their minds and defend themselves. They were brought into Buck's lair.

"Well, well, well, I have you all captured because what you're doing is malicious and evil. You took away my rights. You tried to destroy me by trying to put me in prison, but there's no way that's going to happen. I have you all now. Clayton, you are my captured prisoner and you will remain captured. Will, you have tried to revolt against my leader's government and you managed to kill my leader and take over the leadership position for yourself. Your self-centered beliefs won't cut it with me. I believe that you're wrong because you think who you are. In addition to that, you have tried to commit malicious crimes against Cornelius because you cajoled all of the human beings into revolting against the great power of my leader. My true leader, and by the way, I do honor Communism, Social Darwinism, and evil. I was just kidding with you about that 2009 democrat president. I like them both. When my grandparents became homeless, it was the best thing that has ever happened to me because I was free to go where ever I want. My parents wouldn't be able to tell me what to do. Now, my political opinions do not have anything to do with my hatred towards you. I hate you because you killed my leader Cornelius and you should be ashamed of yourself. And because you killed him, you have just brought forced servitude towards you, your friends, and your fellow humans. Soon, the Starmos citizens will be slaves under the new rule of Jacqueline Langyaw," the homeless man said.

Will answered"You will never be able to get a piece of me because I will kill you before you kill me. Granted, I don't like gnawing through things. Besides, I am not some sort of a woodchuck but I will act like a woodchuck. I will gnaw through the rope and free myself. I'll kill you. I'll drown you, asphyxiate you, and then I will prepare the best meal of your life that features a combination of Mercury and Arsenic. Once that meal is made, death will do its part against you. And you deserve to die. You won't have an abrupt death. You'll have a slow and torturous death. So, I guess there's no way that you will be able to torture me because I will torture you first."

"Who are you to try to torture me? Besides, what on Earth are you talking 'bout that you're going to torture me? Do you realize that this rope is gnaw proof? You can't gnaw through it. After two minutes, I shall free you as long as you do me one favor and you will be Jacqueline's slave. And by the way, all of those humans I've said I killed were actually taken as Jacqueline's prisoners. In spite of my hatred for prosecutors, I like this one. So, you can try and stop her all you want; you can claim that you're going to fight for justice, but one thing that is certain is that you will never be able to win," said Buck.

Will laughed. "Puh, you are not going to win. Besides, you are low life, piece of shit," he replied. "Who are you to call me such a harsh name? You have no right in doing such a thing. So, I must be able to make sure that you are to listen to me. First of all, I will free you, Rubi, and Commissioner Clayton. Once I free you all from the ropes, I will force feed you. It's not going to be something pretty; it's going to be the ugliest things that you've ever eaten. Why don't you all come down from your little perch and have some things," the evil shape shifter answered.

"Do you think that I am afraid of your torture method? I am absolutely not afraid. In fact, I will be the first one to try your slop and once I try it, you are to let me go. Do you understand me? Am I explicit in what I say?" the alien leader asked.

"Oh, yes. You are very clear. I still want you to eat what I feed you. So, come down now," answered Buck. "How do you expect us to come down?" asked Clayton. The shapeshifting homeless man walked up to his brewing cauldron and retrieved a knife, that is sitting adjacent to it. He cut the ropes holding his captives.

He dragged the motley trio to the shale stone table and served them a dish of Crappy Soup. The soup is comprised of Chicken broth and Horse and Cow Excrement.

Unfortunately, the motley trio doesn't know this. "Now, Will, I shouldn't have to force feed you. You are to eat what I am telling you. If you don't eat this, I will slice you and you will be part of this soup. I don't think you want that to happen to you," he said.

"Fine," the alien leader brusquely said. He picked up a dirty spoon. He is the first one to try the meal. He dreadfully gulped the soup down his throat. Rubi followed;

and then Commissioner Clayton. "So, did you enjoy this?" the malicious shape shifter asked. "Oh yeah, we enjoyed this," the motley trio answered in a sarcastic manner. Buck laughed. "I hope you all weren't being sarcastic with me because I know how you aliens and humans think."

"Oh no. Why would we do such a thing?" asked Will. "Well, you humans are nothing but smart asses," the evil shape shifter said. "No, we're not," the alien leader argued. "Arguing is going to get you all nowhere," replied Buck.

Chapter XXIV: Buck's evil side really stands out

The homeless shape shifter is standing in front of a massive boulder. He is watching his captives (the motley trio) eat the gruel that he served them. It is disgusting the way he's mistreating them. "Hurry up. When are you lazy bums going to finish?" he asked. Everybody is stuffing their cheeks with as much gruel as possible. "We're finished now," answered Will. His mouth is stuffed and he was not able to talk in an explicit or eloquent manner. "What's wrong with you? Why do you have your mouth stuffed?" asked Buck.

"What does it matter to you?" asked Rubi. Her mouth tis also stuffed. The trio stood up and surrounded the homeless, malicious shape shifter. "Guess what? I know what you are trying to pull on me. You're trying not to gulp that down your throat. I'm not stupid. Did you not know that I am an alien who comes from Starmos City?" asked Buck. "Oh no, we so did not know that," the alien leader answered in a sarcastic manner.

"Well, I do come from your city. In fact, I am a former guard of Cornelius. Unfortunately, you were the one that had overthrown him because you thought that he was what you liked to call a 'Royal Brute.' He is not a 'Royal Brute.' He was the one that founded the place that you reside in today. He was the one that gave your parents jobs. He was the one that made sure that your parents and you would live in an amazing ultramodern apartment. He was the one that would make all the money and off of the other businesses. He was the one that was a nice leader; and you, being the ignorant jackass that you are, decided to overthrow him because you felt that he was being what you like to call 'too powerful' or 'tyrannical.' He didn't tyrannize that city, you tried to tyrannize it, but now, that I have you captured and now, that you're my slave. You will be doing as I say. And no longer will you have the control over that city. You have waived your leadership rights. You know why? Oh, I have the answer to that question. Because somebody forged your signature and once a document that states that you are waiving your leadership rights is signed in your name, you are no longer the leader. And I don't think you want to know who is the leader. I can assure you that it's not Cornelius," he (Buck) said.

"You know that you or anybody else do not have any way that they can try and waive my leadership rights. And if they do, they will be captured, brought to trial, and if convicted, that individual or those individuals will be sentenced accordingly. The reason why I showed some dissent against Cornelius was because he was a tyrant. He was a cruel, vulgar, sick, twisted brute. He was evil and he was a thug. The reason why I'd overthrow him was to make sure that he wouldn't try and ruin anybody else's lives. He ruined my life. I want to tell you an interesting story, so you better listen to me," replied Will. "Well, should I take out my violin? The snide shape shifter asked. "No, what is so necessary about doing that?" the alien leader asked.

"Because, I want to do it for my entertainment while you tell your oh, so sad and melancholy story," answered Buck.

"Shut the hell up and listen because you're acting like a piece of garbage. Now, one day, my parents came home from work when I was just fifteen years old. I figured it would be a mundane day, but it wasn't a routine day. It was the day when my dad got laid off because the reservoir was closing because Cornelius felt that it had cost him too much money and he wanted all the money for himself. He laid off my dad and all of his colleagues. My mom was the treasurer for my city and she would handle all of the money. A couple of weeks after my dad got laid off, she was fired because Cornelius felt that she was embezzling money by having a salary. Eventually, I came home one night and I discovered that my parents weren't there. I walked outside of the apartment and I walked down the hallway and look down and I saw a bunch of spectators at the Alien Estate. So, I decided to run down to the estate and see what was taking place. I wheedled my way through the crowd of spectators up to the front. That was when I saw four soldiers lined up with M16 Assault Weapons. They were shooting at my parents. Every second, one bullet would have been fired. My parents were tied to the fence and the soldiers were firing at them. After three minutes of shooting, my dad was shot twice in the head and twice in the chest. The worst part is that my mom saw my dad get shot and die right before her eyes.
Eventually, my mom was shot eight times; four times in the head, twice in the chest, and twice in the stomach. She died immediately. That was when my life turned around. I lamented for days afterward. I learned how to get over it. A couple of days after their deaths I went to school, I just

learned how to suck it up and not show any sadness. About two weeks after their death, Cornelius ordered his troops to remove me from my apartment. I kicked and screamed but it was no use. I was dragged over to the Alien Estate and that was when I became a slave of Cornelius. He made me work in the galley until I killed him. That's the primary reason why I hated him, because his tyrannical rule and his despicable behavior directly affected my life. He should be ashamed of himself and he got his just desserts. And he definitely deserved to die because of what he did to my parents," Will said in a sorrowful manner. As he told the story, he was sobbing. He was explicit in the way he spoke. "Oh, it is so upsetting to see that happen to you. It must have been such a miserable sight," the homeless shape shifter sarcastically replied. The alien leader immediately figured out that Buck was being sarcastic and snide. "How dare you even say such a thing! Most folks would be very empathetic towards me. Meanwhile, you are being the complete opposite. No wonder why you are known as the callous, cold-blooded beast. It is actually appalling that you would be so arrogant and disgusting. May God punish you because you definitely deserve to go to Hell," he furiously shouted. "How dare you say those scathing words to me. You're telling me that I deserve to go to Hell. You're the one who created Hell. First of all, you've killed Cornelius a long time ago and that vile act was just bad enough. Second of all, you were converted to Christianity from Atheism and we Stalinist practicing SSGM soldiers do support the idea of Atheism. Besides, we believe that Christians are wrong in what they do. So, that goes to show that you are a traitor. Thirdly, you try and change the justice system in Starmos City. You want to put defendants on trial instead of having them brought before the leader and sentenced at that time in place. Fourthly, you want the citizens to have an opportunity to go in and out of the city if they can't afford an LSC and that was because you built the Starmos Station. Fifthly, you are nothing but a rogue. You lived at the Alien Estate for years out of Cornelius's good will and he didn't have to do that for you. He could have dumped you on the streets to get run over by an LSC. So, my friend, Will, you must be ashamed of yourself because of your arrogant attitude. You are insolent and crude and you are nothing but a bigot. You want the aliens to have to pay taxes so that way your crazy projects get funded. Guess what? I am not going to let that happen. Jacqueline Langyaw is not going to let that happen. You think that it's acceptable to invade an individual's apartment and try and fix it up. It's wrong. If Jacqueine is the leader, then she will fix that place. She will make sure that LSC's are decommissioned so that way fossil fuels are not emitted into the environment. Also, she'll do that because she wants to make sure that LSC's lose their powers to shape shift, so that way they can't enter the Alien Estate. Ms. Langyaw is going to be a much better leader than you. In addition to that, she is much more intelligent and wise than you. All you are is a stupid, world class idiot. You are an accident and you should've never been brought into any dimension or world whatsoever. You think you have all this intelligence. You don't. You think that you can answer any question, but your answers are extremely erroneous and stupid. You think that you have power to do anything you want, but you definitely don't possess that. Face it, Will, you are nothing but, a pathetic loser. You are a failure and you always will be," the shape shifter replied.

"*You* are disgusting. First of all, you think that it is okay to talk to me like that when it is totally unacceptable.

Second of all, the Atheistic practice should have never been forced down the aliens' throats because they should have had their rights to choose their individual religious affiliation. And maybe you don't believe in this, but I believe that all men and women whether you are a human or an alien have rights. These rights are your individual natural rights. They are life, liberty, free movement, fair trials, pursuit of opportunity, and pursuit of happiness. It seems to me that you don't believe in individual's basic rights. That is sickening and you are disgusting. You should really be ashamed of yourself because you are disgusting. You and your five other friends will be captured and punished for kidnapping Light. And if you kidnap him, you will serve an extremely long sentence. You might even get the death penalty if you kill him. I hereby rest my case with what I am saying," the alien leader said. Commissioner Clayton spit the disgusting gruel in the homeless shape shifter's face.

"Clayton! How dare you act the way you're acting. Have you lost your mind? You and your friends are trying to trick me and act as deceptive as possible. Your deception is not going to fly by with me. Do we understand each other?" asked Buck.

"Oh, yes, I totally understand that I shouldn't be deceptive," the police commissioner answered sarcastically. "You better not be sarcastic with me," the homeless shape shifter replied.

"Buck, or should I say, Brutis, you're very intuitive. It is amazing how one can be a homeless, sociopathic introvert, but yet, you are very intuitive. Do you realize that you say the most fallacious statements in the world?" asked Will. "Oh, really? And what fallacious statements do I say?" asked Buck. "Well, let me tell you that you called the three of us deceptive snakes when you, Korbian, Serpianto, Jacqueline, Howard, and Mitchell are the deceptive snakes at the end of the day. You are the folks who possess evil instead of goodness. We possess goodness and you all possess evil," the alien leader answered.

"Why don't you all stay right here and just try not to escape," the homeless shape shifter said. Rubi snickered. "Yeah, we'll do that," she sarcastically said. Buck walked up to his cauldron to receive the three pieces of 50' rope. While he's doing that, the alien leader's girlfriend is contriving a plan to escape from that beast's lair. "There's no way that we can pull this off again because it will be deja vu and this brute tried to change the entrances and exits in this place. So, we must find another way out, she said.

"Well, genius, how do you think we'll be able to get out of here?" the alien leader asked. "I was thinking of making him some gruel that contains a lot of horse excrement," answered Rubi. "That sounds like an ingenius plan," Clayton replied in a sarcastic manner. "Well, thank you," the alien leader's girlfriend said. "No, you don't have to thank me. You should thank yourself for coming up with a stupid plan that is for imbeciles," the police commissioner replied. "Hey, why did you call my plan stupid?" asked Rubi. "Because I don't think feeding that cold blooded shape shifter with any meal. Besides, he's not worthy of food and you would try to feed him what he's fed us. He probably likes that stuff," answered Clayton.

"You are misunderstanding the plan that I have contrived. You see, aliens are immune to all death methods except for poisoning. I was thinking about poisoning him with the excrement. He won't have an immediate death. He'll die in 24-48 hours," replied the alien leader's girlfriend. "How do you expect excrement to poison him?" asked Will.

"You are the smartest fellow that I've ever known and you don't know how excrement poisons somebody. Excrement causes E-coli poisoning, which is extremely detrimental. There's no way he'll be able to get into hospitals because he cannot afford to end up in a hospital. Besides, he's a shape shifter. Only humans and aliens are allowed in a hospital. So, we can definitely poison him. He may have a slow death, but I'd think you would want him dead instead of having him alive," answered Rubi.

"Why do you have such a cold heart? Is my own girlfriend betraying my values?" the alien leader asked. "First of all, don't you believe that all men and women are created equal? Didn't you fight with Mr. Lincoln about equality? And why do you think I am betraying you?" asked the alien leader's girlfriend. "You know something, you're right. I guess I've got a little too carried away. How 'bout we do this; why don't we do things that we both agree on or perhaps come up with a compromise?" asked Will. "Sure, that sounds nice to me. Can I make the decision for this plan to escape because I feel my decision is the wisest decision in the world?" asked Rubi. "Fine then, whatever my girlfriend says," the alien leader answered.

"Thank you very much. Now, I am going to say something to you and Clayton. Do not resist when he ties us up. The reason why is because he has a high adrenaline level right now because he probably knows that we're thinking about escape. So, in order to cover our plan up, we must not say a word about escaping or show that we're going to escape. We must be like pacifists. Granted, I don't support too much pacifism. In some cases, we must not fight nor, should we honor somebody's evil behavior," said the alien leader's girlfriend.

"I object to your opinion because you can't be a pacifist. Look back in history, and look at how pacifism caused a lack of peace and caused war. I know what I am saying sounds kind of ironic. Sometimes, war is necessary in order to maintain some peace. Sometimes war is necessary in order to keep justice, fairness, and equality. Sometimes, war is necessary in order to defeat the villain. Fate is inevitable without resisting against the vicious souls. We must not be peaceful," replied Clayton.

"I object to your opinion because in this case, we can't fight against him. He may look like a weak ragamuffin. He's not weak, he's quite strong. If he suspects that you are acting in a suspicious manner, he will shapeshift from a feeble, homeless vagabond into a Goliath-sized alien. I've seen him in action. When he wants to be violent, he acts violent. You see, some folks are nothing but walking facades. I know you two saw this earlier. Remember when Sarah and I were put on trial for causing Jobe's death? Do you recall that prosecutor and judge? Well, let me just tell you that they were vile and cruel serpents. They were actually Serpianto and Korbian. They were and still are involved with Jacqueline's plan. They made themselves look like hard-working, benevolent civic leaders. In fact, they coaxed the people into thinking that they were the best and into thinking that I was a twisted killer. When they were confronted in front of all the people of that town, they actually showed their true colors of being evil serpents. But because of their evil behavior, that town became a ghost town. It goes to show how some folks cannot keep their deceptive appearance. It also goes to show how some folks try to act like walking facades to hide their evil," replied Will.

"You know that what you said was right. Sometimes fighting is totally not necessary especially in this case. I have different reasons why I don't want to fight or even argue. The reason why is because fighting will not get you or any other individual anywhere. Besides, what's the sense in fighting? It causes you to lose your voice and that wouldn't be good. Fighting and Quarreling is a nonproductive task in my eyes and it is totally stupid," said Clayton. The homeless shape shifter dragged the three pieces of rope up to the wooden poles. The motley trio willingly placed their hands behind the poles. He tied them up.

"You know that it's quite a surprise to see you all very willing to surrender and work as a servant for me. It actually makes me kind of suspicious that you all are so quick to surrender. Typically, a trio of folks would try to kill me. I am surprised that you all are acting respectful," he said. The alien leader grinned. Commissioner Clayton looked at him.

"Let me just tell you that we are not pranking you. Infact, we all are putting up our white flags. Say, how about you eat the rest of your 'stew.' Besides, don't you say its so good," he said. "No, I made that for you, not for me. What do I have to benefit by it? You know that I am super fit. You have to eat it. You all are not strong. I brought you all here to get stronger," replied Buck.

He lied through his teeth when he said that. "I know you are lying. I want you to be stronger than me. Show me your strength. Show me your strength by eating that," the police commissioner said. "What do you want me to do if I don't eat that?" the homeless shape shifter nervously asked.

"Just release me from those bonds that you have put me in and I won't bother you about eating that gruel," answered Clayton. Buck released the motley trio from the bonds. "Is there any way you can repay me for that duty?" he asked.

"No, I just gave you what you wanted. I made sure that you wouldn't eat the gruel that contained E-coli and also, I made sure that we would be your servants," the police commissioner answered. The homeless shape shifter grabbed the giant boulder. The motley trio is staring at him in surprise and disbelief.

"What are you doing?" asked Will. "Oh, nothing. I'm just trying to find my way out of this cave," answered Buck. "Well, you should know the way out. After all, you're the one that is able to have full control over this place. Thus, you should be responsible and know where you're going," the alien leader replied.

"Silence! You are to have no say as to what goes on around here. You and your confidants are slaves. They have no right to speak and they are only allowed to speak when they are spoken to," the homeless shape shifter said. "Let's just get one thing straight! I am your slave for a short amount of time. So, I shouldn't have to be subject or a victim of your evilness. I am not a victim and nor am I afraid of you. You should definitely be ashamed of your attitude because you are of malice and of the devil. You ought not do what you do and may Satan curse your soul," argued Will.

"So, you are asking for my soul to be cursed? Eh? I don't think so because your soul is already cursed. First of all, you were born into an Atheist environment; for you shouldn't be believing in Satan because Atheists are nonbelievers. Second of all, you have made a promise and this promise is not just any ordinary promise. No, no, no; this promise clearly states that you are to be my slave if I untied you from the wooden poles. I could've left you for the dead. why do that? Besides, I have a heart and soul. You've got nothing. You are just a stupid, illegal leader. You shouldn't even be considered a leader because you are an insurgent who revolted against a true, great, and wise leader," replied Buck.

"Let me just object to your despicable and derisive opinions. Firstly, you definitely do deserve to go to Hell. Secondly, Atheists are able to convert to another religious practice. In spite of me being a Christian, I don't think religious practices should influence the government. I am against theocracies or autocracies. Cornelius was an autocratic leader and he wasn't even a true leader. Your statement is a fallacy because you said that I revolted when I did not lead any revolt. I might've led a silent revolt because I was the one who led to the end of that regime, I did not lead any violent revolution. I discreetly captured him and Jacqueline and I was fair with them when they were forced to go to trial. For instance, I made sure that they would go before a trial by jury. I was even nice to Jacqueline because I felt that she was coaxed into working with that brute. I killed Cornelius because he was evil. I am not an illegal leader. I am an elected official because the Starmos citizens voted me in through a direct primary. I would never corrupt my own kind. Finally, you are more of the World class idiot than I am. You often say a lot of fallacious and idiotic statements that are totally wrong. Some of your statements are completely arrogant and I mean it. To conclude this statement, what you say is totally fallacious, condescending, and simply stupid. You may think that what you say is acceptable. And it is totally malicious. You ought to be ashamed of yourself. I rest my case," the alien leader said.

"You think that it is your prerogative to take an attitude with me. You think that it is okay to be bold with me. Even worse, you think that it is okay to be abrupt with me. It is totally not okay. It is unacceptable. The last I checked was that you agreed with me. Better yet, scratch that sentence. You didn't even make an agreement to go free from being tied around the pole. You forced me to untie you and your friends. The reason why is because you wanted me to eat disgusting gruel and you clearly knew the motive was to get out from being tied behind that rope. This so called, 'agreement' was for yourself, not for me. Besides, when you suggested that I ate that gruel, you basically were trying to trick me so I can die of E-coli poisoning. Let me just make one thing clear to you. I am not a stupid individual. Just because I look like a homeless person doesn't make me stupid. I chose to negotiate with you so that way I wouldn't die, but I just thought to myself, 'what's the sense in negotiating when I had full control over the situation?' I could've left you and your friends tied to that pole and you all would have been left for fish bait. I guess I am quite stupid," replied Buck. "Fine then, you know what, you're right. I give up fighting because it doesn't make any sense fighting a morbidly, hopelessly disgusting creature like you. I suppose that I might as well put up my white flag. I hereby surrender myself to you. And so, you can do whatever you want. I guess I give up," Will sarcastically said. He is really thinking about killing this beastly rogue.

He is staring at the rusty knives in the back of the kitchen. "What do you think you're doing?" the homeless shape shifter asked. "Nothing. I am just standing here staring at the beautiful water that you have in the cave," the alien leader answered. Buck snickered. "You are so not doing that," he said.

"Well, yes I am. Quite frankly, I find the water to be nice. It is clear and you can see the nice boulders at the bottom," replied Will. "Like I asked earlier, do you think that I'm stupid?" asked the homeless shape shifter. "No," the alien leader answered in a sarcastic manner.

"Why would you try to make me look stupid even though I'm not stupid?" asked Buck. "Aside from being the alien leader, I am here to be a trickster. I don't just trick folks just to trick them. I trick them for good and justifiable reasons. I have a good reason to trick you and that's because you're deceitful and derisive," answered Will.

"Listen. I am the king of deception and trickery. I know your every move. I know everything you do. And I can assure you that I am not stupid because if I was stupid I wouldn't even be in this hole. I have always been smart. My biggest talent is lying. It may not sound like a talent to benevolent folks like you. it is an everyday thing to me. I lie all the time; my friends lie all the time; even, my colleagues lie all the time. I may not have a job. I do work for Jacqueline. I am her hit man/ kidnapper. I have taken many humans and aliens that I use to enslave and work on my farms and the factories. and I am totally proud of what I do. and I will never give up what I do because it is my passion to be evil. That's what I live for, to ruin the population of humans and aliens that side with the humans. I remember that you have said that different folks have different destinies. So, my destiny is to do evil and get away with it. Besides, doing evil is good and it gives me a ton of satisfaction. Here, I have revealed the truth," the homeless shape shifter replied. "What makes you act in a despicable manner?" the alien leader asked.

"Because I have been possessed by a demon. I am of the devil and I am of Satan. My middle name is comprised of three numbers: 6 6 6," answered Buck. "That's not a sufficient enough answer to explain to me why you act the way you act. Your middle name may somewhat show it. It doesn't give me the reason as to why you do what you do. Give me the answer as to why you act so violent and vicious," said Will.

The homeless shape shifter walked back to the cauldron. He retrieved a long one hundred and fifty foot chain and wrapped it around the boulder. he dragged the boulder. The boulder serves as a door to the outside world. Specifically, in the Atlantic Ocean. You can see a view of the morning horizon. The horizon featured the sun emerging. It is now seven in the morning. The gondola is waiting outside of the cave. The homeless shape shifter jumped on board the small boat. "Why are you bums waiting here?" he asked. "I don't know why," the alien leader answered in a sarcastic manner. He snickered. "I can see that you're nothing but a smart ass. Well, guess what? I am not going to deal with garbage like you. If you are going to act like trash, then, you will be treated like trash," answered Buck.

"What are you going to do about it if I act in the way that you call 'trash'?" asked Will. "Oh, nothing. I am just going to chain you to the stern and instead of paddling comfortably on the boat, you will be dragged all the way to Swinburne Island. So, you better behave yourself," the homeless shape shifter said. The alien leader laughed.

"You think that you're going to be nasty to me? I can crush you. First of all, I am much bigger than you. and besides, I'll kill you in your human form and then you'll never be able to shape-shift into an alien. So, don't mess around with me. I will not stand by and tolerate an attitude of superiority. You are nothing but a piece of trash. You shouldn't be calling me trash because you, not only act like trash. you look like trash. So, don't try and play the role of 'tough guy' with me because I don't play that game," he replied.

"Shut the Hell up. You are nothing but a jealous alien. You did not become the so called 'leader of Starmos City' in a fair way. First of all, you forced your way into the leadership as President of Starmos City. You caused our beloved Cornelius to abdicate the throne all because you wanted to be leader. That is sinister and sickening. That's one way to show that you're a jealous one. Second of all, you are jealous of my powers. I may disguise myself to look like a feeble, impecunious homeless man. the true me is not that. I am an alien. I may not be your normal sized alien, but I am an alien. I do work for the SSGM because I am still committed to Cornelius, but because of your jealousy, you wanted the SSGM to be destroyed and ripped apart. That's not going to happen as long as I am living. Now, just get on board the gondola and put a cork in it," said Buck.

"Do you realize what you're saying is fallacious and slanderous? Do you realize that you can ruin my reputation if your fallacious, disgusting remarks run rampant in my city?" asked Will. "Yes, I want the words that I am saying to run wild. The more they run wild, the more your reputation is ruined. The more your reputation is ruined, the more the citizens will turn against you. The more dissent that goes against you because of my propaganda, the more the folks are going to rebel. Once the rebellion takes place, you will be destroyed. You might potentially be killed and the great Socialist SSGM junta will takeover the government and your life shall be destroyed forever. If that happens, then I will be the leader and the leadership of the real Von Alien, our beloved Cornelius, shall continue and prosper forever. Meanwhile, you will either be in the hole or tied to the fence waiting to be shot at. I will guarantee for that to happen," the homeless shape shifter answered. The police commissioner is becoming angry with the remarks that are being tossed at his friend. His left ear started turning red. He started sweating and breathing heavily. He grunted like an angry bull and he started flaring his nostrils. His muscles started tightening. He showed his bottom incisors.

"Who do you think you are to treat this man like that?" he furiously shouted. "Oh, nothing. What makes you think I'm scared of you? Shoo, shoo, you big oaf. Who cares about you? Besides, I am not afraid of cops like you," Buck snootily answered.

"There are two things about some folks that get me pissed off. Firstly, I hate some folks that slander others and you are clearly slandering Will. You should definitely be ashamed of yourself. Secondly, I also hate some folks who like to defame us police officers. When you are meeting a police commissioner, you are to call him by his formal name. You can't just call him, cop. This unwritten rule does not only apply to police commissioners. it applies to regular police officers. You are to be respectful to them. To me, your actions are uncalled for and you just act evil to cause trouble. You were never battered because I can tell that you want to be evil. You are callous inside and out. You have a

heart to keep you alive. you don't have an emotional heat.
You don't have a Heart for others. You don't even care
about other folks," replied Clayton. "Since when do you
talk? You have no rights to talk because you are nothing
but, a useless human. All you do is bark orders at your
fellow cops. In addition to that, you try to bark orders at me
and act like a big hot shot. I am not going to tolerate
garbage like you. You are totally right. I don't have any
heart because anybody with a heart wouldn't support
Socialism or Racism. I support both. So, that makes me
cold hearted and I am proud of that. Now, you and your
friend are to come with me to the island" said Buck.

"You're right. This benevolent man who has taught
me a lot more than you have is your ultimate target. You
like to try to victimize him, degrade him, and make the
most scathing comments towards him. Meanwhile, he has
worked hard in life and he wasn't trained to work hard. And
he didn't worked hard just to work hard. He crusaded for
justice and he is still in his crusade for justice and freedom
for his aliens in Starmos City and for all of the humans on
Planet Earth. So, you can try and hurt him and ruin him in
every way possible. he is tenacious and persistent to make
sure that he wins this war for fairness. You can try and
bring back Cornelius's tyrannical ways. you are not going
to win. I often say this to the criminals that get detained and
held at the police station. I tell them that evil will never
win. In fact, evil is going to be destroyed and this is
whether or not that individual gets acquitted or convicted.
The time when evil will be crushed is when all evil men
and women meet their Creator or in more universally
accepted terms of God. When man meets his or her Creator,
they will be adjudged and held accountable for his or her
actions. they will have to surrender their sins to God and

that's if that individual believes in God or converts to Christianity on the deathbed. I know what I am saying will give you a shrill down your back, but what else can I say? That's the truth and the good truth shall always prevail Justice will always supercede injustice and evil will be crushed to a pulp and ripped apart into ten million pieces," argued the police commissioner. After those arguments, the motley trio stepped on board the gondola. They were tied together and dragged in the waters all the way to Swinburne Island. The seas are treacherous. It will be a miracle if they survive those harsh currents.

Chapter XXV: Some folks act like walking facades and pull an act to make themselves look different or act different because of life's situations

The gondola arrived in the most Southern part of New York, near Staten Island. They are heading into the New York Harbor from Southern Queens. There is still a long way to go in order to get to Swinburn Island. The motley trio is being dragged in the rear of the boat. Fortunately, they managed to survive the harsh conditions of the Atlantic Oceans. Buck walked to the back of the boat. As he walked to the bow, the weight of the boat shifted backward. He is trying to make sure that his captives are still alive.

As soon as he checked on his captives, Will managed to play dead like a possum. He lied on the top of the water flat on his back. His eyes are closed shut and he held his breath to make himself have a pallid apppearance. The homeless shape shifter managed to fall for the alien leader's phony death. He walked to the stern of the gondola and retreived a key that has been kept in his small, black messenger bag. The key looked like an ordinary key that opens a common lock. He unlocked the alien leader from the chains. Will stopped playing dead. He impulsively started swimming away from the boat. he realized that his friends were still chained to the bow of the gondola. He immediately turned himself around and started swimming back to the boat.

Within a matter of thirty seconds, he reached the boat. He is analyzing the situation thinking to himself about how he is not going to be able to get caught. He needs to make sure that he covers his every move and acts discreet without being killed from Buck. He is punctilious and wary about his every move. He slowly reached his two hands to the side of the boat. He peeked into the boat. The shapeshifting alien is playing Solitaire. The alien leader waited for the perfect moment.

Eventually, Buck walked to the stern of the boat. the alien leader jumped on board. The homeless shapeshifter turned around. "Will, what are you doing here?" he shouted. "Oh nothing," the alien leader answered. "You are so lucky that I fell for your little death hoax because if I knew that you weren't dead and I knew that you were trying to play dead, I would just kill you then and there," replied Buck.

The alien leader looked at the homeless shape shifter with crinkled eyebrows. He has a high adrenaline. "Do you want to die?" he asked. "Are you trying to threaten me?" the homeless shape shifter answered. "Yes, I am and what are you going to do about it?" asked Will. Buck snickered.

"What makes you think I am scared of you? I am not scared of you because you are the most evil individual around. So, if I killed you, you'd be dead. Besides, you are my slave and my captive. I would have to turn you in to the Starmos police and you would be locked up in a hole for the rest of your life. So, you better learn how to not mess around with me. Who the hell do you think you are? Oh, I know the answer to that question. You are a malicious, bold, blunt, and outspoken tyrant. You support evilness. You definitely do not want justice. You want to see anarchy. Surprise, surprise. I have an anarchist right over here. Well, then again, it's not a surprise to me to deal with somebody who is rebellious. As an SSGM soldier, I had to deal with folks who would try and rebel against the honorable and respectable Cornelius," he answered in an arrogant manner.

"Let me just tell you this, Buck. I have said this earlier. I must reiterate these things in order to get them in your stupid and thick head. If you think I am stupid, you must be mistaking. Quite frankly, I believe that you've misunderstood me. You are telling me that I am an individual who fights for the support of Anarchy. You are totally wrong. I would've never won if I fought for the support of Anarchy. Instead, I fought for the support of justice and fairness. Unfortunately, we live in a World, a Universe, and a Multidimensional place where there is unfairness and injustice. We live in a place or places where man supports evilness and cruelty. We witness the rise of tyrannical governments. Unfortunately, I have been affected by a tyrannical government and that was the leadership of Cornelius. Rather than doing the impetuous thing of leading a revolt, I did the smarter thing. I refused to lead a revolt. I acted sneaky in order to cover myself and protect my friends. When my friends and I escaped the Alien Estate, a couple of years ago, we managed to depart from the alien city, which was in sheer chaos at the time of the escape. The prosecution media sensationalist and Cornelius's girlfriend, Jacqueline Langyaw, led a massive attack against the Earthlings of California County in Upstate New York. Cornelius and she placed all of the citizens in time capsules to stunt their growth and development by three days. Eventually, I arrested her and Cornelius without leading a huge revolt. I offered her a plea deal and Cornelius went to trial and he was convicted on all counts. I killed him and took leadership. Unfortunately, division has taken place in my city since the beginning of my leadership as President. All of the citizens were happy that I took leadership. Meanwhile, some former SSGM soldiers were very dissatisfied with the new takeover. Now, you can tell me that I am nothing but a pathological liar and a deceptive sneak. I am not. I fought for justice. I fought for the alien's rights against the Stalinist politics of Cornelius. Killing that brute was justifiable because he directly ruined my life. He tried to cause trouble and put a hole in my heart. That sick, son of a bitch killed my parents because of his ego. Now, I am going to say my final words with you. You are the epitome of evil. You have tried to cause harm to all of the alien citizens. That is despicable and you are an atrocious alien! May God have mercy on your sinister soul because you need all the mercy you can get and the things you have said about me are quite fallacious and disrespectable! In addition to that, those words that you have used were quite unintelligent and they would be words that are said by imbeciles like you. I rest my case. No further statements. To add insult to injury, you treat Cornelius like he is a God. He is not a God. In fact, he is far from a God. He was a tyrant and an evil brute. He made the settlers look at him like he was the type to start a beautiful city. he had a different trick up his evil sleeve. He basically poisoned the minds of his vulnerable alien confidants. He betrayed his peers and he turned Starmos City into a tyrannical regime. Not to sound like I have an ego, but the truth of the matter is that I saved my city from years of more tyranny. One of my goals as the alien leader is to united Starmos City with all of the other dimensions and make one federation of dimensions that share the same principle of fairness, liberty, fraternity, and justice for all men and women. This is a seemingly impossible task, but once the citizens of those individual dimensions unite, they will be able to overthrow their tyrannical leaders," said Will.

Buck started breathing heavily. He started grunting like a boar. His face started turning red and the veins in his forehead started showing. His anger is growing and his adrenaline is high. He angrily widened his eyes so much to the point where they looked like they were going to pop out of his head. He clenched his teeth and started grinding them.

He clenched his fists so tightly that they cramped. He unclenched his left fist and grabbed his aPhone and hit the Shape shifter's application. He shape-shifted from a feeble, swarthy, dirty homeless man into a strong SSGM soldier. Basically, he shape-shifted from the form of Buck into the form of Brutis. His hair started turning brown and he wore his blue and silver SSGM uniform.

His hands doubled in size. His shoe size grew and he grew muscles in this ephemeral shapeshifting process. He also grew a large mustache in this shapeshifting process. He looks totally different from that arrogant homeless man.

He started acting in an animalistic manner. He flared his nostrils like a Rhinoceros at Will. He showed his teeth like an angry shark and he growled like a beastly Lion. The alien leader laughed.

"Oh, I am so scared of you. I don't think you realize this. I do have full control over your job. I don't think you want to mess around with me because I have full control over your criminal status. I can talk to the new prosecutor about bringing you on charges of attempted murder and false imprisonment. I won't do that as long as you don't act intimidating towards me. Once you stop acting like a nut job, you won't have to worry about being a hardened criminal. I have asked you this question numerous times today and you have never really answered the question. I remember clearly asking you why you behave like a monstrosity and why you support socialism and bigotry? Now, I want you to answer this question without giving me a problem. Why do you act like a beast to society?" he asked.

"Fine. I'll tell you why I am the way I am. First of all, people have always misunderstood me my whole life because of the fact that I am bigger than most average sized aliens. When I was younger, I would be bullied at school and treated like a savage when I wasn't a savage. I was just an innocent individual who was bigger than most. When I reached the age to get into Secondary School, I was denied the right to an education because I was too big to receive an education. This was when I was thirteen. I decided to enlist in the SSGM army for Cornelius. I worked my way up from the bottom of the barrel all the way to the cream of the crop. While I was in the SSGM, I started to get to know the one that I call the beloved leader, Cornelius. I thought he was the most genuine and kind-hearted alien that one can ever meet. The reason why I enslave people and aliens is because I was forced to do that in order to stay friends with Cornelius. I do have a heart; I am just sorry for what I've caused. and I didn't mean to be evil. It was just my duty. I want to be a productive citizen. Those remarks about Socialism were false. They were not my words; they were the words of Cornelius and Jacqueline. To be honest with you, I hate Socialism and Racism. I think they are the most evil things that man can do. The only reason why I said those things to you was to sound like a 'tough guy' because Cornelius turned me into a malevolent beast. When I was younger, I was this kind-hearted, misunderstood kid. I was bullied and I joined an organization that I figured that they would build up my self-confidence. they didn't the SSGM turned me into a callous beast instead of a loving and gentle soul. Deep down inside, that's who I am," answered Brutis.

He started showing emotion on his face. His revelation just showed that he is not really a cold-hearted beast. He only acts that way because of his life in the Starmos government and his life in general. He was poisoned by the sinister charm of Cornelius. "That's a terrible story and I am so sorry that I've treated you like a monstrosity. I would've never meant to do that. and we both share similar stories in our lives," the alien leader replied.

"Would you mind sharing your story with me?" asked Brutis. "Sure. When I was about three years old, I was diagnosed with two learning impairments called Asperger's Syndrome and Impulse Control Disorder. I'll explain to you what both disabilities are. Asperger's Syndrome is a learning advancement where you would learn really fast. Typically, in school you would have grades that are up to par or above average. You wouldn't have the best social skills. This disability does not define who I am, but it definitely describes my social skills. For instance, I would have obsessions on certain topics. When I was a young boy, I had dreams about becoming a pilot and I would often look at flight simulators and go in the Cockpit of a jet whenever my parents would go with Cornelius on a diplomacy trip to a distant dimension. When

I became older, I used to have a theater in my apartment and I would often talk about that constantly. Then in my teenage years, I started talking about my dreams of opening up a hotel and the evilness of the Starmos government. In addition to that, I would interrupt conversations and try to get involved in others' conversations just to simply make friends. As a result, my disability caused me to be alienated and bullied in school. Now, we're going to get into my other disability of Impulsive Control Disorder. Along with being diagnosed with Asperger's Syndrome, I was diagnosed with a disability that is known as Impulsive Control Disorder. Basically, I would act impetuous and impulsive. I would often act without thinking constantly. This behavior would take place in the classroom. Because I was academically advanced, I would often not raise my hand and I would call out the answer to the question, in spite of the fact that the teacher did not call on my to answer the question. I would also act brash outside of the classroom. I tried fitting in with the other students because I would constantly joke on the ones that the other students were joking on. Now, it's hard to explain but these two disabilities are related to each other. The reason why is because I would constantly bring up things that happened weeks ago and keep talking about those things. I would also constantly laugh a lot that the students found to be anomalous and even bizarre. I believed that they were clean, fun humor. Looking back, the people who I thought were trying to be nasty and disrespectful to me were here to help me. If they didn't care, they would let me act the way I acted and I would never be able to succeed in life. Later on, I tried maintaining self-control. In my life, I have felt a little misunderstood initially, but when I entered secondary school, I started to discover that my fellow classmates were here to help me instead of pick on me and hurt me. When I was younger, I would cry and ask myself why I was made the way I was made because of my behavior and not being able to make friends. I later discovered that the folks who were knocking me when I was wrong were my true friends," answered Will.

"Granted, it may not sound like the problems that I've dealt with. the stories sound quite similar. We were both sort of alienated because of our impairments, but you were better than me. The reason why was because you overcame the fact that you had learning impairments. and you overlooked the fact that you were bullied in school. I know it must've been bothersome being the one with the disability. I can empathize with you though on this subject. You had quite an interesting story. and it is unfortunate that you had huge obstacles to face, but I guess that this is bitter sweet. The reason why is because you acted a little quirky and bitter. you learned how to adapt and fix those quirks. You learned how to be a better leader and here you are as the alien leader. I feel that you're really going to fix Starmos City and improve the place. So, Will, I shall reprove the comments that I said about you because, I did not mean to demean you or degrade you because I was stupid and wrong. Like I said earlier, I was acting the way I acted because my mind was poisoned and programmed by Cornelius to act the way I acted. and I am extremely sorry. Mr. Von Alien, will you still forgive me?" the benevolent shape shifter asked.

"Absolutely! First of all, you don't have to call me Mr. Von Alien. Just call me, Will. Second of all, you are more than forgiven. Besides, I believe that man pulls an act all the time to try to impress others. at some point they will show their true colors. Those true colors can either be good or bad. To me, your true colors are good. Based on the story that you've told me, you are a kind-hearted soul led in the wrong direction by some naturally evil tyrant," the alien leader replied. "Now, I don't want to sound like I am asking too many questions. can I ask you this one question?" asked Brutis.

"And what would that be?" asked Will. "Can I quit the SSGM and join your side of the force?" the benevolent shape shifter asked. The alien leader's eyes widened and he gaped his mouth open. He is in disbelief and shock. He hesitated because he is dumbstruck and in disbelief. Thirty seconds after the question was asked, he jumped up. "Yes," he shouted in ecstasy. The boat rocked right after he landed back on the wood. "Great, thank you. That was extremely nice and amicable of you to do that especially after how I treated you," replied Brutis. "No problem. Now, one of the first things that you must do in order to show that is to unchain my two friends, who are now your two friends and liberate us from slavery," said Will. "It would be my honor to do those two things. Once your friends are freed from the shackles, we will free the slaves that were captured by Jacqueline and Cornelius. we shall fight against evil and make as many sacrifices as necessary," the amicable shape shifter (Brutis) replied. He walked to the stern of the gondola and retrieved the keys to the other locks.
He liberated Rubi and Commissioner Clayton. he helped them board the boat. Their clothes are all drenched and they have the odious smell of seawater.

"Rubi and Commissioner Clayton, Brutis has something he wants to tell you all," said the alien leader. "Are you going to threaten us?" asked Rubi. "No, I want to ask you two for your forgiveness. I was not showing my true colors when I said that I supported Slavery, Racism, and Socialism. Deep down inside, I have a heart and it's a kind heart. The reason why I acted in such an evil and disgusting manner is because Cornelius poisoned my mind. So, we must fight for justice and stand up against the evils of the Socialist and bigoted tyranny of the callous Cornelius and and sinister Langyaw and end communism, socialism, bigotry, and tyranny, once and all. Who is with me? More importantly, who is willing to forgive me?" asked Brutis.

"We are," both Rubi and Clayton answered at the same time. "Well, I strongly appreciate the fact that you two have forgiven me. Now, let's get ready to attack the malevolent villains. We shall crush Jacqueline and destroy her small militia. I discovered that Will was, and still is, the epitome of true justice and fairness. Jacqueline claims that she supports justice. she is nothing but an evil witch who thinks who she is. She is here to cause trouble and ruin this world. She has no respect for an excellent, new leader like you; and we must fight against somebody like her. She is the epitome of true evil and we must destroy her stone cold spirit and unfreeze her stone cold blood," the alien shapeshiftter replied.

"I hope I am not changing your thoughts when I am saying this. I am going to tell you that it is amazing that one minute you are on the darkest side of the universe, but within a matter of minutes you change into somebody who is siding with the brighter side of the universe. That is quite amazing if you ask me. I didn't think my statement would do much for somebody who acted so cold-hearted, blunt, and malicious. Infact, it is quite bizarre how you change from one side, the evil side, to another, the good side. That is just quite bizarre. Now, I hope that what you're saying is true and you are not going to rejoin the evil side for some crazy reason. I hope that you stay with our side, from now on. If you fight for justice, then you will succeed. and justice will be done if you persistently crusade for your belief. There's only one condition to this crusading idea. The condition is that your idea must be morally correct. You can't fight for the wrong cause," said Will. "Now, I have a statement that I have to say in order to show that I am truthfully apologetic. Each statement will be addressed to you all individually. Will, I am sorry for all of the pain I've caused you by demeaning you, trying to knock you, tying you up, ridiculing your parents, and give lining to an evil beast who killed them. What I did to you was sick and bloody. Now, I am going to direct my next remarks at Commissioner Clayton. Commissioner, I am sorry for ridiculing your job and your fellow brethren's jobs. I am sorry that I used the wrong terms of the word 'Cops' because I can see that I was derogatory and I debased myself below the level of a human being's heart. In addition to that, I show my great apologies for acting violent with you because my violent behavior was unnecessary. Finally, to Rubi; I am sorry for all of the pain I've caused you. For I shall be ashamed of the grief that has happened. I am first going to say 'sorry' because I never meant to poison you. The reason why I poisoned you with the quicksilver or mercury was because Jacqueline told me to do that. She unfortunately has an evil existence all over the place. Once be rid of her existence, we will be safe. she told me to poison you and she threatened to kill me if I didn't do that. So, those are my apologies to you all as individuals. Now, as a group. I have a couple of more apologies. I am sorry for causing pain by using Serpianto and Korbian as a shapeshifting prosecutor and judge. In addition to that, I am sorry for allowing them to bring you all evil and showing intimidation. I do not want to say that I am not holding myself accountable because I am truly holding myself accountable and apologizing. I am sorry for the pain and suffering that I have caused. It was wrong of me to behave the way I behaved and I would never mean to cause that much trouble for anybody. I have wronged you and I definitely deserve to feel ashamed," replied Brutis.

"I don't want to say the things that you've done were okay. To be honest, I believed the things you did were extremely unacceptable and malevolent. You deserve to be ashamed of yourself and you were right in saying it. Not to sound like a preacher. I must tell an important story. Man often makes mistakes in life. He can make as little as one mistake or as many as one million mistakes, but either way, mistakes are mistakes, but decisions are decisions and one makes decisions out of his conscience. If these decisions are bad decisions, some of them can or cannot be reversed. For instance, if one murders a mortal, then that mortal will never be able to be brought back from the dead. That's an irreversible decision. It can be forgiven. that mortal will not be able to be brought back from the dead. If one commits a theft, then that stolen item can be returned back to its proper item because stolen items are definitely reversible and replacable. Sometimes, man makes mistakes or decisions that are irreversible or reversible. Along with that being certain, man can forgive other individuals who apologize for their wrong doings. I feel that you've did what you did because you were told by her to do those malicious and sinister acts. you made a choice. You chose to act vile along with that wench prosecutor, Jacqueline. Besides the fact that I am not a judge, I would not impose a punishment on you because I know that you were bullied as a lad. I am just simply going to say that I forgive you and I am even more happy that you've held yourself accountable for your actions. What makes me even more elated is that a strong, courageous gentleman like you would be here to fight for justice and stand up against the evils of society. and as a united force, we will rip apart Jacqueline Langyaw's brutal group," the alien leader said.

The boat is getting closer to Swinburne Island. Now, one can see the dense forest of oak trees. The boat is approximately two miles from the island. The gondola continued moving all the way to the island. "You were totally right in what you said about me. in order to fight against Ms. Langyaw, we must contrive an important plan. Now, we are going to park the gondola at the defunct dock on the island and secure it, so that way no bandits try and steal it from us. Once we do that, we will search through the rocks of the island to find a map of this island. Then, we will make sure that the map is the correct map. We'll find the trail to the nearest place possible to get a drink," replied Brutis.

"That sounds like such an intelligent idea. You are so contributing to this fight for justice," Will said sarcastically. "Tell you what. I'll come up with the plan when we get to the island. Or, I won't come up with a plan at all and make the idea of discovery do its part," the alien shape shifter replied. "That sounds much better than your original idea," said Will.

"Thank you," replied Bruits. He continued paddling the gondola all the way to the island. The gondola is closer to the island. "I can't believe I am visiting this island. I've never even visited this place. I've only driven past here on my yacht. I would stay away from this island because of the vegetation and there might be bugs on this island. I've always wondered what lied on this place and it would be a pleasure to visit this place. I've always wondered about what lurked in the jungle in this place. It must be quite interesting to see all the natural wonders and wildlife that must've lived here or still lives here," said Clayton. "I hope there's nothing about that former tyrant in Russia or that insane prosecutor in Perugia. I hope that there's nothing about any of those folks because if there is something in existence about those folks, I am going to leave the isl, and" replied Rubi.

"I totally agree with you. I am just here because I want to rescue Light from that beast Jacqueline Langyaw," the police commissioner said. "I don't want anything to do with those two or see anything about them," the alien leader's girlfriend.

"Not to sound nasty but, I have a couple of pointers to tell you. Do you realize who you're dealing with? You're dealing with folks who were associated with that tyrant, Cornelius? You're dealing with Jacqueline Langyaw, a former prosecutor who is just as evil as the prosecutor of Perugia and has the personality of the evil tyrant of Russia. You're dealing with somebody who has an evil personality and evil soul. Then, you're dealing with her confidants. You're going to be dealing with her chauffeur Howard Carterson. You're dealing with Serpianto and Korbian. You're dealing with her accomplice Mitchell. And, of course, you're going to be dealing with her. You never know. She may have some violent streak. She's as evil as sin and she's a beast. Look at how evil she is. For God sakes, she made those two serpents shape-shift into that judge and prosecutor to hurt Will and potentially kill him. This woman is evil and I can tell you that she is worse than a thug. She is here to cause harm to all humans and aliens alike. She only supports the ones that are either Socialist or

Racist. This woman is a snake herself. She is just in the form of an alien. Now, don't get confused because she's not a shape shifter. she is just sick in the head and at the end of the day, she is here to ruin you too. She attempted to cause your death. Fortunately, you survived because of the greatness of God. Now, I didn't tell you this because I didn't want to go on a whole rant. I wanted to get my point across to you and I wanted to be up front and frank with you. Don't back out of the battle because your boyfriend saved you from dying. I would assume that you would want to save your boyfriend from dying. So, I think it wouldn't be such a bad idea to join him in his crusade to fight against the malevolence and despicability of Jacqueline. You must fight with Will and for him. Look what he did. He fought for you and he was with you at all times. He saved you from dying. If we didn't care, we wouldn't travel back to the year of 2047. We would just stay in the mid to late 1800s because it seemed better in those years than this year," said Clayton.

"You know something? You are totally right in what you just said. I wasn't thinking straight because I must've been a little too carried away with being dragged on the back of that stupid boat. I can understand because if Will saw that I was going through a situation like that, he would've been the first to fight with me at that moment. He would immediately take my side and advocate for me. I guess that I was wrong and stupid in saying what I was saying. Shame on me. From now on, when it comes to fighting with or for my boyfriend, I will always be on his side and I will never leave his side because I don't feel that he should be left alone like a lost sheep in the prairie. We should all fight as a team. Besides, an important quote that has been said numerous times was, *A house that is divided cannot stand. And* that phrase was said by somebody who we knew for nearly 7 years. Unfortunately, he is deceased because of some sick, twisted Southerner. his principles do live on, but not to the fullest extant. Unfortunately, we do have bigotry and hatred towards individuals because of their race, creed, or skin color. That's why the Lord created us. We are a united team who will fight against the evils of tyranny and bigotry. and now, it's time to not only get Jacqueline, but, it is time to kill her. Granted, I am somewhat of a pacifist, but in order to keep peace, war is necessary. In this case, killing her would be necessary because she is nothing but a violent, conniving, manipulating, deceptive, deceitful, callous, stony-hearted, condescending, bigoted, sociopathic wench. Instead of red blood cells running through her veins, she has malice running through her veins. For God sakes, this woman is not even an alien or a mortal; at least, she doesn't act like that. She acts in the most beastly manner," the alien leader's girlfriend replied.

"While we've been on this boat ride, you, Commissioner Clayton, and Will have brought up some pretty good points. Now, this is what I think of Jacqueline. She thinks who she is. Although she paid me a lot to capture over 600 humans and aliens and make them her slaves, I rebuke all of the things that I have done for her. Those things that I did for her were totally wrong and I held myself accountable for them. Now, we're going to stop her. As productive aliens, we are going to stop her evilness. Besides, that's the right thing to do. He who lets evil happens is just as evil as the wrongdoer. Therefore, that makes the one who allows the evil to take place, the wrongdoer. We must stop her and we will not honor her twisted and disgusting ways of evil," the shapeshifting alien said. The alien leader is sitting on the boat. Immediately, he feels something odd with the boat. His seat appears to be sinking. He is standing up and he notices his seat sinking further. He raised his right eyebrow. "What's this?" he asked himself.

After thirty seconds of standing on the bow of the boat, he sees a three inch diameter hole in the bottom right corner of the boat. After a minute, his shoes felt saturated. He walked up to the stern of the boat where his girlfriend, Commissioner Clayton, are present. "What are you doing walking on this boat? Aren't you supposed to be sitting in your seat?" the shapeshifting alien asked. "I guess so," the alien leader answered. "Why are you saying you guess so?" asked Brutis.

"I would like it if you would take a look for yourself to see what's going on back there," answered Will. The alien shape shifter walked all the way to the bow of the boat. He noticed that it is all flooded. His eyes widened in shock and disbelief. "Will, what did you do? That's terrible. I can't understand how that happened," he said. The alien leader acted defensive. "I would never mean to pop a hole in this boat. Besides, the boat that you're driving is a beautiful boat. What makes you think that I would want to destroy it?" the alien leader asked. "I don't think you would break the boat. It must've been some debris," answered Brutis. He and the motley trio jumped off of the boat and started swimming over one thousand feet to Swinburne Island. They're heading through strong currents.

Chapter XXVI: The trouble of the wrong trail

It is now half past 8 in the morning and the motley trio and Brutis have arrived on the island. Getting to the island was dangerous heading through those detrimental waters. In addition to that, they were not heading to the best sight one might see. They are in for a rude awakening when they are on the island. They have swum so fast that they weren't able to see the white rocks and grey rocks. The rocks come in various forms.

Some of them are amorphous; while, the others are crystalline and have a full shape. In spite of the fact that Will has never seen an ocean or a pool, he is swimming as fast as a speedboat. Within one hundred feet of the island, and he notices that he is in shallow water. He stopped swimming and stood up. He is standing in an area that is 3 feet deep. He looked down and thought to himself that the ground looks shallower than it feels. He continued walking closer to the island.

As he walked closer, he had seen that the sand appeared to be coming closer to the water. Thus, the area seemed quite shallow. as he keeps walking closer to the island, and the water keeps getting deeper. He is in a state of disbelief. He didn't know what to do and he didn't know how to rescue himself. He is now in seven feet of water. He is starting to notice that he's drowning. Yet, he doesn't know what to do. He doesn't know how to swim back up to the breathable surface. He doesn't even know how to float. Fortunately, he cannot die if he drowns. he is as scared as a cat that is afraid of water, but he is not afraid of the water. He is afraid of the fact that he'll have to deal with drowning. Brutis continued swimming. Will started jumping up and freaking out. "Oh my God, somebody help me! I'm drowning.

I don't know what to do," he said panicking. Brutis, Commissioner Clayton, or Rubi cannot hear him. They just kept on swimming to the island oblivious to the fact that Will is drowning, struggling to breathe. He is trying to breathe. He screamed, "Help," one more time. His girlfriend, the police commissioner, and the shapeshifting alien just kept on swimming. He screamed one more time. Rubi heard a scream. She stopped swimming. Whereas, Clayton and Brutis stopped swimming.

"I hear this noise that sounds like a scream and it sounds a lot like my boyfriend," she said. He screamed again. "There it is again. Let's go check it out," she said. Brutis, Commissioner Clayton, and she continued swimming to the island. They drew closer to the island. By the time they arrived, Will drowned to the bottom of the ocean floor.

"Where's that noise?," his girlfriend asked. "I don't know but, I heard it stop for some sort of crazy reason," replied Clayton. She witnessed her boyfriend's Alien Estate Identification Card floating right before her eyes. "He's dead! Oh no," she screamed. She broke down in tears. Brutis held her trying to comfort her. "Don't worry. Everything is going to be okay. Besides, he's not dead. The only way he can die is if he gets poisoned to death. So, I can guarantee you that he's not dead. I am an excellent swimmer. I'll swim all the way down to the bottom of the ocean in this particular section. I don't think that he's gone too far," he replied. "What do you want me to do?" asked Clayton.

"Not to sound condescending but, we are in a crisis right now. I want you to stay up on the surface and not come down until I ask you to. I think you should help Rubi feel better. She needs a lot of your consolation," the alien shape shifter answered. "Very well then. I'll help her feel better as much as I can," the police commissioner replied. Brutis dunked his body fully into the ocean water. He is swimming in greenish-blue water. The water is totally unclear. The only way that he will be able to find Will's body is if he feels for it. Fortunately, the ground is made of sand. It wouldn't seem hard finding a lump in the ground. He started feeling the ocean floor to find Will's unconscious body. One minute later, he can't find it. Another minute later, he still can't find it. It is now three minutes later and he cannot breathe well. He is using up all his lung capacity. He feels the ocean floor to find the unconscious alien leader one last time. He feels a small lump buried a little beneath the sand. He is feeling a shirt that feels like tinfoil. He then realized that the body is Will's body. He quickly unburied the body from the ocean and swam all the way up with the surface with the unconscious body. He gasped and placed the alien leader's body on the dock.

"What do I do?" he asked nervously. "Perform CPR," answered Clayton. "What is CPR?" the alien shape shifter asked. "It's when you push on somebody's chest in order to bring that individual back to life," the police commissioner answered. "How many times do you want me to do that?" asked Brutis. "As many times as you can until the body comes back to life," answered Clayton. The alien shape shifter jumped back on top of the dock and he started performing CPR on Will. Every minute seemed like an hour to him constantly pushing on Will's chest. Four minutes later, he is about to give up. On the last push, he heard a cough. His eyes widened in disbelief. "Can it be?" he asked himself. He pushed again and he heard another cough, except the cough sounded louder. He pushed three more times and the alien leader coughed up a bunch of sand and water. The last push, the alien leader coughed up more water and he is finally able to breathe normally. He started talking. "Oh my God. I'm alive. What happened?" he asked. "You're talking," Brutis ecstatically said. He embraced Will. "Well, what happened?" asked the alien leader. "Well, I am sorry to say this but, you've drowned. You didn't know how to swim because of your geographical and political location and so you didn't know how to bring yourself up from the ground, but you became unconscious. So, being that I am the most agile one here, I had no choice but, to swim down and rescue you. I performed CPR and you have awakened from the dead," the alien shape shifter (Brutis) answered.

"Oh my God. All this has happened to me in such a short nick of time?" asked Will. "Yes," answered Brutis. Rubi, Clayton, and Brutis walked onto the island from the dock of rotting wood. The alien leader remained there. Brutis walked up to the end of the dock onto the island. "What are you doing there?" he asked. "I don't know what to do. I can't go onto the island, and.." the alien leader answered. "Why?" the alien shape shifter asked. "Because there's a bunch of sand stuck to me and I don't think I'll be able to walk with the wet sand" answered Will. "Well, I know I shouldn't be asking you this question, but can you just dunk yourself into the water without drowning?" asked Brutis. "No, I can't because I don't know how to swim. Sorry, you would have to go without me," the alien leader answered. "Now, don't say such a thing. You created this whole thing and you embarked on these wild adventures. Now, you're just going to sit there and give it up? How could you; this is definitely not the courageous and brave Will Von Alien that I know. Will, would never give up in anything. You need to learn how to pull yourself together. In life, there'll be many dilemmas that you'll be facing and encountering. Some are little, while others are large. This dilemma is a little dilemma and you're going to let this make you give up. That's ridiculous and stupid. Tell you what, I'll jump into the water to keep you safe and allow you to swim better" the alien shape shifter replied. "Fine then, you're right. I'll do it," said Will. He jumped into the ocean water on the right side of the dock. He is being cleansed with the water and the sand is disappearing. His clothes might be clean of sand, but they will have a strong odor when he emerges from the water. Brutis jumped back in to make sure that Will would not drown. Will managed to swim back up to the dock after be ridding the sand that was on his body.

"Wow! You did it. You've learned how to swim on your own," said Brutis. "This sounds quite childish that I learned how to swim at such an old age, but I guess that's what happens when you're not raised with any pools, oceans, or lakes," the alien leader replied.

"You shouldn't say that sounds childish or babyish because I can understand your situation. Now, if it was a human who had a pool, who lived on the East Coast, then I would say it would sound kind of babyish," the alien shape shifter said. "Good point, you must be right," replied Will.

"Very well then. I think we should head on the island to explore what's going on and what's about to take place," said Brutis. He and Will started walking onto the island in seawater drenched clothing. They started heading on a small trail. The trail had a plain appearance with just dirt and mud. Fortunately, the mud is not getting stuck to the alien leader's nor the alien shape shifter's shoes or boots. The trail is surrounded by trees and vegetation. The vegetation has a unique appearance because the trees have a bunch of markings and small mutilations. "Oh my God, this place, looks so generic," the alien leader said.

"Well, maybe we should continue on exploring before we make a judgement. Besides, you can't judge a book by looking at its color," the alien shape shifter replied. They continued walking up the trail on the island. It seems extremely flat, almost to the point where it seems like they are walking on concrete. They are now about two hundred feet onto the island and they're noticing something quite odd. The trail is now increasing in elevation and they are walking up the hill. Also, the forest is becoming much denser almost to the point where they are hardly able to see the ocean.

"It's ridiculous and pathetic that we really have to walk up some crazy hill," said Brutis. "No kidding; I wish we had a quad that would take us up the hill. In addition to that, I do not even want to see some sort of crazy hill," replied Will.

"Not to sound like one who tells proverbs but sometimes in life, you would have to do the things that you dread doing. You also have to make some sacrifices," the alien shape shifter said.

Will just disregarded the comments that were made by Brutis and he continued up the trail. Another, bizarre thing started taking place on the trail. As they continued to walk up, the trail started becoming narrower. They are now heading one thousand feet into the island. It is now a quarter to 9 in the morning and the alien leader is becoming more nervous. he is treading carefully on the island. He is so nervous that he didn't even say one word to Brutis. The trail became narrower to the point where the alien leader has to stand on his side in order to walk on the trail. The alien shape shifter also has to stand on the side. The trail continued becoming narrower to the point that it was only six inches wide.

"How are we going to get through this kind of mess?" asked Will. "We'll keep doing what we're doing; we'll just continue going down the trail without a problem like we've been doing," the alien shape shifter answered. They walked slower as the trail became narrower. Will turned his head to the right. Seen in the distance is a small light. This light looks like the Celestial City.

"What's this?" the alien leader asked ecstatically. "What are you talking about?" the alien shape shifter asked. "Look to your right and you'll see a shining light," answered Will. Brutis looked to his light and he noticed it. "Oh, my God! Well, look at that," he said. Will and he continued walking down the trail. Will moved much faster than Brutis and he stood up close to him, so close that he is in his personal space.

"What are you doing so close to me?" the alien shape shifter asked. "I've just happened to move much faster than you have," the alien leader answered. "Fine then. I guess I need to move," replied Brutis. He continued walking sideways. Suddenly, he fell in the middle of a big patch of grass. Will is the second to fall on the big patch of grass. This grass looks dried out because of the lack of ecology in the area and the roughness of the soil. They looked around and realized that they are surrounded by a dense wilderness. The wilderness is so dense that one wouldn't be able to see the ocean or even hear the ocean. This area is the only place where one would be able to have an unobscured view of the clouds and the sun. This is the only place on the island.

"This place is more unique than Starmos City. For God sakes, take a look at the diverse, mind-boggling terrain that is on this island. This place is quite impressive," said Will. "I am happy that you think this place is unique. we have more important priorities to worry about over here. For instance, I want to know where the Rubi and Clayton are. It's quite important for me to know because I don't want anything to happen to them. I don't thing old man Clayton will be able to survive on this island because he's a human. He's probably fallen on the terrain a number of times. The second priority is that we don't know how to get off of this place. Besides, we won't be able to get off until we find that wench Jacqueline or, at least connections to her. and finally, the third priority is to find a way to live here because this might be some sort of permanent vacation," the alien shape shifter replied. "Well, what if we're not able to find Jacqueline or any other connection to her? Then, what do we do now?" the alien leader asked. "I don't know what to say. We'll scour and scavenge through this island to find her. We will not stop until she or one of her connections is found. As strong individuals, we shall never give up," said Brutis.

"I totally agree with you, but there are 7 different trails that we must take. Each one is marked with a different colored dot. I don't think there's any way for us to get out of here. If we're surrounded by all of these trails. I don't think there's any way for us to get out of here," replied Will. Seen from above is Enkel. He landed on top of Will's shoulder.

"Oh, Enkel, what are you doing here?" the alien leader asked. "I am here to tell you how to get to your girlfriend and Clayton," answered God's messneger (Enkel.) "Well, what trail do you want me to head down?" asked Will.

"I could tell you which trail not to head down," answered Enkel. "Well, that really helps," the alien leader sarcastically replied. God's messenger didn't even realize that the alien leader was talking in a sarcastic manner. "Thank you. I'm here to help you," he (Enkel) said. "Now, if you're really here to help me, would you mind telling me which trail to use?" asked Will. "Sure. Don't head down the trail with the red markings," answered Enkel.

"No, I asked you a totally different question. Let me restate what I've asked you. I'll reiterate the question one more time. 'Can you tell me which trail to go down to find my girlfriend and the police commissioner'?" asked Will. "I can tell that you're being a smart aleck to me. You're on your own and you must make your own decisions. You decided if they are in your conscious or not. That's if you even have any conscious. After all, man has free will. He can do whatever he wants. In spite of being an immortal alien, you fit in the category of man kind. Thus, man has free will. So, you must have free will. Basically, this means that you make choices, but with those choices come consequences. So, you must make the right choice in order to not suffer the consequence," God's messenger answered.

"I won't be able to know the right decision unless you tell me. Whereas, you should tell me which trail to go down," the alien leader said. "Fine. I'll tell you, but I'll give you no more further information. Do not head down the Red Trail," replied Enkel.

"Yeah, you said that earlier. That sounds ridiculous. Red doesn't matter to me. Besides, we all bleed the same color blood. So, what's the sense in listening to you?" asked Will. "Buddy, it's your choice. Like I said earlier, you have choices in life and you make those choices that is based from your conscience. Your choices or decisions can either have good consequences or bad consequences. I've told you that you shouldn't go down the Red trail, but if you do that don't come crying to me for help. For, I have warned you about that trail," replied Enkel. God's messenger disappeared and he returned back up to Heaven. "What do we do?" asked Will.

"Enkel sounds kind of suspicious to me because he says that we're not allowed to take the Red Trail. Then, he said that we shouldn't take it. Then, he said, man has free will. and it was our choice. I don't know what to do. This is like the most mind-shaking situation of my life," answered Brutis.

"You know what? I am not going to listen to that stupid angel. He thinks he has all the sagacity in the World. he doesn't have a pinch of that. He's just spewing stupid words. I'd bet that God wouldn't mind us taking that trail. What does that angel know? He may be immaculate but, he spews a lot of nonsense and stupidity," the alien leader replied. "I totally agree with you. I don't think I'm going to listen to that angel. We must do all it takes to find Rubi and Commissioner Clayton. We can't just sit there and let an angel dictate to us how to make our decisions. He probably can't even see the so called 'Red' trail because of the density of the wilderness out here. That angel is nothing but, a phony, who tells a bunch of fallacious statements. I don't think he's an angel. He's probably some sort of insect," the alien leader replied. "This joke might sound corny, but I'll tell you it anyway. What do you need in order to be rid of a pest?" the alien shape shifter asked. "What?" asked Will.

"An Enkesticide," answered Brutis. "Oh, that's so funny and quite entertaining. Ha, ha, ha," the alien leader sarcastically replied. "Alright, we'll seriously consider on going down that trail because I don't think that angel has any wisdom or intelligence behind him whatsoever," the alien shape shifter said. They started walking down the "forbidden" trail, the red trail. This trail looks like any other ordinary trail in the forest on Swinburne. every tree has a red marker. Eventually, they continued moving about fifty feet onto the trail. "This trail doesn't seem odd to me. That angel must've been telling some sort of fallacy," said Will.

"I totally agree with you. There's nothing wrong with this trail," replied Brutis. They just continued down the trail, not giving a care in the world about what is about to happen to them. The trail is getting wider as they continue moving down. Now, they're five hundred feet into the woodlands. The forest is becoming less dense. In addition to that, the mud on the trail had a reddish appearance. "Now, there's some skepticism in my head. It doesn't look bad to me. It just looks red. Still, I don't think it's a big deal. I can tell you it's not clay because clay would feel kind of muddy. Somebody must've spray painted the dirt over here," the alien leader said.

"To be honest with you. I don't think going down this trail is a big deal. That redness looks like either somebody spray painted that ground or there were vandals that must've come here years back because this redness looks kind of cliched," the alien shape shifter replied. They just continued going down the trail. Now, they're about one thousand feet into the wilderness. There's less vegetation in this part of the wilderness than the other parts. Seen in the distance is a small red brick that is buried in the ground. This brick is thirty feet within the walking distance of Will and Brutis. Thirty-seconds later, the alien leader stumbled upon this brick.

"What's this?" he asked. "I don't know. Probably some sort of ordinary brick," the alien shape shifter answered. They continued walking down the trail disregarding the fact that the trail is really a brick road to an old defunct Quarantine House. This Quarantine House was used to house people that were plagued with diseases that would be considered as too dangerous and untreatable for society. Fortunately, the place is germ free. After walking three hundred more feet down the brick trail, the alien leader stumbled upon another brick. This brick is a loose brick. "What's this now?" he asked. "I don't know why you are asking me such stupid questions about pathetic bricks. Frankly, I think your questions are totally useless and unnecessary about bricks," answered Brutis.

"Buddy, let's not make this an ugly situation that we had earlier, especially over a stupid thing. The reason why I'm suspicious about these bricks is because of three reasons. One reason is that the trail was made of pretty much flat bricks compact bricks, but, this particular part is made of a loose brick. The second reason is that we're on an island that we've never been on. Therefore, I would be skeptical about what trails we must take and what trails we must not take. and the third reason is that Enkel told us not to go on this trail. Now, it's up to you whether or not you're going to listen to him about this trail. I'd strongly recommend listening to him because some of the things that he said were quite important and applicable to life in general," the alien leader replied.

"Oh my God, how dare you say such a thing! How dare you even take his side. Have you lost your damn mind?" the alien shape shifter angrily asked. "In spite of what I said earlier about him and trying to question him about his opinion, I sort of started to agree with him when I headed down this trail. Maybe we should turn back," the alien leader answered. "Do you know what I notice, Will? You don't face your problems headstrong. You need to learn how to fight like a bull when you see problems. Every time you see something suspicious, or every time every little thing happens to you, you whine. That's ridiculous and quite stupid. Whining is not the answer buddy. You are to become a man and fight. How can a 25 year old act like such a 12 year old? That's quite absurd. I am tired of giving you life lessons, but there are some pointers that I must give you. We live in a crazy dimensional and Intergalactic plane. Then, we enter the solar system and before you know it, we enter the most crazy planet of all and that's Earth. When you head to Earth, you are heading to the most complex planet. Then, you head to different countries, that feature a lot of diversity. Before you know it, you enter a country that has an integrated population of all races, all kinds, and all genders. Most of these races and genders congregate and come face to face in a large city. and that's New York. Now, this sounds irrelevant. the immigrants wouldn't come here if they didn't take chances. You're probably going to ask, What chances did they take when coming here? I have the answer to that question. Years ago, I heard that these immigrants would come to this island before they headed to Ellis Island. This island was the place of sheer worry some. This island would be one of the first places that would determine whether they would stay here or go into the country. If they had a little, treatable infection, they'd be forced to be quarantined here and that individual would be quarantined for life, or sent back to his or her country. So, if they were able to take chances by coming here, why aren't you able to take any chances?" asked Brutis.

"You've brought up a pretty good point. Why did a lot of immigrants come here?" the alien leader asked. "You've got to be kidding me, asking such a frivolous and ridiculous question like that. It is a shame that you would even ask that. Besides, you're supposed to be the so called 'genius' around here. I don't get the fact why you are asking me a question that any Tom, Richard, or Harry can answer. That is totally insane," the alien shape shifter answered. "Thinking about it, I was able to answer the question myself," replied Will.

"Thank you. I don't have to throw my larynx to waste then over such a stupid and ridiculous question," said Brutis. "You're welcome. Now, let's see what pulling up this brick would do," the alien leader replied. He pulled the brick from the ground. Anything did not happen. Thirty-seconds later, nothing happened. Still, a minute later, nothing happened.

"Well, I guess we can continue moving down the trail," the alien leader said. He started walking. All of a sudden the ground started to slightly shake. Every step he had taken, the ground kept on shaking even more. the trail started splitting in half. An 6.9 magnitude Earthquake is taking place on that part of the island. As the seconds progressed, the Earthquake started getting worse and worse. Within a matter of two minutes, the trail started splitting in half.

"What do we do?" Will shouted nervously. "I don't know. You were the one who pulled that brick from the ground. Not me. You think of the solution, genius," Brutis answered in a snooty manner. "Don't be such a smart ass. You were the one who was supposed to help me and now you're going to help me. Listen to me. Just tell me what to do in handling this situation," the alien leader nervously replied.

"Fine. I'll tell you. Slowly remove your legs from the sides of the trail and jump down into the crack. Maybe, the crack will disappear and you'll be able to go down the trail comfortably," the alien shape shifter said. Will did exactly what the shape shifter told him to do. he managed to slide down into the bottom of the crack in the ground that the Earthquake made. Eventually, the crack widened and Brutis jumped down into the Earthquake made crater. "That wasn't so hard," he said.

"I know," the alien leader replied. "Yeah, and what makes it even better is that the crack in the ground widened up and became just as wide as the trail. That must've been some sort of supernatural or occult effect that just took place," the alien shape shifter said. "Oh, definitely. Is that all God had in plan for us?" asked Will. "I would say no. This was probably damaging enough. I know it almost tore my leg muscles. If this is not scary enough, then what is? Being at the center of an Earthquake is a nerve-wracking experience," answered Brutis.

"I know," the alien leader replied. "What do we have ahead of us?" the alien shape shifter asked. "I have no idea, but I know that trouble is probably coming down the road next," answered Will. They continued walking down the trail up to a small beach. The beach is made of clay sand. Yet, the water has a crystal clear appearance. The bizarre beach is only eight by eighteen feet. So, it's basically the size of a small tide pool. The alien leader looked out into the distance to view the morning horizon and the sun. All of a sudden, a small bump from the ocean started to appear. This bump has a quite bizarre appearance. It has a yellow and black appearance. The bump kept getting bigger as it drew closer to the shore. About five hundred feet from the shore, a fully circular window is now able to be seen in view. This bump is no longer considered sa mirage. It is actually a vehicle. The vehicle drew closer to shore and it eventually revealed itself in its entirety. This vehicle is an AEV (Aquatic Exploration Vehicle.) The vehicle eventually hit shore. Brutis and Will are skeptical.

"What the hell is that?" the alien shape shifter asked. "Some sort of an AEV, I think," the alien leader answered. "What's that?" asked Brutis. "It's an Aquatic Exploration Vehicle. These vehicles are like miniature submarines. they can only accomidate one or two individuals instead of twenty or thirty individuals like a submarine can. I don't see anybody in the vehicle. Perhaps, I should knock on it," the alien leader answered.

"If I were you, I'd move slowly towards it. If there is somebody in there or, if there's something unfamiliar in the vehicle, then I would run back up the trail. Personally, I'd just move slowly to the vehicle. How 'bout you tiptoe to the vehicle," the alien shape shifter replied.

"Okay, here it goes," said Will. He moved slowly to the vehicle. Every move he makes is a possible life or death situation. His moves are very silent. He knocked three times on the window of the AEV. Nobody answered. About twenty five seconds later, he knocked on the window once more. Not a single noise is able to be heard. He turned around the window dissintigrated into the Ocean. Suddenly, Mitchell jumped out with an assault rifle. He started firing six bullets at the alien leader and Brutis. "What are you doing? It's me, Brutis," the alien shape shifter said. Mitchell stopped firing his weapon. "Oh, it's you? and who's your friend?" he asked. "He's one of Jacqueline Langyaw's good confidants. Treat him well," answered Brutis. "Say, he looks a little familiar? Wasn't he at the consulate trying to get some sort of a passport or green card?" asked the ex-consulate employee (Mitchell.) "I recall he was trying to do that," the alien shape shifter answered. "Oh yeah, he and Clayton were the ones that I got into a fight with. Is this guy's name Will Von Alien?" asked Mitchell. The alien leader hesitated. One minute later, he gave a false name in order to prevent himself from getting shot. "My name is Wilhelm Von Aleon," he said. "Is that your name?" asked Brutis. The alien leader looked at the ex-consulate employee.

"Can I talk to my buddy, Brutis, for one second?" he asked. "Sure, I won't listen to what you folks have to say. Besides, I'm sure it's not that important to me," answered Mitchell. Will and Brutis walked away from the beach to have a secret conversation. "Now, the reason why I've changed my name is because I recognize this guy. He may look like a laid-off employee. he's not. He's a beast that is working for Jacqueline Langyaw. He is paid by her to kill Light. I'm afraid he's going to kill me because him and I got into a large altercation. That's why he got fired because he acted belligerent towards me. Since, I heard he knows her, I'm afraid that he's going to try and kill me before I reach up to her to rescue Light. We did this whole mission to rescue Light," the alien leader whispered. "I don't think you have to change your name, even if somebody is in front of you with a large assault rifle. Besides, what do you have to hide from some folks?" the alien shape shifter asked.

"I have to hide my identity. If I don't hide my identity, then I'll be in serious trouble. I'll be in the worst situation of my life. It's already bad enough losing two parents right before my eyes. Then, to add insult to injury, I was taken from my home and forced to work as a slave in the galley at the Alien Estate. So, I don't want to get into another ordeal and possibly get shot by some human accomplice of Jacqueline," answered Will. They finished their secret conversation and returned back to beach. "So, do you two want to go up to my treehouse?" asked Mitchell.

"Of course, we do," the alien leader and the shape shifter (Brutis) sarcastically answered. They followed the ex-consulate employee to his secret treehouse. This treehouse is located on the opposite side of the island, and right above the rotten dock. After swimming around the island for fifteen minutes, they finally arrived in front of the treehouse. They climbed up the rope ladder and they finally arrived in the treehouse. This particular treehouse looks like any mundane treehouse. The floors are unpolished. There is no air conditioning nor, is there heat. The books are organized and on top of the bookshelf is a small microscope. "Now, the reason why I came to this island was to talk about a conspiracy plan against Light S. Cycle. We are going to meet Jacqueline Langyaw in order to find him. we will hunt him down and burn him at stake. We'll burn him until all of the metal melts. Then, if we don't burn him, we will imprison him until he rusts and dies. I think that sounds like such a great plan," said Mitchell.

"Did you know that we tricked you into thinking that we were siding with you?" asked Brutis.

"Absolutely not. How dare you do such a thing. We've only known each other for fifteen minutes. You can't do this to me. by Jacqueline's orders, she stated to arrest anybody and bring them to the Council for trial and they will have to stand before her and the other four members of that panel. One of those members is me. I hereby cast a spell on you that I shall Arrest you. *Arrestigitis and Dimensiontravelitis shall take place. Once, I cast this spell on you all, you're mine.* He placed his hands in the form of fists as he casted this spell. He placed them under arrest and he is going to bring them to that beastly former prosecutor.

Chapter XXVII: Skull Castle, Being brought before Jacqueline Langyaw

Brutis, Will, and Mitchell arrived at the Skull Castle. This particular place has a dark and lurid appearance. The Castle features twelve gigantic skulls. This castle has an amorphous shape. The Castle has large broad iron gates. On the top of these gates is a large logo that has Jacqueline Langyaw's initials. The black broad iron gates stand at a staggering thirty feet tall. An orange, lava moat surrounds this castle and there are dozens of large volcanoes that surround this place. Every volcano erupts every 10 to 15 minutes. This Castle features five grey Obelisks. These Obelisks are featured on top of the skulls on the sides. Each Obelisk has its own individual height and each one is ornately decorated with its own symbols. The bottom right Obelisk stands at a staggering 60 feet tall and is decorated with different portrayals showing different points in history for the Templars. The bottom left Obelisk stands at 20 feet tall and shows different hieroglyphics portraying the development of the Mayan Pyramids. The middle right one stands at 70 feet tall and shows carvings that depict the history of Scientific innovation and discovery. Then, the middle left one stands at a gigantic 90 feet tall and shows an idea that depicts carvings of Starmos City under Cornelius's rule. This is to show Jacqueline's worship towards that evil brute. A large carving of Cornelius is shown at the top of that particular one.

Now, the top Obelisk shows Jacqueline Langyaw's malicious ego. This top one stands at 200 feet tall and it has a carving that depicts a carving of her. This carving portrays her making an evil laugh. Her sinister grin shows the evilness that she possesses. The hands in this picture show that she is holding the glass sphere of evil. In this carving, she's wearing leather motorcycle style boots that feature spikes on the top of those boots. This carving also depicts her wearing a black leather gown of evil. In spite of there being no colors in this depicted carving, one would be able to see the colors just by the rough texture of the portrayal. This Castle features a number of turrets.

These turrets are made of stones and bones. These turrets stand at the same heights and on the tops of these turrets are animal skulls. In addition to the animal skulls being featured on the tops of the turrets, there are also triangular flags. These flags wave in the constant twenty five miles per hour winds. Although this castle is obviously not some sort of place occupied by pirates, Jacqueline chose flags that showed symbols that would be featured on pirate ships.

There are seven turrets featured at this castle. Thus, there are seven flags. The first flag depicts a portrayal of the Jolly Roger symbol. Followed by that, the next flag depicts a picture Blackbeard stabbing a heart. The third flag depicts a portrayal of Death holding an hourglass. The other flags have variations of the Jolly Roger Symbol. the eigth flag depicts a picture of Jacqueline's cold-hearted face. Mitchell is standing one thousand feet away from the

Castle on top of a large bridge. This stone bridge is about 1/5 of a mile long. He has the Will and Brutis's hands tied up and ankles chained. They will have to be superstrong in order to escape the bonds that have been secured by the human conspirator, Mitchell.

     "Don't even think about escaping these bonds. If you do that, then you'll be killed. So, don't mess around," he said. He started walking up to the Castle. "How will we be able to escape?" the alien shape shifter asked. "I don't think we should be contriving any escape plans because there's no hope right now, but we may possibly be able to escape through that lava that surrounds this place. Once we escape into that lava, we will be able to go to the Supermassive Volcano. Rumor has it that there's an opening featured in the volcano, which would bring us back to Earth, which would therefore bring us back to Starmos City," the alien leader answered.

     "That sounds like such an ingenious answer. You must've done such a good job planning that," Brutis sarcastically replied. "Thank you for saying that," said Will. "Did you realize that I was being sarcastic with you. I would never do what you do by going into a volcano. Have you lost your mind? Granted, we'll not be able to die, but our insides will be burnt and we'll have fourth degree burns on our skins and there'll be no way that we'll be able to even move with such harsh burns. We'll be able to say that we've swam through lava. we will be paralyzed forever with such harsh burns. There's no way that you'll be able to get me to go into that detrimental lava, even if you paid me to do that," the alien shape shifter said. "Fine. I guess there's no way out of this place. We're going to be stuck in Hell forever. When will we get out," the alien leader screamed. As soon as Will screamed, Mitchell ran back to his two detainees. "What's wrong?" he sarcastically asked. "Nothing's wrong. What's wrong with you?" asked Brutis.

"Shut the Hell up. I'll throw you into this lava pool and then you'll shut the Hell up. So, you better not open your mouth especially when shackled," the human conspirator said. "What makes you think that I am scared of you? You can try and ruin me physically, but emotionally and mentally, I stand strong. and I am much stronger than you and I have much more authority over you. At one time, I worked for Cornelius as his SSGM soldier and in order to be one of those soldiers, you must be super strong and weigh over two hundred pounds. You will never be able to win against me. So, get off of your little ego and put up the white flag and make some sort of truce. Otherwise, there'll be war and this war is going to be the most ugly scene that you will ever see. you're not going to be seeing this scene. Instead, you'll be involved. and at the end of the day, you'll be the one being tossed into the lava. and when the Great Windchill takes place, you'll be frozen in the magma. That's when you'll perish. and I last checked that your ego caused you to loose your job at the consulate. That was when you started your job with Jacqueline. So, now this is my final statement to you. If you start working for that wench, Jacqueline, you have just joined the side of evil. In addition to that, it goes to show that you have always had evil in your callous soul. You just didn't reveal it. when you start working for her and collaborating with her, you have just signed the ticket to Hell and Armageddon. One thing that is certain is that evil shall never win. Evil may try to do malicious harm. evil will never win. The good side shall always fight and show the sheer strength. The reason why some folks join the evil side is because they are weak. They have no strength and they are very insecure. So, they'll go to the furthest extant to prove that they are these tough guys. I am done with those words," the alien shape shifter replied.

"Well. I am going to tell you that your words are completely meaningless and totally pathetic. Now, you and your buddy are going to come with me to the Castle," said Mitchell. He is bringing his two captives to the Skull Castle. They willingly followed him. within 500 feet of the castle, they started resisting and dragging. The human conspirator (Mitchell) stopped.

"You low lives are not doing what I am telling you to do or making you do, rather. You are my prisoners and you are forced to come with me to the castle. You are not allowed to revolt. You try and mess with me, I'll kill you. You better keep walking and not disobey me," he angrily said. He is treating them like they're emotionless. He is treating them like they're creatures or savages when they're not savages. He kicked them and beat them. Since they are shackled, they are defenseless. After brutally beating them, he dragged them to the castle.

He stood before the broad iron gates. Above the broad iron gates are two gargoyles. Gargilliam and Gargallon. Gargilliam is the one with the red eyes and Gargallon is the one with the green eyes. Gargallon has a defensive and more conservative personality but, Gargilliam has a more liberal and open personality. Gargallon has ears that are pointy and Gargilliam has ears that are rounded. "Who dares come here?" Gargallon asked brusquely. "It is I, Mitchell, I am one of the conspirators who is out to kill Light. I work for Jacqueline Langyaw," the ex-consulate employee answered. "Well, where's your proof to show that you work for Jacqueline?" the defensive gargoyle asked. "I don't have any Identification on me because I was never given any. she paid me to help in the kidnapping and murder of Light," answered Mitchell.

"Sorry, you're not allowed to come here. No ID; no entry," replied Gargallon. "Sir, is there any way you can let me in without ID?" the human conspirator asked. "Yeah, you can go back to where you came from," the defensive gargoyle sarcastically answered. "There's no way I can come back. Besides, I can't find any dimension traveling portal. I'd appreciate it if you'd just let me come into the place. I am trust worthy," replied Mitchell.

"No, I don't trust you. and if I did, what prized possessions would you be able to bring. Please, tell me," said Gargallon. "I have two prisoners. These folks were trying to rescue Light from the beloved Cornelius Von Alien. The tall and thin blue one is Will. He is the current leader of Starmos City. He is a sneak and a snoop. He killed Cornelius by poisoning him with so much arsenic. Then, on my right is Brutis. He was a former SSGM soldier. He worked for the Starmos Socialist Governmental Militia and he was nothing but, a phony to the good old government. He only did what he was told what to do. he was really against Cornelius and the socialist government all along. So, he's nothing but a traitor and I think we must bring him to justice. So, I hereby ask you to bring my two detainecs to justice because I feel the only way they'll learn their lessons is if they get punished for their wicked crimes," the human conspirator replied.

"Say, is Starmos City the city that Jacqueline Langyaw came from? Isn't Cornelius Von Alien the ruler of that city?" the defensive gargoyle asked. "The answer to your first question is, Yes. Jacqueline did come from Starmos City. In fact, she didn't just come she made a huge number of accomplishments over there. She made the streets safe and crime free. She was the sole prosecutor of that city and she also made sure that the citizens would honor Cornelius and adore him. She worked as the prosecutor until that beast, Will, arrested her, forced her to plea guilty, and revoked her license. Now, she's a nothing. I don't know if you've been listening to me, but I told you that Cornelius was dead. and Will is not only a beast. he's a murderer and he shall pay for his wicked and soulless crimes. We must destroy the murderers in our society. So, I hereby beg you to let us in and we'll bring him to the proceeding and he'll have to pay for his crimes. and when I bring him and his fellow co-defendant in, justice will be done and Starmos City will be free of monstrosities who want to adulterate the population with despicable behavior especially in the government,"answered Mitchell.

"Tell, you what; I'll talk to my fellow gargoyle about letting you in. Granted, I shouldn't let you in because you don't have any ID, but I think I can grant you some access being that you know Jacqueline so well," replied Gargallon. The human conspirator rolled his eyes and sighed in disgust and frustration. Meanwhile, Gargallon flew to Gargilliam's post. "Gargilliam, I think we should let them in because they seem quite familiar. Besides, they are here to fight for justice and that man knows Jacqueline very well. In addition to that, Mitchell had the guts to bring two malicious prisoners to the castle. That takes a lot of strength and endurance. I don't think one individual would be able to do such a thing very easily," the defensive gargoyle said. "Well, may I just tell you my intake on this?" asked Gargilliam. "Sure," answered Gargallon "Now, I disagree with you on this. There are a couple reasons why my opinion is like this. Granted, I have a more liberal approach on folks that are entering. I am not going to be liberal in this case. First of all, a sick, twisted human is supporting injustice because I saw on XOF news that Jacqueline, Cornelius, and his crazy alien army of SSGM soldiers invaded Earth and brutalized the humans. They even attempted to mutilate the humans because they wanted to stunt their growth by putting them inside of capsules. Second of all, I feel that Mitchell is untrustworthy because I don't think he is going to be fair with his detainees. I saw in the distance that he was beating them and dragging them over here. That's just plain sick and evil. Then, he claims that he wants to fight for justice. Meanwhile, he's supporting injustice and cruelty. That's just plain evil and disgusting," the liberal gargoyle replied.

"Let me just tell you these three things. I am in a higher position than you are. My opinions override yours. Basically, I am the one who makes the ultimate decisions and at the end of the day, I decide who is allowed entry and who is not allowed entry. Secondly, that man has a ton of proof and he does have probable cause to enter this place. and it seems to me that he knows Jacqueline so well that he practically lives with her. Thirdly, he is actually here to fight for justice. He is bringing a murderer and traitor to justice. My final words are this. You are not allowed to tell me what to do. You may be my friend, but friends cannot tell friends how to work or in this case, who to let in or who not to let in. I am overriding your opinion and I am letting them in," said Gargallon.

"Remember, what you sew comes back to haunt you. I believe you're sewing a bad seed. Just remember the words that I am saying," replied Gargilliam. "Yeah, whatever," the defensive gargoyle said. He flew back to his post and stared at the conspirator and his detainees. He looked at Mitchell and is prisoners. "I don't say this to often but, I don't let too many people come into this castle. today is the day where I shall be more loose and less defensive. As head Gargoyle guard of this castle, I'll hereby let Mitchell and his two prisoners into the Skull Castle and he should therefore be escorted to Jacqueline," he said.

He slowly opened the large gates. Two minutes later, the gates are fully open. Mitchell dragged his prisoners into the Skull Castle. This Castle features a large cobblestone road that has the appearance of the road to death being that the cobblestones are extremely uneven. All of a sudden a black stagecoach pulled up in front of the human conspirator and his detainees. Mitchell tried opening the door and it wouldn't open.

"What's this?" he asked himself. The stagecoach zoomed away from the detainees and he. "What kind of place is this?" the alien leader asked. "Did I not tell you to Shut the Hell up? Have you lost your mind? There's something wrong with you because when I threaten you, you must listen to me. If you don't listen to me, then you'll have to suffer the potential consequences of death or severe torture. You don't want that to happen to you. At least, I don't believe you want such a thing like that to happen to you," the human conspirator arrogantly answered.

"Do you think I am scared of you? I am willing to fight you right now. Come on, throw a punch at me," replied Will. "Are you sure you want me to do that?" asked Mitchell. "Yeah, in two minutes," the alien leader answered. He always carries a pocketknife to make sure that he can cut through certain objects. He reached his head to his right jeans pocket to grab the pocketknife. He pulled a metallic pocketknife out of his front pocket.

He is biting the sharp object. He placed his tied up hands to the knife and cut the rope in half. He freed himself from the hand bonds. Mitchell turned back around. He noticed that the alien leader freed himself from the hand bonds. An angry appearance is seen in his face. His (Mitchell's) face is turning red and his eyes are widening. The lines and veins in the forehead popped out due to the high adrenaline.

"What do you think you're doing? Do you think you're trying to be some sort of hot shot trying to fool me? Who the Hell do you think you are you sick bastard?" he furiously asked. He lunged at Will and grabbed him in a chokehold. The alien leader kicked Mitchell in the chest and started punching him. "You don't know the damage I can do," he nonchalantly said. "I'll never listen to you because all you do is trick others to get yourself out of a situation. You think you know everything when you don't. I can't stand folks like you," the human conspirator replied.

"You are telling me that I am deceptive and evil when you are disgusting and evil. I never started in with you. You were the one that started in with me. You didn't have to arrest me and bring me to this lurid place. If you would've just let Brutis and I go, we would never be in such an evil situation," the alien leader said. "Well, if you didn't start in with Cornelius and you didn't try to rebel, none of this would happen. Our lives would've been normal," replied Mitchell. "Well, if he didn't kill my parents and if he didn't have a Socialist and tyrannical government, then none of this would've happened. We would've lived in a very peaceful, worry-free place. because he had abominations like you, Jacqueline, and he, Starmos City was evil, but the primary reason why I took over Starmos City was in revenge for what he did to my parents and he definitely deserved to die for committing that wicked crime against humanity," said Will.

"You are forbidden to act so bold and blunt with me. I am your captor and you are to respect me. If you don't respect me, then it's my prerogative to kill you. So, you better learn how to behave yourself and keep yourself in line. Your behavior is so intolerable," replied Mitchell.

"Do you think I would listen to a jackass like you?" the alien leader asked. "Well, if I was you, I would say 'yes' because you were warned that you would be killed. the true answer that I would probably be thinking is 'no.' The reason why I would figure that is because you are nothing but a stubborn, little idiot. You are so quick to revolt instead of listening to others," the human conspirator answered.

"Excuse me. You are telling me that I am not open and that I am ignorant when you're the most ignorant one of all. For God sakes, you're rejecting two aliens for green cards, just because they're aliens. As alien leader, I welcome you humans into our city and we treat your kind with a ton of honor and respect. That's one way to show that I am not ignorant or stubborn. In addition to that, I am not like that old tyrant Cornelius, who had tiles of himself all over the walls of the Alien Estate. I don't have an ego like he has. Instead, I gave five tiles to every citizen in Starmos City; and each tile has been signed with that individual's name. This is another way to show that I am open minded, the total opposite of rank ignorance or stubborn behavior. Unlike you, I listen instead of handcuff," the alien leader angrily replied.

"Like I said earlier, do you realize that I have the right to kill you without getting in trouble for a crime?" asked Mitchell. "Maybe you won't be criminally punished by the law. you will be punished by God. In life, everybody will come face to face with him and he will determine your fate in the afterlife. I want to tell you that at one time, I was an Atheist. I was basically a nonbeliever. The reason why was because I was under a forcefully Stalinist control of that ol' brute and there was no way the schools that I've attended would be able to teach religion. In fact, I didn't know what religion was. when I met God, I was taught about the true beliefs of Christianity and I became a Christian. I wasn't baptized; I've never been to church. religion is not all about going to church. In fact, Christianity is not even a religion; it's a philosophy. If you convert to Christianity, then, you'll be saved, but unlike Cornelius, I am not forceful on my ways of life or religious beliefs or non-beliefs. I let folks make their own decisions in what religion that that individual or individual(s) want to practice. I believe that every individual born in all planets, universes, or dimensions have certain rights. One of those rights is the right to free practice of religion as long as it is not fundamentalist or universally considered illegal or immoral. So, you can kill me but, whatever you sew will come back to haunt you and what you sew will determine your fate," answered Will.

"Good point. Now, can you turn around for about thirty seconds?" the human conspirator asked. "Sure, as long as it's not some sort of trick or use of deception," the alien leader answered.

"Oh. I'm not here to deceive you. I tricked you all along, you see I am here to take you on a more circuitous route to Starmos City," replied Mitchell. He lied through his teeth when he said this. Even though the alien leader hesitated, he just turned around and followed Mitchell's orders. Mitchell pulled another piece of rope out of his pocket and tied the alien leader's hands together once more. he tied them tighter than earlier to make sure that there would be no possible chance of escape.

"My job is done," he said. "Hey, you said that you weren't going to trick me. How dare you do such a thing! I ought to kill you," Will angrily replied. "Well, let me just tell you this. I don't think you remember what happened earlier, but I have a clear recollection as to what happened. I remember when you tried to deceive me. So, in return, I deceived you. Sorry, you deserved it. Don't deceive your peers," the human conspirator arrogantly said.

"Fine. I give up trying to escape. Face it, there's no way out of here. For Godsakes, the place is surrounded by lava, there's no way I can get out of here without being burnt in the scorching, scathing, searing, mind-numbing heat! In addition to that, it would be quite hard trying to find a portal to get back home," the alien leader replied.

"Thank you. You finally learned to be practical. You are finally learning not to think that you're a know-it-all," Mitchell said in a snobby and despicable manner. He continued dragging his two prisoners up the stairs of the Skull Castle. There are six, stone marble stairs that lead up to the broad-iron doors of the castle. The human conspirator dragged his prisoners up the stairs. The alien leader and Brutis sustained little bumps and bruises. they weren't critical injuries. They will be in stable condition.

"Why do you act in the most cruel way possible? What drives you to this point of committing such vile acts of evil and malice?" the alien shape shifter asked.

"Throughout my life, I have always been predestined for evil. You see, when I was younger, I was born with mental problems and behavioral problems. When I was born, I grew up as an orphan because my parents threw me out of the house because I constantly cried as an infant. So, I was sent to the orphanage on Murphy Boulevard. In the orphanage, I did what any other typical orphan would do. I was well-educated and fairly treated by the director of the orphanage, but the kids were mean to me at this orphanage. So, when I was about twelve years of age, I left a note at the orphanage. I remember the exact wording of the note.

In fact, I always keep a copy of this note written in my pocket. I wrote this note to Mrs. Adams, who was the orphanage director. Like any other note or letter, I would adress the name. I wrote the important part of the note. I remember what I had written word for word," answered Mitchell. He pulled the note out of his pocket. The note stated:

To Mrs. Adams,

I am not here to write you an essay; I am here to write an important note. I don't think you've realized what happened, but I have been bullied here by many of my fellow orphans. The bullying was just plain mean and nasty. Granted, my behavior has not been the best behavior, but I have tried to control it. I would like it if my fellow orphans would accept me for who I am. I do not want to stay here any longer because the students have been nasty to me. That's the prime reason as to why I am leaving this place and I do have the right to leave in four years, but my departure will be a little early. I am sorry, but I was basically told that I had to leave based on the feedback that I have been receiving from my fellow orphans.
Sincerely,

Mitchell.

He read the note out loud as he looked at it. "Oh my God, that's so terrible that you had to live in an orphanage.

What was life like after the orphanage?" asked Will. "My
life was a roller coaster after the orphanage. and I am not
talking about the good roller coaster. My life was
tumultuous. From ages 12-18, I scavenged through
dumpsters and trash cans. Some folks would come up to me
and ask if I had parents. Unfortunately, I had to lie to them
so that way I wouldn't be sent to juvenile hall or back to the
orphanage to deal with the bullies. When I was 14, I
enrolled myself in high school. Because of my behavioral
problems, I would often land myself in detention. I
graduated in the top of my class and I made sure that I
would pass the tests in order to get into College. As a result,
I was accepted to a CUNY school for government and
international relations. That was when I started working at
the small consulate, but while I was working there, I would
act impetuous and stupid. Sometimes I would have anger
management problems and I'd lash out at other employees.
That was when I was on a forced leave of absence and I
was sent to a mental asylum. I spent about three years there
taking medication and shock therapy. I was welcomed back
to my job. For thirty years after that, I remained calm at my
job, but even in the workplace, I was bullied and not being
paid enough money. That was when I decided to work for
Jacqueline as a side job. She paid me to be her part time
body guard. I willingly did the job. In addition to that, she
made me feel like I was welcome. None of my co-workers
at the consulate made me feel welcome. She made me feel
great and she taught me how to be superior to all. When
you came to my workplace and Commissioner Clayton
asked for a green card for temporary citizenship, I denied
you the right to a green card and I regret being like that. I
was fired from my job. So, I decided to get back at you and
Light in revenge. Eventually, after being fired from my job,

I snuck back to Swinburne Island and built my own treehouse for entertainment that would divert my mind from the sheer boredom and humiliation of being fired from a job especially due to the bad behavior that I can't help," the human conspirator answered. "I can understand what you went through but, did you ever think that your side was the totally evil side? Did you realize that she caused evil?" the alien leader asked.

"Absolutely not. and I don't think she's evil. She's my idol," answered Mitchell. "I don't think you should idolize somebody like that," replied Will.

"I think you should learn how to mind your own damn business. By the way, everything I said about the orphanage and me having behavioral and mental problems was false; I just wanted you to join my side and be evil. I think being evil is amazing. I am free to do whatever I want and at least I don't have to deal with that crazy boss from my old workplace. I don't care to join the good side and I enjoy being evil. And, there's nothing you can do about it. The reason why I told you this story was because I knew that you had a soft spot and I was trying to deceive you. and I did my job. So, I really don't care if you believe me because at this point, your day is done. You are my captive now. So, it's tough luck for you. and I am out to kill Light. That whole story that I just told was false. I did work at that workplace for a couple of years," the human conspirator said. "It is a shame that you tried to make me weaken my heart for a malevolent beast like you. You are disgusting and you ought to be ashamed of your attitude. You should be ashamed of the fact that you're a pathological liar. I didn't think you were lying because you had a serious demeanor. I can't believe you just lied. I only lied very few times and that was to only save my skin from evil," the alien leader replied.

"Now, shut your mouth because I need to talk to Jacqueline," said Mitchell. He reached his arm up to the door knocker. The door knocker has the head of an Asiastic lion. The door knocker has a stentorian voice. "Who dares enter the hallowed Skull Castle?" it asked.

"It is I, Mitchell. I must enter. I am Jacqueline Langyaw's human conspirator," answered Mitchell. "Can you prove to me that you are a conspirator?" the talking knocker asked. "I don't exactly have any proof because she never gave me any written proof or identification," the human conspirator answered. "I don't care. That is not any probable cause for you to enter this royal castle. You must show me some proof to say that you know Jacqueline," the talking knocker replied.

"Listen, I don't have any proof. I didn't need any proof to go past the gates. and those gates are pretty hard to get past those gates," said Mitchell. "I don't care. It's my prerogative to determine who is allowed to enter the Skull Castle and who is not allowed to enter the castle. I don't need to explain to you why I am not letting you in. I can ask Jacqueline to come to you. I'll call her to the door," the door knocker replied. He called for the beastly female prosecutor to come straight to the door and she willingly did so. She asked about who is at the door and the talking door knocker answered that Mitchell is standing at the door. She opened the door and realized that her human conspirator and his two prisoners are present. She is wearing a black gown. This gown has a similar appearance to a vampire costume. Her face has a wan appearance because of all the makeup she's wearing. Her lips have the color of scarlet red. Her hair is black and curly, a far cry from the hair on the old television show of *Tough Jackie.* Her eyes have a lot of eyeliner. She is wearing a black gown that is twenty five feet long. The gown is also eight feet in diameter. She is wearing platform shoes. She is holding a spear in her right hand. This spear has a six inch long sharp point and the spear has a red tip at the end of that point. This shows her scarlet, evil attitude. In spite of her feminine attire, she has an attitude of a tom boy. For instance, rather than having guards fight her battles for her, she will fight her own battles on her own. Granted, she is a great fighter, but she doesn't fight for goodness and righteousness.

Instead, she fights for evil and injustice. Malice runs through her sinister soul and she is a callous and egotistical woman. She looked at Mitchell and showed a great deal of respect towards him. she looked at his prisoners; she smirked in a cynical manner; and she looked down at them. She showed disdain towards Brutis and looked at him with lowered eyebrows. Her lips tightened and anger is running rampant through her body. She is about to lash out at him and show a great deal of fury towards him. She has a facial expression that shows mortification and shame. Along with that, she is extremely livid because her intuition tells her that he was a traitor. and she was right. Brutis and Will are going to be seeing the lady who is of the devil up close and personal.

Chapter XXVIII: Will and Brutis are brought before the large group of the Skull Castle Council

Jacqueline is infuriated at Brutis. She is looking at him with disgust and anger. She stared at him with eyes as wide as bug eyes. She looks like a daughter of Satan. Brutis is not showing any expression or reaction of Jacqueline's evil behavior. He is just looking at her and doesn't even give a care in the world. On the other hand, and Will is extremely nervous. He is grinding his teeth and twiddling his fingers quite quickly.

He is shaking and sweating. He looks like he is about to faint. He's so nervous that he can't even close his eyes or even blink. His blue eyes are drying up quite quickly. Mitchell is the complete opposite of Will. He is smiling in the most sinister way possible for three reasons. He is primarily happy that he deceived the alien leader and Brutis. Secondly, he is happy that he had the ability to bring his two captives from Earth to Skull Castle.

Thirdly, he is happy that Jacqueline is infuriated with Brutis because he is assuming that she'll treat him harsher than Will. She is staring at all three of them, particularly at Mitchell's two detainees. "What are you going to do about it?" the alien leader boldly asked. She slammed her staff on the stone floor. "Shut up," she angrily answered.

"You have no right to speak. You are nothing but, a stupid criminal and you have no rights around here. So, you better learn not to mess around with me because I don't clown around. If you want to act like a fighter, you will be killed. If you want to act bold, you will be killed. If you want to commit crimes, be prepared to either go to the dungeon or to the plantation to work. If you want to side with the humans, then you also go to the plantation because there are a ton of humans on this plantation and I don't think you want to be there especially during the summer. Spending your summers on the plantations is a living Hell and I don't think you want to be living in Hell."

"Can I ask why do you behave the way you do?" asked Brutis. "Well, I've always been in love with Cornelius. I felt that he was the most honorable and respectable fellow. He was able to build buildings with the simple drop of a brick or cube. That would be extremely hard for any ordinary human or alien folk to do. Cornelius was the one who brought justice to the citizens of Starmos City and he made sure that every citizen would have been treated fairly. He ensured that everybody had an education and a house or an apartment to live in. He would grant freedom of enterprise and freedom of speech. In addition to that, he gave freedom of the press. If you want to see the true definition of a fair leader, look at Cornelius Von Alien. He is the most fair leader of all," the Queen of the Skull (Jacqueline) answered. "I object to your statements. They are quite fallacious. and if you are going to say that you were mislead or misguided, you are a huge liar. He was the most evil leader; he was definitely dishonorable and totally disrespectable. If you want to know a really good leader, it would be me. It seems that I have an ego. I do not have an ego. If I had an ego, I would be fighting for my own justice and not for the justice of the citizens of Starmos City. Cornelius did not grant anybody freedom of speech. One day, my colleague and I were talking about him behind his back because he was nasty and he found out and he threatened to sentence me to ten years in the hole. That was sick. Another time when Cornelius showed his evil powers was when he banned XOF News from coming to Starmos City. The reason why was because he knew that they were going to expand the alien city and he didn't want Starmos City to expand. He also felt that humans should not have been allowed to pay a visit because he felt that they would try and implement the ideas of true democracy. and talk about justice, that brute was the epitome of injustice. He supported the idea of bigotry and slavery and that is the most wrong idea that one can ever support. this was Cornelius's idea. In addition to that, he supported Stalinism, which was a sick method of evil that a communist dictator used to hurt or ruin his people. Cornelius follows that idea because he will kill any political dissenters, in particular my parents. That was also sick. So, you can believe that Cornelius was the great leader. You can believe that he was the most honest leader of establishing a beautiful city. the question that is often asked is did he start that city to develop a large, unpopulated desert, or did he have another trick up his sleeve and was that to spread Stalinism and Communism? I believe he started Starmos City to support and spread Stalinism and Communism," said the alien leader.

"Your ideas are totally sick and wrong. Cornelius was the best and he should go down in respect. How dare you dishonor a dead one! and he is not just some ordinary

dead one. He was thee one who created the place that
you're living in. He was the one that brought your parents
jobs. He was the one that brought you a job and you're
showing a great deal of disrespect towards him? How could
you? You ought to be ashamed of yourself. Anybody with a
right mind wouldn't do such a thing. I guess that you don't
have a right mind. You are insane like I'd figured. and your
insanity made you the alien leader. Along with being
insane, you are also rebellious and cynical. You think who
you are. It is absurd how you think you can just trick the
officers at the front of California County, free the humans,
bring Cornelius and I to jail, and then kill Cornelius. If I
was to say the definition of the worst individual in all
dimensions, you would be on the picture of the definition in
the dictionary. His government was the best government in
all of the dimensions, universes, and planets and an
anarchist like you had to ruin it; a rebellious beast like you
had to pollute Starmos City with a bunch of evil. That is
just plain wrong and I ought to shank you. I am not.
Instead, I am going to punish you in a fair way. Prosecutors
have to be fair; so, I am going to be fair with you. I want to
kill you, but I can't because all of your stupid allies are
going to try to wage war with me. Now, while you're here,
the old Starmos government is coming back from the dead.
I sent King Haggoth from Debilinare, and he will take over
the government as the acting leader of Starmos City until I
come back and while he's leader, he will cut off all ties with
the Earthlings and the Garden City folks. Once he does
that, he will close down the Starmos station and ban all
LSC's from coming into the city. In addition to that, he'll
kill all aliens that are of blue skin pigment. So, there's no
way you can even enter Starmos City. In addition to that, he
is planning on killing humans and mixed aliens. He will

also close down the Star Hotel and all of the businesses. This leader is going to bring back the old order and the citizens will be living in misery like they are supposed to be living in. Granted, my city will look like a Utopia. it will be a dystopian society like its supposed to be. Stalinism will be revived; the courtrooms are going to run the way they're supposed to be and I am not talking about a trial by a twelve alien impartial jury. I am talking about a five minute court proceeding and a sentencing to life in the hole without parole. King Haggoth will be the best ruler in Starmos City because he will bring order instead of ruckus. He will bring absolutism instead of fairness. and most of all, he will respect the true meaning of Starmos City, unlike you. You have no respect towards anything; you just want to either adulterate or change. That is ridiculous and I feel that things should be traditional. The traditional government was the best government and you're government would collapse in a heartbeat. So, the hell with your ideas. It's King Haggoth's and my ideas that count. I am done. You can speak if you want to test my patience," the arrogant former prosecutor replied.

"Let me just tell you that what you're saying is totally fallacious, arrogant, and despicable. First of all, you are not a fair prosecutor even if you tried to be. You are so bigoted it's not even funny. It's not funny that you're bigoted to begin with. You are so quick to lynch the defendant without listening to all the facts of what happened. That shows your rank ignorance and bias attitude. That is despicable. Second of all, you are literally making me sick to my stomach. I am chained up by this monstrosity and you have to say things that I hate that are coming true right now as we speak. That is just plain sick and wrong. I don't think you can get any evil. and I don't even know who the King of Debelinaire is and nor do I care to know because he is in the furthest dimension away from my dimension. He has nothing to do with Starmos City until now. You somehow must know him through a crazy connection and that is just plain arrogant that you know him. I didn't know that he could be just as evil as Cornelius. and what is he doing in my city? Is he trying to cause some sort of war? I don't know about you, but I am not going to give up. My city is not going to go down without a battle. The citizens of my own skin color will not be sent to death camps or any place that has to do with death! Any mixed alien that came from another place will be welcome here and if you have a problem with integration of different citizens, then leave. Besides, I don't want you in Starmos City. For the transient time that I was leader, I intended on changing my city and making it better. I intended on building a liberal society for my citizens. As leader, I have tried to be rid every reminisce of Cornelius and the old regime. Unfortunately, you had a vendetta against me. You are trying to be cruel with me. I was fair with you, but I guess I didn't know the real you, but now I know that you were a beast. I should've never suggested to your assistant to offer you a plea deal because you didn't deserve one. You were just as evil as Cornelius. I should've treated you the same and made you go to trial. I should've poisoned you along with poisoning him. There was one lesson that I learned out of this though. That lesson was not to be too fair to somebody who you don't really know. I knew Cornelius and I had a right to be fairer with him. there wasn't a single way that I could've been fairer. I allowed him to be tried before a twelve member jury of his peers and he was rightfully convicted. Before I took over Starmos City, he would just sentence his criminals immediately without them having a say in the proceeding and every criminal would be sentenced to life in the hole without parole and that was just plain sick. As leader, I would've gotten rid of the hole and only used it for folks who committed really wicked crimes like crimes against humanity, false imprisonment, or felony murder. Cornelius just sentenced anybody who he wanted whenever he felt like it. This is one way to show that he was a tyrant. I am not going to give up. Haggoth may rule for a short amount of time, but I guarantee that he will never rule for as long as Cornelius. For, I will encourage the citizens to rebel and I will send the Earthlings and the citizens of Garden City to come in and crush the tyrannical government of Haggoth. Not only will I crush a tyrant's leadership. I will crush you and anybody who's associated with you. I will make sure that all of the belligerents go to trial and get sentenced accordingly to their role in the revival of the old alien Stalinist dictatorship and freedom and justice will take place," said Will.

"You are not going to do such a thing because I'll kill you, your friends, or any of your confidants before they even get a chance to take a look at Starmos City. I will marry Haggoth and we will rule together and I will have a strong say in the Starmos government. Once I have the say, your city, or I should say, my city will have the stringent principles that are necessary. If I put stringent principles, there will be order. For the two days that you've ruled, ruckus has taken place. A city is not supposed to be run in that type of way. A city is supposed to have order and refinement. A city is supposed to be organized. When you were ruling, tons of citizens and non-citizens came in and out of the city. That was quite unfair and ridiculous. You shouldn't have too many citizens. I don't think you are intelligent to understand this, but I am sure you've heard of Charles Darwin. He said that certain places get overpopulated. If you keep Starmos Station open, then the city will get overpopulated and that ought not be. Instead, close off my city to the outside world. In addition to that, the overpopulation led to the increase of traffic. Now, instead of there being one hundred LSCs on the road, there are six or seven hundred of those. That's a ridiculously high number and half of those LSCs are owned by mixed aliens or blue aliens. That is not fair. The blue aliens and the mixed aliens were the ones that caused the problems and so I feel that it's necessary to kill them to prevent our society from going downhill. Another thing that makes me sick is that you are making alliances with a group that has always hated us aliens. The humans hated us because we drove in different vehicles. By becoming allies with the Earhlings, Starmos City just started heading down tobacco road. You wanted to become allies with monstrosities and beasts. So, I don't think you did anything good by being the leader of Starmos City. Haggoth would know how to enforce the law. He would know what is right and what is wrong. He would know how to treat the aliens. and he would know how to control relations with the outside World," argued Jacqueline. "You know something, you're right. I guess that my leadership was wrong. So, I will not make any fight for any of the alien citizens. They will just have to deal with the problems themselves," the alien leader said. The Queen of Skull Castle(Jacqueline) snickered in a sinister manner.

"Finally, you gave up. I finally knocked some sense into you. Now, I will have Mitchell bring you and Brutis into the castle and you will be brought to the place where you'll be detained before sentencing," she said.

Mitchell handed the chain to the queen and she dragged them down a long dark corridor. Imagine two innocent prisoners being dragged down a cold, hard stone floor. Just imagine that. The floor is made of uneven stones. In addition to that, the ceilings in this corridor are poorly maintained. There are cracks in the stucco ceilings and water is seeping through the cracks almost forming stalagmites. "What are you doing with us?" asked Brutis.

"I am taking you to a place that will be grandiose," the tyrannical Queen sarcastically answered. "Well, why are you treating us like evil creatures even though you are taking us to a place that is grandiose?" asked Will. "Do you realize that I was just being sarcastic to your friend? I would never even take you to a place that is so grandiose. I am taking you to a stone, cold cell. Once you go to the cell, that's when you'll be able to be in some form of comfort," Jacqueline answered in a condescending manner. She continued dragging her two prisoners down the long, dark corridor. As she continued dragging the prisoners, mantles of candles were seen on the walls. The candles brought some light but, not too much light. The place still has a lurid appearance and a scary vibe.

"What made you act the way you are?" the alien leader asked. The evil former prosecutor stopped dragging her two detainees. She lunged at Will and started choking him for thirty-seconds. After choking him, she started punching him and kicking him. She retrieved her staff and pointed it at the alien leader. "I don't think you want to die right now or get seriously injured. I don't think you would be able to sustain such an injury. So, you better be on your best behavior. Don't be a smart ass with me and I won't kill you or beat you," she angrily said. She continued dragging her two prisoners all the way to the cell. This cell had an ugly appearance. The cell featured an iron door that is twelve feet tall and six inches thick. The door is securely bolted and nailed into place. The door also features bars that feature a slide. This slide is only used to keep the detainees quiet at night. All detainees would only stay here for a temporary amount of time. This eight by eight foot cell would be able to accommodate a capacity of 20 detainees. She tossed Will and Brutis in the cell. The cell not only has a scary door and a small size.

The conditions on the inside are gruesome. There are no windows. All the prisoner(s) can see are a bunch of large prison blocks.

These prison blocks have a similar appearance of giant cobblestones The floor is also hard. As a punishment, the floor would often rise to three feet below the top of the ceiling. This is so that way the detainees wouldn't try and escape. Also, being that the room is featured in the basement of the Skull Castle, floods would often take place. Although the cracks between the prison blocks have been sealed off, Jacqueline told the architect to leave one crack open to allow the cell to flood.

She deliberately wanted the cell to flood so that way the prisoners would really be tortured. The alien leader and Brutis have been unchained when they were forced into the cell. After that, the sound of the slam of the prison door was heard. Jacqueline slammed the iron door and she bluntly left the cell. To make matters worse, the alien leader and the alien shape shifter (Brutis) can't complain or rebel because they have been intimidated to the point where fear is instilled into their systems. They don't know what's going to happen. Yet, they want to rebel. They are going to try and contemplate a plan to try and escape from this lurid and harsh place. "I don't know about you, but I want to find some way to escape this place. There's definitely no way that I am planning on staying here forever," the alien shape shifter said.

"I totally agree with you. In fact, I want to be able to come up with the escape plan. there must be some sort of way that we can be discreet," replied Will. ", and how would you expect us to do that?" asked Brutis. "I will try and see a hallway that leads us to the outside of the castle. and then we find Light. I think that sounds like a brilliant idea. Don't you?" the alien leader asked.

"Absolutely not. We must rescue Light first, re-boost his energy and make him like the strong LSC that he was a while ago," the alien shape shifter answered. "You know something. You bring up a pretty good point. we can't plan on rescuing Light right now. We must rescue ourselves first; and then we must rescue him," replied Will.

"How would you expect us to do that?" asked Brutis. "There are only two ways out of here. It's either being covert through the door or, being forceful and killing a few folks," the alien leader answered. "Well, can you explain those plans better? I couldn't quite understand them," the alien shape shifter asked.

"Well, you see the only way we will be able to escape through this door is if we test the bars to see if they're rusted. If they are rusted, then we will get a long piece of string from our clothing and cut through the bars. Will, jump through and be covert in finding Light. Now, I thought of another way to escape this place. I know that Jacqueline will eventually have to open this door to bring us to sentencing, and right at the moment of when she arrives at the door, we will both lunge at her and start choking her. I meant I will be choking her. You will help me push her to the ground because I am not that strong.

After you help me push her, you will stall the guards that are trying to go after me. You will beat those guards up. If you are not strong enough to beat up a number of guards at once, then our plan is screwed and we will have to come up with another plan to escape this wicked place," the alien leader answered.

"I hope you don't think that I sound demeaning when I say this because I don't mean to be demeaning or degrading towards you. I hate to burst your bubble, but there's no way that your plan is going to work. First of all, I don't think we'll be able to cut through those metal bars. I believed that Jacqueline customized those bars not to rust and this castle is new. It's not old like all the other castles. Don't expect the metal over here to rust immediately especially the metallic bars. So, there's no way that you'll be able to cut through those bars with a simple string. You would need a giant cable wire to cut through those bars. I don't think that'll even work. Second of all, your plan will not work by using force. I can tell you that this castle is equipped with super strong guards. Granted, half of them are a bunch of mercenaries, but a number of those guards are a bunch of well trained volunteers. In fact, some of those guards are probably former SSGM soldiers. From my past history of being in the Starmos militia, I knew that the soldiers would have to be very muscular and tall to join the army; and this is according to Cornelius. I believe that Jacqueline is a female version of that old tyrant. She'll probably have this whole place armed with guards just in case of any ruckus especially coming from the prisoners. So, basically, I don't think any of your plans are going to work. There's no way that we can be covert and there's definitely no way that we can use any force because this woman and her guards are monstrosities," replied Brutis.

"You're right. I guess we're doomed here," Will said in a melancholy manner. "I know I'm right. It is a shame that we can't escape. It is quite evil how this beastly woman is treating us like monsters when we're not monsters. We're just revolutionaries who were in the pursuit for justice. We didn't want to curtail and give in to evil. We wanted to make sure that everybody had freedom. And, we totally failed. We should've never even failed. We should've just continued fighting and never gave up, but no we had to be hindered by that callous creature, Mitchell. We had to go down that Red Trail on that island and we had to go down the wrong path with that phony human. That was not only my mistake. The other mistake was that I had the compassion to ask him about why he acted the way he did and about his youth hood. That was also stupid on my part because I didn't know that he was going to be a liar. And, me being the stupid individual, I started feeling bad for him. Then, at the moment where I started showing some empathy he outright admitted to lying and he did this with great zeal. That's just plain wrong. None of this would've happened if I didn't revolt against Cornelius and made his plan backfire on him. If I just would've not rebelled and remained a fugitive, these ordeals would've not even have happened. If I didn't overthrow him and kill him, Jacqueline would've been quite happy and she would've probably left me alone. and I don't think we'd be here right now. We'd probably be safe and home in California County or Starmos City. I guess I am a total failure and loser. It doesn't make any sense continuing. I am probably going to put up my white flag and say, 'I give up. I surrender," the alien leader remorsefully said. "You don't have to be sorry for anything. It was Cornelius and that wench who had the warped minds. They are the ones that should be ashamed of themselves. You shouldn't have to be ashamed of yourself. In fact, you deserve to be proud of yourself. I am much bigger than you and I would never have the guts to stand up against a beastly dictator like Cornelius. That is just impressive enough. You also got a lot done in two days of being in office. Granted, the first day was not really considered as a full day in office. You made sure that there'd be a fair justice system. Before you took over, a criminal would stand before Cornelius and be sentenced to life in the hole without parole. That is just plain crazy. You established laws for certain crimes. In addition to that, you made sure that all criminals would be entitled to a fair trial by an impartial jury that is made up of twelve aliens. You also set rules for judges that they are to give criminals fair sentences within the guidelines. You did a lot of fair things just in that realm alone. You also had plans to revive the Star Hotel and the reservoir. I also heard that you've opened up a train station for those who can't afford an LSC. That's an excellent accomplishment because you brought Starmos City to all dimensions and the world.

That is just amazing enough. So, don't say that you're going to give up or surrender because surrendering is not my option. We mustn't surrender especially against some beastly tyrant, who commits wicked crimes. Will, maybe you aren't so good at contriving escape plans. you're good at a number of other things. So, you shouldn't be so quick to put yourself down and knock yourself. In fact, you shouldn't knock yourself. You definitely deserve a pat on the back for your excellence and heroism. I can assure you that I wouldn't be tenacious and strong like you. I would never be able to have the ability to do that," the alien shape shifter replied. It is now high tide on the outside of the castle. The lava is slightly rising. a slight rising of lava would cause the cell to partially flood. Besides, the cell would be used as some sort of a drain. Will felt a burning sensation on the right part of his neck. He looked up and realized that something quite unusual is taking place.

"Oh my God. The lava is leaking into this cell. We definitely must find some way to get out of here because I am not planning on staying here to be buried in any magma or get fourth degree burns with lava. We must find some way to get the hell out of here," he said. "You know something. I am tired of this place too. It's one thing for two aliens to be placed in an eight by eight foot cell. it's another thing to be stuck in some sort of a torture chamber or even malevolent death trap. We must find a way to get out of here," replied Brutis.

"Well, what would you do?" asked Will. "Just start banging on the door like crazy," the alien shape shifter answered. He and Will walked up to the metallic door and placed their hands in fists. They started banging in a boisterous and crazy manner. Within a matter of thirty seconds, Jacqueline arrived at the door. She opened the door. "What the hell is going on in here? Do you morons have anything better do in your pathetic lives?" she snobbishly asked.

"I would appreciate it if you would've listened to us and didn't talk to us like that," the alien leader said. "Fine, then. What do you want to tell me before I take you to the council for sentencing?" the former arrogant female prosecutor asked. "I don't want to be placed in a cell that has scorching hot lava that comes down from the volcanoes," answered Will. "Well, I wasn't on planning on keeping you here for long. This place is only for detainees that are awaiting sentencing. Now, I want you and your friend to come out of this cell without resisting and follow me down to the council room. I will talk to the members of the council to decide your sentencing. She chained the prisoners' ankles and marched them down the corridor all the way to the room of the council. They walked past three large doors. The council room is at the end of the corridor. Jacqueline opened the large wooden door to the council room. This room has a similar appearance to a black box theater. There are four seating areas. Each seating area features one hundred seats. There are four hundred members of the council. The council determines the extant of an individual's crime and punishment. The defendant sits at a small table in the center of this large room. The seating areas are made of polished wood and the seats have similar appearances to Church seats. The cherrywood in the seating areas are polished. The walls are comprised of wooden panels and a chandelier hangs in the center of the room. There are four arched windows that view the side of Skull Castle.

The alien leader and Brutis walked on the red carpet to the circular table. The two detainees are looking around the room. They appear to be sort of confused about the setting. Although they are extremely intelligent and they know about most of the multidimensional and international justice systems, they don't have any understanding of this justice system. The members of the council are all members of the former SSGM, so there's a high chance that they'll rule against the two prisoners. Jacqueline walked up to the podium.

"Good day, ladies and gentlemen. You all have come from Starmos City to do your duties as productive members of society and you have done an excellent job fighting. The ultimate test is now your decision making. This decision is probably one of the most important decision of your lives. This decision I can assure you is not some sort of ordinary decision. You all will determine if the two prisoners sitting before you deserve a lengthy sentence. They have done a ton of evil. Let's start off in the beginning. Cornelius Von Alien was the former leader of Starmos City, and he decided to invite Light S. Cycle, who is on the work plantation right now. he wasn't the real perpetrator or perpetrators. He was just an individual caught in the middle of this whole ordeal. the ones who are the real troublemakers in this whole ordeal are Will Von Alien and Brutis. Let's start off with Will. Will is the former leader of Starmos City, but the big question is about how he became leader. I have the answer to that question. He basically freed his friends from jail and aided them in their escape. He then brought them over to California County in upstate New York and he led us on a wild goose chase. Then, he decided to go to Garden City to meet Emperor Gairdon about being a supporter for his fight for his so called 'justice.' After doing that, he returned back to California County, which was under our jurisdiction at the time. After that, he rammed over a number of SSGM soldiers and arrested Cornelius and I. He placed Cornelius through a horrible and mind-boggling ordeal and that was by bringing him to trial. After doing that, he decided to be a vigilante and decpetively kill him. Now, in your right minds, I don't think you all should even think about exonerating him or giving him a minimal sentence. I feel that you all should give him the strongest sentence possible. Will was not only a revolutionary. he was a jealous traitor. Cornelius was the one that provided his parents with jobs and he also provided him (Will) with jobs. That was not the only good thing that he did, he also took Will under his arm when Will's parents died. He helped to raise and nurture him. and I am sure you know what happens to somebody as benevolent and kind like that, Death. Will Von Alien is a sick, twisted, jealous murderer and he deserves to get the harshest punishment possible. I rest my case with this defendant. Now, Brutis is the next defendant who is the worst defendant in the World. He is the beastly one. He is the one that ought to be chained. He is also the representation of betrayal and jealousy. He didn't take a single ounce of any pride in his job as a soldier. He took an oath and that oath was to fight, never give up, and never show perfidiousness or disloyalty to the government. and you know that he had shown a great deal of disloyalty to Cornelius. He joined the SSGM. I don't think he joined it to fight for the justice in Starmos City. I felt he did that to access Cornelius and show a great deal of betrayal. Now, my final words are that my prisoners are the most evil prisoners that I've ever dealt with. Will is the worst. So, I'm going to reiterate what I said earlier. Sentence these prisoners, especially Will, to the maximum sentence because they totally deserve it. I rest my case. It is now up to all of you to decide," she said. The Four hundred members of Council deliberated for a short amount of time. The judge representing all of the council members walked down from his box all the way to the podium. "On behalf of all four hundred Council Members for the Skull Castle, we believe that the defendants Will Von Alien and Brutis shall be sentenced to twenty five years on the plantation in the back of the Skull Castle" he said.

      Jacqueline threw a fit when she heard this. She wanted to give the two prisoners life. the judge gave them

25 years on the plantation. Now, there's a possible chance of escape.

Chapter XXIX: The beginning of relief

The alien leader and Brutis have just been sentenced by a panel of 400 former SSGM soldiers to many years on the plantation for the alleged crimes that Jacqueline decided to fabricate. They are being dragged out by two guards of the Skull Castle. These two guards have brown hair and almond brown eyes. They are wearing Gold plates on their shoulders and knees. They are wearing laced leather sandles that reach up to their kneecaps.

These soldiers are wearing a metallic helmet with spikes on the top. These soldiers are twins. Will started kicking and screaming. "There's no way that you're going to do this. You idiot police will pay. You deserve to die. Just let me go, you crazy nut jobs. Please, I didn't do anything wrong. That witch Jacqueline never gave me a chance to speak in front of the panel. If I would've had a chance, I would've been exonerated. I wish that this prosecutor didn't have any power or say anywhere because she is extremely irresponsible with her powers. She is evil and malicious and I can tell you that she has a vendetta against me. You two don't understand because you two are just guards and you are forced to act like robots. If you would've had some understanding, you would've let me go on with my life. You would've let Brutis go on with his life. We are both innocent. Jacqueline is the one that is guilty as sin. She deserves to be placed on that plantation. She deserves to be in the cell that has lava. She deserves the harshest punishments, not me and definitely not Bruits. I have always been innocent. Our good ideas have been turned into malevolent crimes. Our fights for justice have been turned into wrong doings. That ought not be because fighting for justice is a good thing. So, I beg for you guys to give me some mercy. If you give me mercy, I would be strongly appreciative. I would make you the President of the Starmos Military. You would be making sure there would be fairness. You would fight for the citizens' freedoms. You would do what is right and not what is considered as evil. In addition to that, you would've been treated fairly on your jobs. So, I would appreciate that you guys would let Brutis and I go because we aliens are innocent. Jacqueline is evil," he said.

The soldiers stopped dragging him. The one on the right said, "I am sorry that I've been doing this to you. Jacqueline is the one who has forced me to do this. It's my job. Quite frankly, I don't want to be doing this. I'd rather be fighting for justice. I'll tell you my name. My name is Waldon and his name is Norman. We come from an old castle in Debelinaire. This Castle was known as the Magic Castle. Since, the citizens of the outside town decided to revolt and occupy the building. Haggoth and all of the guards had to revolt. When the revolution had taken place, my brother came back from the dead and so we decided to find work and this was the place. It was the perfect setting. Granted, we had to make some sacrifices. We had to forfeit our horses and change our uniforms, but we found this place to be a better place for us. Besides, Skull Castle is more of our kind of Castle. It's not generic like the one in Debelinaire."

"What was life like in Debelinaire?" the alien leader asked. "Debelinaire was totally different from this place. Debelinaire was quite entertaining and more secure. For instance, there would be a colosseum there that you would be able to watch a prisoner and Bedlam fight. In addition to that, there were a lot of occult effects that had taken place over there. Over here, there aren't any occult or supernatural effects. This place is extremely boring. In addition to that, every guard was entitled to his own individual manor. In this place, every guard is treated like an animal. The guards over here are forced to sleep on the outside of the castle on the plantation. That's just plain cruel. So, I don't like Jacqueline, but she is the only one that provided us with guaranteed jobs," answered Norman. "Do you honestly believe that we're innocent?" asked Will. "Absolutely. You guys are more innocent than some moron that we've dealt with a while ago," answered Waldon. "Who was that man?" the alien leader asked.

"He wasn't actually a man. He was a dragon. he did associate with his immature, pathetic friend. This dragon was an arrogant beast and he was the size of a small shack. This dragon went by 'Iron Steel.' He was a muscular beast and one wouldn't want to mess with him. He was the one who almost killed my brother. He threw a potion on top of him and that was what killed Norman. Fortunately, my brother eventually resurrected from the dead. he wasn't the same, but let me tell you the story about Iron Steel. I remember it was a Friday afternoon and the winds were really strong. All of a sudden, my brother an I see a huge black dragon come on down to the castle. This dragon was dangerously large and he had an intimidating aura. I didn't show any fear because I knew that fear would be the ultimate danger. He and his friend forced themselves into the Castle. They went after Bedlam; and then, they killed three guards when they were sentenced to die. Those two prisoners were the most interesting and the most intimidating. My brother and I have learned some valuable lessons. I think we should've been more diplomatic and accepting. a higher, more bigoted influence, Haggoth ordered that we don't let any dragons or non-caucasians into the Castle," answered Waldon.

"Not to try and burst your conversation, but we have to continue walking to the plantation to escort the Will and his buddy," said Norman. "These guys don't seem like they're up to no good. I think they're very well behaved and I think they'll be extremely nice and respectful. They're not like the world class idiots that we dealt with a few weeks ago at the old castle," replied Waldon.

"Fine, you can talk to your prisoners, but I will not be responsible if Jacqueline comes by and sees us talking to Will and his friend," said Norman.

Loud footsteps are being heard in the corridor. A 25 foot long gown is seen in the distance. The wan face of Jacqueline Langyaw is appearing. She approached the two guards, the alien leader, and the alien shape shifter. Her lips tightened and her ears are red. She looks like the Scarlet Female Satan. She is extremely furious with the guards.

"You morons! You rogues! You lowlives! You ought to be ashamed of yourselves and you definitely deserve to go to Hell because you two are the most evil guards that I have ever met. I ought to shank you two because you are totally despicable. How can you be so nasty and snide with your attitudes? You guards are supposed to be dragging these two prisoners all the way to the plantation. You must be stupid or spiteful. I don't think you two are stupid because you've worked at the Magic Castle in Debelinaire for a while. If you were competent to work over there for a while, I would think you'd be competent to work here. I think that you're being spiteful. Is that correct, Norman? Is that correct, Waldon? Is what I am saying true?" she angrily asked. "Yes," both guards answered.

"So, tell me why you're being spiteful with me?" the arrogant Queen asked. "Because you have been nasty to me. For Godsakes, you don't give us any salary, you have been cruel to us. You didn't treat us like how King Haggoth treated us. Haggoth gave us two manors to live in. You give us two simple quarter rooms to live in. Haggoth treated us like royalty and you treat us like we are dirt. I can assure you that this castle would not be protected if it wasn't for us. Second of all, your prisoners are innocent. I am not just talking about these folks. I am talking about all the prisoners that you have detained. The prisoners that you have detained were innocent and the reason why you have imprisoned them was because of their race, religion, creed, or nationality. That is racist and bigoted and we must destroy bigots like you. You have been cruel to us and you want to imprison the humans. It's like you want to use them as a scapegoat for the problems that you've dealt with. the humans are completely innocent. Jacqueline, you should blame yourself for all of the things that have happened to you. If you did not side with Cornelius, none of this garbage would've happened to you. When you sided with him, you have turned into a monstrosity and a malicious, callous beast. When you learn to be fairer, then, we will respect you. But, for now, we will hate you because you deserve all of the hatred in the world. You are the most evil individual that I have ever met. Once I leave this place, I will not want to even see you again. I don't even want to know you any more. The only reason why my brother and I came here was because the people of Debelinaire were tired of the old government and they led a revolution and my brother and I had to flee and so we were out of work for a while. you decided to act like a walking facade and say that this place would ensure that we would have jobs and housing and we figured that these jobs would be good jobs, but they are jobs that have a protocol to make us do malicious things and that is definitely not who we are. We are excellent guards who have been born to fight for justice and fairness. and so these two prisoners are not here to cause any evil. They are here to make sure that there is fairness and equality in all lands. They are the exact opposite of your personality or views. Besides, your political views are sickening and sinister:," answered Waldon.

"Who are you to even talk to me like that? You and your brother are nothing but traitors and you two ought to be ashamed of yourselves. I have a special place for the two of you, but before I give you the imposed sentence for treason. I will give your brother an opportunity to speak. You see? I am fair with guards. So, don't think that I am unfair because I am extremely fair. When I sentence a guard to a punishment, I give him the opportunity to speak. So, I already gave you the opportunity to speak. Now, I will give your brother the opportunity to speak. You already got your chance. Now, he has to get his chance. So, you better shut the hell up and listen to what your brother must say. Besides, your brother has more wisdom than you and he wouldn't question me. Your brother is the type to be acquiscient to the environment that he is in and he will definitely not protest or try to revolt against my revolt against my rules," said Jacqueline.

"Right now, it is hard for me to get the perfect words that I have to say, but I am going to say them right now. Jacqueline, I usually believe that whatever the leader says is correct and whatever the leader does is the right thing. I don't think that you are a righteous leader. Face the truth. You are nothing but a tyrannical beast. You are not even worthy enough to be called an individual. You are what is known as the scarlet creature. I feel that you get pleasure out of committing sadistic acts. That is despicable and you are the most evil woman that I have ever met. It is sickening that you get pleasure out of dragging your prisoners and bringing them over to plantations. This makes me sick that you enjoy that. Lady, you better learn how to look in the mirror and make a change because you are wicked and your acts are heinous and cold-blooded. Now, I initially said that I would just let my brother get in trouble on his own for talking to the two prisoners. I will get in trouble with him because; if he goes down, I am going down with him. My twin brother and I are a team. and we don't consider these two standing in front of me to be prisoners. We don't consider Will and his friend to be criminals. Instead, we consider them to be heroic. They are here to fight for justice and fairness and you are not here to do that. You are here to cause malice and evil. You are as nasty as sin. You are of the devil. You are a true daughter of Satan! May you go to Hell because that's where you belong. In fact, all 600+ prisoners that have been held captive over here were all innocent. The reason why you decided to hold them captive was because you had a vendetta against all the humans on Earth and all of the alien dissenters against Cornelius, who was also a tyrant. That is just terrible the way you acted. So, if my brother gets the maximum sentence, I want the same exact sentence as him. Remember, we are both here as brothers and we will go down as one. And, we are not only going to go down as one, we are going to go down for the right cause. We are not going to stand by and curtail and give in to an unfair justice system! We will stand up and fight! We will rebel and we will make sure that the prisoners on the plantation rebel! So, you can do all you want to us, but we will stand up against evil," declared Norman. "Do you realize that you and your brother's declarations have no meaning? At the end of the day, what I have to say is what counts. So, you get up here and whine all you want and try and profess that you're a crusader. You are definitely not one at all. You and your brother are not crusaders or fighters for justice. So, you can get that idea out of your little heads. Now, I will impose a lengthy sentence. First, I am going to make you relinquish everything you have including the gold plates. You will give me your keys to the chains also. In addition to that, you will be forced to work on the plantation and you will be chained to all of the other prisoners. and you will live the rest of your lives in bondage. I am done. and I have officially imposed the fairest sentence that should've been imposed a long time ago," the cold-hearted Queen said.

"Yeah, whatever," replied Will. "Shut the hell up. You are already in enough trouble as is. Now, to all of the prisoners, I want to tell you that you are to call me by Queen Jackie or Queen Jacqueline the first, not Langyaw and not even Mrs. Langyaw. You and your fellow prisoners definitely deserve the sentences that you are receiving. I am officially done with what I have to say and I am going to drag you two to the plantation," said Jacqueline. One of the former SSGM soldiers presented Waldon and Norman with blue and black striped plantation uniforms. The twin brother guards walked into the cell and changed into a blue and black striped plantation uniform. Once they finished changing, Will and Brutis walked into the cell to change into plantation uniforms. Once they changed, Jacqueline pushed her four prisoners to the ground and dragged them on the cold stone floor all the way to a wooden door. This wooden door features a lock on the inside of the castle and a handle on the outside of the castle. She opened the door and made them walk onto the grassy Plantation. This plantation features all human men and alien dissenters. Jacqueline grabbed her four prisoners and tossed them onto the plantation. This plantation is a wheat plantation. "Hope you four enjoy it here because you are going to spend a very long time here and you might be able to enjoy it here. So, I hope you have such a splendid time here," she said in a snooty manner.

 She slammed the wooden door. "What do we do?" asked Will. "Well, I would say just work here for the rest of our lives. Face it, we are not going to live here for long. We are slaves and we are not allowed to eat. We'll probably not be able to sleep tonight because of our hungry stomachs. Face it, we don't have any beds, no tents, no nothing. We would be forced to sleep on the wheat plantation. We are going to be living our lives in Hell. We will not be able to see anybody that we know ever again," answered Brutis.

 "Well, my brother and I are not going to stand by with this evil whench. She will have to deal with me because I am not going to die on this plantation. I will fight against her evil ways. and I will get all 600+ prisoner slaves to listen to me and rebel against her. We can't live in a place like this. Man needs freedom. His heart and mind must run wild. This idea of forced servitude that Jacqueline strongly supports is totally sick and wrong. For Godsakes, this is a method to deprive our senses. This is the true epitome of sensory deprivation. This is the true idea of evil. It is malicious and disgusting and we must find some sort of way to escape it," said Waldon.

"And, how do you expect us to escape this?" the alien leader asked. "Well, we can't be covert. So, the second way to escape is to coax all of the male humans and aliens to push through the door to get out of here. Once we all do that, we will hunt Jacqueline down and arrest her. we will bring every individual back to his place of residence. Once we do that, we will try Jacqueline on crimes against humanity and all of the necessary criminal charges that should be brought against her. we will hunt down Haggoth and try him for accessory to those charges and we'll make sure that we deny him bail. we will make sure that they get the death penalty, but if they act evil before they go to trial, we'll just shoot them like they deserve," answered Brutis.

"No, let's just shoot them with the ray guns to vaporize them and they'll have nothing to do with our lives ever again. We will not only shoot them. we'll also shoot Mitchell, who also deserves to be shot with the ray gun," replied Will.

"Doesn't it sound a little childish to shoot war criminals with a ray gun? What is a ray gun?" asked Norman. "A ray gun is a gun that turns an individual into a vapor. I will turn Mitchell, Howard Carterson, Jacqueline Langyaw, and Haggoth into a vapor. Simply, I'll just make them disappear," the alien leader answered. "That sounds like a good idea," replied Waldon. "Thank you," said Will.

Jacqueline looked out the kitchen window facing the plantation.

"Start picking," she shouted. "Picking what?" the alien leader asked. "Have you lost your mind? I am telling you to pick the wheat in the fields. It doesn't take some sort of rocket scientist to figure that out," the scarlet queen answered. "Shut the Hell up. I'll do whatever I want whenever I want. and there's nothing you can do to stop me," the alien leader replied. "Excuse me, but the last time I checked, I was higher in ranking that you are. You are not even considered an alien or a human.
You are just a slave. This is the place where alien political dissenters and humans belong on. You are now my property and do not make me come out there and crack you with the whip! and you better not make the guards come out there. That's when trouble will take place," Jacqueline declared.

"Do you think I am scared of you? Come on. Bring it on. I'll beat you to the point where you'll have such hard internal bleeding that you'll get blood poisoning. Thus, you'll die," said Will. "Are you threatening me?" asked Jacqueline.

"Yes, I am. In fact, I am proud of threatening you. Somebody like you deserves to be threatened. Face it, you're nothing but, an arrogant witch. You definitely deserve to die. If it was up to me; I'd serve you a drink filled with quicksilver," the alien leader answered. "What's that?" the arrogant queen asked.

"Puh, you think you're so intellectually superior and powerful. you're not. Quicksilver is Mercury. I am going to poison you to death with that. So, you better not let me work as a chef over here," answered Will. "If you think I am scared of you for one second, I am definitely not. If I was scared of you, I wouldn't enslave you. I wouldn't even threaten you. You're just trying to pull some sort of an act with me. You are a nothing in my life. You are just like all the other 600+ slaves over here. So, like I said earlier, shut the hell up and continue on working," replied Jacqueline.

"Just remember that the Universal Declaration of Human Rights and the Bill of Rights clearly states that nobody should be placed in forced servitude. So, you're not only violating the Bill of Rights; you're also violating the Universal Declaration of Human Rights. You are a criminal on Planet Earth. So, you better not go over there. In addition to that, the Starmos Common Law states that nobody should be forced to work unless they are being paid. You are violating the Starmos Common Law. So, you better not go over there. and you are violating the Celestial City's Law. You are violating the rules of God. There's no way that you can escape the crimes you have committed and I believe that you'll be punished for eternity. Unlike you, I believe and you don't. You know who God is. the idea of Stalinism has reached your mind. That idea will never be able to escape your mind because you are of the devil. As I told you earlier, you are nothing but a daughter of Satan. So, you are just as guilty as the devil. and you are just as evil as he is," the alien leader said. "I don't like your attitude. Infact, I am coming out there right now," the evil queen answered. "What makes you think that I like your attitude?" the alien leader asked. Jacqueline sickened.

"Your bold and blunt attitude is going to get you nowhere. You have no right to be blunt. and you have no right to be aggressive. You are nothing but a slave. So, shut the hell up before I crack the whip on top of you," she said.

"I am not scared. You don't get it. Go right ahead and whip me. You can kill me if you want to. All I want to know is that I am fighting for justice. I am not the type to be so quick to die. I am willing to die for the right things. I am willing to die for the right values. I am willing to fight for righteousness and fairness," replied Will. "That's it. I am getting my whip," the evil queen said. She was sitting at the table in the alcove in the kitchen. she walked into the rear of the kitchen into the pantry. This pantry features a number of food products. These food products are either canned products or sun dried products. Hidden behind the food products are two whips. One whip is used for horses and another whip is used to rip the skin and flesh off of one's body. She hesitated. She thought about using the Cat O' Nine Tails for one second, but she used the whip that is used to direct horses. This whip will only cause an individual to have a small blemish. She grabbed the keys that are on top of the wooden kitchen counter, walked into the corridor, and opened the door. She walked over to the plantation. All of the slave prisoners stopped their worked and stared at her. She stared back at them with a face of anger. Her eyes are squinted.

"Get back to work, you cretins," she said. All of the 600+ slave prisoners continued picking the wheat except for Will, Brutis, Norman, and Waldon. "The only one who shouldn't be working right now is Will. Besides, I am going to paint his back red. He'll remember this day," she continued. She walked up to Will.

"Like I told you earlier, you low life, I am not going to work. I can assure you that I am not scared of you. So, you can whip me as many times as you want. you're not going to win. You can try to be as dominant and condescending as you want to be. You can try to be a know-it-all as much as you want, but guess what? I am not scared. I am very willing to fight you. Face it, you're nothing but an evil whench," the alien leader said. "I hope that you're trying not to be belligerent towards me because I have a Cat O' Nine Tails in the castle that is perfect for slaves who think they can be bold or try to act cute with me. I am just giving you a little leniency. I shouldn't be giving you any leniency. In fact, you should've been dead a while ago. I could've forced you to poison yourself. I didn't do that. The reason why is because I am not evil. I am a good woman fighting for justice," replied Jacqueline.

"You have got to be kidding me. You just claimed that you fight for justice. You have just claimed that you weren't evil. You are totally evil and absurd. You have an ego the size of an elephant and a heart the size of a small rock. You are the most callous creature that I know. I can assure you that you are not one of God's creatures because one of God's creatures wouldn't commit the wicked acts and barbaric acts that you have committed. May you be punished for the evil crimes that you have committed," said Will.

"Shut the hell up. Go to Hell," the evil queen abruptly said. She swung the whip back and she flogged the alien leader the first time. He fell to the ground. She continued flogging him. After twenty three flogs, he passed out. She started kicking him. and she cold-heartedly kicked dirt in his faced. she shuffled her boot in the ground and walked back in to the Castle. After that, she slammed the door and walked back into the kitchen to continue eating her lunch. This woman is a vicious beast. While innocent individuals are in forced servitude, not able to have a single roll of bread, she is able to eat a fancy lunch of a delicious Arugula Salad. She opened the window. "I bet you cretins and dumb asses are enjoying working on the plantation. If you're not enjoying life out there, then it's too bad and it's tough luck. You brought your own problems. and you got what you deserved. You all should've gotten this punishment a long time ago," she said.

She snickered after she said those disgusting comments. Brutis stopped doing his job and he walked up to the kitchen window. "You are disgusting! You are terrible and sinister! You may be tall in height. you are short in character; by throwing degrading comments in our faces and trying to lower our self-esteems, you are debasing yourself. You're acting like a piece of garbage. I hope that you perish forever and I hope that nobody is ever haunted by your spirit. I hope that your spirit gets erased," he shouted. "Do you want to get the same punishment as your little friend?" asked Jacqueline.

"No. don't belittle us because we have hearts, souls, and minds. Maybe you don't have one, but we do and we care about life. We humans and aliens act in a humanitarian and benevolent manner. We are here to help each other. I can assure you that we are not egocentric. We are modest with our attitude and we are not cruel like you. We are fair and we have respect towards one another. We care about each other. We aliens are not callous. So, my final words are that you deserve to be on this plantation more than anybody else. You are just as evil as Cornelius, if not worse. and if you think that's a good thing, that is definitely not a good thing. That is an evil feature that you have and you must be rid of all evil. I would help you change if you're willing to get some help. it seems to me that you're not willing to get any help," the alien shape shifter said.

"You are absolutely right. You have officially won the jackpot. I am cold-blooded and I am proud of it. and if I was even willing to get help, I would have already gotten it. I do not care to do good. Besides, I was born to be an evil doer. I have been born to commit wicked acts. Can't you tell that I am of the devil? Can't you tell that I am a daughter of Satan? I know I am evil and I am proud of it and I don't care about what you think of me because; time and time again, I have said that my opinion counts. You are nothing but a slave; you have no say and your opinion doesn't count," replied Jacqueline.

"You may be saying that now. when you come face to face with your Creator, he will see what you have done. He will see how evil you've been. and you will be sent to Hell," said Brutis. "I don't care about Hell. Hell is my true origin. Have you not remembered that I am the daughter of Satan? I love Hell; I love fire. I love thirst and hunger. Infact, I love looking at it. It is quite enjoyable to me and even entertaining," the evil queen replied.

"Maybe you don't understand what hunger and thirst is. You have emaciated these innocent aliens and humans to satisfy your mind. That is quite wicked! How can you even act like this. You don't even have a heart because if you had a heart, you wouldn't be doing this despicable behavior. You wouldn't even think about doing this behavior if you had a right mind. and if you even had a soul, you would be fighting for real justice, not 'Jacqueline' justice. So, you better look at yourself in the mirror and make a huge change. You are nothing but a callous and malicious beast. You ought to be ashamed of yourself. I don't know anybody who would even think about committing the vile acts that you have committed," the alien shape shifter said. "Come here. I have a little surprise for you. It's a gift," replied Jacqueline. "You can get up here and profess that we are all cretins and say that we are all stupid. You can say that I am stupid because of my size. I am not stupid. I am intellectually fit for society. I may not be as smart as Will, but I am smart enough not to fall for some stupid, deceptive trick. I know that you are a sinister woman. I know that you have evil up your sleeve and I know that you are the most evil creature. You may be a female alien in a physical form, but you are extremely heartless. You do not show any mercy. If you had shown any form of mercy, you wouldn't put us in a cell that has lava leaking into it. If you had shown any mercy, you wouldn't be forcing male humans or male aliens to work on a plantation without any pay," the alien shape shifter said.

"Just come over here; I'm not going to trick you, nor am I going to hurt you. Just get over here and shut up," the evil queen replied. "Fine then, I'll do what you've told me. The only reason why I am listening to you is because I don't want to get flogged with a strong whip," said Brutis. He walked up to the kitchen window. She opened the window. she decided to act like a nasty witch and toss the salad on top of the alien shape shifter's head. She snickered. "I hope you enjoy that. and I have to add one more addition to that," she said. She started spitting at him and started making demeaning comments to him. "That's what happens to low-lives like you. I told you that you were intellectually inferior to me," she muttered. Brutis walked away from the kitchen window with a chip on his shoulder. He returned back onto the plantation. He clapped his hands twice. Everybody stopped working.

"I want you all to listen to me. Jacqueline is a piece of garbage. Look at what she has done to you all. She is the most evil woman in the world. She is here to cause trouble. It is already bad enough that she tried to ruin my friend by flogging him so many times. She ruined all of you and she tried to ruin me. This woman is a beast. She is not even considered a woman or female alien. She is a callous creature! She must go down and in order for that to happen, we must rebel. We can't just sit here and act like robots working; we have to fight for justice. We were brought into this world to do that. We will not curtail and give in to tyranny. We will not somebody who's evil and cold-hearted. This woman must be stopped. Her confidants must be stopped. The only way that we can do that is leading a violent revolution. and in order to lead this revolution, you all must listen to me. So, I have a plan, but before we do anything. I want Light S. Cycle to come over here and I also want Will Von Alien to wake up from the dead. Light all of a sudden started walking up to Brutis. His robotic legs are chained and so are his hands. The alien shape shifter is filled with ecstasy. "We have to rescue Will," said Light. He walked up to the alien leader and commanded him to wake up. Will awakened. He stood up. Brutis also stood up. He raised his voice to make sure that it's loud. "Now, I want you all to line up and push me through the wooden door. I will jump to the side and we will raid the castle. You all are to act like hooligans and scare the guards. some of you will find the 600+ keys and free yourselves from the shackles. Then, one of you will free me from the shackles. After that, the beginning of the end of our fight for justice has taken place," he declared. Everybody lined up and rammed through the wooden door of the Skull Castle. Every slave prisoner is leading the strongest revolution that has ever been led. The castle is being raided, books are being burnt, and the guards are fleeing. Jacqueline has barricaded herself into the kitchen pantry. Mitchell joined her in hiding in the pantry. When everybody stormed into the castle, Brutis jumped into the kitchen. After he jumped into the kitchen, everybody freed themselves from the shackles and stormed out of the castle. The only ones who didn't storm out of the castle were Will,

Light, Norman, and Waldon. Will walked up to the alien shape shifter. He unshackled Brutis. the alien shape shifter (Brutis) opened the pantry. "Well, look what I have here. My two prisoners. Guess what, you two are under arrest. and we will detain you over in California County while we go to war for justice in Starmos City," he said.

Jacqueline and Mitchell resisted arrest. They were shackled and this is the beginning of the end of evil.

Chapter XXX: The war to end all wars in all of the dimensions and true justice takes place

The slave prisoners have just revolted against the wicked Jacqueline Langyaw. They freed themselves from the shackles. Will, Brutis, Waldon, and Norman shackled Jacqueline and Mitchell. They are now in the kitchen. The evil former prosecutor and her human conspirator are resisting arrest. They are kicking and screaming. They are filled with anger.

"Since when did you four become the police officers? Since when were you royal guards of this castle? and who gave you the proper warrant to apprehend us? You have no rights. This is not going to play well in court. You are the most evil alien that I've ever met. This is not justice! This is anarchy! You are a beast! Will, you ought to be ashamed of yourself because you started this whole thing. If you would not have led that movement of what you call 'democracy', none of this would've happened. I would've still had my job in Starmos City. I would've had my job! You better learn not to mess around with me because you'll pay. You hear me? You'll pay. So, let me go from those shackles. It is wrong to treat a woman like that," shouted Jacqueline. "Well, I don't think enslaving men and alien dissenters is justice either. What you did was cruel and despicable and now, you're paying for your crimes. and you will not only spend the rest of your life in prison. you will have to look at the prospect of a Ray Gun. That's when you'll be turned into a vapor and nobody will be able to see you or think about you ever again. You have tried to prosecute my friends and I. and you had a vendetta against me and you had a deceptive and deceitful plan to hurt me. your plan backfired at you. and it's a good thing that it backfired. You claim that you're an innocent woman. you're not an innocent woman. You're really a vile creature that is trapped in a female alien's body. Oh yeah, I must tell you that what I am doing is not anarchy. What you did was anarchy. This whole ordeal would not have happened if you didn't kidnap Light. You took us on some sort of a wild goose chase to find him; and you thought that we were stupid. we followed many leads and we were guided over to this place, the lurid but, anomalously shaped castle. One thing that is for certain is that evil will never win. Good is always going to be the winner. So, your diabolical scheme disintegrated quite quickly," the alien leader replied.

"Excuse me, but you don't talk to a woman like that. This woman gave me some job. and I believe that you are the most evil alien leader in all of the numerous dimensions. Do not even try to mess with me because I will kill you. and if you think I can't escape those shackles, you better think again. I am a genius and an escape artist. You have no right to mess around with me. You think you can be evil whenever you want. you can't. The reason why I conspired to kidnap Light was because I felt it would be the right thing to do in revenge for what you did to Starmos City. You've adulterated that city with your nasty attitude and your so called ideas of 'democracy.' The other reason why I helped in the kidnapping of Light was because he deserved to be kidnapped. He was the one that helped you go anywhere. and without him, you would've gone nowhere. So, I saved you a little work," said Mitchell.

"Shut up. Do you realize that you're an imbecile? Light is not a piece of work. Light is a big help in my life. In addition to that, the reason why you probably got fired from your job was because you were a communist and that is totally wrong. Communism and Socialism are evil ideas of government and you supported that. You are going to go down. Those who are evil and those who support evil will fail and somebody like you deserves the most severe punishment in the book. I rest my case with you," replied Will.

"I am hereby objecting to your statements. You think that you can try to be condescending towards this wonderful man, Mitchell? Who do you think you are to take such an attitude with me? You are extremely despicable and you ought to be ashamed of yourself. You have betrayed the aliens of Starmos City and I will show how you had betrayed them. You are the most evil alien that one can ever meet. and you are the most bold alien that I've ever met. I am not talking about the bold in the good way. Instead, I am talking about the bold in the evil, most abrupt way. You think who you are and you think that you can do whatever you want whenever you want. you can't. You are nothing but a stupid, little alien. I have more power than you. Remember, I've been all over the Starmos television. I've been in the world much longer than you have been in existence. Thus, I have more power and more wisdom over you. You have no rights, Will. Do you hear me? No rights whatsoever. So, you better shut your little mouth and unshackle Mitchell and I," said Jacqueline.

"I am definitely not going to unshackle you. and by the way, I do have a ton of rights. I have the right to whip you with the Cat O' Nine Tails. I am not going to do that because that's not me. Unlike you, Jacqueline, I have a heart. I care about people and aliens. I care about all creatures whether they are creatures of God or the Devil. I am a very compassionate individual. You are not; you're just plain evil. And, I am definitely not surprised by that. I am definitely bold and I am proud of it. The reason why is because I fight for justice and fairness, you definitely don't do that. You fight for injustice and unfairness. You support cruelty and evil. You curtail and give in to an evil tyrant. You call this evil tyrant your boyfriend. he's not. He's just plain evil. and may he perish without leaving a single trace. In spite of his death making a strong impact on the aliens of Starmos City, his spirit is starting to disappear. This starts with the renaming of some streets and the removal of all of the tiles with the portrayal of Cornelius. In addition to that, I wrote the Starmos Common Law and I started drafting the Starmos Constitution. So, yeah, I may not have been the best leader and I may have acted like an Anarchist in your eyes. I am not one who supports that idea of Anarchy. Instead, I support the ideas of justice and fairness. I have given all of the alien citizens rights. individuals like you, Mitchell, Haggoth, Serpianto, and Korbian have caused trouble. That hindered me from making the place of my origin a better place," the alien leader replied.

"You have no rights. You are extremely immature. Besides, you're only twenty-five years old so, you're still just a stupid, little kid. What you're saying sounds ridiculous and like I said earlier, you have no right arrest me or Mitchell. I am done with what I have to say and I guess that I will have to surrender," the evil former female prosecutor said. The alien leader escorted her and Mitchell outside of the Skull Castle. Everybody is waiting on the long, brick sidewalk in front of the Castle cheering that they are free. When Will escorted the two monstrosities on the sidewalk, the crowd went wild. Everybody is chanting, "Go Will, Go Will, Go Will. Justice for who? Justice for Starmos City! Justice for who? Justice for Earth!" All of the 600+ former prisoner slaves kept chanting this. "Thank you," the alien leader shouted. Everybody stopped chanting to let him announce his speech. "I may want to tell you all that we have arrested Jacqueline Langyaw and Mitchell. Light is going to shapeshift from a robot into an LSC to head over to Planet Earth. we will have them held captive in California County and they will stand trial in Starmos City.

　　　　While they are in jail awaiting trial, I am going to fight the war against Haggoth and his fellow associates. In addition to that, Light will pick you up and return you to the places that you belong. He will take four of you at a time. Some of you might have to wait over two hours to be brought back to your places of origin. As long as you get there safe and in one piece, that's all that matters. So, now, I will make my departure with my two prisoners and they will be awaiting trial. Now, I want to thank you all for your cooperation because; without your cooperation, this whole thing would've not happened. There wouldn't have been any justice. So, I want to thank you all for working with me," he said.

　　　　Everybody stepped to the sides and Light shape-shifted from a robot to an LSC. He opened the door and the alien leader escorted the two war criminals into the rear of the LSC. and to make sure that they wouldn't do anything stupid or disgusting. He place spit masks on top of their heads. Will slammed the door shut and sat up front. Light made the ultimate departure from the evil Skull Castle. He moved from zero to mach 600 miles per hour. Shortly after the ultimate departure, Jacqueline started to complain about the surrounding.

"I ought to shank you. You are the most evil one that is in existence. I am going to tell the authorities that you are mistreating Mitchell and I. You have no right to put nets around our faces. That is just plain cruel. To add insult to injury, you are nothing but a hypocrite. The reason why is because you claim that torture is wrong. You're torturing us. Individuals like you make me disgusted. How can you preach stating that torture and cruelty to prisoners is totally wrong? Yet, you violate the rights of the prisoners. If you think that prisoners are innocent, then Mitchell and I must be innocent. and you're violating our rights. We can bring you to an International Tribunal and try you on crimes against humanity," she said.

"Is there something wrong with you? You have no right to call me a hypocrite because I am not torturing you and your friend. Just because I am putting a spit mask around your head doesn't mean I'm torturing you. The reason why I am doing that is so that way you or your friend wouldn't do anything stupid. By the way, police officers and bounty hunters are allowed to put spit masks on criminals heads if they feel that they are going to be a threat to them. I am not a police officer. I do have the rights of a bounty hunter. and in addition to that, I don't believe that all prisoners are innocent. I believe that all of your prisoners who were on the plantation were innocent victims of an evil wench. and I do believe that torture is wrong and it is a crime against humanity that you have committed on numerous occasions to different individuals. You are the most cruel creature that I have ever met. So, you ought to be ashamed of yourself because; you are atrocious. You have done the most evil and heinous things that one can ever do. You are the epitome of a sinister monster," the alien leader replied.

"Fine. You win. I'll shut the hell up. I am innocent; Mitchell is innocent. We didn't do anything wrong. We did what we were supposed to do. We imprisoned the ones who we felt had to be imprisoned. That was all of the male humans and the alien political dissenters who despised our old beloved Cornelius. Will, what you did was unnecessary. You should've never tried to revolt. If you didn't revolt in the first place, none of this would've happened. I am done trying to tell you because what I say to you goes in one ear and out the other. Screw you," the evil former prosecutor said.

"I don't get angry on too many occasions and I don't really open my mouth too many times. In this case I am going to open my mouth. When individuals have a quarrel inside of me, I become very angry; and the one who keeps opening the mouth is you, Jacqueline. Just shut your trap because I don't want to hear a word from you. Face the facts, your day is done. You and your fellow accomplices will never be able to reign again. Evil will be destroyed; and you are evil. Stop trying to proclaim your innocence because you are definitely not innocent. Stop trying to make Will waste his breath. Just shut up and enjoy the ride to prison. Look at your fellow accomplice. He hasn't said a word since he's boarded. We might even talk about striking a plea deal with him because of his good behavior and cooperation. We are definitely not going to even think about striking a plea deal with you because you are the most evil creature that exists. There's no way that I can be so nice to such a callous creature," replied Light.

He departed from the Skull Castle Dimension and arrived in California County. He landed on Goodluck Street and everybody stared. The Labor Day block parties on the numbered streets are taking place. Some of the old folks are staring at Light due to his impressive size. He headed down the municipal street and dropped of Jacqueline and Mitchell. Johnstone is standing on the steps. He is wearing a blue police uniform with a gold sheriff star on his shirt. He pointed his nine millimeter gun at Light.

"What are you doing here?" he abruptly asked. "I am a citizen of this town. I have two prisoners that I have to drop off for a little while because I have to fight a war in Starmos City. Don't worry, I'll come back for them later. I would appreciate it if you guys keep them here for now," the shapeshifting robot (Light) answered.

"What are they like?" the police officer asked. "One's an alien and one's a human. The alien is a female and the human is a male," answered Light. "I don't think you get what I'm asking you. I'll rephrase that question. Are they hardened criminals?" asked Officer Johnstone. "Yes, they are. They're charged with over 600 crimes against humanity, 2 counts of conspiracy, 600 counts of false imprisonment, 4 counts of attempted felony murder, 1 count of treason, and 1 count of first degree attempted murder," the shapeshifting robot answered.

"Oh my God. You bettter not be lying to me," the police officer said in a brusque manner. "I am not a liar. I will never lie. They are charged with all of those crimes and they are as guilty as sin. They ought to be ashamed of themselves because they are hardened criminals. I am telling you that they're beasts and they're creatures and I am

not talking about God's creatures. I am talking about evil
creatures that belong to Satan. These individuals have no
hearts whatsoever. They are bold and sneaky. Personally, I'd
recommend you keep them away from all of the other
prisoners because they're going to cause trouble. Put them
in Solitary Confinement because; that's where they belong.
I do not want to hear any bad reports about their behavior
and make sure that they don't escape. Keep them in Solitary
Confinement," said Light.

"Okay, now I have one more question before I take
them out. Where's Starmos City?" asked Officer Stone. "No
time for further questions. Just take them out of me and put
them in solitary confinement without booking them,"
answered.

The police officer did as Light had commanded him
to do. He opened the door and tried pulling Jacqueline out.
She started resisting and she tried to bite him on the hand.
The officer tasered her. She was forced to sit on the marble
steps. Mitchell willingly walked out of the vehicle. He sat
on top of the marble steps. "I am not going to deal with this
garbage and I can assure you that I am not going to let you
manhandle me," said Jacqueline.

"Shut up," replied the police officer. He brought her
and Mitchell into the police station. He brought them over
to Solitary Confinement. Meanwhile, Will and Light
departed from the police Station. They returned over past
the Town Square all the way to Goodluck Street. Light
made a loud vroom that sounded exactly like a motorcycle
engine. He launched at high speeds of mach 600 hundred
miles per hour.

He left the Earthly dimension and arrived on
Highway D, which is also known as the Dimensional plane
or the Dimension Highway. He and Will started contriving

a plan in order to fight the war to end all wars. "So, Will, what do you want to do?" he asked. "Do what?" the alien leader asked.

"I am talking about the war that we must fight. What do you want to do in order to fight this war?" asked Light.

"Well, we should start off coming in a slow and discreet fashion. So, I'd recommend you'd slow down right now. So, that way we wouldn't cause any disturbance. Besides, rumor has it that Haggoth banned LSCs and any blue alien. We must enter slowly and in a sneaky manner. This is probably one of the most covert missions that we're going to embark on and it's probably going to be the most dangerous mission. When we arrive, go straight to WVA Boulevard and that's when you'll shape shift from an LSC into a robot. When you do that, I'll walk behind you and I will follow you to the Alien Estate. Once we do that, we'll be covert in entering and then we will beat up one of the guards and steal a ray gun in the tower. we'll vaporize Haggoth and justice will be done. This is if everything goes well. We might have a slight possibility of something going wrong," the alien leader answered. "What happens if there's some sort of a change?" the shapeshifting robot asked. "Then, I'll let you know how to handle the change. the plan I just told you is known as the 'perfect plan.' The only way it can stay perfect is if we act quite discreet and covert. I think we have the capability of doing that," answered Will. "Fine, whatever you say goes. After all, your wish is my comm, and" replied Light.

"Don't be like that. You have a say in this mission too," the alien leader said. "Thank you for being so kind and fair with me," the shapeshifting robot replied. "It's no problem. That's what I'm supposed to do. Besides, that's

who I am. I'm not like that whench Jacqueline", said Will.
"I totally agree with you," replied Light. After 10 minutes
of driving on Highway-D, the alien leader and the
shapeshifting vehicle/robot arrived in Starmos City. The
place looks quite normal. it is not a bustling city metropolis
as it was earlier. The place looks like a desolate colorful
town. Light is heading through the orangish, sandy dunes.
"Oh my God, this place looks so desolate," said Will. "I
know," replied Light. "Why would you think this place is
the way it is right now?" the alien leader asked.

 "Well, there are only two things. A, the citizens fled
before Haggoth arrived or B, the citizens are being held
captive in the hole," the shapeshifting robot answered. "I
hope its not B," replied Will. "I hate to burst your bubble,
but it's most likely choice B. I don't think that any of the
aliens would know that there'd be an invasion without
warning. If they knew that there would be an invasion
taking place, then we would have to go through a security
barrier in order to get in," said Light.

 "Well, I don't know about the fact that we don't have
to go through security checkpoint. You see, I heard that
Haggoth had a policy where an alien of blue skin color
would be automatically executed. I am of blue skin color.
And, anybody who is an ordinary LSC would not be
allowed in," the alien leader replied. "Perhaps, I can sneak
you in," the shapeshifting robot said. "What you just said
was ridiculous. How on Earth can you sneak me in without
getting in trouble? How can you even sneak yourself in?"
asked Will. "I am not just any ordinary LSC. I am Light. I
was Cornelius' old chauffeur. They'll be able to recognize
that by blue checkerboard tag that I have on my side,"
answered Light. "How will you be able to hide me?" the
alien leader asked.

"Did you forget that my windows are tinted? If I make my windows pitch black, nobody
will be able to see inside. If nobody sees inside, then we'll be able to get in," the shapeshifting robot answered. "Good point. You have some pretty good ideas that sometimes can prove me wrong," replied Will. "Thank you," said Light. He and the alien leader finally arrived right in front of Starmos City. All of a sudden, two large police cruisers pulled up right in front of the LSC. These police cruisers look like orange flying saucers. Two humanoids are featured in these cruisers. Their names are Bar and Sar and they are both brothers. "What is your name?" the humanoid on the right, Bar, asked. "Light S. Cycle," the shapeshifting robot answered. Bar hesitated. "Hold on there mister, you're an ordinary LSC. You're not welcome here. Get lost and go back from where you came from," he said. "Don't tell me that. How would you like it if I told you to get lost and go back to your own placed of origin?" asked Light. "This is going to be a failure," muttered Will. "Who said that? Is there anybody in the vehicle?" Sar abruptly asked.

"No," the shapeshifting robot answered. "That't a good thing. I guess I can let you in. You don't seem like you're here to do any harm," replied Bar. The two guards opened the gates. the alien leader and Light were let into Starmos City. Now, they will be able to witness the war zone of a city. All of the windows are smashed in every single one of the buildings. The beautiful colors of all of the buildings are defaced and desecerated with graffiti saying hateful words about all the aliens. The buildings are all gutted and destroyed. Water is leaking from the sides of the buildings and the furniture is scattered throughout the streets. The once bustling and beautiful Star Hotel looks like a defunct mess. Numbers of jobs have been destroyed and the gold entrance has disappeared.

The outdoor carpet in front of that hotel looks all worn out and wrinkled. It even looks dirty due to the tumbleweed that has passed by. The firehouse looks like it has been set on fire by the invaders from Debelinaire. The shining red tiles have been coated with ash and soot. The blue tiles have been ripped off from the building. The municipal buildings have stones in front of them because King Haggoth wanted to retrieve all of the documents and destroy them.

All of the LSCs look like they're all useless. Light drove Will all the way down to WVA Boulevard. The street signs that show the name of WVA Boulevard have been torn down. According to King Haggoth, the street is supposed to be renamed Royal Avenue. "This looks like a crime scene that was committed by a ruthless individual. Who would do such a thing?" asked Will. "Buddy, you've got to be kidding me. You're asking about who would do such a thing? This is all done by Jacqueline Langyaw. She's the menace behind all this evil. She has ruined this city. and she must die for her crimes. She requested that Haggoth would come here to invade too. So, Haggoth is just as guilty as she is. I believe that we should go after all of the perpetrators and that's when justice will be done. Don't ask such a stupid question," the shapeshifting robot answered. "There are a number of perpetrators. After a while, it gets confusing," the alien leader said. "You still should remember. After all, you were the one who started this whole thing to begin with. and you definitely started this whole thing for a good and justifiable reason and that was to fight against the evils of Socialism, bigotry, and injustice. You have been definitely doing the job the right way; so, if you continue doing the job the right way, then you'll be able to finish and win your ongoing war," replied Light. He continued driving up the boulevard all the way to the Alien Estate. The fountain is off and the mural of Cornelius Von Alien has been revived. Will is mortified to see this. His eyes are widened in disbelief. and he is still wondering who would do such a thing.

He is just in a state of shock. Light finally pulled up to the Alien Estate. He is waiting behind the gate. The guard in the tower is staring at him. The guard all of a sudden realized that Light is present. He opened the window and retreived his assault rifle and started shooting at the shapeshifting robot.

Will started panicking. "Where's the gun? Where's the gun?" he frantically asked. "It's in the trunk," answered Light. "Good," the alien leader replied. He crawled into the trunk the receive the Mercury 3000. This gun is the best assault rifle that one could ever have. It just doesn't shoot any ordinary bullets. This gun shoots bullets that explode into poisonous, detrimental quicksilver. The alien leader shot two hundred bullets into the guard tower. Within a matter of seconds, the evil guard died.

"Yes, I am extremely happy and I am thrilled to death. It's like I'm in Heaven. Now, 1 don't know what to do," said Will. "That is the most stupid thing I've ever heard come out of your mouth. I'll tell you what to do. Go in the guard tower and fetch me the ray gun. Once you do that, we'll barge through the gates and you will enter through the doors and hunt down King Haggoth and his army. once he's dead, you'll rescue the prisoners and give them full amnesty. After that, we'll return back to California County to bring Jacqueline and Mitchell to stand trial for the crimes that they've committed," replied Light.

"Okay," the alien leader said. Light opened the door and Will jumped out. He dashed all the way up to the double doors of the Alien Estate. He slowly opened them. he dashed and raided through all the rooms. Finally, he entered the kitchen. He found King Haggoth, who is sitting on a Gold Throne. His wife is sitting adjacent to him. "Who are you?" the king asked. "It is I, Will Von Alien. You have ten seconds to get out of her before I forced you out," the alien leader answered. ", and what happens if I don't move?" asked Haggoth. "Then, I'll shoot you," answered Will. The king (Haggoth) jumped up from the throne and angrily slammed his staff onto the floor.

"What did you just say?" he angrily asked. "I said that I would shoot you if you didn't leave this estate," the alien leader answered with great pride. "I am not afraid of you. You can try and make yourself look like the tough guy all you want. you're not the tough guy. Infact, you're the infidel, the scoundrel, and the rogue one. You don't belong here because you are inferior. Besides, do you realize that it is my perogative to execute you?" asked Haggoth.

"Yes, I do. if you want to execute me, you are making a horrible decision. I don't deserve to be executed because I was the alien leader before you took over. and besides, who died and left you in charge?" asked Will. "Apparently, I was told by Jacqueline that you died and that I was next in line to take the throne. and I decided to pass a law stating that LSCs and blue-pigmented aliens are banned from here because I don't like the color or the advanced technology," the tyrannical king answered. "Shut the hell up," the alien leader said. "Guards," shouted Haggoth. The royal guards entered and tried grabbing Will. He started resisting. He shot the king and his wife with the ray gun and the disintegrated. he shot the guards with the ray gun

and walked out of the Alien Estate. He walked all the way
to the Artillery room, which featured a number of weapons
such as rifles, ray guns, and other weapons. He retrieved a
miniature cannon of Arsenic gas and fired it at the estate.
He killed all the guards in the place. he opened the Hole
and freed all of the one hundred and fifty prisoners. He
jumped back into Light.

"Did you kill him?" the shapeshifting robot asked.
"Yes, I did. He's dead. I also killed all of his possible
successors and justice was done. Now, all we have to do is
return back to California County, pick up our two criminals
and bring them to trial," the
alien leader answered.

"Say, did you happen to kill Serpianto and
Korbian?" asked Light. "Yes, how do you know who they
are?" asked Will. "Those two are Haggoth's pet snakes.
They became his pets after his dragon, Bedlam was killed
by Iron Steel, who was an old friend of mine. I like him
until he betrayed me," the shapeshifting robot answered.
"Did you know that I was taken through time and brought
to trial?" the alien leader asked. "Yes, I am very intuitive. I
know everything that goes on in your life because I get
word from some folks immediately. I also recalled that I
received some telegrams from you," answered Light.

"Well, that's quite impressive that you know all
that," said Will. "Thank you," the shapeshifting robot
replied. "Now, let's return back to the county to get those
beasts, the real perpetrators," the alien leader said. "Very
well then," replied Light. He made a quick departure from
Starmos City and returned back to California County. he
and Will arrived at the police station. "Who should go in?"
the alien leader asked. "You'll do it," answered Light. He

opened the door and Will jumped out. he entered through the double metallic doors of the police station.

Thirty seconds later, he arrived at the reception desk. This desk features a granite counter with two aComps, the most technologically superior computers. Officer Johnstone is typing a report regarding the status of Mitchell and Jacqueline. Will knocked on the desk. He didn't get any response. he knocked louder on the desk. Still, no response. Then, he knocked on the police officer's forehead. "What do you want?" Officer Johnstone asked brusquely. "Where are my criminals?" the alien leader asked.

"I didn't realize that you were coming back here quite early. You're here actually way to early, but if you want to have them right now, you're more than welcome to have them. I hope you get a conviction," the police officer answered. "Thank you. I am very confident that I will get a conviction. After all, they're guilty as sin. They were the ones who supported injustice and unfairness and all I just wanted was fairness. They were the evil ones, not me," replied Will. Officer Johnstone walked out from behind the desk and escorted the alien leader to the jail cell. There, Jacqueline and Mitchell are waiting; they're sitting on the concrete bench. The police officer opened the cell door.

"There's a visitor waiting to bring you two to stand trial. You'll need all the good luck for a jury to believe that you're innocent because you're guilty as sin. He's going to bring you back to Starmos City, but before anything, I am going to put your spit masks on," he said. Surprisingly, the two beasts didn't resist and they were brought into the LSC to stand trial. They didn't say a word the whole ride there. Light arrived back into the alien city. All of the buildings are back to its original shape and none of the buildings look like they have been destroyed. This place looks terrific. The alien citizens are walking the streets. "Did some miracle happen?" the alien leader asked. "Yes, some sort of miracle. It must be a work of God," the shapeshifting robot answered.

"You might be right," replied Will. "I know I'm right. With all the destruction that this place felt, there's no way it would've been fixed by man so quickly in such a litle nick of time. The place has been fixed by God," said Light. He pulled up to the courthouse. The alien leader walked out of the shapeshifting robot/vehicle and he met Brutis, Rubi, and Commissioner Clayton. "Where were you?" asked Brutis. "I was finishing my fight for justice," answered Will. "We were so worried about you. We didn't know if you even survived," the police commissioner replied.

"Well, all that matters is that you're home and that I have my criminals. and I want to congratulate you on being the best bounty hunter," the alien shape shifter answered. "Speaking of which. I have the real criminals. They're right inside of Light," the alien leader replied. "Good. I'll take care of them. You go into the courtroom and wait for the trial. I'll read them their rights," said Brutis.

He read the two beasts their rights and they were brought into the courtroom after they had their rights read. While the trial proceedings had taken place, Light returned back to Skull Castle to rescue all of the 600+ former slave prisoners and he returned them back to their home locations. Meanwhile, in the Starmos Courtroom, both Jacqueline and Mitchell entered not guilty pleas to all 600 counts of crimes against humanity, 2 counts of conspiracy, 600 counts of false imprisonment, 4 counts of attempted felony murder, 1 count of treason, and 1 count of first degree attempted murder.

If convicted, the defendants face the death penalty. Jacqueline has such a huge ego that she is her own defense attorney. She's also Mitchell's defense attorney. The prosecuting attorney is her (Jacqueline's) assistant. Opening Statements and Direct Examination had taken place in the morning and closing arguements and Cross Examination had taken place in the evening.

Finally, the jury reached it's verdict. The aliens in the courtroom are excited to hear a guilty verdict. The jury is now about to read the verdict. Will is crossing his fingers.

"Madam clerk, you may publish the verdict," the presiding judge said. The clerk read the verdict, "For the aliens of Starmos City versus Jacqueline Langyaw and Mitchell, the one who doesn't have the last name. We the jury, duly, paneled, and sworn, upon our oath find the defendants as to counts 1-600 of false imprisonment, guilty; counts 600-1200 of crimes against humanity, guilty; counts 1201-1205 of attempted felony murder, a lesser included offense, guilty; counts 1206-1208 of conspiracy, a lesser included offesne, guilty. We find that this defendants also commited treason and first degree attempted murder while committing those crimes." "Does any counsel want the jury to be polled?" the judge asked. "Yes, I would your honor," answered Jacqueline. The jury was polled. The jury found Jacqueline and Mitchell guilty on all counts.

"Jacqueline Langyaw and Mitchell, I adjudge you to be guilty on all counts. Now, I believe the jury has also came to an idea for what sentence you shall face," the judge said. "Is the clerk ready to read the sentencing verdict?" he asked. "Yes. As to the charges of crimes against humanity, false imprisonment, and treason, we the jury believe that the aggravating factor is clear to state that Jacqueline Langyaw and Mitchell are to die by getting shot with a ray gun. They are to be vaporized and they are erased from memory. Basically, we unanimously agreed to the death sentence while we were deliberating," the clerk said.

"Will Von Alien, you will march the defendants out of the courtroom and you'll shoot them with the ray guns," the judge declared. "Thank you, judge," the alien leader ecstatically said. He shot Jacqueline and Mitchell with the ray guns. The crowd went wild and everybody cheered. The citizens are extremely happy and ecstatic and proud. Rubi, Clayton, and Brutis walked out of the courtroom. The alien leader faced his girlfriend, Rubi. "Will you marry me?" he asked.

"Yes," shouted Rubi. They kissed and this is a marriage made in the alien city. The crowd showed feelings of awe when the alien leader proposed to his girlfriend. Later that night, a firework and muscical show had taken place. and this is the beginning of the new Starmos City. Evil has ended and goodness has prospered. The memories of Cornelius, Jacqueline, and Mitchell have been erased from all of the alien citizens. and everybody, not only in Starmos City; but around all of the dimensions and the world are filled with joy because of this remarkable milestone in the fight for freedom.

Epilogue

Injustice will always take place. the power of justice will destroy injustice. The power of team work will destroy one who commits evil. In society, man kind has to face evil, injustice, and unfairness every day.

Man has to be wary of everything he or she comes across, but we can't let that wariness overtake us. Sometimes our confidants need us to fight for them and their justice, which might cause a great effect on us at the end of the day. So, in order to crush injustice, man must fight as a team.